John E. Southall

Wales and her Language

considered from a historical, educational and social standpoint with remarks on

modern Welsh literature and a linguistic map of the country

John E. Southall

Wales and her Language
considered from a historical, educational and social standpoint with remarks on modern Welsh literature and a linguistic map of the country

ISBN/EAN: 9783337238438

Printed in Europe, USA, Canada, Australia, Japan

Cover: Foto ©Andreas Hilbeck / pixelio.de

More available books at **www.hansebooks.com**

WALES

AND

HER LANGUAGE

CONSIDERED FROM A

HISTORICAL, EDUCATIONAL AND SOCIAL STANDPOINT

WITH REMARKS ON MODERN

WELSH LITERATURE

AND A

LINGUISTIC MAP OF THE COUNTRY.

BY

JOHN E. SOUTHALL.

NEWPORT, MON.

J. E. SOUTHALL, 149 DOCK STREET

LONDON:

E. HICKS JUN., 2 AMEN CORNER, PATERNOSTER ROW.

PREFACE.

A PREFACE is the place for apologies and explanations plus anything else, that may set off the Author's work, or give wings to his vanity.

I shall not apologize to the Welsh nation, because I feel rather indignant that none of them has attempted a similar work, and I shall not apologize to the English public, as this was not primarily intended to meet their eye, if they read it, it must be at their own risk, whether they find it dull or unintelligible, especially as I have in certain instances given quotations without translations, though it might be affectation to deny that a circulation in England would be gratifying.

It is a nauseous practice which some writers in Wales fall into, of giving translations without the original, sometimes for the benefit of a minority only of their readers. It is easy to say, why cannot Welsh be served up in a translated form? Personally, I do not believe that one language can be translated into another, to say so is almost a contradiction in terms, and if Welsh prose is partially untranslatable, Welsh poetry is much more so.

If English people want to become acquainted with the Celtic genius as manifested in Welsh literature, they must learn the language, not merely the scholastic dry bones of it, but they must in some way acquire the accent from living lips who know its power. It will then be demonstrated that Welsh is not a succession of uncouth sounds, but can produce rare combinations of forcible and melodious utterances.

It was, as I have said, not principally for the English that this book was written, but to rouse the Welsh nation and prevent the premature and artificial extinction of their language,

by a system which is condemned by a preponderating weight
of evidence on almost all hands, as will be seen by the following pages, and to point out that quite independently of the
question of the desirability of preserving the language or not,
by properly applying the means within their reach, the managers
of elementary schools can secure the basis of a much more
efficient literary education, than is yet the case in Wales, if
they cause their instructions to be bilingual in every stage.

Talk as we may about technical and scientific education,
important as they are, a sound basis of *literary* education,
should after all, be one of the chief aims of elementary schools,
and in many cases they will have time for little else.   The
Welsh language then should be looked upon as a means to
extend this basis, *i.e.* a means by which at a *minimum* of
mental *labour* to himself and the teacher, and of material
expense to the community, the scholar has the opportunity of
rising into a higher sphere of knowledge, through the training
direct and indirect, thereby afforded.   When I say a minimum
of mental labour this presupposes a Welsh *Code* which enlightened educationalists, ought to strive for, as well as previous
training on the part of the teacher, the deficiency of which is
at present a hindrance to education.

If Welsh dies, should the reformation here proposed become
general, well and good, let it die : but it is a fact to-day,
therefore treat it as a fact affecting not merely a few districts,
but the greater part of a whole nation.

It would have been a comparatively easy task to have presented to my readers a hodge-podge of miscellaneous facts and
fancies about "Wales and Her Language," pitched-forked
together in an undigested mass, without much regard to rhyme
or reason, but this was not aimed at, and how far I have
steered clear of such a course, the reader must decide.

Literary faults, there are, of which some are felt by the

author himself, but when it is considered that indifferent
health occasioned frequent delays in the prosecution of the
work, and that he has seldom felt physically able to attend to
it for more than short periods of time at once, the severity
of criticism may be mitigated. The principal scope of the
book can be compressed under three heads—

I. A demonstration of the defects of the present educational system, in its relation to the language.

II. A historical record of the position of the Welsh
language, in 1892.

III. A commendation of the language to the attention of
English people, especially those resident in Wales.

I have to add that " *Wales* " in these pages refers to the
thirteen counties. I do not believe that Henry VIII., when
he divided the country into assize circuits, and tacked Monmouthshire on to an English one, had any idea of defining the
limits of Wales, but that it happened to suit his convenience
to make this arrangement.

If this is so, until the limits are fixed by law, " Welsh " is
simply a conventional term of the same character as the
" Midland Counties," or the " East of England," which has
rather by force of custom, than law, become limited to twelve
counties. Welsh people do not all admit the custom as a
respectable one to follow.

My thanks are due to Principal M. D. Jones, of Bala, who
has kindly read through most of the proofs, although so much
new matter has frequently been added before going to press,
that he cannot be considered responsible for any errors that
may occur; also to Col. J. A. Bradney, of Tal-y-coed Court,
who has given me valuable information on the geographical
limits of Welsh, to Dr. Burlingham, of Hawarden, and Henry
Tobit Evans, J.P., of Neuadd Llanarth, as well as other
friends for the service they have rendered, and to my subscribers

for supporting a man (unknown to most of them) in a comparatively untrodden track.

It may be observed that in the case of certain names, the Author has either dropped the usual prefix of St., or put it in quotation marks. Some of the persons to whom this prefix is applied were beyond question Saints, *i.e.* they lived in a heavenly atmosphere above the general spirit of the world. There are however, some serious objections to the use of the term as a formal distinctive—one is, that thereby the men who put such epithets into circulation as current coin are in effect telling the world, "these men and women were holy Saints, they lived in quite an unreachable plane, or one to which a very few need aspire, therefore you may be satisfied to remain as you are—unholy sinners." Another objection is that the authority, which guarantees the fact of so-and-so being a Saint, is the excathedrâ voice of the man who, on a given occasion, professed to hold the power of the Keys. What guarantee have we that these men have at any period lived so near the infallible Spirit as to be able to inwardly discern beneath the surface (without any promptings from Cardinals, Jesuits and the like), who deserved the epithet of Saint, and who not. Take Patrick, of Ireland, for instance— an honest, simple-minded, earnest, God-fearing man : but has one Irishman been inclined to a saintly life through putting him outside the level of every-day life, and calling him Saint Patrick ?

It will also be noticed, that I have abstained from calling any places built of stone and mortar *Churches*. I believe that a religion which attaches any sanctity to PLACES, is nearly nineteen hundred years out of date, at least, when an opportunity is afforded to know better.

JOHN E. SOUTHALL.

6 mo., 1892.

CONTENTS.

CHAPTER VI.
SOCIAL INFLUENCES.

CHAPTER VII.
STUDY OF THE LANGUAGE AND LITERATURE.

CHAPTER VIII.
WELSH NATIONALITY.

CHAPTER IX.
GEOGRAPHICAL LIMITS.

CHAPTER X.
CORNISH AND IRISH.

CHAPTER XI.
THE PAST AND THE FUTURE.

CHAPTER I.

THERE are probably not many persons cognizant of the fact
that at the commencement of last century there were no
less than eight *native* languages spoken in the British Isles,
viz :—

ENGLISH	GAELIC IN THE HIGHLANDS
WELSH IN WALES, AND PARTS	ERSE IN IRELAND
OF SHROPSHIRE AND	NORSK IN THE ORKNEYS
HEREFORDSHIRE	FRENCH IN THE CHANNEL
CORNISH IN CORNWALL	ISLANDS
MANX IN THE ISLE OF MAN	

In the following pages it is my intention to take notice
of historical or present day facts in connection with the use of
some or all of these languages, but the one which pre-eminently
will claim our attention is the Welsh.

The author cannot lay pretensions to being a Welshman,
having been born some eighteen miles east of Clawdd Offa,
but within sight of the Welsh hills on the other side, in
Radnor and Brecon. It is perhaps some advantage that an
Englishman should discuss the history and topography of the
Welsh language and its claims on Welshmen, provided it is
not to him a wholly foreign tongue.

If we hold a book too close to our eyes the letters become
blurred and indistinct; if too far off they again lose their
characteristics : so with the Welsh language, it lies too near

A

Welshmen for them, and their relation to it has been such of a character that they are in many cases scarcely able to form an unbiassed opinion of its educational value ; to some it seems the badge of nationality, which must be maintained at all costs ; to others a millstone round their necks which must be got rid of. Similarly the language lies too far off Englishmen who are ignorant of it and perhaps occasionally nettled by reason of their ignorance in dealing with servants and work-men, or who lack a mind to appreciate its beauties.

I do not write for such if they have no ears to hear, but principally for the more intelligent portion of the English speaking inhabitants of Wales, and those who have more or less influence in its educational arrangements, to call their attention to the fact that they have in their midst a *gem*, which is capable of being used, not simply as a curiosity or an ornament, but for cutting fair and harmonious characters on the mental mirrors of Welsh children, if it is properly handled and in a way that has hitherto been scarcely attempted.

Starting from the axiom that education in Wales is far from being in a satisfactory state, I endeavour to shew that in one direction at least a considerable and solid improvement may be made, and fortify myself by adding to what might be considered individual fancies, the opinions of practical teachers and others.

Whatever the future of Wales may be, she is now in a transition state—socially, religiously and linguistically.

Socially in so far as a more educated and wealthy middle class is arising. *Religiously* in so far as the simplicity and zeal of sixty years ago appears to be disappearing, before the influence of custom and fashion. *Linguistically* in so far as the monoglot Welsh-Welshman is much more rarely to be found, and in some districts his duoglot successors are being replaced by monoglot English-Welshmen, reared under the influence of the nineteenth century, and an English Government, backed by the educational traditions of generations; although the transition lies in the fact that a knowledge of English is more and more spreading, while it is at the same time possible, that during the last ten years the aggregate of the Welsh speaking population has increased.

Much that is said here, has been said before in one shape or another during the last five or six years. Some things will perhaps be new to most, if not all of my readers, and at any rate what has before been mostly in a fragmentary state, not easy of reference, is here brought together in a collected form ; while the map and various statistics will, it is hoped, serve the purpose of present information and interest, and as an *historical monument* of the year 1891.

The late Dan Isaac Davies' dream of "Tair miliwn o Gymry dwy-ieithawg yn 1985" (three millions of Duoglot Welsh in 1985) may or may not be realized, yet a future generation can hardly fail to reap some instruction as to the laws which govern the use or disuse of language, by reference to the facts that may be gleaned from a linguistic map printed in this last decade of our eventful century.

One thing remarkable however at the present day, is the considerable amount of ignorance which prevails even among those who are well-informed—some of them Welsh speaking people—about the linguistic condition of the country.

If what I have written tends to cause the question of language in Wales to be regarded more intelligently, both in its social and educational aspects, and tends to the better development of the life of the nation, I shall feel that this book and its appendage have not been written nor drawn up in vain.

This is not, however, intended principally for English eyes, but, as I intimated above, rather for those whose lot lies west of the Severn and who by birth, association, or intercourse are intimately connected with Wales, or interested in its welfare, inviting them to use the past as a key to the present, and as a possible index to the future.

English people are usually taught to look upon themselves as Anglo Saxons, and are unaware how much they owe to other races or nations, either in the way of blood or ideas, nor what lessons may not be learnt by even humble and prosaic facts presented in the history of the tongues of such other people.

To begin with we will now briefly consider the influence of Welsh on the nomenclature of the speech of England, not in an exhaustive or very scholarly fashion, but within a short compass, which will, nevertheless, point to a new field of thought and observation.

A slight knowledge of Welsh is not, it is true, sufficient to give a new meaning to every place named on the map of England which cannot be explained by reference to Saxon roots, but it is historically instructive and fruitful in awakening the intelligence.

The following names of English Counties all contain roots of Celtic* origin which are indicated by capitals—

North-UMBER-land	WOR-cester
DUR-ham	CAM-bridge
YORK	DOR-set
CUMBER-land	DEVON
LAN-cashire	CORN-wall
LIN-coln	KENT
DER-by	LEI-cester
WAR-wick	BERK-s

---

* I use the word Celtic here in a general, not in a strictly scientific sense; possibly some of these names have really come down from pre-Celtic times.

Of the thirteen Welsh Counties we include all except Montgomery (which is only indirectly Celtic), Radnor and Anglesea. The two latter have, however, Celtic names of their own.

Many of these Celtic roots of County names arise from the names of rivers or from towns named from rivers, which indicate that the river was named before any town was built, or from physical characters of the country, e.g.,—

NORTHUMBERLAND—The country north of the Yorkshire Humber.

DURHAM—The old Anglian Kingdom of *Deira*: the country between the *dyfroedd* of the Tees and Tyne.

KENT—A singular confirmation of reputed history here presents itself. According to popular account the first settlement of the Saxons in Kent was a peaceful one, their leaders Hengist and Horsa being invited by Vortigern, the British King to assist him in military operations.

However this may be, there is corroborative evidence that a large British population remained on the soil and perpetuated traces of their language in some of the place names with the name of the County as well as to the custom of inheritance of land known now as *gavel (gaffael) kind.* *(See appendix A.)*

Vortigern comes to us as a proper name, but in reality he was simply the Gwr Tigern* (*c.f.*, modern Welsh *Teyrnaswr*) = the man or Ruler of the Kingdom ; just as *Brennus*, who, long centuries before at the head of his victorious hosts of *Cymry* and *Teutones* entered the seven-hilled city, was simply the *Brenhin* or King of the *Cymry.*†

---

* *Tiye* (modern Welsh, *Ty*) as the house and the name applied to the patriarch of the house appears to have gradually become applicable to the head of a confederation ; *c.f.* Irish *Tighearna* = a lord.

† It seems probable that the word *Cymry* itself simply means the *federated hosts.*

DOVER is pronounced by our French neighbours almost exactly as their Gaulish forefathers pronounced it, some two thousand years ago, when it was as now, the main point of reaching the *dwfr* (or water) which separates England from France ; the Saxon settlers were sufficiently in touch with their neighbours to call the place (for probably no town existed there) by the same name, but unwitting that it simply signified water, hence to the present day when speaking of going from Dover to Calais we are really saying from Water to Calais, a proof of the extinction of the Welsh language in the district, but evidence also, if I am not mistaken, that it was gradual and not attended with the bloody slaughter which must have taken place in the Eastern Counties, and would have caused the Celtic name to become obsolete.

The WAR in Warwick and the WOR in Worcester are undoubtedly the same word, and the root survives in WYRE Forest near Bewdley, and in Caer *Wrangon* the Welsh name for Worcester, probably also in the Roman City of Uriconium, and in *Erging* the foundation name of the *Archen*field district near Ross, Herefordshire.

CUMBER-land reminds us of the once extensive Cymric Kingdom of Strath Clyde (Ystrad Clwyd) which embraced the tract from the Clyde to the Mersey, bounded probably on the east by a line running through the West Riding Dales. The Celtic names in South West Scotland are however more Gaelic than Cymric ; *e.g. Sanquahar* = Hen Gaer.

The " Lan " of Lancaster, doubtless, comes from the Celtic root of the river LUNE, but the Welsh name *Caer hir fryn*, reminds us at once of the long ridge, the *hir fryn* or elevated country, forming the backbone of the county about which the cotton mills are congregated.

In DEVON we find testimony to the deep brooks of the old red sandstone, the dyfneint (*dwfn* deep, *nentydd* brooks).

CORNWALL was originally Kernyw. Kernyw Wealas, were Welshmen—foreigners who dwelt in Kernyw.

The term Wealas whence Wales we find illustrated again in the name of the modern European State Belgium. The Belgians, a people older than Cæsar, were formerly *foreigners* to some Teutonic neighbours, just as the Germans were at the same time Ellmynwyr = All-man wyr, *i.e.* men from another place—to the Gauls and are still so called by the Welsh, while the French call them Allemands; so indestructible amid the rise and fall of Empires have been personal names once conveying simple ideas when fixed on a nation on or before the times of early history.

Of those Counties not in the above list two at least deserve notice.

GLOU-cester may be wholly Roman, and if so was originally Claudii Castra, which was Cymricized as Caergloyw—its name to the present day. It is difficult to understand the usual Roman name *Glevum* arising from anything we should find reproduced as Gloyw. *Glevum* was certainly the Latinized form of an old Celtic place name.

SOMERSET is a remarkable and historically instructive name: at first appearance it is wholly and solely Saxon and to mean the settlement of the *Somers* folk. Without a knowledge of Welsh, however, we have no real clue to the name, and at first sight, the Welsh name for the district, viz: *Gwlad yr Haf*, used even in the nineteenth century, does not suggest what appears to be the true derivation.

I venture the following conjecture of its origin: when the Saxons had penetrated as far in the country as Somersetshire, they were not mere hostile and alien invaders, but had become used to the country with its residual British population and were to some extent bilingual. They asked the natives what they called the district and were told it was Gwlad yr Haf.

These Saxons possessed Welsh enough to know that
Haf meant summer, but were ignorant that the Severn was
Yr Hafren, hence they jumped to the conclusion that they
were in the summer country and called themselves
Somersetas.

In a neighbouring county the new comers were also called
settlers—Dorsetas, from the old Roman town of Dorchester
(W., *Caer dor.*)

Another curious case of the mistranslation of a Celtic name
occurred in the fifth century. All readers of Church
History are acquainted with the name of Pelagius, a Briton
whose doctrine was firmly opposed by the noted Augustine,
Bishop of Hippo. His original name was *Morgan*, and some
of the learned of that time wishing to translate it into a classic
form took for granted that the MOR meant sea, and that
Morgan meant, "born by the sea." They accordingly dubbed
him Pelagius from the Greek word *pelagos*, the sea. The real
meaning of the name I take to have been *Great Head ; cean*
being the Gaelic form of Welsh *pen*—the head. . Possibly he
was a Monmouthshire man, as Gaelic was spoken here,
according to Professor Rhys, as late as the fifth century ; in
any case he was one of the numerous clan of " Morganiaid,"
who have given their name to the *Gwlad Morgan*, known by
the Saxon as Glamorganshire. Malcolm *Ceanmore*, King of
Scotland, bore the same surname, but the adjective *more*
[great] followed the noun.

That there may have been a certain amount of bilingualism
among early English in the south of England—perhaps
Somersetshire—is borne evidence to by a poem of the 13th
century, given in Prof. Henry Morley's History of English
Literature, the refrain of each stanza in which is " Quoth
Hendyng." In reference to the latter the Professor says,—

" As for the name Hendyng, I believe that it suggests only

the wisdom of age and experience and is one of the vernacular words drawn from the Celtic part of the population for *Henddyn,* means in Welsh an aged person."

The following stanza is from the original, the second is the same translated into modern English.

> Yef thou havest bred ant ale,
> Ne put thou nout al in thy male,
> 　　Thou dele it sum aboute.
> Be thou fre of all thy meeles,
> Where so me any mete deles ;
> 　　Gest thou not withoute,
> Better is appel y-geve than y-ete,
> 　　　　Quoth Hendyng.

> Hast thou of bread and ale, no lack,
> Put not all in thine own sack,
> 　　But scatter some about.
> Art thou free with thine own meals
> Where another his meat deals ;
> 　　Goest thou not without,
> Better apple given nor eaten,
> 　　　　Quoth Hendyng.

Names of important hill ranges, rivers and mountains in England are nearly all Celtic or pre-Celtic :—The Mendips, Quantocks, Chilterns, the Tors, Cheviots, Cotswolds, Malvern, Bredon Hill, Helvellyn, Pendle Hill.

Sometimes however a Celtic name is lost, as *y Van* near Abergavenny, now called the Sugar Loaf, and while its companion the Skirrid is still Celtic : unimportant hills are generally English, even in Herefordshire as Brierley Hill, Foxley, Lady Lift, &c. Abergavenny (w., *y Fenni*) was Gobannium in Roman times—*Go* being an intensitive prefixed to *ban,* a high mountain.

B

Among the names of English towns, not being County names as well, we find the following which bear evidence of the presence of the Celt—

MALDON	LEEK	MANCHESTER
KELVEDON	LEEDS	LIVERPOOL
CROMER	RIPON	CHICHESTER
ARUNDEL	WINCHESTER	CARLISLE
LYNN	"ST." ALBANS	WIGAN
ROMNEY	COVENTRY	LUDLOW
LONDON, including	BATH	COLCHESTER
LUDGATE AND	PENRITH	SALISBURY
BILLINGSGATE	CIRENCESTER	

These, however, are merely samples, the number of place names with Celtic roots must amount to several hundreds.

LUDGATE and BILLINGSGATE :—Each of these names that romancing historian Geoffrey of Monmouth, who lived as far back as the 12th century connected with the history of mythical kings, viz., *Lud* and *Beli* respectively, so with LEICESTER (Caerleirion) which name he originated from "King Lear." Somewhat singularly there is a place in Leicestershire still called *Leir*; just as there is a place near Gloucester called *Cleere* which appears to correspond with the old term Glevum.

Most probably, such a man as "King Lud" never existed, but *Lud*gate contains a very ancient name; undoubtedly the same one occurs in the present day Welsh poetic name for London—*Caerludd*.

BILLINGSGATE has all the appearance of being derived from a Saxon patronymic *Billing*, but it is scarcely credible that the Saxons should have transmitted a name to that ancient structure, ancient even in the days of the Conqueror which the Welsh would have recognized in their *Porth Beli*; so that I take Billingsgate to have a simulated Saxon derivation, but, and in reality, a Celtic one.

OXFORD seems again thoroughly *Saxon*,—in reality it was the ford of the [Taf]wyse, thence Wyse or Uskford and Oxford. Later on, the Welsh, oblivious of the old derivation, translated Oxford by *Rhydychain* = Oxenford.

LICHFIELD is a striking instance of a Celtic name, being translated by a Teutonic speaking people, who found it called *Maes y Cyrph*—"the field of corpses" from the bloody slaughter of Christians there in the days of Diocletian. George Fox when he passed through the streets of Lichfield beheld them with his spiritual vision, streaming with blood, while he believed himself inspired to cry aloud, "Woe, woe to the bloody city of Lichfield,"* and little knew that the very name of the town bore evidence of the fact which he saw by revelation, before he was acquainted with the historical narrative of what had taken place there some 1300 years before.

As we approach the West, Celtic names become more frequent, till in Cornwall we get a preponderating majority of them. In Lancashire we should find a good crop, but for the fact that until modern times Lancashire was one of the poorest portions of the kingdom, almost the poorest County, and many now important towns could have had no existence when the Cumbrian language was still spoken there, possibly down till the thirteenth century, but MANCHESTER (*Manceinion*), and LIVERPOOL (*Llynlleifiad*) still bear evidence of Celtic influence.†

The nomenclature of the Continent of Europe, presents many interesting facts to the Celtic student.

Here he sees in the CRIMEA a name that must have belonged to that Peninsula for three thousand years at least, and a

---

* *Leiche* = a dead body, hence the "*Lich*-gate" before burial grounds.

† The English reader may be surprised to learn that the Welsh names in italics are still used in current literature to signify those great towns.

primeval home of the Cymry.   The word APPENNINE at once
becomes eloquent to him as *pennau wynion,* the white historic
peaks of the backbone of Italy.   The PYRENNEES become the
Bar wynion,—the white ridge, keeping the Celtic name in
spite of the Basque population still adjacent.

He comes across the AAR in Switzerland and finds it
represented on the borders of Wales by a river bearing the
apparently English name of the ARROW (near Leominster), but
which was undoubtedly the Aarwy (*Araf,* slow, *wy,*
river,) while he is not slow to recognize that the DOURO in
Portugal was simply *the water* to a primitive people.

Near the ARROW he finds the LUGG (llugwy) and sees in the
busy town of LYONS (Lugdunum) evidence that the same
people have wandered in uncultivated simplicity by the banks
of the Lug and of the fast flowing Rhone, while they have
transmitted identical relics of their speech in the distant cities of
VEN-ice and WIN-chester.

Near the Anglicized Town of Newport he finds the CEFN
as well as elsewhere in Wales ; and in the South of France
the *Cevennes* : the radical idea of a ridge or back being the
same in each case.

In the historical city of MAG-deburg he sees the identical root
which has been preserved in *Magor,* a Monmouthshire village
and in many places in Ireland.—(*c.f.,* Manx, *Magher* a field).

Turning now from English and Continental place-names to
the English language itself, an observer, familiar with both
languages, finds that a larger share has to be assigned to the
Celtic than is generally supposed.

The Authors of students' handbooks and examiners in
English at Universities are generally all but ignorant of a
Celtic vocabulary and more so of Celtic grammar ; consequently
they are incompetent to deal with an analysis of the Celtic
elements in the English language.

Into anything like an exhaustive or thorough treatment of the subject I am not qualified to enter, nor has it ever been seriously attempted, to my knowledge: what is here said is not put forward authoritatively, but rather to indicate that just as in the case of place-names, a knowledge of Welsh throws light on the history and condition of England in past times, so the English language itself is not untinctured by expressions which betray Welsh influence.

A careful examination of English idioms alone would probably confirm this, and apart from phrases, if we only consider verbal constructions, there are instances which arrest our attention—*e.g.*, the peculiar use of *do* as an auxiliary verb. "I *do* not see him." "*Does* he walk quickly"? Where do we find similar constructions in any Teutonic tongue; and yet, in Welsh, as an affirmation, we hear *gwnaf*, "I will do so," in answer to a command such as "Lock the door"; and in Breton it is even more prominent, as *mond a rann*—"I am coming," literally "Come, I do."

I am writing, with but a simple present signification is or might be expressed by a somewhat similar compound in Welsh, *yr wyf yn ysgrifenu*; but not usually in German or Danish.

No one has ever, so far as I am aware, made out a complete list of Celtic words incorporated in the English language. The total it is true, is not comparatively large, but it is larger than such authorities as I have hinted at give, and I suspect too, that technical terms would yield a good harvest in this direction.

When the farmer's wife picks out her *addled* eggs, and scatters *barley* for her new *brood* of chickens, then, after she has chopped her *suet* in the *kitchen*, she sits down with a *clean apron* and makes *gussets*, and *hems* her *flannels*, or sews on *buttons*, while the goodman is preparing his *bait* for vermin. He goes out of the *gabled* house and looks at his

hogs and *rams* and walks a *brisk* pace on the *road* to the
common, where he finds an *adder* which he *hurts* with his
pitch-fork (*pig* a beak); and passes his *hired* labourers *tedding*
hay and some of which is destined to go into a *rick* and some into
a *loft* with *laths* under the tile roof, while his fields are manured
by aid of *carts*, drawn by horses fed on *bran* mash, from the
lime *kiln* and worked up into *ridges* with *mattocks*; and his
hedges are trimmed with *bills* (*bwgell*). He eats his morning
meal that has been prepared on the *griddle*, looks at his infant
in the *cradle* while he is *coaxed* by his elder children to have
a *romp* with them, and all the while if he is an Englishman,
is quite unaware that many of the words I have italicized were
borrowed by his ancestors from their British neighbours: others
of them are very similar in Welsh but cannot safely be
included, though it is possible that a certain number of such
words entered the Anglo-Saxon or Icelandic languages through
contact with Celtic speaking people long ages ago.

The engineer talks of *blocks, bosses, butts, chisels, cranes,
funnels, cams, plugs, spigots, scuttles, cogs, gimlets, tow,* and
probably many more things which from their technical character
escape the cursory notice of Philologists, but which bear
similar relations to the corresponding Welsh words.

As intimated above, the number of Welsh words permanently
incorporated in English is small, but it would have probably
been very much increased had it not happened that
modern English is most nearly derived from a dialect similar
to that spoken in *Northamptonshire*, where Celtic influence
must have been very much smaller than in many other parts
of the kingdom. Had the dialect of West Mercia, or
Wiltshire, or even Derbyshire, ruled the formation of English,
many Celtic-English words, now only confined to local *patois*
or else obsolete altogether would have become part and parcel
of the "Queen's English."

The mere resemblance of an English word to a Welsh one is
not in itself sufficient evidence of the former being derived
from the latter as such words admit of being divided into
three classes, viz. :—

    I.   Words which are alike by reason of English and Welsh,
       being both branches of a common Indo-European stock,
       from which they divided long before the Christian Era.

    II. Words which the English has borrowed directly or
       indirectly from the Welsh, and which may amount to
       two hundred or more.

    III. Words which the Welsh has borrowed from the
       English.

Considering the relations of the two countries during the
last six hundred years, the number of the latter is surprisingly
small. I believe very few English scholars have ever given due
weight to this fact, or perhaps been acquainted with it. That
a language which has been exiled from secular schools and
colleges, with small exceptions for centuries, should be written
to-day, with such an unmixed vocabulary as it is, can only be
adduced as a proof of its wonderful vitality. English emerged
from the ordeal of the supremacy of Norman French saturated
with foreign expressions, in fact she may be said to have lost
half her old face, and to have reappeared half Latin and half
Saxon. Breton has somewhat similarly been drenched with
French words, so was the later Cornish with English, so now
is the colloquial Welsh of Gwent and Morganwg, but when
we come to read Y *Geninen* and Y *Traethodydd*, although
they perhaps scarcely lay claim to be models of style, we find,
notwithstanding all defects, that the proportion of English
words is very much less (especially in the poetical portions),
than a stranger would have expected.

CHAPTER II.

THE history of Wales proper from the point of view we are now considering it, might be said to begin with the formation of Offa's Dyke, in that is to say, whereas previously we could scarcely give any limits to the extent of the language, we can now afford pretty much to confine our attention to the limits of this Dyke, although I have no doubt that communities of Welsh speaking people were to be found in England, outside Devon and Cornwall for centuries afterwards.

I incline to think that beyond perhaps a few years, the effects of the Dyke in restraining attacks of Welshmen was comparatively small and that the penalty attached to a Welshman being found on the other side could not be strictly enforced, otherwise how is it we find native Welsh spoken East of the Dyke to the present day in Shropshire and also that this was the case some sixty years ago in Herefordshire. ?

How is it too, that only a century after Offa's time a learned Welshman, *Asser*, was attendant at King Alfred's court for six months in the year, though his property lay in West Wales?

Offa's Dyke was completed about the year 780 and the Welsh language was spoken right up to the edge of it, from Chepstow to Chester with little or no absolute break for no less than 900 years, except that the contemporaneous use of English was current along the greater distance of it during the latter portion of that period; but throughout the middle ages, the area of spoken Welsh in Wales and the Borders must have been remarkably constant.

Circumstances, however, were imminent which affected Wales, and ultimately modified her future history, as they did that of her Saxon neighbours. The Northmen who ravaged the East of England, carrying terror and desolation along with them, did not spare the West coast, and left permanent relics of their presence in various names on or near it, as the Nash (*naes* = nose of land) in Monmouthshire, and also in Glamorgan; the *Holms* islands, *Lundy*, the *Skerries*, and the important port of Swansea—the *ea* representing the Norse *ei* for island, while further up we get Port*dinorwic*, near the Bangor slate quarries (the Norwegians' port); the Orme's Head, and Bard*sey* Island, also *Caldy* Island in Pembrokeshire. Swansea is still called by the Welsh *Abertawy*, in preference to the appellation given it by foreigners. Compare also Anglesea—W., *Ynys Mon*.

A more remarkable instance of the persistence of Welsh names occurs in Herefordshire where a monastery was founded in 660 by Merewald, King of Mercia, a Saxon—Ealfrid being the first Abbot. In the 10th century, however, the monks were supplanted by *nuns*, but about the time of William the Conqueror, the nunnery ceased and the monastery was restored; though the name Leofrici Monasterium evidently connects with the days when Leofric, a Saxon general under King Canute, repaired the building, with a great "bravery of gold and silver."

This monastery was a cell of the Abbot of Reading, and for many centuries, English influences must have been prevalent in the district, as the names of the surrounding villages are mostly Saxon, and were so, even at the advent of the Conqueror.

Notwithstanding these cogent facts, the Welsh name *Llanllieni* (*llieni* = nuns), referring to the nunnery, still survives. The writer has heard an old Radnorshire woman, hailing from Abbey Cwmhir, near Rhayader, repeat the doggerel which she had heard many years before :—

"How many miles, how many
Is it from Leominster to Llanllieni ? "

and he is assured that Leominster is still known by some Welsh people as Llanllieni. Those were days in which a well-to-do woman who could have afforded to have ridden, *walked*, 40 miles from near Llanidloes into Leominster butter fair, and sold her butter the same day; "and now," said my old friend almost indignantly, "you take a train to go to Hereford,"—thirteen miles.

Why the Welsh refused to recognize the 11th century monastery, and only spoke of the nunnery when they referred to the town is not clear, unless it is, that by the time the monastery was well established they entered the town as strangers, speaking a foreign language, and did not wish to trouble themselves about any new-fangled name coined by the Saxons.

After the Northmen had come and gone, or else settled down and had become incorporated with the people, a great Englishman—no less a man than King Harold—pitched his tent, in the shape of a hunting lodge, in a corner of Wales, at Portskewett (*Porth Ysgewin*), near the "Moors" (the *Morfa*) of Monmouthshire, which Roman skill had in time past reclaimed by a sea wall, remains of which exist to the present day, more or less entire. Traces of his settlement of the low land, may not, improbably, be found in the Saxon names of *Whitson, Redwick, Goldcliff*, and *Itton*.

King Harold's day was short; and with his fall came the subjugation of the Saxons; for 300 years it was the

Fraine or *Norddmein** rather than the *Saeson*, whom the Cymry feared: then was ushered in the era of huge castles, with gloomy vaults, where the ray of hope scarcely entered, while the common people toiled on in unrequited serfdom.

Wales was, at this period, in far too weak and divided a state to offer much permanent resistance to these Norman spoilers, who erected stronghold after stronghold all along the eastern borders and the southern coast of Wales.

Directly, however, the Norman rule did not much affect the language of the people, but it was the means of extirpating the Welsh language from two districts, viz., South Pembrokeshire, and Gower near Swansea, by the introduction of Flemish Colonies. Whether or no the populations there had been very much reduced through the Norse invasions, I am not able to decide.

How far the Welsh flannel trade is originally due to Flemish industry I will not attempt to decide; but in the case of family names ending in *kin* the Flemings have left lasting traces, as the frequently recurring *Watkins*, *Jenkins*, *Hopkins*, will testify. Not that the holders of these names necessarily have a drop of Flemish blood in their veins, but such became current in Wales, people adopted them for their children, and then, in the third generation, a Robert ap Siencyn ap Einion Ddu would, if he lived in the time when patronymics were becoming fixed, be simply known as Robert Jenkins.

Ivor James, the Registrar of the South Wales University

---

*Llywarch Brydydd y moch, writing on Llewelyn ap Iorwerth, says,—
" Ai gwell Franc na ffrawdus Gymro."
(Is a Norman better than a conquering Cymro.)
Einion Gwgan, about 1244 :—
" Golud mawr ystrud ysgryd Norddmein."
(Great was our happiness to put the Normans to fear and consternation.)
Quoted in " Specimens of Ancient Welsh Poetry," by Ieuan P. Hir, Pryse's Edition.

College at Cardiff, contests the fact that these districts were mainly settled by Flemings : the evidence adduced by him in support of his view is partly based on the absence of Flemish family names there.   He has overlooked the force of the above mentioned fact, and even if not, the objection should not carry great weight as many family names are of comparatively recent origin, even in England ; and in Welsh Wales very few of the family names can be older than the 16th century, when the first name of a father came to be borne by his son as a surname, and then by his descendants in perpetuity ; and when it also happened that custom ran in the direction of such first names being from a few of English, Norman or Hebrew, rather than of national origin, the choice accordingly admitted of but little variation, hence great confusion has resulted to the present day.

Thus, we may suppose, that a Griffith ap Conan had a son in the 16th century whom he named—in deference to prevailing ideas—John : this John ap Griffith's son was named Risiart ; this Risiart ap John would be called Richard Jones ; and thus, Jones be established as a family name ; so with the Edwardses, the Davies, the Robertses, the Jameses ; ap Harry and ap Huw becoming Parry and Pugh.

Sometimes, however, family names were adopted which entirely broke the ancestral connection, for instance, Dean Gabriel Goodman, of Westminster, was a Welshman, who, if I am not mistaken, assumed the name *Goodman.*   An ancestor of the Mostyn family assumed that name at the suggestion of Roland Lee, Bishop of Lichfield, of whom we shall hear later on.   Some names of Welsh origin but scarcely to be met with in Wales, are found in England, *e.g., Walwyn,* in Ross, Herefordshire, *Gough, Craddock, Camm, Says,* &c.   The ancestors of these people must have lived away from Wales when this casting-off of vernacular names went on.

Whether Wales will be satisfied as population increases, to allow such a poverty of family names to continue, I do not know : one well-known Welshman—living at Manchester—R. J. Derfel has made a move against it by adopting the name Derfel for his family instead of Jones.　Though no movement of any magnitude in this direction has set in, a somewhat curious custom prevails of individuals bearing three names, the second a distinctively Welsh one, and being generally known by the second and third name, sometimes the initial only of the first name being mentioned.　Thus we have Cynddylan, Einion, Ossian, Illtyd, Tudor, Ceiriog, Gwynfe, Teganwy, prefixed to more or less common surnames.　For instance, John Ceiriog Hughes—always known in bardic circles as *Ceiriog*—would, if he had been a lawyer, or doctor, and not an author, have probably signed himself J. Ceiriog Hughes.　Among writers the difficulty is almost entirely removed by the adoption of *noms de plume* (*enwau barddonol*).

In England, it is the exception rather than the rule to speak of a standard author by an assumed name, or for the latter to exist : in Wales, authors are frequently better known in the latter way, even when there is no attempt to hide the personality.　Few people in Wales talk of William Rees, or William Thomas, but many of " Gwilym Hiraethog " and " Islwyn" : there are, however, exceptions—Goronwy Owain's name is sufficiently poetic and distinctive by itself, and was the name given him at birth.

In early times there was a considerable variety of personal names in Wales ; in the appendix I give a list of some which have been preserved to us in the names of *places* ; many of their possessors were Christians of the fifth or sixth centuries ; had I also included personal names, handed down in historical documents, the number might have been indefinitely enlarged.

One difficulty which Welsh parents would doubtless find in

re-introducing them is, that their English neighbours would
be likely to mangle the sounds of the double letters ; and
ignore the *n* sound of the *y*. There are, however, some in the
list which might, with advantage, be used, even though the
sounds be not English.

Several of the old Saxon names of men and women are now
extinct, as Ethelwolf, Athelstan, Edwy, Kenelm, Leofwin,
Ella, Edgiva ; a larger proportion, however, than in the case
of Welsh ones have survived, such as Alfred, Edward, Egbert,
Harold, Margaret, Winifred ; besides this there appears to
be a tendency to revive some previously extinct ; why should
not the Cymry do the same ?

I have mentioned above that the Norman Conquest did not
greatly affect the language of the people in Wales. It was,
however, the means of introducing into it many warlike terms
and words used in legal administration. As regards English
itself, or to speak more correctly a late form of Saxon, and its
social and literary status, the effect was much more marked,
for we must recollect that during most of the time under
review, it was a despised, down-trodden language. Eight
hundred years ago it had ceased to be the Court language
or the language of legal affairs, and probably many of the
nobles were unable to hold a conversation in it. We know
that Henry II. could not, nor possibly Edward II.

Two hundred years later when the old enmity between
English and Normans had pretty much passed, the chance for
English to become the permanent tongue of the land appeared
even smaller ; Norman French was considered the language of
education and culture and not simply a badge of political
superiority.

In the schools English was ignored much as the
education department affected until recently to ignore the
existence of Welsh : children had to construe in French,

and perhaps less than ever was the English language *written*.

In the reign of Edward I. Acts of Parliament and public letters were written in French, it was not till 1385 that children at school began to construe in English, and not before the reign of Henry VI. or nearly *four* hundred years after the Conquest, was French disused for legal proceedings. Students of law books may still find in the Norman French terms used there, relics of the degradation of English.

There are still parts of the British Isles where a stranger finds that English is no longer *the* Imperial language ; where the supremacy of the same language which the haughty Normans spoke is maintained.

Why is French allowed to be legal language of the Channel Islands while Welsh is still out of court in Wales ?

Is it because Englishmen now have any more love to French than to Welsh ? No.

The reason is that, when utility demanded the abolition of French in England, the French speaking population of those islands were allowed to retain their native French in legal proceedings, because they had precedent and the lingering respect for Norman customs in their favour : but in the case of Wales, whatever precedent, there may have been in Plantagenet times, under semi-independent governors, it was evidently feared later on, that there would be an element introduced antagonistic to the stability of the government by permitting its use in the law courts.

Robert of Gloucester (strangely anticipating John Edwards of 1651) says about this period: "There is no nation that holdeth not to its kindly* speech save England only." It is thought probable that the French wars of Richard III. turned the

---

* *Kindly* here means *native*.

scale and encouraged the use of English, which to this day contains an almost unparalleled proportion of words of extraneous origin, and as the historian Freeman remarks, has lost the power [which Welsh still possesses] of forming new compound words from the original stock, which power he regards as the " test of a really living language."

This shews us that the linguistic condition of Wales has been to some extent anticipated in the past history of England and the fact that Welsh is scarcely allowed to enter a course of secular education, further than it can be used as an instrument to learn English, is no argument against its inherent worth or that it should not receive a larger meed of recognition.

At the close of the fifteenth century, I take the boundary of spoken Welsh to have embraced the whole country west of Offa's Dyke, with the exception of South Pembroke and Gower, and perhaps a district near Chepstow, and to have included the whole, or nearly all Herefordshire South of the Wye, some portions of the Forest of Dean, Clun Forest in Shropshire and the country west of Shrewsbury. We may have to except some small portion of North Herefordshire, west of the Dyke.

The great baronial families had to some extent become absorbed in the Welsh speaking populations; and the Scudamores of South Herefordshire were pretty certainly Welsh speaking; so were the Herberts of Raglan, who amassed a large Welsh library ; probably also the Turbervilles of Glamorganshire, the Aubres of Breconshire and possibly the Pulestons of North Wales ; other leading families were themselves of directly Welsh descent, such as the Morgans of Tredegar, and the Wynns of Gwydir.

It was a frequent occurrence for the sons of Norman barons to marry into Welsh families, even the Mortimers did this,

hence it would easily happen that these descendants would be
Welsh speaking. For instance*—Nest, daughter of Trahaern
ap Caradog, married Bernard de Newmarch; Nest, daughter
of Iestyn ap Gwrgant, married Robert Fitz Hamon. Margaret,
daughter of Llewelyn ap Iorwerth, married John de Breos.
On the other side, Dafydd ap Owain Gwynedd married a
daughter of Henry II. Llewelyn ap Iorwerth—Joan, a
sister of King John; and Llewelyn ap Gruffydd—Elinor
de Montfort, while Rhys Gryg married the daughter of Earl
Clare. Later on, than the preceding, Sir W. Scudamore
married a daughter of Owain Glyndwr. It was at Kentchurch in Herefordshire, the seat of the Scudamores, that Sion
Kent, the Monk bard of the 15th century, found protection
in those troublous times; he was a learned man, and, even
up to this nineteenth century, a marvellous, traditional
character has been given him among the peasantry of Gwent.

Two other reasons might be adduced for this Cymricizing
tendency—One was the state of semi-independence in which
some of the leading men liked to remain, hence their
attachment was naturally lessened to the Court language,
which was, as we have seen French for some centuries.

Another, was the influence of the Arthurian romances and
the story of the Trojans being the ancestors of the British,
which latter, though without a shadow of a foundation, was
sufficiently generally believed, to be adduced as evidence of
the high birth of Henry VII. and it is not surprising to find
L. Glyn Cothi writing of him :

> Evo yw'r atteg hir o Vrutus
> Er wedi Selyf o waed Silius
> O ddynion Troia lwyddianes vonedd
> Ac o ais Gwynedd ar ysganus.†

---

* See " *Hanes Llenyddiaeth Gymreig*," page 279.
† See translation next page.

D

This process of absorption into Welsh nationality was undoubtedly somewhat similar to that which took place in Ireland during the same period, and it proceeded there to such an extent, that the English Government was aroused to the danger of the Anglo Norman families becoming more Irish than the Irish themselves; so by the statutes of Kilkenny (Edward III. *circ* 1362), marriage with an Irish woman was declared *high treason.*

Linguistically, this fact is worth some consideration : Celtic languages have shewn in the past a much greater power of vitality than Scandinavian ones. Within a few generations after the settlement of the Northmen in Normandy, their language was unknown there and they had become French speaking ; perhaps the same thing could be said of Sicily.

In the Isle of Man where Norse or Scandinavian existed side by side with the Manx, it became extinct centuries ago ; in the Orkneys it also died out, long before the age of steam had time to interfere.

After the final conquest of Wales in 1283, there was no effort made to destroy the distinctive nationality of the people : in fact, various different laws and customs were retained and nothing like the statutes of Kilkenny was put in force ; but the provision for even-handed justice must have been weak.

The oppression of one of the border lords at Ruthin— probably one who had not been " Cymricized," drew forth reprisals from Owain Glyndwr, which eventually, involved nearly the whole of the marches from the Dee to the Wye ; and

---

[TRANSLATION].
† He is the great (*long*, literally) support descended from Brutus,
Though after Selyf from the blood of Silius,
From the men of Troy of successful origin,
And from the ribs of Gwynedd on his wanderings.

the House of Commons in 1431, when requesting that the forfeiture of his lands might be enforced, declared that had he been successful, the English tongue would have wholly and for evermore perished.

In consequence of this outbreak, and as early in its course as 1401, Parliament passed ordinances, calculated to promote in an eminent degree the evil they were directed against, or, at least, to inspire hatred of England, and discord among neighbours.

Among these provisions, after allowing an Englishman sued by a Welshman to be sued *only in England*, it disenfranchised all Englishmen married to Welsh women ; no victuals or ammunition might be imported into Wales except by permission of the King and his Council ; the Welsh were forbidden to keep their children at learning, or apprentice them to any occupation in any town or borough in the realm.

How far these merciless ordinances were actually carried out, I have been unable to ascertain, and as Wales was lost to English law for some years subsequently, they cannot have had much immediate effect beyond that of calling the Welsh from the English Universities or towns, whither they had gone for study or for purposes of trade, to enlist in the cause of Glyndwr, who is reputed to have died at Monnington, Herefordshire, shortly before the battle of Agincourt.

Among the Welshmen engaged there under Henry V., was Owen Tudor, son of Meredith ap Tudor, and a descendant of Prince Llewelyn, who was subsequently attached to the English Court.

Here he gained the affections of Catherine de Valois, Henry V's. widow shortly after death of the latter, and in 1428 was married to her, thus becoming the son-in-law of Charles VI. of France, Owain Glyndwr's former ally.

We can scarcely imagine an English Queen-dowager

marrying a representative of the Welsh royal line, and a scion of the Welsh nobility, which had been a few years before bitterly opposed to the English crown and almost everything English. Nor was it so, a peaceful domestic union of a Welshman with a Frenchwoman did more to bring about the final reception of Wales on equal terms into the councils of England, and to remove the sores of centuries, than the ebullitions of national hatred and the devastations of fire and sword had done in generations past.

Two sons were born of the marriage, Edward who was made Earl of Richmond, and Jasper who played an important part in the Wars of the Roses. Edward married Margaret Beaufort, heiress of the Lancastrian line of Plantagenets and died about 1456, leaving one son *Henry, Earl of Richmond,* who after the battle of Mortimer's Cross in 1461, and the subsequent execution of his grandfather Owen Tudor by the Yorkists, was imprisoned by order of Edward IV. On the accession of Henry VI. to temporary power in 1470 he was released and escaped to France, after receiving we may reasonably believe, a Cymric education at his place of confinement with the Herberts of Raglan, or at Usk, where, also, Edward IV. and Richard III. passed part of their time.

For fourteen years, Henry, with his uncle Jasper, appears to have found it necessary to be absent from England, till seizing his opportunity in the summer of 1485, during the unpopular reign of Richard III., and with the assistance of Rhys ap Thomas, Governor of South Wales, Evan Morgan, ancestor of the present Tredegar family and other Cambrian leaders, they effected a landing at Milford Haven, with some three thousand French or Breton troops.

After strengthening various positions on the border, and receiving reinforcements from Wales and a few Shropshire men, Henry marched to Bosworth field in Leicestershire, with the result known to all readers of history. Richard III., it is said, perished by the hand of Rhys ap Thomas, an ancestor of the present Lord Dynevor, and Henry was crowned on the battle field by Lord Stanley, who, with his Welsh followers from Chirk, Yale and Bromfield had seceded to his cause, "pitying" (so says the historian Powell) "the miseries of the Welsh."

With the accession to the throne of Henry Tudor as Henry VII. a new era begins for Wales, old things were passing away and a new order, of which we see the effects to-day, was beginning to appear. The ceaseless tumults, pillagings, forrays, heart burnings and wanton disregard of life and property which had prevented both high and low from receiving the benefits of civilization and honest employment, and also had stood in the way of Christian principles spreading among the people, though not perhaps wholly terminated, became more and more things of the past, and the husbandman felt he could at last, till his ground without fear of his crops being burnt or trampled on.

Whatever were the bad qualities of the Seventh Henry, Welshmen cannot say that he was ungrateful. Not long after his accession he repealed the odious ordinances of Henry IV. and actually granted the Abbot of Neath a charter for a *University of Wales.* How the project fell through, is not known, but if we had had another Cymric speaking, Welsh-bred King, it is probable that four hundred years would not have passed and the want still be unsupplied. (I have no positive evidence as to this qualification of the King, but consider it most likely, as he passed part of his youth in Wales). Lewys Morganwg in 1490 thus writes—

"A University at Neath ! A subject of celebration ! "

During the early years of Henry's reign, he was a frequent visitor at the border town of Ludlow, where Arthur, the young

Prince of Wales, was being brought up under the care of Sir Rhys ap Thomas, and we can hardly doubt but that Cymric influences largely directed the actions of the vice-regal Court of the Marches. Providence saw meet to cut short the career of this promising youth in 1502, and the government of Wales was then conducted by a council under a chief officer, styled the *Lord President of the Marches*, the first of whom, strange to say, was the *English Bishop of Lincoln*.

The semi-independent rule of the Lords Marchers does not, however, appear to have entirely ceased with these events, and the common people were deprived in greater or less degree of the ordinary protection granted to English subjects. One historian, Woodward, says—" Writs issued in the King's name were of no authority in the Marcher Lordships, but only such as bore the signature and seal of the Baron of the district." Even in Edward III's. time they were reminded "not to yield obedience to any one who might chance to be owner of Wales."

The Statutes of Rhuddlan given forth when Wales lay prostrate at the feet of Edward I., although destroying what remained at the political entity of the Welsh nation, scarcely took the Welsh language into consideration at all, it placed Wales in the hands of officers of the crown, and without any regular representation in the government. As may be gathered from what precedes the various offices were filled to some extent, perhaps nearly entirely, by persons of Welsh speech and sympathies. We get some trace in this in L. G. Cothi's poems, *Dosparth* I., 24, where he eulogizes Rhys ap Sion* of Glyn Neath, who would neither appoint an Englishman to fill any public office under government, nor even allow them to be empannelled in a jury (circ 1470.)

*Senedd vawr llys Nedd yw ro
" Lutenant" a'r wlad tano.[1]

Na welir Sais diddirwy
Na Saeson mewn Sessiwn mwy
Na dyn o Sais yn dwyn swydd
Na deu-Sais na bon' diswydd.

*   *   *

Ni ad Rhys ail entrio Sais.[2]

At this time, so far as the *pendefigion* (nobles) were concerned, there was in fact no great inducement for them to become Anglicized; the English tongue was only lately recognized as a medium for publication of the laws, and it had as yet, but a comparatively scanty literature; they had no call to the English Parliament, and on the whole they could do without English in Wales and attain as much culture as their neighbours the English landowners of Worcester and Gloucester. A great change, however, was near at hand, which shortly profoundly affected the relative position of the two languages.

This change was brought about by the following principal causes—

I.   The provisions of the Act incorporating Wales with England.

II. The increasing importance of English in England itself, as the official and literary language of the Country, after its long abasement.

III. The introduction of Printing into England—a mechanical

[TRANSLATION].

[1] He is a lieutenant of the great Council of the Court of Neath,
And the country subject to him.

[2] Let not an unfined Englishman be seen,
Nor Englishmen in the assizes any more,
Nor an Englishman in office ;
Nor two Englishmen, nor gentry, without office.

*   *   *

Rhys will not suffer an Englishman to be twice entered
[on the jury list.]

art which could only be practised under great difficulties in a sparsely populated country like Wales.

IV.   The Reformation which tended to popularize literature and freedom, and which made itself, at first, the most felt in England, and in those parts of England which lay nearest the continent, so that it came to Wales and Cornwall as an *English* movement.

V.   All the above facts tended to make an English education a thing more to be desiderated ; and they came to the view of Wales, without meeting there any national organization, which could produce social, and educational results of an independent character.

The *Reformation and the Discovery of Printing*, two great boons to the human race, happened near each other in point of time, and powerfully contributed to the breakdown of the Feudal system, and to render the whole country amenable to one central, civil authority.   The spirit of enquiry and of progress were abroad, and now that the old enmity was in good measure subdued, a general desire seems to have been spread abroad, among the more intelligent classes to learn English, which was fostered by the ruling powers, while any systematic instruction in the native language was ignored to the great loss of the nation.

The country had evidently suffered severely from this want of a centralized power and was too much in the condition of a conglomeration of semi-independent baronies and lordships, under which it was impossible to obtain due redress for grievances, nor could it make the progress it would have done under a responsible and impartial Government.

This state of things was somewhat in accord with the traditions of the middle ages, both in Great Britain and on the Continent, as well as Ireland ; but as further light and education spread among the people, law and order followed in their train.

To illustrate further what I mean,—the principles of the Reformation, and the invention of printing, came to the English from the Dutch and Germans; while the Revival of learning, which diverted men's minds from the narrow sphere, of the schoolmen's speculations, was partly of Latin (*i.e.*, Romance) growth. All these mighty levers, which transformed the character of the age, were appropriated in England, as part of the national life, and naturally made their power felt through the medium of the English Tongue, which, at the same time, received considerable additions from Latin sources; although it was still the few, and not the many who had the privilege of being able to read: but they were not appropriated in Wales, in so far as it was a part of England, and under the influence of English Universities and English laws; and because, in Wales, there was no Welsh University providing for an educated class of men capable of writing Welsh, and no Welsh laws involving its being spoken.

Just so, we may suppose, that if these events had happened three centuries before, when Norman-French was uppermost, they would have given a great impetus to the use and study of French, perhaps establishing it as a permanent tongue; but there would have been still this great difference—that, however much French might have been taught in the schools, and exclusively adopted in the courts, it was nowhere the language of the mass of the people; hence the comparison is not a perfect one between the relation of English to Welsh now, and the relation between English and French in the thirteenth century; neither does it follow, that, because the English people failed to be permanently bilingual, as remarked by Professor Jones in 1887, before the Royal Education Commission in London—

E

that Wales may not be so, under the different circumstances in which she is now, or may be placed.

The Welsh people, or a few of them, and from what part of the country I know not, addressed a memorial to the King in which they expressed a desire for Union with England and the introduction of its laws, and in which they promised to study English, were it but to learn how they might " better serve and obey his highness."

This was an appeal to a sovereign, who like his father, had felt obligations to Wales, and partly, if not wholly as a result of it, was enacted the statute of 1535 by which Wales was finally united to and incorporated with England; if we except the measure passed in 1689, whereby the remaining shadow of the Court of the Marches was abolished.

The text of the commencement runs thus—

Albeit the dominion, principality and country of Wales justly and righteously is, and ever hath been incorporated, annexed, united and subject to and under the imperial crown of this realm, as a very member and joint of the same, whereof the King's most royal Majesty of mere droite and very right, is very head, King, lord and Ruler, yet notwithstanding, by cause that in the same country, principality and dominion, diverse rights, usages, laws and customs be far discrepant from the laws and customs of this realm: and also because that the people of the same dominion have, and do daily use a speech nothing like ne consonant to the natural mother tongue used within this realm, some rude and ignorant people have made distinction and diversity between the King's subjects of this realm, and his subjects of the said dominion and principality of Wales, whereby great discord, variance, debate, division, murmur and sedition have grown between his said subjects. His highness, therefore, of a singular zeal, love and favour that he beareth toward his subjects of his said dominion of Wales, minding and intending to reduce them to the perfect order, notice and knowledge of the laws of this his realm, and *utterly to extirpe all and singular the sinister usages and customs differing from the same* and to bring about an amicable concord and amity between English and Welsh, declares Wales incorporated with England, with like liberties to subjects born there as in England; and the extension of the laws of inheritance and other English laws to Wales.

The statute annexes Lord Marcherships to counties already established, creates the fresh Counties of Monmouth, Brecknock, Radnor, Montgomery and Denbigh. Divides Wales into the north and south Wales assize circuits and gives Monmouthshire to the Oxford circuit. Provides for Parliamentary representation. Appoints the *sole use* of the English language in all courts. *Interdicts* the enjoyment of any kind of office throughout the King's dominions to persons USING THE WELSH TONGUE ON PAIN OF FORFEITURE, unless they adopted the English speech.

It is evident, from the above, that the Act was conceived in a kindly spirit toward the Welsh, and in part that it represented their own aspirations.

The last two provisions were, however, eminently unsatisfactory. I cannot regard them as expressing the will of the people; it is almost incredible to believe, that they could be immediately carried out. Who was responsible for them? Was it the king himself, or was it Roland Lee, who undertook the office of Lord President of the Marches in 1535, and was remarkably active in his post? Whoever it was, the author must have been an Englishman.

Referring to the said Roland, the antiquarian, Thomas Wright, in his history of Ludlow Castle, calls his a " mission of reforming and civilizing," but I suspect he started in it, devoid of one important qualification, viz.: A literary and colloquial knowledge of the Welsh language; which would have given him a proper understanding of the peculiar

condition of the people, whose good he should have served.
For all we know, this active Lord President of the "reforming
and civilizing" turn of mind was an official of the class
represented by the school inspectors (or masters) more frequent
in former days than now, whom a Glamorganshire teacher
speaks of as "rank Englishmen whose hobby is to stamp
out the Welsh language altogether." (*See Teachers' replies
Chap. IV.*)

If it had been enacted that all judges to try cases in Wales,
should have a competent knowledge of both languages, and
that other government officials should be subject to the same
rule, the material power of Wales in succeeding generations
might have been substantially increased, and its educational
status have been on a much more satisfactory basis than it is
at present.

As it was, these provisions contributed to give rise to a
state of things, wherein, almost all the educational advantages
which follow in the train of an advanced civilization, were
made to flow through a foreign medium, and as an even more
serious disadvantage, those whom the people naturally looked
up to as leaders, became gradually so thoroughly Anglicized,
that they partially lost that position, wherein mutual benefit
would have accrued to both rich and poor, from hearty
sympathy and mutual understanding with what was good
and worthy to be admired on either side.

On the other hand, however, we may remark that
Nationality, in those days, was dangerous stuff, although
language does not always affect it in the way sometimes
imagined; the son of the king, under whom Poyning's Act
was passed to Anglicize the Celto-Normans of Ireland, and
discourage the use of the Irish language, was probably not
sorry of an opportunity to consolidate his own kingdom by
having, even in its most remote districts, officials attached to

one language, and *that* the language of London—the central seat of power—and we must acknowledge Wales has, in many other respects, enjoyed untold advantages from the Act of Union. Poyning's Act, by the way, was of a similar character to the Statutes of Kilkenny.

Edward I., in 1284, had promulgated the Statutes of Rhuddlan, by which he intended Wales in future to be governed, and for this purpose the laws of Howel Dda were read before him and his counsellors : some of them he retained, in particular the provision for the division of land among all the sons of a deceased man, except that illegitimate sons were excluded. In 1542, however, the English Parliament passed another measure sweeping away the remainder of Howel Dda's laws, which had been retained for so long a period, and introducing primogeniture according to the English custom, though as will be seen in the appendix, under head of Gavel kind, certain parts of the country were allowed to retain the old custom.

I have hinted at a gradual extension of Welsh influence among the ruling class up to the fifteenth century ; but after the Act of Union, increased facilities for an education which was much moulded by English ideas, and the conditions in which they were placed, gradually tended to create an artificial separation in aims and feelings between them and the mass of the people which is painfully to be felt at the present day; to this state of things the practice of intermarriage with the English nobility has powerfully contributed. We have already seen that in pre-Tudor times the descendants of such marriages, if brought up in Wales, frequently became Cymry ; but after the Act of Union it was hardly to be expected. Henry VII., for instance, found a wife for his cousin, Charles Beaufort, in the person of the heiress of Raglan, and grand-daughter of William Herbert, Earl of Pembroke.

For some years, however, such as Lord Herbert of Chirbury
(author of the "Trioedd Arglwydd Herbert"), Sir E. Stradling
of Glamorganshire, patron of John David Rhys, the Mostyns,
and the Pulesdons were more or less Welsh in speech
and feeling.

Henry VII. was probably a Welsh-speaking sovereign;
Henry VIII. not; and had the former undertaken this
business, we cannot believe that he would have initiated such
a one-sided policy.

About 1542, Henry VIII., in the presidentship of the same
Roland Lee, gave license, to transfer the canons of Abergwili
College, which had been founded by Bishop Beck in 1323,
to Brecon, and founded there what is known as Christ College,
on the site of the Friars Priory, which had lately been
suppressed. One of the objects in establishing this college,
*evidently, was to spread the knowledge of the English
language.* The charter says,—

And, whereas, also our subjects dwelling in the southern parts
of Wales being oppressed with great poverty are not able to
educate their sons in good letters, nor have they any grammar
school; whereby both clergy and laity of every age and condition
are rendered rude and ignorant, as well in their offices towards
God as in their due obedience towards us; but they are so
little skilled in the vulgar-tongue of England, that they are not
able to observe our statutes in such cases enacted, and that,
which they ought, and are bound to perform, they are unable to
understand on account of ignorance of the English language.

In the days of manuscripts, Welsh literary undertakings
had flourished in proportion to the population in a greater
degree than in England; *now* it was a recognized fact that to
be abreast of the age a man must learn English; and that
through the English press, he must mainly look for literary
enlightenment and instruction, besides which, there was the

difficulty of finding a sufficiently numerous clientèle of readers
to make Welsh printing remunerative in those early times, as
well as that, of not having such a central point for publication,
as London presented for English works; so that, for 150 or
200 years there was remarkably little printed in Welsh except
a few religious treatises and books, some of which were
designed indirectly or directly to spread the knowledge of
English; even the Bibles of 1588 and 1620 were chained with
the English Bible, that the people might learn English.

W. Salesbury, in the introduction of his English and Welsh
Dictionary, thus writes to Henry VIII :—

Your excellent wisdom has caused it to be established, that
there shall be no difference in laws and language, considering
how much hatred and strife arises from difference in language,
and community of language is a bond of love and friendship; and
it is also, in the judgment of all wise men, particularly suitable
and convenient, that those who are under the government of one
head, and a most generous King, should use one language.

He goes on to say, that as many in Wales could read Welsh
perfectly; by means of his dictionary they might teach
themselves and others also [to read English], so that, in the
quickest way, the knowledge of the English language might
spread through the whole country.

The result of these views was, that, except in the case of a
select few, Welsh, as a medium for intellectual education, or
for acquiring general knowledge, was almost wholly neglected,
of which neglect Bishop Davies complains in 1567, and Morris
Kiffin in 1595.

John Edwards, translator of the "Marrow of Modern Divinity
in 1651," says, "no nation cultivates such enmity to their
language as the Welsh!" While Vicar Prichard leaves his testimony in 1630, that not one per cent. of the people could read
Welsh : although, eighty-seven years before, W. Salesbury says,

that many could.   Possibly these readers had come from schools
taught by the monks ; and a future historian may be able to
tell us how such as Salesbury himself, learned to read Welsh.

Just 100 years after the John Edwards above-quoted,
Thos. Richards wrote in the preface to his dictionary :—

" I know too well there are some who have such an aversion
to their mother tongue that they profess a hearty desire of
seeing it entirely abolished, that no remains of it may be left in
this Island.   So great an eyesore is the language of their forefathers become unto them *   *   *   their prejudice and ignorance
render them altogether unfit to pass a right judgment upon it "
[The Dictionary].   And again :—

" Fe edrych pob iaith yn chwith ac yn anhyfryd i'r neb ni fo
yn ei gwybod. Ac onid yw yn gywilydd-gwarthus iddynt hwy
fod mor wybodus oddigartref, ac mor hyfedr a chyfarwydd mewn
ieithoedd ereill, fod, ar yr un pryd yn anwybodus gartref, heb
fedru siarad yn iawn, chwaethach darllen a 'sgrifenu Iaith eu
Mamau."

In addition to these testimonies there is that of John Penry
(quoted by Ivor James), when petitioning the Queen and
Parliament in 1587, he says, there is no market-town in Wales,
where English is not as common as Welsh.   From Chepstow
to Chester, all round the country, and the sea-shore, they all
understood English.

These facts—with those I shall advance further on—indicate
that up to the time of the publication of the Welsh Bible, and
for years after, Wales was not far from running neck and neck
with Cornwall in the process of Anglicization ; there were,
however, forces at work which limited its extent, and which
up to the present day have tended to build up a nationality
that may yet have a further development in the next century.
On the one hand we see a process of disintegration, and what
the writer of " Siluriana " has called " denationalization and

deodorization," and on the other we shall see that there has been a contrary tendency expressive of individuality and national feeling clothed in that language which can most adequately express it, and coincident with a knowledge of the cosmopolitan English.

If it was a Tudor who gave the language a deadly thrust, it was a Tudor, on the other hand, who assisted in its preservation; for a principal mainstay against this tendency, which had lately been initiated, was an order for the publication of the Welsh Bible by Queen Elizabeth and her Parliament in 1568, and which was carried into effect in 1588; although there were then persons not unrepresented in the present day, who feared that such a measure would revivify the language.

Dr. Morgan, Vicar of Llanrhaiadr-yn-Mochnant, to whose labours the Welsh are indebted for the translation they now are privileged with, in his Latin dedication of the Bible to the Queen,* says that the Act sets forth, at the same time, "our idleness and slothfulness, because we could neither be moved by so grave a necessity, nor be constrained by so favourable a law, but that such work (than which there could not be anything of greater importance) was allowed to remain almost untouched." Closs in his history of the Church of England in Wales, says, that there was a desire on the part of the bishops to suppress the Welsh language, and they thought that if they refused to translate the Bible they would thus compel the Welsh to learn English.

It is some consolation to look back to that period and feel that twenty long years of waiting preceded an event fraught with so much importance to the future of Wales, and which is still bearing daily fruit, also to feel that apathy,

---

* A revised translation got out by Bishop Parry. which is now the standard version, was published in 1620.

F

indifference, and delay in the nineteenth century do not necessarily impose impassable barriers on the attainment of such a desirable object, as the general recognition of the language of the people in educational and legal matters. Had the Welsh Bible never existed, how different would the future of Wales and her language have been?

We may look to Ireland, what would not she have gained had a similar measure been secured for her? It was true that there was a spirit of greater opposition there to the English Government than in Wales, but perhaps not an invincible one. In a future chapter remarks will be made on the educational position of the Irish language, which differs from the Welsh in having no background of modern literature.

It should be remarked that while the Government allowed their order for a translation, reviewed by the five bishops (Hereford included), to "be printed and used in churches by the first of March, 1566," to become a dead letter, the object was in fact attained mainly by a country priest, one of the very few in the diocese at that time who actually preached at all. Here, then, is encouragement again to private individuals to wrest the palm from supine officialism.

A learned book called *Institutiones Linguæ Britannicæ*, by Dr. John David Rhys, appeared about the same time as Dr. Morgan's Bible. It was framed, some have thought, with the idea of giving Welsh parsons a scientific knowledge of the tongue that they might read and understand the Bible better : the former was presented to Queen Elizabeth* by the wife of John Scudamore, of Holme Lacy (an M.P. for Herefordshire in successive sessions), a favorite at court, and member of the family, who had kept Sion Kent, at Kentchurch, and had taken up arms for Owain Glyndwr.

---

* See *Llyfryddiaeth y Cymry*, p., 66.

Queen Elizabeth was mindful of her Tudor descent, and one of her maids of honour was Blanche Parry, of the Golden Vale, Herefordshire, which was then a Welsh speaking district. The poet Spenser introduces a Scudamore, prominently, in the "Faerie Queene," Book iv.   Whether in Herefordshire, or elsewhere, Spenser seems to have picked up some Welsh :—

> " How oft that day did sad Brunchildis see
> The green shield died in dolorous vermeil ⌈vermilion⌋?
> That not *scuith guridh** it mote seeme to bee,
> But rather *y scuith gogh* signe of sad Crueltie.   Book ii.

Again :

> And Twede the limit betwixt *Logris*† land and Albany.
>
>   [Book iv., Canto xi. 36.]

What English poet these days would think of alluding to England, as *Logris* land ?

In Elizabeth's reign it is probable that most of the County landowners were familiar with Welsh, perhaps more so than with English, in spite of her father's enactment that offices must not be filled by any person using the Welsh tongue. What was the practical interpretation of that claim ? I am unable to say; it may have simply prohibited Welsh as an official language; but the tendency, doubtless, was to foster the growth of a class of people in Wales whose national place would have been as leaders, but who are separated from their neighbours by a chasm, artificially caused by their exclusive use of a foreign idiom; which tendency, has of course, been much developed and strengthened by the banishment of Welsh from the higher schools and colleges.

The seventeenth century was a comparatively uneventful one for the Welsh language ; but during that period perhaps even

---

* These stand for *ysgwydd werdd* (a green shield), and *ysgwydd coch* (a red shield.)

† *Logris* land, of course = the Welsh *Lloegr*.

more than now, was English well established as the official
language; and during the Civil Wars, as remarked by Ivor
James,* the appeals to the country on either side were almost
exclusively issued in English. After the accession of Charles
II., however, it was ordered that the book of Common Prayer
should be provided for Welsh speaking districts in the Welsh
Dioceses, and in that of Hereford.

The total number of Welsh Bibles printed from 1600 to 1700,
averaged only some 3,200, every decenniad, being very
much below the wants of the population. One of the bene-
factors of the country towards the end of that period was
T. Gouge, who instituted schools to teach the poorest children
to learn English. Rees, the author of " Protestant Nonconformity in Wales," while highly admiring his piety and
philanthropy, says this was a "great mistake," and rendered
them comparatively useless to the children of the poor. It is
somewhat singular to find in a report of the work carried on
by T. Gouge, and his friends in 1674, it is mentioned, that 32
Welsh Bibles had been distributed, which were "all that
could be had in Wales or London." The opposition to Welsh
similar to that of the sixteenth century, cropping up again in
the seventeenth, as is thus referred to by Rees :—

The promoters of Welsh literature at that time were greatly
discouraged, and even opposed by many persons of influence and
authority, who thought that no books should have been printed
in the Welsh language, in order to induce the people to learn the
English. That opinion has operated most disastrously against the
intellectual and spiritual advancement of the Welsh nation, ever
since the Reformation. (2nd Ed., p. 195.)

Towards the beginning of the eighteenth century *political
reasons again* were influential in discouraging Welsh nationality

*See Y Traethodydd—1886.

when the attachment of the people to the house of Hanover
was by no means strong.

Another change, however, was at hand, which has profoundly
affected the History of Wales, we may almost call it a second
great tidal wave of the Reformation, rolling in two centuries
after the event. The first tidal wave had, as we have seen in
conjunction with other causes, rather depreciated the status
of Welsh, as a medium to reach the intelligence, and improve
the culture of the people ; the second, which the last decades
of the eighteenth century, saw rapidly rising to its height, has
been largely the means of creating a modern national literature,
in which every cottage, and every hamlet, in extensive districts
of the country has, more or less, a direct interest ; so that
Welsh literary culture no longer was confined to the John
David Rhyses, the Dr. Davieses, the Edward Llwyds, and a
few *clerigwyr*, and representatives of the old well-known
families, but was participated in, though in a necessarily
imperfect fashion by the farmers, small tradesmen, noncon-
formist preachers, and even working men who took the places
of the gentlemen bards of the fifteenth century.

Religion, undoubtedly, lay at the root of the dispositions
which principally facilitated this change, and, as it should
be regarded principally from this standpoint, it will be out of
place for me here to criticize its history, but this much is
said, lest any should think that undue prominence is given to
the indirect, secular effects which followed in the wake of the
movement.

Of course I am alluding to the great Methodist arising,
which, apart from any religious teaching it afforded, was the
means of acquainting the great mass of the Welsh people with
the power and discipline of organization, and of giving them
the opportunity of learning to read their own language ; at
first, the Bible ; next, a denominational vernacular literature ;

which speedily sprang up, not only among the Methodists but among the other leading dissenting bodies ; which, while giving the facility to read indirectly, paved the way for *writing Welsh* to become a common self-taught art (though, as will be seen later on, by no means so universal as it might be), and thereby furnished a stepping-stone for the dissemination of a secular and vernacular literature, which in the branches of poetry is by no means inconsiderable.

This work had partially been anticipated early in the century by Griffith Jones, of Llanddowror, who, seeing the inefficiency of schools conducted in English, established circulating schools] for a few months at a time, at a place. By means of his effort, a large number of persons, including adults, were taught to read, and thus the way was gradually made for the later Methodist and other dissenters, under whose auspices it became a rare thing to find any adult brought up with them, unable to read his or her language.

All the while we must recollect, or at least since 1790, Welsh was practically excluded from the day schools, ; it was the establishment of schools on the first day of the week, which this revival made possible, that so vastly increased the number of readers in the vernacular ; and it is probable the increase has gone on from that day to this. Such an impetus was strengthened early in the nineteenth century by the establishment of the Bible Society and the issue of cheap Welsh Bibles, so that in Welsh-Wales instead of there being only one per cent. who could read Welsh, as in Prichard's time, there was certainly a very much larger proportion in 1820, about the time when the Eisteddfodau began to be a factor in the national life.

It is a suggestive fact that Methodism broke out first, and most extensively in those districts, where the poems of Rees Prichard and the schools of Griffith Jones had exerted the most powerful influence. Some of my readers not familiar with the history of Wales, may need to be told, that Rees Prichard was a Vicar of Llandovery, who died about 1644, and whose religious and didactic poems, entitled "*Canwyll y Cymry*," so commended for their colloquial style by the Rector of Merthyr in 1887, to the Royal Commission on Education, became almost a household book in Wales, and have been again and again reprinted, the last edition being quite a recent one by Wm. Jones, Printer, Newport, Mon.

Had it not been for this change, there is, humanly speaking so, some ground to believe that the Bishop of David's would have been correct when he said, not long ago, that Wales was "only a geographical expression." Perhaps, however, in his case, the wish was father to the thought.

The author of the Prize Essay on the "Character of the Welsh as a Nation," published in 1841, undoubtedly takes cognizance of the indirect effect of this multiplication of readers on Welsh literature; he says—

During the last twenty five or thirty years, a great revival has taken place in Welsh literature; but it is remarkable that the interest felt in its cultivation, has by no means impeded but rather assisted the diffusion of the English language. (p. 23.)

The consideration of the educational and linguistic state of Wales during the great industrial era which embraces the last fifty years, I propose to consider in the next chapter.

CHAPTER III.

In 1846 the Government undertook to direct an enquiry into the state of Education in the Principality of Wales, especially into the means afforded to the labouring classes of an acquiring a knowledge of the English language.

The terms of the enquiry called forth the following able criticism from the acute and learned Bishop Thirlwall of David's, well known in English literary circles as the author of one of the Standard Histories of Greece. He acquired sufficient knowledge of the Welsh language to be able to preach in it, and was the only Bishop who had the courage to vote for the Disestablishment of the Irish Church. He says in 1848 :—

"I think it is to be regretted that, according to the terms in which the object of the enquiry was originally described, it was directed to be made, not simply into ' the state of education in the principality of Wales,' but ' especially into the means afforded to the labouring classes of acquiring the knowledge of the English language.' I think this addition was unnecessary, because the investigation of this point must have formed a main part of a full enquiry into the state of education in Wales; while the putting it thus prominently forward was attended with two unhappy effects : one is, that it lent a handle to those who wish to represent the Commission as an engine framed for the purpose, among others equally injurious, of depriving the people of Wales of their ancient language. The other is, that it tended to suggest or confirm an exaggerated conception of the efficacy of schools, in producing a change in the language of the country. This I regard as one of the most pernicious errors that beset the subject ; and I am afraid that it prevails very extensively among persons who have great influence over the management of schools. It might have been thought, that a very little observation and reflection must be sufficient to convince every one that a school, however well conducted, must, of itself, be almost utterly powerless for such an object, where a language taught in it for a few hours in the day is one which the children never think in nor use at any other time. It ought, I think, to be evident, that a general change in the colloquial language of the country is only to be expected from the operation of very different causes ; though the school learning may, in conjunction with them, contribute to promote it. But the persuasion of its adequacy for the purpose is not simply a theoretical error, but one which, so far as it prevails, tends most seriously to obstruct the progress of good education. For, under this impression, the managers of schools prohibit, not only the learning of the Welsh letters, and the reading of Welsh books, but all use of the language in school hours."

Now I wish my readers, though I fear some of those I desire to reach will fight shy of this volume, from the very beginning, would just give due weight to these words,—"one of the most pernicious errors;" "tends most seriously to obstruct the progress of good education." Are they the words of an hot-headed Eisteddfodwr, or of a man of one sided culture, on whose opinions the successors of the broken down schoolmasters of 1846, look down with indifference from their superior vantage ground of 1891. No, they came from the "*Esgob call Tyddewi,*" who has left his mark in English literature, not a Welshman, but an Englishman, who deserved to be listened to because he knew what he was talking about, which could not be averred in the case of nine out of ten utterances on the subject by representative persons.

G

The names of the Commissioners were R. R. W. Lingen, M.A., Jelinger C. Symons, and Henry Vaughan Johnson, each of whom furnished the Lords of the Committee of Council on Education with a report on the district,* undertaken by them individually. These reports contain valuable information, and will doubtless, be again and again referred to by future historians of Wales. We must, however, bear in mind, that they were drawn up by men to whom Wales was a foreign country, and who were obliged to accept much evidence at second-hand without using such discrimination as would have laid in their power, had the sphere of their labours been in London; we must also bear in mind that their reports shew very little evidence, that they were, in the first place, any way adequately acquainted with the social, moral, and intellectual state of the labouring class in England. If they had been, I think, they would have received the facts presented to them in Wales, with a judgment tempered by a wider range of experience. It is true they were not called upon to give a judgment, so much as to collect and classify evidence, which they did in a laborious and, in some respects, admirable manner; nevertheless, the inferences drawn from the facts were not, on the whole, adequately representative of the reality.

The reports evoked forth quite a storm in Wales; the whole incident was called *"Brad y Llyfrau Gleision."*† Sir Thomas Phillips, a Welsh speaking Welshman—the Mayor of Newport who withstood the Chartists in 1839, appeared in the lists as the Champion of Wales, and shewed clearly that on the score of morality, instead of Wales being, as might have

---

* R. W. Lingen took Carmarthen, Pembroke and Glamorgan. J. C. Symons —Cardigan, Brecknock, Radnor, and part of Monmouth. H. V. Johnson— North Wales.

† "The Treason of the Blue Books."

been gathered from the Commissioners' report, utterly in the shade, side by side with England—though they did not say so in so many words—so far as statistics of illegitimacy are indications, six out of nine English districts, including Yorkshire and the Northern Counties, were worse than Wales; and, moreover, that the worst county in Wales in this respect Radnorshire is almost entirely Anglicized in speech; Montgomeryshire and Pembrokeshire being the next, neither of which are thoroughly Welsh counties.

Many of the Commissioners' remarks on the extremely inefficient and defective means of intellectual and moral training would, doubtless, have applied to some parts of England as well as to Wales. Even Wm. Howitt, the son of a man of property, "went to a dame school, and then to one kept by a merry little man, the baker of the village. This schoolmaster was wont to come whistling out of his hot bake-house to hear his pupils read, and to set them their copies in the intervals of setting his bread."*

Events move rapidly in our days: the railway and the telegraph, and almost an universal system of schools under efficient, trained teachers and inspectors, are now taken as matters of course, and we almost forget how near we are still living to the time when the machinery of education was on an altogether different basis, when these and other developments of civilization were still in their infancy.

Since the publication of this Report, in 1848, a new generation has had some time to grow up, and now mainly occupies the scene of action. To many of them it will appear almost incredible, that Wales was what it was at that time; they will, however, bear in mind that the description of the country, given by the Commissioners, does not illustrate an *all-round*

---

* See *Records of a Quaker Family.* London: Harris & Co., 1889, p. 181.

view, but rather some aspects of it, as presented to the minds
of persons who had apparently the disadvantage of no previous
common bond of sympathy or association with the people
they went to visit.

J. C. Simons and R. W. Lingen, in particular, naturally
looked to the Established Church, and its dignitaries, to perform the office of Virgil, when he conducted Dante into
purgatory, and the last mentioned Commissioner was provided
with powder and shot in the shape of introductions to the
Lords Lieutenant and the Bishops of his district. The former
(J. C. S.) had letters of introduction from the Bishop of
Hereford, and a circular letter from Connop Thirlwall, Bishop
of "St." David's.

Although, as will be seen, education has put on a new face
since the time of the Commissioners, I propose to take up
some pages of this book, with extracts from the reports, which
will, I believe, not be altogether unwelcome to many who
may not readily be able to refer to the originals, and which
are necessary to my purpose of endeavouring to present
materials for an historical manual of Welsh Education in its
relation to the language. The pages refer to the 8vo. edition.

In the Government instructions issued to the Commissioners,
they were reminded of the fact that "numerous Sunday
schools have been established in Wales, and their character
and tendencies should not be overlooked in an attempt to
estimate the provision for the instruction of the poor." The
Reports, accordingly, contain a mass of statistics of these
schools, which would be out of place for me to attempt to
reproduce here. I will however, include some of them
bearing on the question of language, besides various remarks
made by the Commissioners, or other persons which appear
worthy of attention.

For convenience sake the extracts will be grouped together

under separate headings, one of which will refer to those called Sunday schools, and others to day schools in English speaking parts of Wales, others to the Teachers, the condition of the school houses, School Patrons and Managers, character of the teaching, Welsh language and literature, and General Remarks.

FIRST DAY (SUNDAY) SCHOOLS.

A prominent feature in the Report was a full amount of detail of the schools on the first day of the week, known as Sunday Schools. Here, the Welsh language, excluded from the day schools, found, and does still find, a place—and an important place; but the real fact remains, that in consequence, much *secular* instruction was given in the way of teaching reading in that language: and this did not escape the notice of Commissioner Symons, who uttered a protest which has been repeated by some of the friends of Wales of late years.

I cannot close these remarks on Sunday-schools without venturing to express my disapproval of the practice, common alike to Church and Dissenting schools, of allowing young children to learn and read in them. This is surely a perversion of the object and spirit of the institution. I have frequently seen persons occupied in teaching little children to spell and pronounce small words, not only engrossing their time with the drudgery of elementary instruction, but disturbing the rest of the scholars. Schools thus conducted cease to be seminaries of religious knowledge and sink into week-day schools of the lowest class. It is a fallacy to say that no secular instruction is given in Welsh Sunday-schools: this *is* secular instruction, and of the most profitless and least spiritual kind. (*Symons*, p. 285.)

The Commissioner objects to the burden of teaching reading, in these schools, which afforded the only opportunities for the mass of the population to learn to read their mother tongue, and yet he objects to the more preferable way of teaching it in the day schools. If reading had not been taught there, what could have been taught except *viva voce*? He embodies in his report, without comment, the testimony of John Saunders (Independent preacher), that these schools supplied much of the *deficiency* of the day schools.

This was an evil then, and it is an evil now : the proper place for secular instruction is the *day school*—not a gathering professedly for religious purposes. Is it not surprising that the leaders of the people have not long ago given due weight to the considerations which occasioned the above quoted remarks?

What is the remedy? Plainly, nothing else than to *teach* Welsh children at the *day schools* to read Welsh in all districts where there is a considerable proportion of them attending Welsh classes and Welsh preaching on the first day of the week.

Henry V. Johnson, the North Wales Commissioner, gives some very apposite remarks on the educational effect of these schools ; and although it would not be true to say that the resources of the language in every other branch, except theology, are meagre, the character of the demand for current Welsh literature is very considerably modified by the fact that the terms used in many books of a secular character are too unfamiliar to make them popular. He says—

The language cultivated in the Sunday schools is Welsh ; the subjects of instruction are exclusively religious : consequently the religious vocabulary of the Welsh language has been enlarged, strengthened, and rendered capable of expressing every shade of idea, and the great mass of the poorer classes have been trained from their childhood to its use. * * They have enriched the theological vocabulary, and made the peasantry expert in handling that branch of the Welsh language, but its resources in every other branch remain obsolete and meagre, and even of these the people are left in ignorance. (p. 519.)

What wonder that its resources in other branches remained obsolete, when no further means of cultivating it were afforded.

The following two paragraphs illustrate Lingen's attitude to these schools:—

They gratify that gregarious sociability which animates the Welsh towards each other. * * The Welsh working-man rouses himself for them. Sunday is to him more than a day of bodily rest and devotion. It is his best chance, all the week through, of showing himself in his own character He marks his sense of it by a suit of clothes regarded with a feeling hardly less sabbatical than the day itself. I do not remember to have seen an adult in rags in a single Sunday school throughout the poorest districts. They always seemed to me better dressed on Sundays than the same class in England. *(Lingen, pp. 5 and 6.)*

Most singular is the character which has been developed by this theological bent of minds isolated from nearly all sources, direct or indirect, of secular information. Poetic and enthusiastic warmth of religious feeling, careful attendance upon religious services, zealous interest in religious knowledge, the comparative absence of crime, are found side by side with the most unreasoning prejudices or impulses, an utter want of method in thinking and acting, and (what is far worse) with a wide-spread disregard of temperance whenever there are the means of excess, of chastity, of veracity, and of fair dealing. (do., p. 9.)

If this isolation from secular information is so prejudicial, why be so jubilant (as will be seen further on) that there should be no secular institution for a distinctively Welsh education, which might pave the way for a wider scope of mental ideas.

A 1st day (Sunday) school teacher in the Welsh part of Caio hundred, Carmarthenshire, sent the learned Commissioner a letter, from which the following, *verbatim et literatim*, is extracted :—

I am very please to take little trouble to answer your letter about the Sunday Schools, in hope that your Searching about the Daily and Sunday Schools, will come to good consequence to the Welsh Nation.

Our Creator make many of them a People of Strong Abilities, and a possessors of various talents, but because their ignorance Spend their time in poverty to get their living in Slavery as a pig and his snout in the ground they got no advantage to make use of their abilities in defect of learning and knowledge. But Some of the young people are under good education, the Children of the Noblemen and Gentlemen farmers but the greater part of them in Towns: and in the countrys one here and one there. The major part of the welchmen, not knoweth in what quarter of the world they live? this thing I think is very true.

In the time ago riseth up some Excellent people in Philosophy and Theology among the welch Nation as one of the *welch Poet say's about one of them, called The Reverend Mr. Rowlands Llangaetho,

> Talentau ddeg fe roddwyd iddo
> Fe'i marchnattodd hwy yn iawn
> Ae* o'r deg fe'i gwnaeth hwy'n gannoedd
> Cyn maihludo 'i haul brydnhawn.

I hope that you'll not be angry with me, because I have on my mind to desire on you, Sir, to give me a little presant, that is, the Map of the land of Canaan. (do., pp. 185 and 186.)

At Llanelly, in connection with the Capel Als School (Independent), some of the parents objected to their children "being taught Welsh on Sundays." This objection would now be scarcely so likely to occur.

---

* William Williams, Pantycelyn. The stanza is given as printed, but I am inclined to think that the errors in the Welsh spelling were due to the compositor or the transcriber.

The following observation is undoubtedly just:—

[Gilead School, wholly Welsh . Readiness and propriety of expression, to an extent more than merely colloquial, is certainly a feature in the intellectual character of the Welsh. (*Lingen*, p. 136.)

J. C. Symons says of the Dissenting schools, that the routine is admirable, and of the "Church Sunday Schools," they want life. The whole system is spiritless and monotonous and repulsive instead of attractive to children;" and in the way of general remarks—

I have heard very curious and recondite inquiries directed to solve even pre-Adamite mysteries in these schools. The Welsh are very prone to mystical and pseudo-metaphysical discussion, especially in Cardiganshire. The great doctrines and moral precepts of the Gospel are, I think, too little taught in Sunday Schools. They are more prone to dive into abstract and fruitless questions upon minute incidents, as well as debatable doctrines,— as for example, who the angel was that appeared to Balaam, than to illustrate and enforce moral duties or explain the parables. (*Symons*, p. 285.)

Somewhat contrasting with the remarks of Lingen on such schools are those of the third Commissioner, H. V. Johnson, he says:—

As the influence of the Welsh Sunday school decreases, the moral degradation of the inhabitants is more apparent. This is observable on approaching the English border.

         *   o   *

The humble position and attainments of the individuals engaged in the establishment and support of Welsh Sunday schools enhances the value of this spontaneous effort for education; and however imperfect the results, it is impossible not to admire the vast number of schools which they have established, the frequency of the attendance, the number, energy, and devotion of the teachers, the regularity and decorum of the proceedings, and the striking and permanent effects which they have produced upon society. (p. 519.)

H

It may interest some of my Welsh readers to consult the following tables, which may be taken as fairly correct for 1846. I have only inserted the statistics of some counties for fear of swelling the list to an immoderate size.

STATISTICS OF "SUNDAY" SCHOOLS BELONGING TO THE PRINCIPAL DENOMINATIONS IN VARIOUS COUNTIES, SHEWING PER CENTAGE AS TO LANGUAGE IN WHICH INSTRUCTION IS GIVEN.

CARMARTHENSHIRE.	Total number of schools.	Welsh only per cent.	English only per cent.	English and Welsh per cent
Episcopalian	48	18·8	22·9	58·3
Calvinistic Methodists	78	68·0	1·3	30·7
Independents	110	46·4	·9	52·7
Baptists	55	45·5	—	54·5
GLAMORGANSHIRE.				
Episcopalian	92	4·3	79·4	16·3
Calvinistic Methodists	90	72·2	4·5	23·3
Independents	99	52·6	5·0	42·4
PEMBROKESHIRE.				
Episcopalian Schools	52	9·6	82·7	7·7
Calvinistic Methodists	44	50·0	25·0	25·0
Independents	57	38·6	31·6	29·8
BRECKNOCKSHIRE.				
Episcopalian	40	10·0	77·5	12·5
Calvinistic Methodists	45	80·0	4·4	15·6
Independents	51	43·1	2·0	54·9
MONMOUTHSHIRE.				
Episcopalian	30	3·3	80·0	16·7
Independents	34	11·7	20·6	667
Baptists	40	5·6	22·5	72·5
CARNARVONSHIRE.				
Episcopalian Schools	16	18·7	25·0	56·3
Baptists	16	80·0	—	20·0
Calvinistic Methodists	137	99·2		·8
Independents	49	93.7	2·1	4·2
DENBIGHSHIRE.				
Episcopalian	32	6·3	28·1	65·6
Calvinistic Methodists	104	83·7	7·7	8·6
Independents	40	72·5	7·5	20·0

RADNORSHIRE—6 out of 53 schools were conducted in English and Welsh.

What difference in these proportions is observable in 45 years I am unable to say. The figures do not afford a trustworthy index of the proportion of the population speaking Welsh, because they give per centages of schools and not of scholars; and as R. W. Lingen remarks of those in both languages in his district, the English class is generally very small; he says, in reference to indirect means for spreading English—

The Sunday schools in nowise conduce to such an end. Thirty-eight per cent. of them are conducted in Welsh only, and 36·4 per cent. in both languages. In the latter, however (excepting the Church schools), the English class is generally *very small*, being composed either of those children who are going to a day school, and whose parents object their being taught Welsh on Sundays, or else of those adults who are not of the labouring class. (p. 51.)

We find, however, that the Episcopalian body are foremost [then under English bishops] in carrying forward what Lingen and Symons regarded as the important work of superseding the Welsh language. In Glamorganshire, 79·4 per cent. of their schools were conducted in *English* only; but 72·2 per cent. of the Calvinistic Methodist schools, in *Welsh* only.

The following table of Pembrokeshire statistics shew that these schools were attended by a larger proportion of the population in the Welsh speaking district, than in the English.

COUNTY OF PEMBROKE.	Total per cent. of population attending 1st day (Sunday) school.	Per cent. of Scholars attending Episcopalian.
Castlemartin Hundred (English speaking District) ...	10½ ...	82·0
Dewisland (Welsh speaking District)	25 ...	7·0

That is to say in Castlemartin of the small proportion of the population, viz., 10½ per cent., who went to the "Sunday" school, four-fifths attended those managed by the Episcopalians, whereas in "Dewisland" 93 per cent. were attenders in Non-conformist schools.

DAY SCHOOLS IN ENGLISH-SPEAKING PARTS OF WALES.

R. W. Lingen remarks on the greater number of resident gentry and proprietors in the part of Pembrokeshire called "Little England beyond Wales," and connects this fact with a superior class of day schools, which he says " compensates for the absence of Sunday schools." (*Report*, p. 174, *Castlemartin hundred and Borough of Pembroke.*) It will be seen, how-ever, by the following extracts, that very much had to be said on the other side.

— Davies, Independent minister of Golden, near Pembroke, considered that in and about Pembroke there was a general care-lessness on the subject of education, and that, as regards religious knowledge, the people were inferior to those in the Welsh districts. The Sunday schools are fewer, and worse attended.

The master of the Apprentices' school [at Pater] said—

It was difficult to realize, except by experience, the backward-ness or rather utter absence of secular education in Wales. * ⁰ The style of the Scriptures, their only reading-book, did not enable them to read with intelligence the most ordinary work upon subjects of common information. Such was the experience of a man who was coming into daily contact with what are rather the *élite* of the Welsh labouring classes in an English-speaking part of the country. (p. 175.)

The reader will here note—inability to "read with intelli-gence the most ordinary work," in a place which has been English speaking for centuries.

It is not uncommon to hear the Welsh advised to learn

English for the sake of its literature, but I venture to say now, and shall have reason to repeat myself, that the mass of the English people have not yet learned English in the sense of the authors of those platitudes. Barbarian manners and inability in the Welsh to master literary English are largely ascribed to the influence of their language. Why not ascribe all the torpidity of good, honest Hodge to the influence of his language. On the whole it is very much to be doubted whether the limited range of ideas which Lingen notices was greatest in the Welsh or the English speaking districts, and if so, what ground has he to say of the Welsh workman that his "language keeps him under the hatches." If it was true of poor Taffy going from his mountain hut to the ironworks, why not of the above-mentioned Hodge. Probably the latter had fewer difficulties in some directions to contend against in working his way to be overman, and then to be manager, but the former had a skill in dialectics which the other did not possess, and which was not so easily marketable in £ s. d., as mechanical ability.

The statement above referred to was a slipshod one, which though made 44 years ago, I have seen quoted in 1890. There was *no evidence* to warrant R.W.L. in saying this ; he had ample evidence for saying that ignorance of English kept Welsh workmen under the hatches; but knowledge of English, as the passport to advancement in the material world, does not necessarily imply ignorance of Welsh. He would with much more justice have said that a faulty system of education had that depressing effect.

What of the late David Davies, chairman of the Barry Dock and Railway Company ; what of Edward Williams, son of Taliesin ap Iolo, late manager of Bolckow, Vaughan and Company, Middlesbro'? The writer happens to be acquainted with the shipping agent for a large and well known firm of

colliery proprietors, who remarked not long ago, " While I am
speaking to you I am translating from Welsh (mentally) into
English ;" at any rate that fact did not disqualify him for a
responsible position.

Pursuing the point further—

" The non-comprehension of what they read is by no means
confined to the children who speak Welsh, and read English ; it
prevails also amongst those of whom English is the mother tongue.
The reason is that the English they read is not the English they
talk. * * * I found children who read fluently, constantly
ignorant of such words, as ' observe,' ' conclude,' ' reflect,'
' perceive,' ' refresh,' &c." (*Symons*, p., 255, 256.)

He rightly observes that one reason of this is that English
children are Anglo-Saxon born, while the books use words of
Norman-French or Latin derivation. It does not seem to
have occurred to him that Welsh children receiving information
on an abstract subject through the medium of Welsh would
have, in this respect, an advantage over English ones of
the working class, in that little or no time need be wasted
in drilling the meaning of the words into them.

A schoolmaster's wife in the English part of Radnorshire
informs him—

The parents do not wish it ¡questioning on mental teaching :
they do not send their children to day-schools to get religious, or,
in fact, any *mental education;* they send them purely from a
money motive, that they may advance themselves more easily in
life ; and to this end, reading English, writing, and ciphering, are
esteemed certain and sufficient means. (*Symons*, p. 242.)

At *Presteign*, Radnorshire, endowed school :—" The children
evinced no symptoms of mental culture of any kind."

At *Buttington*, Montgomery (H. W. Johnson's report) :—

All were ignorant of Scripture ; and a scholar in the first
class believed that St. Matthew wrote the History of England.

At *Bersham*, in the county of Denbigh, scholars were questioned on outlines of Scripture History :—"They were ignorant of everything."

Ignorance of English was not confined to teachers who were natives of Wales: the master at Holt, Denbighshire, "speaks English with a broad Cheshire dialect, and very un-grammatically."

At *Northop*, Flintshire :—

English is spoken in this part of the parish of Northop ; but notwithstanding this, the children recently admitted could not tell me which was their right hand and which their left. (p. 499.)

SCHOOL-HOUSES AND SURROUNDINGS.

Very little comment is needed from me under this or the succeeding head, the paragraphs given, will, it is hoped, elucidate the History of Wales in the second quarter of the nineteenth century.

The school was held in a room, part of a dwelling-house; the room was so small that a great many of the scholars were obliged to go into the room above, which they reached by means of a ladder, through a hole in the loft ; the room was lighted by one small glazed window, half of which was patched up with boards ; it was a wretched place ; the furniture consisted of one table, in a miserable condition, and a few broken benches; the floor was in a very bad state, there being several large holes in it, some of them nearly half a foot deep; the room was so dark that the few children whom I heard read were obliged to go to the door, and open it, to have sufficient light. *(Lingen, p. 21.)*

This school is held in the mistress's house. I never shall forget the hot, sickening smell, which struck me on opening the door of that low dark room, in which 30 girls and 20 boys were huddled together. It more nearly resembled the smell of the engine on board a steamer, such as it is felt by a sea-sick voyager on passing near the funnel. *(do., p. 25.)*

This school is held in a ruinous hovel of the most squalid and miserable character; the floor is of bare earth, full of deep holes; the windows are all broken; a tattered partition of lath and plaster divides it into two unequal portions; in the larger were a few wretched benches, and a small desk for the master in one corner; in the lesser was an old door, with the hasp still upon it, laid crossways upon two benches, about half a yard high, to serve for a writing-desk! Such of the scholars as write retire in pairs to this part of the room, and kneel on the ground while they write. On the floor was a heap of loose coal, and a litter of straw, paper, and all kinds of rubbish. The Vicar's son informed me that he had seen 80 children in this hut. In summer the heat of it is said to be suffocating; and no wonder. (do., p. 25, 26.)

This school is held in the church. I found the master and four little children ensconced in the chancel, amidst a lumber of old tables, benches, and desks, round a three-legged grate full of burning sticks, with no sort of funnel or chimney for the smoke to escape. It made my eyes smart till I was nearly blinded, and kept covering with ashes the paper on which I was writing. How the master and children bore it with so little apparent inconvenience I cannot tell. (do., p. 26.)

The schoolroom was originally a cow-shed, converted into a schoolroom without any attempt even to mend the paving of the floor, which was well worn and so uneven that the rough benches in it were propped up by large stones; the walls were of mud, the roof of decayed thatch, without any attempt at a ceiling; and there were only two small windows at each end, affording little light in the middle of the place. Each child had a book, and nearly all were reading aloud, each by himself. The master, a poor half-starved looking man, came out rod in hand to met us. Our visit, he said, was not unexpected, as he heard we were going about. *(Symons, pp. 274, 275.)*

Until the winter was far advanced, although the weather was

most severely cold and damp, fires were rarely found in these desolate places in Cardiganshire. p. 239.

I found the schoolroom used as a receptacle for churning materials, gardening-tools, and sacks of flour. * * Of these [49] only 14 knew the alphabet.

At Mydrolin, the room in which the school is held is a low, dark, damp building, erected partly of stone and partly of mud, and thatched with straw, altogether unfit for a place to conduct a school in. The floor of it, on the day I visited it, was completely covered with mud and water, worse than some places on a country road on a wet day. *(Symons, p. 277.)*

A Radnorshire school—The door guarded by a pig!

Having been assured it was at the church, I tried in vain to gain access to the building itself; and as I was turning away in despair, I heard the hum of a school in a wooden hut, in the last state of decay, with extensive plains of mud in front, and a pig asleep at the door. The thatch was mouldering away, and there was scarcely a whole board in the entire building. Having passed through a sepulchral sort of kitchen, I obtained access through it to the school-room—an inner room, or rather a slip of one, in which it was not easy to steer one's way safely through the beams and rafters by the dim light of two minute windows, one at either end. A handful of children were ranged on rude seats along the walls. [Nantmel, English speaking district.] *(Symons, p. 272.)*

THE HEADMASTERS DESCRIBED.

The present average age of teachers is upwards of 40 years; that at which they commenced their vocation upwards of 30; the number trained is 12·5 per cent. of the whole ascertained number; the average period of training is 7·30 months; the average income is £22 10s. 9d. per annum: besides which, 16·1 per cent. have a house rent-free. *(Lingen, p. 53.)*

Of course, these figures apply to his district—Carmarthen, Glamorgan and Pembroke. Imagine the schools of Wales, in

I

1891, being staffed with teachers that is, *head* masters and mistresses (for in those days paid assistants were so few as to be unlikely apparently to affect the return), whose average income was only £22 10s. 2d. per year, and that only 16·1 per cent. lived rent free. In North Wales the gross average income from all sources, so far as returns were given, was £26 19s. 2d.

The list of previous occupations of these so called teachers presents a miscellaneous medley, affording room for reflection *e.g.*, it includes clerks, carpenters, cooks, drapers, milliners, farmers and farm servants, labourers, mariners, and married women, whereas only one in eight had served any apprenticeship to it. Think, moreover, of a private school, " somewhat superior," when, after attempts to fix a charge of 10s. a quarter, it was found necessary to make a separate bargain for each child, according to the means and willingness of the parents.

J. C. Symons remarks that "the established belief for centuries has been that it requires no training at all" to be a schoolmaster; but even in those early days there was a certain amount of negative uniformity among the masters, as indicated by the following, in which it transpires that they were usually found doing anything but teaching, while in this instance "blindman's buff" supplied the place of a fire.

It is singular that in three or four instances only have I found a schoolmaster occupied in teaching on suddenly entering a school of the common class. I have far oftener found them reading an old newspaper, writing a letter or a bill, probably for some other person, reading a Welsh magazine, or doing nothing of any sort. At one school, near Aberystwyth, I was attracted, while passing along the road, by the boisterous noise in school, and on entering it found the whole of the scholars playing at blindman's-buff, or some similar game, though the dust and confusion prevented me from ascertaining what it was. I found that the master was absent, and had gone to warm himself at a neighbouring cottage: and on arriving he said that he told them "to have a bit of play, just to warm them."

The following paragraph refers to the usual equipment of schools:—

A Welsh schoolmaster of the ordinary description thinks himself well supplied if he is provided with two long tables and one short table, two or three forms for the children, a chair for himself, a score of Bibles, slates, and Vyse's spelling books, a few copy books, plenty of primers, two or three Walkinghame's Tutor's Assistant: an old newspaper, a rod, and if it be winter, a heap of peat in the corner, complete the sum of his wants, and of the recognized requirements of the scholars. The area of the room is often ludicrously insufficient, and at other times uncomfortably large. (*Symons*, p. 240.)

II. Vaughan Johnson, after referring to mere youths being put in charge of wholly undisciplined and ignorant scholars, says, still worse results are occasioned by employing aged persons and cripples, *e.g.* the master at Kilkin, Flintshire, was a miner, disabled by ill health.

I will however summarize some of the notable features of the schoolmasters in his district in short sentences following the name of the place they belonged to.

PENBLEDDYN—Income, £19. Apparently induced to accept these terms by the loss of one eye.

PENTRECAEHELYG (Vale of Clwyd)—A quarryman fractured his leg. Determined to commence teaching, but studied Latin and Greek! for nine months instead of undergoing any training.

LLANBRYNMAIR, MONT.—A village shopkeeper—children laughed at everything that was said to them.

PENYGROES, MONT.—Untrained, made innumerable errors in catechizing the scholars, pronounced wild *weeld*, region, *ragion*.

HOLT, DENBIGH.—Englishman, spoke very ungrammatically, when he thought a blunder was committed, corrected it by committing another.

HALKIN, FLINT.—Englishman, says *whoole* for whole, *han* for an.

ABERFFRAW FREE SCHOOL.—Master assured H. V. Johnson that the children understood nothing of what they read in English, but he attempts no kind of explanation.

"CHURCH" SCHOOL, RUTHIN.—An Englishman, with no system of interpretation. Scholars all Welsh. His questions few, slowly conceived, and commonplace.

DOLWYDDELEN, CARN.—Master 54. Previously cattle dealer and drover. Scholars positively laughed at his attempting to control them.

OVERTON (English Flintsh.) Free School.—Only 2 out of 6 who profess to know arithmetic, could work a plain sum in addition.

EFAILRHUD, DENBIGH.—Formerly a farm servant. His method of teaching grammar is unusual. He reads the book and the children repeat after him, as if making responses at church.

"CHURCH" SCHOOL, LLANDYSILIO.—A mere boy (19), untrained, knew but little Welsh, while only one scholar knew English.

"CHURCH SCHOOL," LLANYNYS, DENBIGH.—Pupils stated that Pharaoh was king of Israel, and the master commended them, saying, "very good." Called British, *Brutish*, and the like.

GRESFORD (English part of Denbigh).—Master in a public-house at 10 a.m.; boys playing with all their might. Afternoon, master again absent, boys playing at horses.

LLANFYNYDD, FLINT.—Master did not attempt to suppress the tumult, uproar and disorder prevailing during the visit. Commissioner feared lest a general fight should ensue before examination was finished.

"St." David's "Church" School, Festiniog.—Continual uproar. Girls sweeping the school floor unbidden, and struck the heads of the boys with a broom while the examination was going on.

Rhyl.—Had taught for four months only. Was extremely deaf. Cannot detect mistakes nor ascertain when scholars are making a disturbance.

Llandyrnog "Church" School—Aged and infirm. Appears to have had no education.

Rhiwlas, Llansilin.—Formerly a blacksmith, for *father* he said *fayther* and *gounzillor* for *counsellor*.

"Church" School, Ruthin.—Master trained for eight months at Westminster. The following extract is really of too outré a character to be condensed:—

Neither master nor scholar appeared to have any idea of manners or discipline. While I examined the school, all remained sitting, including the master; I could not do the same, as there was no seat left. The boys sat lolling luxuriously with their hands in their pockets, and answered or not, just as they felt inclined. In the mean time all business was abandoned by the rest, who collected themselves in groups, looking on and talking. One or two monitors amused themselves by wandering about, striking the younger boys, but indiscriminately, and with no useful object in view. I could with difficulty walk across the room without catching the saliva which the boys were spitting in all directions—not through disrespect, but from habit.

Please note—The Commissioner standing, boys lolling luxuriously, amusements of the monitors, the "difficulty" of walking across the room, &c.

British and Foreign School. Ruthin.—One of the best in North Wales. Master inspired the pupils with a desire for knowledge, but neglected discipline. The Commissioner

regrets that scholars so intelligent, and making such progress
in all subjects, should not be taught manners.

Few schools in North Wales were found destitute of a cane
or birch rod.

PATRONS AND MANAGERS.

A large class of the promoters of schools were unqualified
to "select masters or superintend institutions." For instance,
the promoters of a British school of great reputation, represented in high terms the extent of instruction and attainments
of the pupils, but when examined, in grammar, it was found
that the pupils had never heard of the singular or plural
number.

H. V. J. next describes how the children are specially coached
up to answer questions gone through beforehand, so that when
" the gentry visit them "　　*　　*　　"they gain great
approbation and obtain the credit of being excellent institutions."

Speaking of schools richly supported by the "clergy and
wealthy classes," H. V. Johnson says—

The visitors and promoters of such schools appear to have overlooked the defect which lies at the root of all other deficiencies -
the want of books expressly adapted, and of teachers properly
qualified, to teach English to Welsh children. The majority appear
conscious (sic) that English may remain an unknown language
to those who can read and recite it fluently; others have frequently
assured me that Welsh parents would not endure any encroach-
ment upon their language —an argument which would seem to
imply great ignorance of the poor among their countrymen, who,
as I have already stated, insist on having English only taught in
the day-schools, and consider all time as wasted which is spent in
learning Welsh. (pp. 477, 478.)

The complaints have been generally made by persons among the
higher classes, who, through neglect, have allowed their schools
to become extinct, or, through misapprehension of the character

and temper of the inhabitants, have failed to adapt the style and subjects of instruction to the requirements of those whom they professed to teach. (p. 486.)

A fatal delusion has misled the promoters of schools in North Wales. They have supposed that, if children make use of the Bible as a handbook to learn reading from the alphabet upwards. and if catechisms be carefully committed to memory, the narratives and doctrines therein contained must be impressed on their understandings and affections. (p. 500.)

Bear in mind, good reader, that we are now adverting to persons who were the victims of a "fatal delusion," and permitted in the schools under their care a defect which lay at the "root of all other deficiencies." Did they belong to the lower stratum of society? No; we may reasonably suppose that some of them had received an English University education, and yet in the year 1891 there is evidence that exactly the same defects would be found in the schools under the care of their successors, had not they in some respects reaped the benefit of other men's labours; and in one important matter—the want of books expressly adapted for teaching English to Welsh children, the "clergy and wealthy classes" are content, and many of them very well content, with the system which the Commissioner of 1846 condemned, which degrades Welsh without properly elevating English; while they appear to receive with stolid indifference any outcry for a more reasonable and more natural method.

In the discharge of his duty the North Wales Commissioner collected some valuable evidence about *endowments* and school funds which it would be out of place to reproduce, at any great length, in this book. In North Wales the endowments exceeded £4,000, excluding a large amount under litigation. Of this a considerable proportion was misapplied.

At Bryneglwys, Denbigh, for instance, there was an endowment, but the school was closed. The clergyman appointed himself master, *i.e.*, pocketed the stipend of one.

LLANERFYL, MONT.—A valuable endowment. One of the trustees farms the charity estate without accounting for rents, in return for which he professed to act as schoolmaster. Had eight scholars, and was frequently absent. Outbuildings out of repair and occupied by geese, hatching.

RUABON GRAMMAR SCHOOL.—Valuable endowment of £100 per year.

I found the school-room, which would accommodate 81 scholars, partly filled with coals, and the remainder used as a lumber-room, being covered with broken chairs and furniture. The glass of the windows was broken, and the room neglected and filthy in the extreme. The lumber and dirt appeared to have been accumulating for several months, and, except some tattered books, without covers, in the window-seats, there was no vestige of the school which is said to have been held there.

DEYTHUR, MONTGOMERY—Endowment reduced by Law Suits; £88 paid to the nominal master, a clergyman; school conducted by an usher, previously an agricultural labourer, and was inferior to the average of the lowest schools in North Wales. Pupils understood more English than Welsh.

Here is plain speaking about supporters of National Schools, giving a notable illustration of *pleidgarwch* or *sect-yddiaeth* in the Establishment.

In addition to the above-mentioned abuses, it is important to state that it is a practice in North Wales for the trustees of endowed schools which are not absolutely connected with the Established Church, to allow waste and dilapidation, and to neglect to visit and examine the scholars, with the professed object of inducing their parishioners to consent to have the schools united with the National Society. I allege this upon the authority of their own statements, in which the practice and the motives of it were avowed.

We can imagine such pious trustees holding up their hands in holy horror at the wrangling in the denominational literature of the benighted Dissenters; for this, it is evident they had but two remedies; one was to extinguish the Welsh language, the other to drive the wanderers back to the bosom of their Mother Church.

H. V. Johnson finds that out of the funds of 517 schools the rich subscribe £5,675, and the amount raised by the poor is £7,000, adding—

It is important to observe the misdirection of these branches of school income, and the fatal consequences which ensue.

The wealthy classes who contribute towards education belong to the Established Church; the poor who are to be educated are Dissenters. The former will not aid in supporting neutral schools; the latter withhold their children from such as require conformity to the Established Church. The effects are seen in the co-existence of two classes of schools, both of which are rendered futile—the Church schools supported by the rich, which are thinly attended, and that by the extreme poor; and private-adventure schools, supported by the mass of the poorer classes at an exorbitant expense, and so utterly useless that nothing can account for their existence except the unhealthy division of society, which prevents the rich and poor from co-operating. (p. 511.)

The report further speaks of parents purchasing exemptions from the rules requiring conformity in religion by payment of a small gratuity, to increase the "slender pittance" of the master—of expulsion where poor parents held out—of a compromise in other cases, the children being cautioned by the parents not to believe the Catechism, and to return to the "paternal chapels" as soon as they have finished schooling—of the "inexpedience" of such a system being not yet apparent, except to a few; and moreover when speaking of private adventure, and dame schools of an utterly worthless character,

"that nothing can account for their existence except the deter-
mination on the part of Welsh parents to have their children
instructed without interference in matters of conscience," while
such schools exhaust the greater part of the £7,000 contributed by the poor towards education.

The intellectual results produced by the present class of Church
schoolmasters, reduced as they are to such extremities, has been
already seen in the ignorance of scholars, not only respecting the
distinctive doctrines of the Church, but of the first element of
Christianity. (p. 512.)

H. V. J. complains respecting indifference as to education on the part both of parents and children. After alluding
to the fact that many scholars walked eight miles a day, he very
justly remarks, considering the value of the instruction, they
cannot be expected to "expend more time in an occupation
so unprofitable."

WELSH LANGUAGE AND LITERATURE.

In dealing with the Welsh language and literature, as might
be expected, the three Commissioners were very largely
dependent for information upon other persons.

Lingen and Symons pass by the phenomena of existing
Welsh literature with very scant notice indeed. Johnson, on
the other hand, makes what appears to be an honest attempt
to analyze its character, though he was far from doing it
justice. Lingen and Symons adopted a directly antagonistic
position to the existence of the language. Johnson stood
more on neutral ground: the two former, however, obtained
the ear of the Government, and not long after the publication
of the report Lingen was given the important post of Secretary
to the Committee of Council on Education, and it may well
be believed that his subsequent attitude towards Welsh
education was very much influenced by the judgment he had

previously formed on imperfect data, and more or less in conjunction with preconceived opinions.

He comes across a characteristic of Wales, though a by no means universal one, parents wishing to exclude Welsh from the secular education of their children (this is much more the case in thoroughly Welsh districts, than partially Anglicized ones), coincident with their choice of Welsh as the "natural exponent" of nearly every social relation and all religious exercises.

Yet, if interest pleads for English. affection leans to Welsh. The one is regarded as a new friend, to be acquired for profit's sake; the other as an old one, to be cherished for himself, and especially not be deserted in his decline. Probably you could not find in the most purely Welsh parts a single parent, in whatever class, who would not have his child taught English in school: yet every characteristic development of the social life into which that same child is born—preaching—prayer-meetings—Sunday schools—clubs—biddings—funerals—the denominational magazine (his only press), all these exhibit themselves to him in Welsh as their natural exponent, partly, it may be, from necessity, but. in some degree also, from choice. * * He ⌈the Welshman⌋ possesses a mastery over his own language far beyond that which the Englishman of the same degree possesses over his. (p. 10.)

Couple this statement with the confession of Symons, that children at Presteign, where Welsh has been extinct for generations, evinced "no symptoms of mental culture of any kind," and with the evidence of Rees, the publisher of *Yr Haul* :—

The Welsh peasantry are better able to read and write in their own language than the same classes in England. Among them are many contributors to Welsh periodicals. *(Lingen,* p. 10.)

The process of instruction being conducted entirely with English books led, however, to the following remark :—

It would be impossible to exaggerate the difficulties which

this diversity between the language in which the school-books are
written and the mother-tongue of the children presents. In proportion as the teacher adheres to English, he does not get beyond
the child's ears; in proportion as he employs Welsh, he appears
to be superseding the most important part of the child's instruction.
How and where to draw the line—how to convey the principles of
knowledge through the only medium in which the child can
apprehend them, yet to leave them impressed upon its mind in
other terms, and under other forms—how to employ the old
tongue as a scaffolding, yet to leave no trace of it in the finished
building, but to have it, if not lost, at least stowed away—all this
presupposes a teacher so thoroughly master of the subjects which
he is going to teach, and also of two languages most dissimilar in
genius and idiom. that he can indifferently represent his matter
with equal clearness in one as in the other. *(Lingen,* p. 52).

Why should he be so anxious to leave "no trace" of the
old tongue, to which he is a stranger, in the "finished
building" of the completed education of the youth in Wales.
A person entrusted with such a responsible post should have
seen at once that English *per se* is *not* "the most important
part of the child's instruction." Many thousands of English
agricultural labourers have learned English from their early
childhood, but they are still "under the hatches," and their
intelligence remains comparatively undeveloped.

In 1847, as now, the parents of Welsh children were eager
to have them taught English almost without exception, and
being themselves ignorant, were quite content with the mentally
wasteful way which is continued down to the present day of
having all school-books solely in English.

We see in the above extract how the Commissioner appears
nearly to come to the conclusion of the Welsh Utilization
Society, that it would be best to employ bilingual books, but
he shrinks from expressing it, evidently from the fear that

while the children are learning English they will also learn the language he wishes to see extirpated from the country.

Although he acknowledges that the language cannot be "taught down" in schools, yet, the idea of an advanced bilingual education scarcely seems to have entered his head, as he speaks of schools not being called upon,—

To impart in a foreign, or engraft upon the ancient, tongue a factitious education conceived under another set of circumstances (in either of which cases the task would be as hopeless as the end unprofitable). but to convey, in a language which is already in process of becoming the mother-tongue of the country, such instruction as may put the people on a level with that position which is offered to them by the course of events.

Now, what the meaning of this mass of verbiage was, it is not easy to discover, but it is squarely evident that in substance it amounted to a repudiation of Welsh as a subject of instruction, and yet he acknowledges that the best mode of teaching *English* was found at the Venalt Works School, where the class was taught to translate, clause by clause, into Welsh: a system which he compares to the Hamiltonian *viva voce*. How is it possible to carry this excellent method into practice without interfering with the idea of employing the "old tongue as a scaffolding," and leaving "no trace of it in the finished building?" I venture to assert it is an impracticability, and is repugnant to the laws of the human mind. How was it again, that when R. W. Lingen's name figured as Secretary to the Education Department, and he doubtless had the power of initiating many reforms, that this "best mode of teaching" English was not recommended to all schools receiving the Government grant in Welsh schools?

Amid the gross inefficiency of the schools in his district J. C. Simons sees one gleam of light, but we fear it was a short-sighted vision : he says :—

"There is one most striking and important peculiarity in

them, which will be a subject of the utmost satisfaction to
every friend to Wales : it is the fact that there is but one day
school out of the entire number—the three counties of
Brecknock, Cardigan, and Radnor — where the Welsh
language is taught. It seems scarcely to have occurred to
him that it is impossible to teach an English boy the French
grammar without, to some extent, teaching him English ;
likewise, that a Welsh boy taught English thoroughly and in
the most expeditious way, would have to be taught his mother
tongue as well."

It is this fear of children learning Welsh, and which
exists at the present time, that has been and continues to be
one of the drawbacks of the intellectual progress of Wales,
and has degraded Welsh schools from being the arenas of
rational intellectual exercises of a higher stamp than those
met with in English school life, into scenes of mechanical,
irrational drudgery.

Notwithstanding the fact which Symons says, was "a
subject of the utmost satisfaction to every friend to Wales,"
he has to admit that teaching English by the methods then in
vogue were a failure.

Any inference, therefore, that the children were extensively
learning English, drawn from the facts that the schools everywhere
try to teach it, would be utterly fallacious.

It is strange that with the many improvements of modern
education there are still schoolmasters, and possibly inspectors
too, who cling to the old injurious system of excluding Welsh
entirely from the day schools except for the purpose of simple
explanation, so as to admit no books whatever printed in that
language.

For otherwise well educated people in responsible positions
to ignore Welsh as a medium of *direct* mental culture, and to
regard it as an inconvenient obstacle to progress, appears rather

a sheepish following of custom and tradition under the influence of the Government regulations in force until recently, than the result of a well matured and honest endeavour to fit the minds with which they are brought in contact for the circumstances.

I say that schoolmasters cling to the old method, not simply because they have been obliged to—although there is no obligation to read the *English* Bible at the commencement of schools—but because they, or at least their managers, have generally evinced so little disposition, to change a system condemned by such varied and respectable authorities, as are adduced in the course of this work, for one which would develop a better standard of intelligence in English. although involving a better mastery of Welsh.

J. C. Symons says the "Welsh language is a vast drawback to Wales, and that it is not easy to over-estimate its evil effects," and that there is no Welsh literature worthy of the name, although he had never read a page of what there was, while in a note he utters a half sneer at the Cymreigyddion y Fenni then in existence, and at their making English speeches once a year in defence of Welsh literature, saying, " Its proceedings are perfectly innocuous.

If what he and his modern representatives say is true, how is it that in Radnorshire and east Breconshire, where Welsh is extinct, we do not find the people intellectually far in advance of Carnarvonshire ? Let them give a proper answer to that question before being so persistently dogmatic on an unstable foundation.

Of course, my readers will bear in mind that some of the evidence must be looked on with suspicion; we find for instance the magistrates' clerk at Lampeter says, " the Welsh monthly magazines do more harm than good," and he believes there is not a single Welsh weekly newspaper in existence.

The following is from the pen of E. C. Hall, a barrister at
Newcastle Emlyn:—

The two languages are a great facility to perjury. The want of
accuracy in the knowledge of the language seems to remove the
feeling of degradation   *   *   The Welsh language is
peculiarly evasive which originates from its having been the
language of slavery!! (p. 345.)

Did it never occur to this man that if barristers, such as he,
and the Judges of Assizes, and Chairmen of Quarter Sessions,
were not allowed to perform their duties without a knowledge
of Welsh, it should put a stop to some of the perjury he
speaks of; and if he is so shocked at perjury, why does he
bring in a shameful mis-statement about the Welsh language.
Would he have called Ieuan Gwynedd's language, which I
shall refer to presently, evasive had he been able to read it?

Colonel Powell, Lord-lieutenant for Cardiganshire, complains
of people being disposed to shew less respect to the old
families of the county than they used to be, and that the Welsh
language is a great obstruction to the improvement of the
people.

A land agent at Aberystwyth who held courts leet for the
Lord-Lieutenant, echoes his master's words, and says that the
language is an impediment to the improvement of the people;
but he adds that the people are very much attached to it,
although a preacher in the same county says they would not
value a school teaching Welsh.

Now, while Commissioner Symons dismissed the subject of
Welsh literature as scarcely worth discussion, and Lingen
scarcely alludes to it all, Vaughan Johnson took the trouble to
prepare an abstract of Welsh literature, or rather, I suppose,
employed some one to do it for him, in which it appeared
that at that time there were current 405 works (Welsh) printed
and read in North Wales, of which 64 were books of poetry,

46, prose works on miscellaneous subjects. Although he ventured to remark about the latter, that most of them, besides books on domestic medicine, and diseases of cattle, were of a "frivolous character," he is candid enough to say that he was unable to obtain an impartial statement of the character of the periodicals, and accordingly printed in his appendix a translation and brief abstracts of their contents.

A "communication" is given on the "Exclusive character of Welsh literature," from which I extract the following:—

The poverty and indifference of the Welsh people, and the difficulty of withdrawing any of their attention from questions of theology and polemical religion, forbid all hope of extending Welsh literature, without the hearty and continued co-operation of the wealthier classes. No person would venture to set up a periodical of a merely literary or scientific character, unless he had the support of some religious party; and such a support cannot be obtained to any extent. (p. 251).

How can the wealthier classes co-operate, if they too are shut out from a knowledge of the medium whereby they might share their superior advantages with their poorer neighbours.

Take away every field of activity but one, from a Welshman as such, and why blame him or his language because he appears to be exclusive. Religion was undoubtedly intended to leaven the whole life and not to be the foundation for the battering rams of party animosities, or a vain love of disputation, which perhaps after all has been a form of intellectual restlessness finding vent in an unusual way, but going unhappily under the name of religion, while the paths of general knowledge are made unnecessary hard and rugged.

The Commissioner alludes to numerous periodicals published in Welsh by means of which "all that goes on in England is known in Wales, being read by the quarrymen and tradesmen, but not by the farmers, they read nothing.   *   *   It matters

L

not how plain and colloquial the style of a book, the farmers complain that they cannot understand it."

A sixpenny or at most a shilling book of a religious character is the only safe publishing speculation in the Welsh language, and even this would be a loss, if it were not "pushed" in religious circles. It is by no means an uncommon thing for books to be advertised from the pulpit, in dissenting places of worship. (p. 522.)

To some extent, though not nearly so much as formerly, this remark holds good to day. There are populous sections of the country where Welsh theological works occasionally sell well, considering the class of buyers. Yet if a person were to write a general treatise in Welsh on a scientific subject, say agriculture, the same readers would find a difficulty in understanding him, and the sale would be small.

This is explained, not by lack of interest in those subjects, but because the opportunities of the people have been too limited to acquire a sufficiently extensive Welsh vocabulary (other than in the domain of Theology) to read general literature with interest.

I was not long ago at Mountain Ash, among a mining population, where a bookseller, with a Scotch name, assured me that he had sold one hundred copies of the 2/6 edition of Principal Edwards' *Esboniad ar yr Hebreaid* (Commentary on the Hebrews). This is the more remarkable, as English is the usual language of the children; but the probability is that some of those very children will be added to the circle of Welsh readers, at least to that of Theological ones. In this instance, the large sale is accounted for by the Hebrews being at the time, a subject of examination among the Calvinistic Methodists. The same bookseller also told me that he had sold several copies of another religious work at 5/-.

Now so long as the language is scouted, frowned at, and thwarted in its growth in the day school, and the people are denied secular instruction in it, would it be a matter of wonder that "its resources in the other branches remain obsolete and meagre"? Would it be a matter of wonder that books on general subjects do not find a ready sale? It is however not correct to affirm that the resources of the language are meagre, and the wonder is that they have been developed so much as is the case.

Symons and Lingen, both of them comment on the extraordinarily unintelligent way in which Education was carried on, yet neither of them suggest such an improvement as bilingual books; although David Charles, Principal of Trevecca College, very sensibly said in a communication to J. C. S.—"I would also recommend that the Welsh receive their knowledge of the English language through the medium of their own, at first by means of Welsh books. The want of this mode of instruction has been a great drawback which I have often desired to get removed."

Not merely did David Charles make this objection, but another leading dissenter, Lewis Edwards, of Bala, held the same view, as shewn in the following translated extract from the *Traethodydd* of 1850. (See *Traethodau Llenyddol*, p. 120):—

From the bottom of our hearts we give our consent to every word that is said by Sir Thomas Phillips about the necessity of teaching Welsh children in the Welsh language. *   * The truth is, that the easiest way for them to learn English is to give them a taste *for* and knowledge *in* the Welsh language.

The North Wales Commissioner displayed more practical ability than his colleagues, in severely commenting on the exclusive use of English books, and the English language, and says that the promoters of schools appear unconscious of the difficulty (as some are to-day), and the teachers of the possibility of its removal.

After saying that he had found no class of schools in which
an attempt had been made to remove the children's difficulties
of first learning English, he makes the following general
remarks:—

Every book in the school is written in English; every word he
speaks is to be spoken in English; every subject of instruction
must be studied in English; and every addition to his stock of
knowledge in grammar, geography, history, or arithmetic, must be
communicated in English words; yet he is furnished with no single
help for acquiring a knowledge of English. As yet no class of
schools has been provided with dictionaries or grammars in Welsh
and English. The promoters of schools appear unconscious of the
difficulty, and the teachers of the possibility of its removal.

Speaking of the Grammar School at "St." Asaph,

Those who learn Latin are provided with grammars, dictionaries,
and vocabularies; but here as elsewhere no hand-books have been
provided for learning English, although English is to many of the
pupils as unintelligible as any dead language.

Nearly fifty years have passed away, Welsh education has
been very much in the hands of the English Government,
clerical officials, and other persons, who have sought a share in
its management, and yet this monstrous anomaly so disgraceful to the civilization of the nineteenth century remains, and
it is even defended by a certain class of teachers bred under
the influence of long standing customs and English laws.

H. V. J. introduced into his report a mention of the "Welsh
note," a stigma of disgrace transferred to the last boy
heard speaking Welsh. Among other injurious effects this
custom has been found to lead children to visit stealthily the
houses of their schoolfellows, for the purpose of detecting
those who speak Welsh to their parents, and transferring to
them the punishment due to themselves."

The same Commissioner speaks of the impediment to efficient teaching offered by the prejudices of Welsh parents against the employment of their own language, even as a medium of explanation : " In the day schools we want our children to be taught English only ; what good can be gained by teaching us Welsh? We know Welsh already." There are too many School Boards in 1891, where this kind of ignorance appears to prevail—concomitant recollect, with a genuine attachment to Wales."

The following table may be of some interest :—

CLASSIFICATION OF DAY SCHOOLS ACCORDING TO LANGUAGE IN 1846-7.

Language of Instruction.	Carmar-then.	Gla-morgan.	Pem-broke.	Car-digan.	Breck-nock.	Rad-nor.	Mon-mouth. (Part of.)
Welsh only		--	—	1		—	
English only ..	52	258	155	75	88	43	120
Welsh & English books	9	1					
English books only* but Welsh spoken in explanation	118	63	48	25	8	---	7
Grammar of English..	74	127	67	57	35	12	37
„　of Welsh ..	—						
„　of both ..	2	2	1				

It should be borne in mind that Welsh spoken in "explanation" may simply mean that an ignorant schoolmaster used that language as the ordinary medium of converse with his scholars. It does not appear that there was any systematic bilingual instruction except in a few schools, and those where the habit prevailed to get the children to commit to memory the English of certain Welsh words.

He says (though incorrectly) "of this amount one-half have always spoken English"; thinks that English has not dis-

---

* For Pembroke, Cardigan and Radnor, information simply states "instruction given in Welsh and English." North Wales—Particulars not given.

placed one-tenth part of Welsh; and looks to good schools to expedite its progress.

Symons estimates the amount of population in his district, of whom English is the fireside language:—

> In Brecknockshire, 23,500 out of 55,603 speak English.
> In Cardiganshire 3,000 ,, 68,766 ,,
> In Radnorshire 23,000 ,, 25,356 ,,
>
>   50,000 ,, 149,725

A Brecon Curate, named Jas. Denning, writes to J. C. S.:—

I cannot too strongly express my opinion about the necessity of getting rid of the Welsh language. * * The bigotry of the preachers would be driven away. (p. 359.)

Lingen gives no estimate of this kind, but alludes to the district within which the English language may be considered as the mother-tongue of the people, as lying south of the London mail road—roughly speaking, we should say the Great Western trunk-line—from Cardiff to the coast of the Irish sea, except between Swansea and "St." Clears, which may be considered to have been Welsh.

Is it not a striking fact, that more than 40 years have passed since these enquiries were made, and since it was found that Welsh books were wholly excluded from the day schools with very trifling exceptions, and yet, that the Welsh speaking population has increased probably 20 per cent. : and there is more Welsh literature now than ever.

GENERAL REMARKS.

Symons alludes to the small proportion of the whole number of children in day schools who ever learn to write, but speaks highly of their proficiency in arithmetic, saying he had never witnessed more, after so small an amount of instruction, in any school either in England or on the Continent. "Wherever the children remain long enough in school their proficiency in figures is wonderful."

"Though they are ignorant, no people more richly deserve to be educated. In the first place, they desire it to the full extent of their power to appreciate it; in the next, their natural capacity is of a high order, especially in the Welsh districts. They learn when they are even badly taught with surprising facility."

The perpetual Curate of Builth (R. H. Harrison) writes:—

"The Welsh people are much quicker than the English. I have been much concerned in schools in England, and have succeeded well with them; but the Welsh have much better and readier powers of perception; their reasoning powers are much less developed. There are, however, beautiful faculties lost here for want of proper cultivation. They would learn quickly and profit greatly by good schools." (p. 341.)

This was in an English speaking district—nearly entirely so. I have, however, heard a Welsh schoolmaster say that the reasoning faculties of bilingual boys were better developed than when they know one language only.

The following, from the pen of a witness, then President of the Independent College, Brecon, only recently deceased, who was, I believe, intimately acquainted with the language and habits of the people:—

Taken as a whole, I believe the Welsh peasantry are decidedly superior to the English. Having spent twelve years as a minister in England, and in daily communication with the poor, I may perhaps be allowed to speak with some confidence. But all the other classes among us are immeasurably inferior, in point of information, to the corresponding classes in England. Nothing can be more worthless than the schooling ordinarily given to the children of our small farmers and shopkeepers. This is especially the case with respect to girls all through Wales. Let me add, the

whole community suffers from the absence of that teaching, which
would tend to fit boys to excel as mechanics or artizans. (p. 361.)

There have been ministers among us, men of great mental and
moral power and prodigious influence, men whom we need not blush
to class with England's best, and whose memoirs will be instructive
to the end of time, but who nevertheless knew nothing of English,
and never were able to write their names! In hundreds of our
cottages, at this day, you may find men of most elevated habits of
thought and feeling who never read a page in their lives but the
Bible. (p. 362.)

Johnson speaks of the true method of teaching geography
being inverted—that of home being neglected, children per-
fected in definition, can point out islands, straits, &c., yet
suppose that such phenomena have no existence in North
Wales.

Grammar—not taught a science, but as a matter of memory,
a fault to which doubtless the Inspectors of 1891 could also
attest.

The definitions and explanations in these works 'Murray's
Grammar, &c.', which would be difficult to an English scholar,
are incomprehensible to Welsh children, and the teacher, even if
competent to interpret, neglects to do so. No part of the
subject is illustrated by familiar examples suited to the capacity of
children ; and in the conversation of the teacher, the rules of
syntax and grammar are far more frequently broken than
observed.

MONMOUTHSHIRE.

As J. C. Symons subsequently devotes a special Report
to the eighteen westerly parishes of Monmouthshire, with a
population at that date of about 100,000, and as I am writing
in that county, my readers will, I hope, deal leniently with
the desire to notice it a little more prominently than its
relative importance warrants.

It is impossible not to admire the ability and integrity displayed in this production. It is evident that the previous few months' experience had fortified him for the undertaking. The electors of the Monmouth Boroughs, we fear, did not allow themselves to be much benefitted by it, as they shortly afterwards sent to Parliament, Crawshay Bailey, one of the ironmasters of the district, whom it may be lawful to make an *exception* to the rule, *de mortuis nil nisi bonum.*

At the period of which I am writing the population of the county had increased at a faster rate than that of any other in the kingdom, being 36·9 per cent. between 1831 and 1841, when the Glamorganshire rate was only 35·2. The population, it must be recollected, was by no means exclusively a Welsh one, there having been then, as is the case now, a considerable immigration from England and Ireland, which, combined with the exclusion of Welsh from the day schools, has undoubtedly done much towards diminishing its use as a *family* language, though there are at least 130 Monmouthshire congregations in 1891 to whom Welsh is preached weekly.* Possibly this immigration and other facts which the report brings to light, had something to do with the low standard of attainment in Government examinations, which was shewn by the county not many years ago, and for long after a much more perfect system had been established.

In this county there was an improvement in the school-teachers, but a custom was frequent in the large works for the masters to make a deduction from the workmen's wages for the support of the school, and in some cases the Commissioner had to state that there was ground to believe that the masters made a profit on it, and the workmen did not "derive an equivalent from the fund usually raised from the wages, and to which they are compelled to pay."

---

* In the Appendix I hope to give exact statistics of each denomination.

M

As regards training or mind teaching "it exists only in one or two schools, and there too owing to the shortness of the stay of the children among the older classes alone."

The understanding of ninety per cent. of the children who pass through these schools is just as little improved or informed as when they entered it. There is the same book-labour and rote-labour as in Wales, with the same utter inactivity of mind. There is the same absence of thought and of desire to be taught to think. Schooling is desired simply because it is deemed a stepping-stone to gain, and a means to advancement in life. On that account is it alone sought for. The Bible is universally read in the day-schools, both great and small. Little children are found stammering through the Pentateuch or the Revelations, who may be reading the Koran with equal profit. (p. 379.)

I am writing in a time when much attention is being devoted to Welsh Intermediate and Higher Education, and with the consciousness that Welsh-Wales has produced, and has now within her borders many self-taught men, who are able to make mental comparisons, suggested by times and conditions, other than those by which they are immediately surrounded, and of whom it would not be just to say the discipline (schooling if we like to term it) to which they have subjected themselves, has been "desired simply because it is deemed a stepping-stone to gain;" but while this much is said, it applies to those who have a higher ideal of education than the average school manager in Wales. There is too much of the spirit of 1847 left behind, too much of the idea of turning Board schools and intermediate schools into money-making machines.

Quite true it is that there is a need for an education that shall better a child for after life, and so far as a more practicable scheme than the current one can be introduced, let it be so. The discrepancy really lies in the interpretation of the term "after life." Members of School Boards are too apt to confine it to the technical work of the office, the shop, or the work-shop. Perfectly necessary in their way, as these are, a real educationalist applies it to the tout-ensemble of the future man, so far as any mechanical or material course of training can affect it. He of course sees the intimate connection between language and the use of ideas, hence he cannot afford to allow a vocabulary acquired in infancy to be dormant while he is endeavouring to develop the power of using and developing ideas and knowledge, entirely through a medium to become familiar with which involves a long period of mechanical drudgery. It is his clear duty (in Wales at least) to induce familiarity with this foreign medium, but to do it at the expense of sacrificing all culture in that which nature has provided ready to hand, as is done in the majority of schools in Wales, means a needless delay of the child's development.

At TREDEGAR TOWN SCHOOLS, under a wealthy Company, in which Samuel Homfray had a leading position, and for which he had selected an able master, the funds appear to have *entirely* come from the stoppages in workmen's wages.

Much dissatisfaction was expressed at the children being compelled to attend the Church Sunday School though many of the parents are Dissenters. Some of the men are therefore compelled to pay for schooling which they cannot conscientiously avail themselves of for their children. (p. 387.)

SIRHOWY DAY SCHOOL—Belonging to the Company. To persecute one [scholar] said meant to preach, and none could set him right   *   *   Two thought the people in Scotland black.

Speaking of schools held on First day ("Sunday") he says—
The Dissenting schools are superior to the Church schools in every respect as means of religious instruction; the far larger

attendance of teachers, sitting each with their own classes, reading
with and questioning them, would alone give this superiority. I
should fail in my duty, were I not to give a prominent place to
this source of the slight moral right which prevails among this
population; but one-sixth part of whom it thus appears are subjected to this discipline, and their attendance is irregular. (p. 291).

Somewhat mournfully J. C. S. adds—

The clergy are scattered and few in number, and can make little
way with the people against the combined numbers and activity
of the Dissenting bodies, who are inspired no less by emulation
among each other than by zeal for the sake of truth.

Speaking of the population generally—

Whatever is unsettled or lawless, or roving or characterless
among working-men, as long as bodily strength subsists, has felt
an attraction to this district, and a surety of ready acceptance
and good wages which very few other districts have afforded in so
great a degree.

The whole district and population partake of the iron character
of its produce; physical strength is the object of esteem, and
gain their chief god. (p. 394.)

In fact, it seems to have been the policy of some ironmasters
or colliery proprietors of that day, to collect together a band of
ruffians, if they could get no others, settle them down to spread
corruption among a population less deeply steeped in vice,
and then keep them under their thumb by means of the truck
system, or otherwise favour their being penniless. For instance
"one or two benevolent ladies tries to get up a Provident
Society," to encourage the men to lay something by, and
applied to a large mine proprietor for his contribution and
patronage.

"Indeed," he said, "I cannot give you either, for if I did, I
would be arming the men against myself, and enabling them to
strike for wages. I want them to spend their earnings and not

hoard them." This was an unusual case of candour, but by no means unusual policy. I mentioned it to a neighbouring magistrate, who told me he firmly believed it; and I heard from others, in whom I can place confidence, that the desire to deprive the men of the means of striking for wages, and to subjugate them to their employers, is said to animate their conduct, and it appears to be even more at the root of the truck-system than the immediate gain which springs from it. (p. 398.)

What a trust in Belial! It reminds one of that concern existing at the present day called the Rhymney Iron Company, Limited, whose sphere of operations is in or near Rhymney, Monmouthshire; they own a good part of the town, consequently can manipulate houses and tenancies at will, they are reputed, moreover, to carry on an underhanded species of compulsion to induce workmen to deal at a large shop close to their works, and have on two occasions had to pay legal punishment through carrying out a miserable system of putting on the screw which led to positive contraventions of the Truck Act.

They also own a large BREWERY close at hand, which, I am informed by a local tradesman, is worth about half-a-million. Providence has so far prospered the endeavours of this beery-irony-grocery Company, as to enable them recently to declare a dividend of £0 0s. 0d. per cent. If the property is shortly in the market, it is to be hoped that it will fall into the hands of persons who will confine their attention to coal and iron. Having a number of Irish workmen, the Company is obliging enough to their priest to make stoppages from the men's wages (by their consent) towards his salary. In return for this service, it is scarcely beside the mark to suppose that they (the Company) expect a *quid pro quo* in the shape of influence on his flock in their favour.

We must however go back to Monmouthshire in 1846.

Even the physical condition of the people seems almost as if

contrived for the double purpose of their degradation and the
employers' profit. Some of the works are surrounded by houses
built by the Companies without the slightest attention to comfort,
health, or decency, or any other consideration than that of
realizing the largest amount of rent from the smallest amount of
outlay.   *   *   An immense rent, in comparison to the accommodation, is paid to the Company or master for these miserable
places.   (p. 397.)

The Commissioner regarded the degraded condition of the
people as "entirely the fault of their employers," and found
the "grossest ignorance prevailing;" but on religious subjects
they were generally better informed, when they knew anything,
than any other subject.   He issued a circular letter to various
persons in the county, containing 11 questions, mostly referring
to education and morals, one of which was—

Is the English language gaining ground; and is it desirable that
it should be better taught, and if so, for what reason?

I make bold to give my reader extracts from the replies
which reflect in some degree the state of mind of influential
persons in Monmouthshire at that time, but apparently they
mostly belonged to the Episcopalians, so that we are somewhat at a loss to know in what light the mass of the
population were regarded by educated persons of other per-
suasions.

E. H. Phillips, M.D., of Pontypool, says—

It is impossible to think of the social and political conduct of the
people without alarm.   Their dissolute habits, their recklessness
of living, their contempt for authority, their "speaking evil of
dignities," must, if unchecked, bring on a state of things in this
country which it is frightful to contemplate.   I would not need-
lessly make invidious remarks, but I cannot help observing that
much of that turbulent insubordination, and that haughty independence which spurns control, manifested by the people, may be

attributed to the violent and inflammatory harangues which they often hear from platforms and pulpits of dissenters. (do., p. 400.)

One of the reasons Dr. P. alleges why English should prevail more than than at present is that—

It would extend the influence and power of the Established Church, because it would remove the cause of complaint on the part of many Welsh persons that they cannot get Welsh exclusively in the Establishment, which they forsake for Dissent, where this exclusiveness is generally found; and consequent upon this would be the general improvement of the people in due deference to their superiors and respect for the law of the land. (do., p. 401.)

This is followed by a short laudation of the "more peaceful and submissive character of the lower orders," who are members of the Church of England, over those of other sects.

The author of this book never had any personal acquaintance with Dr. Phillips. At the time in which he wrote, English was the prevailing language at Pontypool, as is proved by the fact that within a few years afterwards, say 1860, Welsh was abandoned in the dissenting pulpits of the town, and its use has only quite recently been resumed. It is however doubtful whether the *mother-church* has correspondingly extended her "power and influence." Of course the reader will recollect that the terms "turbulent insubordination," "haughty independence," "inflammatory harangues from the pulpits of dissenters," were written before there was a local Daily Press to pass its comments. Whatever the character of the Daily Press is, and I will not venture to stand as its apologist, it certainly would not be behindhand in giving Dr. Phillips an amply sufficient audience, even if one not much inclined to enter into the state of "alarm" in which he found himself.

Owen Phillips, Pontnewydd, speaks of great ignorance among the poor, chiefly those from Gloucester and Somerset, and of the natives of the Principality, being for the most part tolerably well informed, especially in religious subjects.

Jas. Hughes, Rector of Llanhilleth, writes from the point of view of the semi-educated Welsh Episcopalian with whom his own language is a "nuisance."

The English language is gaining ground but very imperceptibly. As the Welsh language has no valuable writings, either in prose or poetry, and as the Welsh people have not one single interest unconnected with the English, I consider the language to be a nuisance and an obstacle, both to the administration of the law, and to the cause of religion, imposing on pastors a double degree of work (or duty), by their having the Welsh and the English portion of the community to attend to.

He however speaks very plainly on the extremely harmful custom of agents of works keeping public houses, where the men are expected to spend their earnings.

Again—

I have met with Welsh cottagers capable of arguing on the most abstruse theological points, and taking them as a whole, they are very well acquainted with the Bible; but the Welsh have absolutely a distaste for any other kind of reading. Seldom will you see a Welshman reading a newspaper, but he reads with unusual fondness such publications as extol his religious party or expose the failings of those sects to which he does not belong. This fondness for divinity subjects, to the exclusion of all secular knowledge, I ascribe in a great measure to the absence of day-schools, which were nowhere to be seen in Wales until of late years.

Did it never occur to Jas. Hughes, and to others who have made similar remarks that if some secular instruction were imparted in Welsh it would naturally open the way for the acquirement of secular knowledge? He may have been a well-meaning man, though it seems he was in the habit of putting on green spectacles when he looked at his countrymen.

Let not my English readers go away with the idea that
Welshmen do not read newspapers; they do, probably much
more in proportion than Englishmen out of large towns. I
speak of vernacular papers, though there is now a considerable
coexistent circulation of English papers including much trash,
especially in South Wales. As to the language having no
"valuable writings," and being a "nuisance," it is scarcely
necessary to say that such statements, and from such a quarter,
should be met by a sufficiently prominent warning,—"Beware
of the dog."

The Incumbent of Trevethin writes,—

One need only read the Welsh publications to be convinced of
the non-utility of the language for any practical purpose whatever,
religious, or commercial, and the sooner it becomes dead the better
for the people.

How could it be of religious use when the country was
swarming with Dissenters, who disseminated their schismatic
principles by means of it, when, for some unexplained reason,
the people took more kindly to them than to the holder of the
Episcopal crook? How could it be of political use when it
had not long before been proved that it was a stepping
stone for "noisy demagogues" to get the ear of the people?
As for commerce, Welsh was not much used therein, and
therefore one did not need to read the periodicals to be
satisfied of the fact.

Augustus Morgan, Rector of Machen, considered it very
desirable that English should supersede Welsh for three reasons.
1. So that judge, counsel, and jury, in law courts may not be
dependent on an interpreter. 2. To insure a more regular
attendance of the rising generation in "parish churches."
3. Because revolutionary meetings had been held in Welsh, so
that their proceedings might not be discovered.

N

In the winding-up of this Report, the following outspoken paragraph occurs, indicating the judgment of the Commissioner, that this tax on wages as the only method of providing educational funds was an unhealthy one:—

The fierce struggle of interests (believed to be adverse) is ever present, fomenting envy, bitterness, malice, and all the inhumanities of hatred. It pervades the entire conception of the relation between labour and capital. There is, therefore, no confidence in the class through whose medium the remedy should be administered; nor are they inclined to administer it by other means than a tax on wages, which renders it repulsive to the recipients, whose sympathy and appreciation it is so essential to secure. No effective voluntary efforts on the part of the people to obtain sound education can be expected whilst they are too ignorant to value it; nor will any voluntary exertion be made by those who can so well afford it, whilst that feeling prevails among the majority of the employers of labour which it has been my painful duty to develop and attest.

So much for the work of the three Commissioners and their reports, which displayed undoubted ability, and on the whole a desire to conscientiously fulfil their duties.

As far as the writer is aware, those portions of the reports which dealt mainly with education, did not call forth any great degree of comment in Wales. The Welsh people were generally aware of their deficiencies, and glad to have them rectified, but were unable, from various reasons, to oppose intelligent criticism to such of their conclusions as appear to have been other that the fruit of a well balanced, well informed judgment, though it will be seen that these weak points were not wholly unnoticed.

What was however keenly resented, was the very strong language used in each report on the moral character of the people. As to whether or not this judgment was formed on evidence arriving from prejudiced sources I will not take upon

me to decide. It is however quite clear that in some parts of
the country customs prevailed which had an exceedingly
deleterious effect on the people. In the *Traethodydd* for 1850
Lewis Edwards, of Bala (father of the present Principal
T. C. Edwards), dealt with the subject calmly and clearly.

He said, "We cannot do less than express our conviction
that the reports of the visitors should get a greater hearing
than they have done.' It was natural and proper to turn from
the misleading descriptions they gave, but in the zeal to disprove untruth, the truth that they contained has been too much
overlooked."

Quite of another spirit was the stinging lampoon of Ieuan
Gwynedd, which appeared in the *Almanac y Cymry*, 1849,
published by John Cassell. He there describes the commotion
caused by the books of the "Three Spies."

> Mae'r wlad yn llawn o ddwndwr,
> A chodwyd fi drwy cynwr';
> 　Ac achwyniadau sydd heb ri'
> 　Ar lyfrau tri Ysbïwyr.

He then alludes to the clerical informants of the "Spies,"
"who (Balaam like) taught them—the Commissioners—to run
us down" *(diraddio)*.

> Y gwŷr mewn dillad duon,
> A elwir offeiriadon,
> 　A'u dysgent i'n diraddio am
> 　(Fel Balaam) lwgr wobrwyon.

How thoroughly Welsh it is to drag in a Scripture simile
when possible. The Parliament he gives credit for picking
out "sharp lawyers" for the work.

> Anfonodd dri Ysbïwr,
> Pob un yn llwm gyfreitbiwr;
> 　A'r tri yn Saeson uchel ben,
> 　I Gymru wen mewn ffwndwr.

Y tri wŷr awdurdodol
A aent mewn brys rhyfeddol,
  I gasglu pob budreddi cas
Yn llyfrau glâs anferthol.

     *   *   *   *

Ar ol eu cael yn gryno,
Hwy aethent oll i lunio
  Rhyw dri o lyfrau gleision hyll,
Wnant yn mhob dull ein beio.

The four bishops are touched off in a verse each. Here is
the long-headed Connop Thirlwall (*call* is scarcely translatable
by any one word in English) advising a Government grant
from *Sioni* (Lord John Russell), which Ieuan fears will be for
the purpose of "buying" over the children.

Mae Esgob call Tyddewi
Yn dweyd mai callach tewi,
  Ac ail ymdrechu prynu'r plant
Drwy geisio *grant* gan Sioni.

Ieuan treats with biting sarcasm the charge brought by the
Commissioners against the morals of the people, but the impartial reader will find that the evidence was of far too decided
a character in each of the three reports to leave room to doubt
that in *some* country districts, away from the polluting influence
of large industrial centres, with their unsettled populations,
the standard of popular feeling with regard to chastity was
a low one, though at the same time the Methodists, and
other religious bodies, had endeavoured to purify the atmosphere,
evidently with some success. It is certain, as shewn
before, that statistics failed to substantiate the imputation
that Welsh-Wales was worse than England, and we cannot
but feel that R. W. Lingen, in particular, made one or two
unjustifiable remarks when dealing with the matter.

In Volume II. of *Yr Adolygydd*, a quarterly periodical for

"November," 1851, appeared an excellent article on "*Aninweir-deb*" (unchastity), dealing in very plain, and yet not too plain. terms with the subject. Probably the Commissioners' report had called the writer's attention to the subject. He ends with this beautiful and metaphorical language, after calling on his countrymen to sound the trumpet of war against the evil*—

Os rhaid arloesi anialwch, codi pantiau, palu mynyddoedd, sychu corsydd, a hollti creigiau, na ddigalonwch, mae Duw o'ch plaid. Os parhewch i fod yn ffyddlon, cewch weled eich gwlad wedi ei gwaredu, eich cenedl wedi ei phuro, a'ch mabonau yn rhodio yn rhydd. Pan waredir Cymru oddiwrth y gelyn mawr hwn, dawnsia ei mynyddoedd gan lawenydd, llama ei bryniau gan orfoledd, a chura ei choedwigoedd eu dwylaw gan falchder. Pryd hyn bydd gorfoledd ar y ddaear, a llawenydd yn y nef.

We must not dismiss without further notice the hostile criticism offered to the Reports by Sir Thos. Phillips, then a barrister in London, who published in 1849 a volume entitled "Wales: the language, social condition, moral character, and religious opinions of the people, considered in their relation to Education." He writes from the Episcopalian standpoint, mildly chiding some of the shortcomings of that church in Wales, and apologising, as it were, for the existence of Dissent, with which he was not wanting in sympathy.

He desires teachers for his own denomination, who will "train up the young of her flock in accordance with the solemn vow, promise, and profession made for each of them when they were grafted into the body of Christ's Church," (he evidently thinks the "grafting" took place when a little water

---

* If you have to clear the wilderness ground, raise the valleys, lay low the mountains, dry up the bogs, rend the rocks, be not discouraged, God is on your side. If you continue to be faithful, you will see your country delivered, your nation purified, and your sons walking free. When Wales is delivered from this great enemy, her mountains will dance for joy, her hills will leap with rejoicing, and her forests will clap their hands for gladness. Then there will be praise on earth and joy in heaven.

was sprinkled on the child's face), and quotes Archdeacon Williams:—

The parish schoolroom is now the battle-field of the Church: and within its walls must be decided the share of influence which she is to exercise over the hearts and affections of the next generation. Her influence, her very existence as an establishment, are at stake: they must be won or lost upon this cast.

I refrain from quoting more, but the assumption of the Archdeacon in the next sentence, that the spread of *true religion* is at stake in this matter, is astounding.

Sir Thos. Phillips did not unite with the attitude of the Report towards the Welsh language. He says in his Preface—

The opinions expressed by the Commissioners on the language of the country, to which they attribute injurious influences on the character and condition of the people, have provoked much controversy, and are opposed to the views of competent judges.

And he thus alludes to the statement as to moral character—

Such imputations, instead of being cast at random in public Reports, which, from their character, give force and poignancy to the charge, should be conveyed in language carefully weighed, and strictly limited by the extent and character of the evil. When indiscriminately scattered abroad, they excite a strong sense of injustice.

It is the admission of men, who have travelled far and seen much, that in no country have they found women of greater gentleness and interest than the peasant girls of Wales.

Owing in good degree to the efforts of Sir T. P., the Committee of Council on Education, made an important concession to Wales in 1849, by allowing a good and systematic knowledge of Welsh to be accepted in pupil teachers' examinations in lieu of two subjects, and a less perfect knowledge in lieu of one subject only.

Shortly after, however, R. W. Lingen, was appointed Secretary to the Committee, and whether from this cause or from the lack of facilities, whereby pupil teachers were able to attain this "good and systematic knowledge," or from any other reason it was not much acted on, and many years ago the privilege was abolished, which were it revived now, could much more easily be made available on account of the great increase of Welsh educational books.

There is additional evidence that elementary education was in a most neglected state, not merely in Wales but also in England, if not contemporaneously with the visit of the Commissioners, only some seven years before.

The following paragraph from the introduction of Gibbs and Edwards' "Code of 1876," summarizes the state of things in England and Wales prior to 1839:—

Good schools were few and far between, the school houses were often squalid, with miserable furniture, few books, and scarcely any other school appliances. The attendance of the children was irregular, their attainments were wretched. The teachers were often ignorant adventurers, who had adopted the profession when they had proved their utter incompetency for any other calling, while those who possessed any knowledge were ignorant of good methods of imparting it. Riot and disorder were kept under only by the most savage discipline."

In 1839, Government grants were first made to assist in the erection of schools. In 1843 they were extended towards the purchase of apparatus and the erection of training schools for teachers. In 1846, the year of the appointment of the Welsh Commissioners, in order to assist in keeping up a body of efficient teachers, provision was made for the augmentation by Government of the salary paid by managers to teachers who had obtained by examination a certificate of merit, and whose schools were well reported annually by Inspectors, and where satisfaction was also given to the managers themselves.

In 1853 and 1856, Capitation Grants were made, by which from six shillings to four shillings were paid per head for each child under certain conditions.

The result of these successive educational advances was such a change over the face of the country that when W. E. Forster's Act of 1870 was passed with Compulsory Education in its train, there was no short and sharp transition between such destitution as had existed only 30 years before that, and the completed system we see in form to day. I say complete with regard to its exterior mechanism, as to the completeness of the results, I will here abstain from expressing an opinion.

As regards Wales, in particular, there are not many facts to add, but having noticed an article in *Yr Adolygydd*, for 1851, which appeared to indicate that the period of inefficient teachers had then passed away, I wrote to Wm. Williams, M.A., Chief Inspector for Wales, who has kindly sent a communication, from which I extract the following:—

I have a slight recollection of the article to which you refer in *Yr Adolygydd* on " *Yr Ysgolfeistr fel y mae*," and I may say confidently that it could refer to only a comparatively small number of teachers, *i.e.*, to the few teachers who had been trained between 1846 and 1851, at the British and Foreign Training College, Borough Road; the National Society's Training College, at Battersea; the Normal College started at Brecon, about the beginning of 1846, removed to Swansea in 1848, and conducted by the late Dr. Evan Davies, who was the author of the articles in *Adolygydd*, and possibly a few trained in Scotland.

The number of Church and National Schools in Wales increased, comparatively rapidly, from 1846 or '47, and this was due to several causes. The grants towards the erection of schools were from about this time increased and were very liberal, amounting, I believe, to about 40 per cent., and as the value of school sites, which were often given, and the cost of haulage often done without pay, could also be counted in the expenses, the grant in many cases amounted to probably 50 per cent of the actual money spent.

During this time Dr. Davies, of the Normal College, Swansea, and some of the leading Nonconformists in South Wales (like the late David Rees, of Llanelly), were opposed *in toto* to receiving grants towards the erection or maintenance of schools, and this greatly retarded for a time the spread of British and undenominational schools, and allowed the ground to be covered by Church schools. The Nonconformists of South Wales subsequently decided to accept grants, and British Schools spread comparatively fast from about 1855 to 1870, whilst a considerable number of the Church Schools fell into a state of inefficiency, or were closed.

By 1870 accommodation had been provided in Wales for probably from one-third to one-half of the population, but this was very unevenly distributed, and there were large tracts of country with no efficient school in them.

By what precedes it will be seen that the advancement of Welsh and English education was nearly collateral, and to ascribe the backward state of the former to the deleterious effects of the Welsh language, in spite of the strange adventures of the *tri wyr awdurdodol*, is an unfair inference.

For another generation, however, the people of Wales ignored secular education in Welsh, hoping that they might thereby learn English better, notwithstanding the more enlightened views of some of their leading men; and the Government ignored it both with that mistaken notion, and with the additional hope, there is ground to believe, of shortly effecting a linguistic *bouleversement* in the country. Just as Llewelyn ap Gruffydd's head was welcomed outside the Tower of London with savage delight, so there have not been wanting men of position who would hail with satisfaction a bulletin conveying intelligence of the last expiring groans of the language spoken by that ancestor of our present Sovereign.

CHAPTER IV.

THE preceding Chapters having been principally devoted to an elucidation of the state of Elementary Education in Wales from forty to fifty years ago, it will be necessary in the present one, to revert to the same period, briefly noticing some facts affecting intermediate and higher education, before following out at length the controversy started a few years ago by a Welsh Society in London, and afterwards more or less in the country at large, as to the desirability of a radical alteration in the existing methods of dealing with Welsh schools principally with regard to elementary ones, but also to some extent, including the whole educational system.

In Wales the ingenious educationalists of two or three generations past, contrived a remarkable expedient for the employment, if not amusement of the boys in middle class schools, which consisted in hounding their language down by means of the *Welsh note*, which was a stick of wood passed on from one boy to the next, who was heard speaking Welsh. At the end of a certain period, the last possessor of the "note" or "stick" was punished.

The custom was not confined to middle class schools, as appears by the following in H. V. Johnson's report of Llandyrnog, Denbighshire:—

My attention was attracted to a piece of wood, suspended by a string round a boy's neck, and on the stick were the words, "Welsh stick." This, I was told, was a stigma for speaking Welsh. But, in fact, his only alternative was to speak Welsh or to say nothing. He did not understand English, and there is no systematic exercise in interpretation. (p. 452.)

We ask what kind of metal were the masters of those times made of, when we learn that "among other injurious effects, this custom has been found to lead children to visit stealthily the houses of their schoolfellows for the purpose of detecting those who speak Welsh to their parents, and transferring to them the punishment due to themselves? See also *Appendix* D.

I have had occasion to allude to the attitude, and think I am justified in calling it the prevailing attitude at that time, of representatives of the Established Church towards the Welsh language. I shall not, however, be understood to imply that this was universal. The year 1847, saw the foundation of a scheme which, though under the care of the Established Church had for one of its express purposes the colloquial and literary cultivation of the Welsh language, and is at the present day (apart from questions of religion) one of the best, if not the best higher class school in Wales.

The following extract from a summary of the provisions of the Deed of the founder, viz., Thos. Phillips, a London Welshman, who bestowed nearly £5,000 for the purpose, gives some idea of his views:—

The scholars will be instructed in Welsh reading, grammar, and composition; in English, Latin, Greek, and Hebrew, arithmetic, algebra, and mathematics; in sacred, English and general history, and geography; and in such other branches of education as the trustees, with the sanction of the visitor, shall appoint. The Welsh language shall be taught exclusively during one hour every school day, and be then the sole medium of communication in the school; and shall be used at all other convenient periods as the language of the school, so as to familiarize the scholars with its use as a colloquial language. The master shall give lectures in that language upon subjects of a philological, scientific, and general character, so as to supply the scholars with examples of its use as a literary language, and the medium of instruction on grave and important subjects. The primary intent and object of the founder (which is instruction and education in the Welsh language) shall be faithfully observed.

So far we say so good, but the crucial test of a middle class school in England or Wales now-a-days, is generally looked for in its ability to prepare for the preliminary examinations of English Universities, few schools, if any, unless carried on under exceptional circumstances, think they can afford to work to entirely independent standards of their own. This has directly or indirectly affected the course of instruction at Llandovery, so that the intentions of the founder have not probably been carried out to the fullest extent, although they have been so far as to materially increase the usefulness of the institution.

I have mentioned that Llandovery school was (and is still) under the care of the Established Church, so is that called "Christ's College," Brecon, with a good organization and an annual endowment of £1,200; other Welsh endowments were mostly either denominational or inadequate, and for a number of years it was felt that the needs of the country demanded considerable improvement in the facilities for Intermediate Education, especially in such as Nonconformists would be likely to freely avail themselves of.

In 1880, in compliance with representations made to it, the

Government appointed a Committee, to enquire into the condition of Intermediate and Higher Education in Wales, consisting of the following persons,—

LORD ABERDARE

VISCOUNT EMLYN

H. G. ROBINSON (Prebendary of the Established Church).

HENRY RICHARD, M.P.

PROFESSOR RHYS

LEWIS MORRIS.

The main scope of the enquiry of this representative Committee was confined to the question of the utilization of endowments for middle class schools in Wales, and the best method of supporting such in the future.

As might be expected from its constitution, the Welsh Language received considerably more respect from the Commission than from that of 1847. Its power and vitality were acknowledged, but the Report offered no suggestions as to any improved method of coping with the difficulties, created by the existence of a household language, side by side with a system of education which ignored its existence.

The immediate result of their labours was the establishment of University Colleges for North and South Wales, and the giving of an annual subsidy to the one at Aberystwyth, which, after considerable demur, the Government wisely consented to retain.

A very important recommendation was made by them, viz.:—the creation of what amounted to a Welsh University, with the representatives of the leading colleges on its Governing Board, which was not, however, carried into effect; but, perhaps we may, in some measure, trace the passing of the Intermediate Educational Act for Wales, with the powers it conferred on County Councils for the establishment of middle class schools, to the labours of this Committee. Nor

was the work of the Commission in any way directly related
to that movement, the rise, and progress of which I am about
to trace; but inasmuch as the establishment of these University
Colleges has given some educated Welshmen a vantage ground
to co-operate with it, and as no single part of Welsh education can be looked at without reference to the whole, it
may not have been out of place to give a few brief hints at
its work.

At present this movement is confined within comparatively
small limits, and although it has gained some victories, there is
still a possibility of its retiring from the field without permanently occupying the ground gained. It has, however,
within itself the germ of an educational revolution for Wales,
which may yet wonderfully modify the future history of that
country. Be that as it may, there has been so much of interest
bearing on the relation of the language to the social and
intellectual life of the people, evolved by enquiries and dis-
cussions set up in connection with its operations, that a wise
historian cannot refuse to notice them, and in a work of this
kind, it is deemed necessary to give details somewhat more at
length than may perhaps please some persons to whom the
power exercised by the language in the past and in the
present, is an unsolved and unsolvable enigma.

In 1884 the Cymmrodorion Society, having its head quarters
in London, appointed a committee to enquire into certain
points relating to Elementary Education in Wales, which
were in brief the alleged defects of teaching English, and the
proposal that it should be taught through the medium of
Welsh. Questions bearing on these points were sent round
to about thirty leading educationalists in Wales, including Wm.
Williams (the senior Inspector of Elementary Schools). It
was found on receipt of replies that only one correspondent
positively expressed depreciation of Welsh as a subject of

education, while the Principal of the Normal College, Bangor, was one who strongly advocated its introduction.

The next step of the Committee was to address an enquiry to the head-masters and mistresses of primary schools in Wales, as follows:—

Do you consider that advantage would result from the introduction of the Welsh language as a specific subject into the course of Elementary Education in Wales?

In the Spring of 1885, 628 answers were received, of which 339 were affirmative, 257 negative, 32 neutrals. For a tabulated statement of these replies, arranged according to counties. See Appendix E. By this it will be seen that Flint and Pembroke were the only counties that shewed negative majorities. Somewhat singularly, the county of Monmouth, where Welsh is not much spoken as a family language, shewed a majority in the affirmative, while the busy, industrial county of Glamorgan, shewed no less than a majority of 57 per cent. of affirmative over negative replies.

The replies of these teachers form in the mind of the writer, one of the most interesting contributions to the literature of Wales, that have appeared during the present century. To reproduce the whole would take up too much space, I therefore propose to give selected extracts from them, or summaries ranged under their respective Counties.

The original printed report of the Cymmrodorion and the appendix, giving the replies in full, are perhaps not easily accessible to most of my readers, and as the negatives touch on nearly everything that can be said now against any similar proposal, it is well they should be heard, although for the most part their arguments were decidedly the weakest, except where any of them felt that Welsh as a class-subject would meet the case better than as a specific.

It must be borne in mind that these replies were written

before the subject had been canvassed by public discussion,
and that early prejudices doubtless biased some of the writers,
from whose school and collegiate courses Welsh had been
excluded.

They are however valuable as the independent witness of a
number of intelligent men with trained minds in different parts
of the country, and surrounded by very different conditions.

I have not quoted the reference numbers given in the
original, except occasionally for the sake of clearness, but the
reader will bear in mind that each separate paragraph is
written by a different teacher, and that it does not in every
case comprise the whole of the answer.

ANGLESEY.

NEGATIVE.—I don't think that Welsh parents would welcome
the introduction of "Welsh" as a subject into our schools. They
want us to prepare their children to fight the "battle of life."
But I am of opinion that the Government ought to make some
allowance for the difficulties we have to encounter in teaching
English to our pupils.

The greatest opposition would be offered in this district to
Welsh being introduced, as all parents with whom I am acquainted
are most anxious that it should be altogether excluded from school
work. My opinion is that "well" is best *let alone*. So my answer
is "No."

No. For: (1) Parents would not stand it. (2) Welsh is amply
cared for by our Sunday schools and literary meetings. (3) I cannot see the utility of the proposal. (4) Our schools are Welshy
enough as it is. (5) After eight years' experience I find the best
plan is to use the Welsh language as sparingly as possible. Of
course we all love the old tongue, but school life is not a matter of
sentiment, but a serious preparation for the battle of life. (6) I
am certain if you succeed few teachers would care to teach it, as
it would seriously interfere with other more important work.

No. Reasons: (1) Sufficient latitude is already given by the Educational Code for the employment of Welsh as a medium of teaching English. (2) Teachers having no knowledge of Welsh, and those who entirely discard it in teaching Welsh pupils, are highly successful as such in Wales. (3) If Welsh were included as a specific subject in the Educational Code, I, in anticipation, assert that no more than one out of ten teachers would adopt it. (4) My knowledge of people of both mining and agricultural districts enables me to say positively that the teaching of Welsh in our schools would be much objected to. (5) The introduction of Welsh into the curriculum of the schools would greatly hinder the teacher in endeavouring to encourage English conversation among his scholars.

AFFIRMATIVE—The introduction of Welsh as a "specific subject" will be of great benefit to schools where the children are entirely Welsh. Many children now leave school when they can neither write English or Welsh correctly.

Most of the young men, after passing the fourth standard in a day school, as well as attending Sunday schools, are unable to compose either Welsh or English. Whereas if they were all grounded in their "mothers' tongue" in elementary schools it would be an inducement for them to compete at literary meetings, Eisteddfodau, &c., and at the same time it would assist them to understand the English language.

(1) It would afford a highly interesting (because thoroughly understood) mental training, and English would be more efficiently taught than at present, on the natural principle of proceeding from the known to the unknown. (2) A child would comprehend the grammatical structure of his native tongue, and compose in it with ease; thereby acquiring a power and model to deal with English and other languages. The majority of children leave school with very imperfect notions of English composition, and none of Welsh, as far as school teaching helps them; and parents justly complain that their children cannot write correctly "either an English or a Welsh letter." (4) Such being the universal complaint, it follows

P

that the present mode of teaching English has lamentably failed (except to a few talented youths in each school), and some course akin to the suggested syllabus must be adopted before any better results can be obtained from the great majority.

It would be a great boon to the children in order to aid them to understand the English language. It would create in their minds when leaving school a thorough love for higher education in science and literature.

The study of such a BEAUTIFUL, POETICAL, and EXPRESSIVE LANGUAGE as the Welsh would carry its own intrinsic value in the possession of the full command of such a language to clothe his thoughts.

Though an Englishman, I have been very much struck with the slight knowledge of Welsh grammar as evinced by the working class with whom I have been brought in contact.

By placing the Welsh language among the specific subjects, I do not think that any English teacher would find that he was handi-capped in the matter. I thoroughly endorse the opinion of Mr. Edward Roberts, B.A., H. M.'s Inspector of Schools.

CARNARVONSHIRE.

NEGATIVE—No; because (a) Welsh children's knowledge of Welsh being for the most part only of colloquial Welsh, they would have to unlearn a great deal before any progress could be made, (b) The parents of English children in Welsh schools would very probably object to their children learning Welsh.

Our literary associations and Sunday schools are ample means of supplying the required knowledge of the Welsh language.

No, a thousand times no. A discreet use of Welsh in the lower standards is commendable, and may be for some time yet indis-pensable.   *   *   Every Welsh teacher I have yet spoken with emphatically condemns the idea. Indeed, most of us have not even acquired a knowledge of the rudiments of Welsh grammar, so utterly purposeless is its acquisition to successful teaching.

No. Perhaps it would be an advantage to teach it to the pupil-teachers, as this would in time largely increase the number of Welsh writers. The Government might be asked to set papers in the Welsh language at the scholarship and certificate examinations. I think I am not wrong in stating that at present there are but very few of the Welsh teachers who can write Welsh.

AFFIRMATIVE—Yes, provided it should be taught as a class subject, and not as a specific subject.

Welsh-English translation being under existing conditions copiously practised, I do not see that any material extra labour would result from the adoption of Welsh as a "specific," nor that it would necessitate the dropping of the ordinary class subjects. Though there is a cry for English, yet parents are quite as anxious for their children to be able to write respectable Welsh letters. I say yes, on financial and educational grounds.

I maintain that nothing but a parrot-like knowledge of English can possibly be imparted to scholars in Welsh-spoken districts, as far as Standard III. inclusive. without freely using the Welsh language. This being done in the majority of elementary schools in Wales, the teaching of Welsh as a *specific subject* would require so little *extra work* that there would be no need to drop any of the ordinary, in order to introduce it. Having been engaged in schools in Welsh-spoken district over fourteen years, I hope you will excuse me for giving expression to the above statements.

It would be a good foundation for the learning of English. I have been repeatedly asked by parents to teach Welsh composition (letter-writing) to their children; of course, without neglecting English in any way.

Yes, I believe that the introduction of the Welsh language into the curriculum of elementary schools, will greatly facilitate the teaching of English in purely Welsh schools.

I do really consider that the introduction of the Welsh language as a "specific subject" would enhance even the speedy acquisition of English, and a better grounding of the Welsh language than we have hitherto possessed, providing that a Welsh grammatical primer suitable to the capacity of the children would be supplied, containing sentences that would render a mutual aid to acquire a sound elementary knowledge of both languages. Whatever is said of Sunday school teaching, my experience assures me that many a Sunday school scholar does not know the difference between *i'w* and *yw*, and *mae* and *mai*, and in this respect it is a complete failure, and the only remedy would be acquired by the introduction of Welsh as a specific subject.

Being a most ancient and original language, its knowledge could not fail to be AN INTRODUCTION TO A CLASSICAL EDUCATION. In Welsh-speaking districts I consider the vernacular the best medium of teaching English and of improving the general intelligence.

Yes. It would be far more serviceable than Euclid, &c., to the lads of the Welsh-speaking districts of Carnarvonshire, &c.

Few English families reside here, but I find that the English children in a very short time are able to talk Welsh, and will insist upon speaking it every chance they obtain.

Yes. It is an act of justice to an ancient people and their language. It will give the rising generation an intelligent and grammatical, as well as a practical knowledge of their native tongue, and enable them to correspond with facility in Welsh, whereas at present many Welsh people correspond with each other in English.

Before the schools of Wales will be on an equal footing with those of England, your plan should be adopted.

NEUTRAL—It would be of great advantage to these, if they were able to write and compose in their native language. But they have had no practice and no opportunities to learn these useful acquirements.

DENBIGHSHIRE.

NEGATIVE—No, I do not. I confess that English could be *better and more thoroughly* taught through that medium, but it would very much retard the progress of the scholar. The greatest objection I see to it, is the fact that *few* schoolmasters, although Welsh, can write or understand Welsh correctly. Also, it would take as much trouble to get the children to understand the *proper* Welsh language as it would to do the English. I say proper.

because children *do not* speak it properly—and differently in different districts.

Decidedly no. Because there is too much division in the British empire now, and the giving legal sanction to another language will only increase the division. Because there are too many subjects taught already.

No. But I think it would be good to give a small piece in English language as home lesson, to be translated into Welsh, such as a letter from a friend. I have been doing so, and found it to do good.

I would most decidedly say "Yes" if it was introduced as a *class subject*.

AFFIRMATIVE—Yes. I believe the knowledge of even two languages (Welsh and English) to be stimulative to the mind, by exciting comparison and enquiry. Welsh, being a root language, gives a good insight into the construction of languages.

In my humble opinion, which is based upon a residence of more than twenty-five years in North Wales, *all the schools would do well to teach the Welsh language as a " specific subject,"* as I fully believe that quite four-fifths of the children understand and speak the native tongue. I would except the eastern portion of Montgomeryshire, and perhaps two or three schools at Rhyl and Llandudno. A boy who is conversant with both languages has, in more than one way, an advantage over a boy who simply knows English. * * * I deem it a great advantage to know a BEAUTIFUL, PHONETIC, EXPRESSIVE language, such as the Welsh is.

FLINTSHIRE.

NEGATIVE—Rather than introduce the Welsh language as a specific subject, it would be more fair to the teachers in the Principality for the Committee of Council on Education to acknowledge the *disadvantage* under which they work, especially in rural districts, and draw up a simpler and special CODE for the WELSH SCHOOLS, in order to put them on a more common-sense level with the English schools, where the children know nothing but their mother tongue, English, from their birth. What would the English teachers do if they had to teach every subject in the French language to children who had been taught English from their birth, and who heard nothing but English at their homes and while at play; and those children again to be examined in the same subjects as French children of the same age? The use of both languages must be made by the Welsh teachers before English can be taught in the schools of the Principality.

No. At least nine out of every ten of the teachers would require special training.

AFFIRMATIVE.—I do. I have had an opportunity of (more than once) lecturing on Welsh grammar before " Young Men's Literary Associations," and in each case a decided craving for such a move as you recommend was manifested.

As an old pupil of the Rev. Jenkin Davies, Rector of Bottwnog, Caernarvonshire, I consider his method of teaching English one of the best for beginners in a Welsh country school — e g.: The Verb "to be" Indic. Pres. *Singular.*—I am=yr wyf fi; Thou art yr wyt ti; He is =Y mae ef. *Plural.*—We are yr ydym ni; You are yr ydych chwi; They are y maent hwy. The introduction of the Welsh language as a specific subject into the course of elementary education in Wales would, I firmly believe, be of great advantage to both teacher and scholar. The most successful teachers use it freely.

MERIONETHSHIRE.

NEGATIVE—And what a disadvantage a Welsh teacher and the children under his charge would be labouring under in comparison with an English-speaking teacher, even in Wales, and much more so in comparison with an English-speaking teacher in a district exclusively English, who one and all are expected to produce the same or similar results, independent of circumstances over which they often have no control, or be involved helplessly in professional ruin. See reply to No. 7 B., the said H. M. Senior Inspector. *"Edrych yn y drych hwn dro, gyr galon graig i wylo."*

No. The introduction of any Welsh into this school would be

very unfavourably met by the parents; even now they will blame
the teacher for explaining difficult passages in English by means
of the Welsh language.

Reducing the number of readers in Welsh schools, so as to give
teachers more time to cultivate intelligence by means of *translation*,
as prescribed by the Code, would secure the same result.

AFFIRMATIVE—I consider that great advantage would accrue.
I may state that the Welsh is now universally made use of in the
lowest standards; and ideas, when expounded in Welsh, seem to
adhere longer to pupils' minds, especially in purely Welsh speaking
schools. By the adoption of the proposed scheme, both the Welsh
and English languages would be more thoroughly known in the
Principality.

There is no doubt but that a very great advantage would result
from it, because the Welsh language is not properly taught at our
Sunday schools, &c., as asserted by some; but really it puzzles me
to know how it can be introduced into the course of elementary
education in Wales with the present requirements of the Code.
The best teachers already groan under the drudgery.

Although my Welsh is very imperfect, I vote strongly for its
introduction into Welsh schools, not as a medium for teaching
English, but as a SEPARATE SUBJECT paid for by the Education
Department as a class subject in the same ratio as our other class
subjects; and I would furthermore suggest that in Welsh schools
all teachers may have the option of teaching grammar (English)
and Welsh, instead of grammar and geography.

NEUTRAL—After advocating beginning Welsh in the early
Standards, "There will, I know, be too much *timidity* to ask for
such a radical change in the Code, until Welshmen who would be
listened to by the Department discover the dreariness and the
unnaturalness of the present methods of teaching in our infants'
and junior classes. The handful of Gaelic-speaking population in
Scotland seem to have more official cognisance in this respect than
our Welsh-speaking population of *one million*, with a living
literature to boot."

MONTGOMERYSHIRE.

NEGATIVE—[Answers 11, 12 and 13 allude to the prevalence of English in their districts.]

I think no advantage would result from its introduction as a "specific subject." (1) It would tend to isolate Wales from becoming assimilated with England in every sense of the word. (2) No adequate return would be obtained in after-life. (3) It would unnecessarily burden the already hard-pressed teacher in rural districts. (4) It would tend to exclude English teachers from taking charge of schools in Wales.

AFFIRMATIVE—Yes, especially where the Welsh language is likely to be forgotten.

I have only been a master in Wales for a few weeks *   * as far as I can tell I think it would be greatly advisable.

As long as the object of the Education Act is to teach English, the least of Welsh used in schools the better, until the children have learnt to *think* in English. When that point is reached, as in upper standards (sometimes), Welsh may then be taken without being a hindrance to their learning English—the original object.

I do: (1) The study of the Welsh language is as much a means of MENTAL DISCIPLINE and development as the study of the Latin, the French, or any other subject at present mentioned in Schedule IV. of the new Code. (2) If a child speaks the Welsh language, and is likely to use it during its lifetime, a grammatical and systematic knowledge of it would render it of much greater value to him or her than would be the mere power to speak it.

As a teacher of public elementary schools for upwards of thirty-four years, I would most strongly advocate that teaching Welsh should be made compulsory in *all* schools located in Welsh-speaking districts. There is not a better mental culture, or one so well calculated to enliven and bring out the mental energies of Welsh children, than to combine the vernacular with English.

CARDIGAN.

NEGATIVE—[Along with other references to parents' objections.]
The chief request of all the parents that call upon me is to

make their children learn plenty of English.   *   *   I have had experience in two schools in different parts of Cardiganshire, and the chief and great desire of the people is for the spread of English in those parts.

The introduction of Welsh in any form would seriously retard progress in English.

AFFIRMATIVE—Yes.   *Reason:* In so much as I love Wales, and in particular the Welsh language, I have always felt grateful towards St. David's College, Lampeter, where the Welsh language is studied, and am glad of this present opportunity of voting for the future *existence* of my mother's tongue.

Yes, as a "specific subject" if examined by Welsh inspectors. This would bring Welsh children to have some regard and admiration for their own language.

Yes, for it seems ridiculous that the present generation of children should be able to express themselves better, *on paper*, in the English than in their mother tongue. Welsh, as a *written* language, is falling fast into disuse in Wales.

I am at a loss to see any objection, on the part of teachers, to its being introduced as such. The correct rendering of Welsh in writing is most imperfectly known in these parts. The Sunday schools do nothing more than teach the mechanical part of reading Welsh, leaving grammar, &c., entirely out of the question.

Yes. (1) I think the children would learn English better by such means than by the present SLIPSHOD WAY of teaching, or rather not teaching it. (2) It would be an invaluable exercise for the mind—*i.e.*, the comparing the two languages would be. (3) It would tend to keep alive the Welsh national spirit, and although an Englishman myself I think this an HONOURABLE AND GOOD motive. (4) I think there is no doubt that Welsh literature would gain immensely by such an introduction.

I do not hesitate for a moment to say "yes." But I am afraid that the want of a proper staff in the majority of Welsh schools to conduct the teaching of it as a *specific* subject will be a severe check to the advantages thus to be derived. I should be inclined

Q

to place it among the *class* subjects, or at least to include it in the
present *class* subject English.

RADNOR.

NEGATIVE—[Reason assigned by two writers—Welsh unnecessary.]

AFFIRMATIVE—Welsh parents have been, and still are, more or
less anxious that their children should learn the English language,
but the feeling in my opinion is not so strong now as it appeared
to have been ten years ago, when the almost convincing and loud
cry was raised that their old and dear language would in a couple
of years die out never to revive again. The inhabitants of the
Principality at the present time, however, and after ten or fifteen
years' experience of such hue and cry, are not the least terrified
about the extinction of their language; in fact, the Welsh as a
nation begin to feel jealous of their language; they think it worthy
of attention, and indeed heed is paid to it now more than ever,
and in a much higher sphere than hitherto. *   * To learn, even
a little, of the Welsh grammar, and to write Welsh correctly, would
be of advantage to Welsh boys and girls in after years. I was
asked last Christmas twelve-month to adjudicate some poetry at a
competitive meeting written in English and Welsh. The Welsh
idea was superior to the English, but the spelling was wretched.

BRECKNOCK.

AFFIRMATIVE —I believe the more intelligent farmers here would
like very much that their children should be taught to write Welsh
correctly, in addition to being able to read it, which they are now
taught to do in our Sunday schools.

PEMBROKE.

NEGATIVE—No Welsh spoken—Parents' objections—Majority
of teachers English.

Again, the parents of children would soon repudiate such a
step; the unanimous feeling is to see their children progress in
English, for "they can get as much Welsh as they want at home,"
and any shortcomings of the same would soon be noised abroad.

AFFIRMATIVE—Virtually I should say there would be an advantage to the children themselves, but many Welsh localities would discountenance such teaching, owing to the notion that sufficient knowledge of Welsh is being got at home, and that the school course should consist in the teaching of the language of practical business, &c.

I am of opinion that children would be greatly delighted and interested in learning a subject so familiar to them, and it would be a great step towards bringing out their intelligence.

I feel compelled to answer "Decidedly yes," as I am unable to teach my Standard II. children nouns and verbs in the English language, and am obliged to resort to corresponding Welsh nouns and verbs. This is more difficult as I am English.

CARMARTHENSHIRE.

NEGATIVE—Parents are very anxious that their children should learn English well, and those who have learned English grammatically have little difficulty in writing a letter in Welsh fairly. They learn to read in the Sunday schools in Welsh, and nearly every family takes a weekly Welsh paper in this locality. Welsh is spoken by 99 per cent.

Children and teachers overpressed.   * The POPULAR DELUSION [that of parents thinking the Sabbath school (so called) sufficient for picking up Welsh] must first be removed before any general teaching of Welsh be obtained.

Children, however, on leaving school take up Welsh or English papers, no matter which. But although the rising generation is well able to speak English in their business affairs (which I cannot say their parents can do), the language at home is essentially as "Welsh" as ever.

This district is entirely Welsh, but, strange to say, no one writes or carries on correspondence in Welsh; all is done in English.

No. I speak from an experience of eighteen years as a master of schools in strictly Welsh-speaking districts. The teaching of Welsh as a specific subject will not be advantageous because it

will increase and not lighten the existing pressure.   * As
a practical teacher, and as a warm advocate of the retention of
the Welsh language, I should suggest as practicable and advantageous the substitution of Welsh translations for the present
burdensome and often useless learning by a rote of a number of
lines of poetry with meanings and allusions.

AFFIRMATIVE—Yes; but I believe that parents would be very
much opposed to it.

In my opinion considerable advantage would result, but the
parents would object.

It might prove advantageous, especially when such encouragement as that offered by Dr. John Williams, of 11, Queen Anne
Street, London, is given in the form of an Exhibition of the annual
value of £27, tenable for four years, at The College, Llandovery,
or Christ College, Brecon, to lads under fourteen years of age from
elementary schools in five surrounding parishes, one of the subjects
for examination being: " *Welsh—Reading and translation from
Welsh to English,*"

It would also be the means of cultivating the intelligence of the
pupils. It is a great pity, if not shame, that we (Welshmen) do
not study our language properly, so as to be able to enjoy the
writings of our excellent authors, in poetry and prose.

[Particularly thoughtful answer]. In my opinion it would be a
decided advantage, particularly so in country districts, where few
attractions are found for young people to employ their leisure time.
It would be the means of fostering a love of study, inasmuch as
children leave school before their thinking powers are greatly
developed, and they require some subject as a connecting link
between the subjects adapted to the capabilities of boys and men ;
and I believe that starting with a fair knowledge of Welsh would
open the field for more extensive reading.

Yes; for I believe it would improve the Welsh children in
English and in Welsh.

Yes. After reading the "Elementary Report" you sent me
carefully and studiously, I was surprised to find these gentlemen

differ so much upon a subject which ought to receive more attention from every true Welshman.

I sometimes, and now often, write on the board colloquial Welsh expressions for translation, and I find the children soon pick up the idiom in English. But there is no time for a teacher to take this method too freely, as his labour is not acknowledged; for a Welsh teacher would not willingly pass over false orthography in Welsh. But apart from benefiting the children in Welsh, I am of opinion I could teach them English more *thoroughly* by such a method.

Would be welcomed by many teachers as a boon, both to themselves and the scholars, as the teaching of Welsh would be less laborious in Welsh schools than other subjects now taught ; and it would thus, to a certain extent, relieve the over-pressure which now exists in Welsh district.

By taking Welsh as a "specific subject," the time (and labour) spent in conveying English instruction through the medium of the vernacular tongue (as is the case in the great majority of Welsh country schools) might be turned into direct *pecuniary advantage.* The *mental training* it would produce would be of considerable *"educational"* advantage.

It would be a *moral* advantage. By the omission of the teaching of it in school some children are led to regard their mother-tongue as being something to be ashamed of, and (Dic-Shon-Dafydd-like) to be forgotten and cast aside as soon as possible.

I beg to state that I heartily approve of some such scheme as your "Honourable Society" has suggested, provided it undergoes some modifications. Text-books should be provided for all the standards—conversational dictionaries, somewhat like the book of the Rev. Kilsby Jones, Llanwrtyd, with enough of work for one year. Unless you limit (a work for each standard, to form a foundation to the next standard), the superstructure will collapse, and Her Majesty's Inspectors will annihilate the "plan" and the teachers. I have adopted that method of teaching English through the medium of the Welsh for about fifteen years. If I had text-

books we could succeed better. We simply use the black-board
for half an hour daily. We take special care with the irregular
verbs, pronouns, moods, and tenses. We make lists also of idiomatic
phrases; those stumbling-blocks are unsurmountable to the Welsh
children but for the above method of elucidating them. I do not
approve of preparing a "specific subject" to be examined in Welsh;
I think there is ample work to learn English in general by some
such means as above. But some method should be adopted too to
measure our extra labour, and to pay for it according to the results.
I do not know in what standard in the "Elementary School" you
intend your Schedule IV., Welsh, to be applied. From my experience
of the labour required, yours is too hard after considering the time
we have at our disposal. There is a vast difference between
translating Welsh to English and English to Welsh. Brilliant
children will not do the former, while they can do the latter with
ease. So I would confine the latter to the 3rd Stage; but with
better advantages, such as home-lesson books, and the subject
becoming honourable, perhaps indeed yours could be adopted.
*   *   The Education Department cannot form an idea of the
WEARY WORK of teaching the children to comprehend the most
commonplace words in a consecutive order. Should this scheme
ever come into a practical form, I would be glad to see in each
series English diphthongs grouped together, according to their
sounds in Welsh. I teach the infants to read English in that way,
using the phonetic system through the medium of Welsh. I need
not explain, you understand the system better than I. I beg to
thank your Honourable Society for labouring on behalf of us teachers
and our beloved language. "*Oes y byd i'r iaith Gymraey.*"*

It would be becoming, and also polite [to the Welsh] to allow
them the use of their much-loved language, and make it a "specific
subject" for schools.

I am afraid that but few men clearly perceive what immense
advantage would accrue from the introduction of the Welsh

---

* This long answer is inserted nearly entire through an error of the
compositor. Having been set up in type I leave it stand.

language into the Code as the *thin end of the wedge.* The subject should have been well discussed in the Welsh newspapers and periodicals before soliciting an expression of "opinion" from all teachers, &c., indiscriminately.

The introduction of the Welsh language, in Welsh-speaking districts, as a *special school subject,* would greatly sharpen the intellects of the children for the reception of moral impressions when in attendance at religious services (inasmuch as the colloquial Welsh in all districts is very imperfect), making them virtuous in life; and certainly accelerate the acquisition of English.

GLAMORGAN.

NEGATIVE.—[Eight replies from districts, considered unsuitable for the experiment.]

No. Generally speaking the answers to this question will, to a very great extent, reflect the ability of the teacher to teach the Welsh language.

No. Neither H.M. Inspector nor parents would approve of it, and it would be of no benefit to the children as a class.

The Welsh children of my district (Waunarlwydd, near Swansea) understand Shakespeare better than they understand Islwyn. The teaching of Welsh, therefore, would require much time. Because the knowledge of Welsh possessed by some children is far more extensive than that possessed by others. Because Welsh people in fairly good circumstances ignore the Welsh language and discourage it in their children; such is the fact.

Children in the Rhondda speak English habitually in the playground; this results from the immigration of English people. *Summary of Objections* (1) Many refining influential *English* teachers incapable of taking up the subject. (2) Many Welshspeaking teachers quite unable to *teach* Welsh. (3) Districts like the Rhondda too mixed; English increasing. (4) To teach it as a "specific" would only add another burden to the already over-taxed powers of the children. (5) Welsh too elaborately inflectional. *Suggestions*—(1) That it be taken up in night schools. (2) That a suitable set of Welsh *readers* for Welsh Sunday schools, with illustrations, be compiled to make the Welsh reading therein interesting and attractive, thus utilizing *Welsh* teaching already in existence with great effect.

No.   Because the Inspectors do not allow children the privilege of answering a question in Welsh at present, although the Code stipulates that such a liberty should be allowed.   The great majority of Inspectors are RANK ENGLISHMEN, whose hobby is to stamp out the Welsh language altogether.   There would be great difficulty in conciliating the parents to such a course.

In this district (the Ystradyfodwg) we have scarcely any mistresses able to teach Welsh: the masters, as a whole, would be able to do so.   *   *   Englishmen, as a rule, do not possess "very strong love" towards anything Welsh, and rather than assist it would prefer crushing it under foot.   As a thorough warm-hearted Celt, I would gladly hail this new attempt at perpetuating the old language, but cannot see any hope.

AFFIRMATIVE—Yes; and not only at elementary schools, but I think that at higher schools and universities it should have a place amongst the other languages taken, and candidates for degrees, &c., should be allowed to take it as an alternative language, just as they now can take French or Latin, Greek, &c.

Yes, to Welsh country schools.   (1) Country teachers have often told me that they have recourse to the Welsh language to make the lessons intelligible: therefore, by its introduction into the Code, they would get some credit and pecuniary benefit for labour which is now often unrecognised and unpaid for.   (2) It would materially aid towards securing Welsh Inspectors for Wales, who can properly sympathise with Welsh-speaking children, and understand the difficulties they have to contend with in grasping the subjects.

Yes.   The children attending my school are not conversant with the language, although their parents are as a rule Welsh.   This seems a pity.   If Welsh were taught as a specific, it would, in my opinion, be an inducement to Welsh parents to bring up their children in the mother-tongue.   Again, it would be the means of aiding those who are already Welsh-spoken to obtain an accurate knowledge of their language. It is to be regretted that but few in comparison can speak and write Welsh properly.

Having been the head master of, probably, the largest schools in the Principality for a period of over forty-one years, and having observed the comparatively little change in the use of the Welsh language among the resident population of this district during that time, I venture to express my decided opinion that "advantage would result" from the introduction of Welsh as an optional "specific subject."

Yes. I believe it could be taught with great advantage. I find it easier to teach French to a child who knows Welsh. The meanings and allusions in the reading lessons are better understood in many cases where the explanation is given in Welsh. English boys and girls strive to learn it if they hear the teacher explain the reading matter thus, and the petty jealousy between the races diminishes.

Yes. Welsh children naturally speak English veiled in Welsh idioms. This is a great obstacle in the way of teaching English effectually. The introduction of the study of the Welsh language into our elementary schools would give teachers an opportunity to teach children how to translate properly. As a consequence the children would learn to express themselves in purer English.

I feel certain that much advantage in every way would result therefrom; chiefly, the intelligence of the children would be greatly improved thereby, and school would be more of a pleasure to them. I know that these things would follow from their having done so in my school by my taking my upper standards through a Welsh grammar side by side with an English one, and I have no doubt but that it would be the case to a much greater extent were Welsh taught as thoroughly as it would be, were it a paid subject.

Yes. The knowledge, intelligence, and the thinking powers of the children would be increased immensely; instead of their being as they are at present, learning everything by rote.

I am not a Welshman, but I sincerely appreciate your intention. I have always felt a desire to introduce *Welsh* as a "specific

subject" into my school. My experience as a teacher enables me
to confirm Professor Powell's remark, "that the Welsh language is
a powerful agent of education."   *   *   It is a mistake to think
that our boys and girls will become better Englishmen and English-
women by ignoring what one recently called "our beautiful Welsh."

Although I do not understand Welsh, I am of opinion that a
grammatical knowledge of their own language would be a much
greater advantage to the Welsh working classes than most of the
ordinary specific subjects.

I find it easier to teach French to a child who knows Welsh.

Our pupils speak *fairly good English* but *very bad Welsh.* (My
experience extends as far as West and North Pembrokeshire and the
Glamorgan Valleys.) (1) It would be a good mental discipline.
(2) It would tend to accuracy in expressing ideas. (3) It would
enlarge both vocabularies (English and Welsh). (4) It would give an
excellent opportunity for learning the *idioms* of th English language.
Welsh teachers have quite enough to do in preparing for the
Government examination, and as Welsh counts for nothing at the
certificate examination, it is of course neglected. To remedy this
some good Welshmen should establish classes in connection with
the Welsh colleges, and the Welsh professors should hold periodical
examinations and grant diplomas to those who have attained a
certain standard of excellence. As Welsh *is learnt now it is simply
a hindrance to progress in English,* and consequently in all other
subjects of a common school education. Schedule IV. More
stress should be put on a thorough knowledge of the accidence and
syntax, and also on the idioms in translation.

Advantages: (1) The usual mental discipline in the systematic
learning of any language. (2) The language would in the future
be spoken in a much purer and more correct form than at present.
(3) It would stimulate patriotism, so necessary to the well-being of
the community. (4) The realisation of the "prophetic dreams" of
our old bards. (5) Being placed amongst the specifics there is no
possibility of its interference in the acquisition of English, which
is of such vital importance.

Much is said about "cultivating a taste for reading." I cannot conceive of a better aid. Children in this district read English in the Sunday schools until they are about thirteen or fourteen years of age, then they prefer the Welsh classes. Objections: Masters are not capable of teaching the subject. The Code demands too much already. Many inspectors I am afraid would be unfavourable to it, hence disheartening those who would take it up. There are different opinions with regard to the merit of our literature, but I find that those who read Welsh as well as English (although they are lovers of Milton, Shakespeare, Wordsworth, Tennyson, and Morris) feel they cannot afford to neglect Hiraethog and Islwyn.

NEUTRAL—The English language ought to be taught in Welsh districts (such as Anglesey) the same as any foreign tongue would be taught—viz., by means of the vernacular. I believe that if the children were systematically taught the English language instead of picking up what little they do by accident, that in twenty or thirty years a revolution would have taken place in the mental condition of the people. For this purpose we would have to go in for a *Welsh Code* (optional, as some schools in Anglesey, and most in other parts, such as Glamorganshire, would prefer working under the English Code). * * As a Welshman, I am afraid that such a course would accelerate the death of our dear Welsh language, and gwell fuasai genyf byny na gwrthod allwedd fawr pob gwybodaeth i blant ein gwlad.

MONMOUTHSHIRE.

NEGATIVE—No. I consider that its introduction would result in greater "over-pressure" in schools in Wales. Managers would insist upon its being taken up in all schools to increase the Government grant.

AFFIRMATIVE—Yes, as it would be a great assistance in teaching English to the Welsh children. From my twelve years' experience as teacher in Welsh districts, I have found it necessary to impart my instruction by means of the Welsh language, and I know that the knowledge of the English language, which is gained by the

Welsh as a channel is far more sound and perfect than that which
is acquired by leaving the Welsh entirely out of the course of
instruction. In spite of the prejudice which some of II. M.
Inspectors have against Welsh, I have never failed to give the
children as much instruction as time would allow me in their
mother's language.

Most decidedly. It ought to be an extra subject in every school.

My children, although they were instructed first in English, but
now being able to converse in Welsh, would be benefitted by a
further knowledge of the Welsh language, and to the Welsh it
would be a greater advantage.

The educational advantages would be very great, and surely the
adoption of such teaching would add a delightful work to many a
Welsh teacher and scholar and help to keep "*yr hen iaith*" alive.

To the scholars themselves it would give a sense of reality to
grammar which the subject does not now possess. And by its
giving a power of comparison it would greatly facilitate the
teaching of historical English. The great drawback is the ignorance
of Welshmen of the grammar of their own language. I may state
that the village in which I live has four English places of worship
and six Welsh ditto, the size of the latter being to the former as
two is to one.

Yes. Those of my scholars who read with *true expression* have
a knowledge of the Welsh language. They are certainly ahead of
those possessing no such knowledge.

It is the case in this school, which numbers over 200 children,
all Welsh except eight. I frequently use Welsh to explain difficult
terms, and the last school report contains this remark: "The very
intelligent work of the three highest standards is deserving of
special mention.   *   Many look at it now with contempt and
as a thing to be forgotten; if introduced into school it would be
looked at in quite a different light.

It *does* seem very unscientific to attempt (more correctly to
continue) to make Welsh children learn English by literally
gulling them with it. We hear much of "bi-lingual difficulty."

This I don't admit; the "difficulty" is altogether in the *means used* to teach English.

I heard the advocates of an alteration in the present system of Welsh education spoken of lately by a person who had been a Carmarthenshire teacher, as a "few agitators.' The answers that are given above will sufficiently disprove such a crude assertion, at least for the recent date of 1885. Persons who make similar statements, and adopt a hostile attitude, are frequently either Welshmen who have, through an imperfect education, had to suffer disappointment in some way or other, and blame their language instead of the system, or else persons who are really in good degree, ignorant of the language, at least from a literary point of view.

Bearing in mind that we are not dealing with the views of impractical enthusiasts, but with the opinions of practical men, although in fact they had no experience of systematic teaching of the language, except in a few isolated cases, also bearing in mind the magnitude of the changes which might be expected to take place in the event of the bilingual system being universally adopted, I subjoin further summaries of leading points in the answers, which may enable the reader to obtain a still clearer view of the arguments for and against, than would be obtained by a cursory perusal of the foregoing pages.

REASON FOR.	REASONS AGAINST.
Would assist in acquiring English.	Would hinder English conversation.
In Welsh-speaking districts intelligent farmers wish their children to write Welsh letters.	Children would have to unlearn colloquial Welsh.
Parents' desire for children to write Welsh letters.	Parents would object.
English boys try to learn it when teachers explain in Welsh, and race jealousy diminishes.	Would isolate Wales from complete assimilation with England.

REASON FOR.	REASON AGAINST.
Would be a pecuniary, an educational, and a moral advantage.	Want of utility.
Young people *now* unable to compose Welsh letters.	"Sunday" schools and literary meetings provide for it.
Successful teachers use Welsh freely.	Some successful teachers do not understand it.
Would aid in securing inspectors who could properly understand the difficulties of Welsh children.	Inspectors rank Englishmen.*
Children could then be taught to translate properly.	Present Code gives sufficient latitude.
Stimulative to the mind.	Language too inflectional.
English children insist on speaking Welsh every chance they get.	English predominant in certain district.
Means of mental discipline —*systematic* knowledge of great value.	Most teachers ignorant of Welsh, and would require special training.
Should be COMPULSORY ON ALL SCHOOLS.	Because a special Code for Wales is wanted worst.
English taught more thoroughly thus.	
Would require little extra work.	
Children would be greatly delighted.	
Would foster a love of study.	
Open the field for more extensive reading.	
Would induce parents to bring up their children in their mother-tongue.	
Easier to teach French when Welsh is learnt.	
Would enlarge both vocabularies.	
Especially [wanted] where Welsh is likely to be forgotten.	

---

* It would not be fair to speak of the Inspectors of 1891 as *rank Englishmen*. There are now notable exceptions to the old rule, but the Department is not yet sufficiently alive to the advantage of having Welsh-speaking Inspectors and assistants, even in bilingual districts.

RESULT OF PRESENT SYSTEM.	PREDICTED RESULTS OF PROPOSED SYSTEM.
Present mode has lamentably failed except to a few.	Would create a thorough love for higher education and science.
Parrot-like knowledge of English in most elementary schools.	The study of it would give full command of a beautiful and expressive language.
Many "Sunday" school scholars does not distinguish between *i'w* and *yw*.	Would be an introduction to a classical education.
Best teachers groan under drudgery of the Code.*	Would keep alive the Welsh national spirit.
Present methods dreary and unnatural.	Welsh literature would gain immensely.
Welsh as a written language going into disuse.	Would relieve over pressure.
"Present slipshod way of teaching, or rather not teaching English.	Would sharpen the intellects of the children for the reception of moral impressions during preaching.
Children ashamed of their mother-tongue.	[Under a Welsh Code] in twenty or thirty years a revolution
Weary work.	would have taken place in the mental condition of the people.

It will be admitted that if we except, on the negative side, the parents' objections, induced by what Carmarthen (61) styles "a popular delusion," and the much more reasonable fear of overpressure, or inability to keep pace with the then requirements of the Code in other respects, that the affirmatives had an immensely preponderating weight of evidence on their side, tending to strengthen the opinion that there were solid grounds for introducing Welsh, experimentally at least, as a specific subject, and in some places as a class subject. It is to be feared that the Education Department, with their inspectors, have done but little to remove the popular delusion referred to. Yet, one of the primary objects of education is to improve the judgment, weaken superstition, and healthily expand the

---

* This was written under the old Code, but doubtless is still true to a large extent in Wales.

mental powers, in attaining which latter object competent judges allege, as will be seen in this chapter, that the present system of ignoring Welsh is sadly defective.

As a matter of fact, School Boards, composed in many cases of persons of narrow or inferior education, continue, apparently, satisfied with results which, although fairly good in contrast with the rest of the country, are by no means the best attainable under a more intelligent system.

Considerable excuse however, must be made for many of these, because it is not long since, as we have seen, the "Welsh note," was in use in certain schools, so that the meaning of the term *education* in the minds of many teachers, as well as parents, who observe how necessary a knowledge of English is for purposes of material advancement, rather excludes the idea that Welsh may at the same time, if properly handled, be made a powerful instrument of education in the correct sense of the term, conducive to habits of correct speaking and thinking, and supplying, in conjunction with English, a means of mental discipline even to boys in elementary schools, far superior to that evinced by the present "slipshod," hap-hazard, rule of thumb-way, in which there is ground for believing many Welsh children think and speak.

Even in semi-Anglicized districts where the mother-tongue of most of the boys is English, but they are more or less familiar with Welsh, either by hearing it spoken, or by connection with the religious denomination their parents belong to, a course of Welsh can be introduced in the higher standards, without much, if any strain on the teacher, as has been practically proved where the experiment has been tried. Any other bilinguistic training involves far too large an expenditure of time and talent to be at all practicable in elementary schools. The attempt would, intellectually speaking, be expensive. It is held that a bilingual method as advocated here would, in the same sense, be remarkably cheap.

It should be borne in mind, too, that the objectors were speaking for the most part of what they had not tested by actual experience, and very few of them have done so, even up to the present time. This is true of the affirmative, but the onus of proof, to shew that such a proposition should not be tentatively adopted, lay with the negatives, which proof they failed, on the whole, to establish.

Although I am somewhat anticipating my subject, I may mention the singular fact that while theoretically the most thoroughly Welsh schools in Wales would seem the most to need instruction in the language, in the practical working out of the idea, it is in bilingual districts where English prevails more or less largely, that the teachers or school Boards have shewn most willingness to make the necessary changes, for instance, Ruabon in North Wales; Merthyr, Gelligaer, Mynydd-islwyn, in South Wales; while the teachers in the country around Merthyr, which is more Welsh than the town, have opposed the scheme. There are, however, one or two exceptions such as Llanarth, in Cardiganshire, but this was previously an exceptionally well taught school, and though in a thoroughly Welsh district, is ahead of most in Wales or England. Probably this peculiarity is due to the fact that hitherto we are only dealing with Welsh as a specific language taught to the higher standards only, and it corresponds to the idea of one teacher—"especially where Welsh is likely to be forgotten."

To resume now the thread of our history, very soon after the Cymmrodorion Society had drawn up their reply, giving teachers' replies in *extenso*, the National Eisteddfod in Aberdare, of 1885, was held, and presided over by Dr. Isambard Owen: it was decided to form a Society for promoting the utilization

of the Welsh language in education, and agreed to leave the
organization to Dan Isaac Davies. D. I. Davies, B.Sc., was
a Sub-Inspector of Elementary Schools, who had served the
Education Department some years in England, and then
returned to Wales under the impression, as he expressed it,
in 1887, that he should find the Welsh language fast receding,
almost disappearing, but "at every step since my return on
the 1st October, 1882, rather more than four years ago,
I have found the Welsh language has turned the corner, and
it has passed out of the time of, we may say an English
teaching reaction, I am glad to say not into a time of
Welsh teaching reaction, but into a time of bilingual teaching
reaction."

In his earlier life it appears that D. I. Davies was inclined
to depreciate Welsh. He called himself an "Anglophile," but
now at once threw himself heartily into this movement so contrary to what had been for years, the general current of
education feeling in Wales, and so contrary to the traditional
policy of the Department in London.

As an illustration of the character of the opposition that
was evoked, I will quote the *Western Mail*, 8mo " Aug." 28th,
1885, which, in the course of a long leader, remarking on the
increased facility which it was said systematic instruction in
Welsh in day schools would give to the children in understanding
sermons etc., said—

We were rather surprised to find in a report drawn up in the
interest of a people so determinedly opposed as the Welsh have
been represented to be, to all religious instruction in their
day schools the statement that, "by accustoming the children
to correct Welsh, it would greatly improve their understanding
of the religious instruction given in that language." This, if
it mean anything, means that an adoption of the Committee's
recommendation, that Welsh be taken as a specific subject in the

day schools, must eventuate in a tremendous accession of strength
to the Sunday schools.

Think of that, you Nonconformists. Here is a champion
of the Established Church fearing that if systematic instruction is given in your language, a "tremendous accession of
strength" will accrue to your schools.

At the meeting in Aberdare above mentioned, a somewhat
singular scene took place; D. I. Davies said that Tudor Evans
(a Cardiff architect)—

Had impugned the action of the Committee of the Cymmrodorion
Society in appealing for information to the teachers of Wales, and
had said that other persons ought to have their say. There was a
strong feeling that he, as one of those other persons, should come
forward, and have his say now.

Mr. Evans, who occupied a front seat in the body of the hall,
and who resolutely declined to comply with repeated appeals made
that he should ascend the platform, said he was not prepared
that morning to be immolated on the altar of bigotry (Cries of
"Shame") !

D. I. Davies did not remain satisfied with the initial steps
to organize this Society, he wrote a series of six letters to the
Western Mail on the "Utilization of the home language in
Wales," in the last of which he said—

We owe an apology and an explanation to our readers. We
have seldom written to the Press, and lay no claim to literary ability
and yet we have ventured to take up their time. Our life has been
devoted to the spread of English in Wales, and yet we have felt
compelled to say a word for Welsh in the interests of our people.
Our University degree proves that our own tastes flow in the
direction of exact mathematics and science and not towards literature and languages, and yet conviction urges us to plead, however
imperfectly, for a side of education which better qualified men
should have placed in its true light. We are personally disposed to

think that Welsh should be used as a frequent means of illustration
in teaching the infant classes and lower standards, and taught as a
specific subject in the upper standards, the secondary schools, the
Colleges, and the University, and not as a means of teaching English,
and yet see that we ought to give a patient hearing to those
teachers who claim that English can only be taught effectively in
Welsh-Wales through the medium of Welsh. We feel that we
must rest our case on purely practical educational arguments, and
fear not the result of any fair experimental trial of the plan we
recommend, yet our Cymric heart cannot help glowing at the
thought that the fair trial asked for will show that the practical
utility of to-day and the ancient glory of our race or nation
(whichever "Gwyliedydd" may prefer) will be found to be
inseparably bound up together. Some of our poetical countrymen
are fond of making touching references to the death of the Welsh
language. *   *   * Infinitely to be preferred to the sentimental, cruel tenderness of those who love to contemplate the
agonies of what they think to be an expiring language is the
healthy, inspiriting advice of Dean Vaughan, which we take from
the valuable volume referred to in Letter III.:—

'I take things as I find them, and I presume to say that the one
hope for Wales of to-day, her one hope of learning, or of influence,
or of usefulness, is that at least she be bilingual. No nation ought
to part willingly with her distinctive speech. She ought to cling to
it with all fondness. The only limit to this tenacity should be
that which common sense and self-interest conspire to impose upon
it. If the language isolates her from all nations, if it risks her
cosmopolitan character, as the disciple of the wise and the instruc-
tress of the ignorant, then, and then only, should she accept the
omen, and make the very best of the inevitable. But what then?
Is she to fling away the speech which was her *differentia* among
the nations? Only treachery and cowardice would counsel it. She
has a patriotic and a religious duty still towards the tongue in
which she was born. She has, first, to see that it be articulately
and grammatically formed and shaped in all its particulars, so that

it shall be no *patois* of chance and trick, but a language worthy of the respect of other languages, worthy to become the study of the learned and the training speech of the young. Next. that it shall have a literature all its own, a literature without a knowledge of which the education of a scholar shall be confessedly incomplete— a literature unapproachable save through its language, and, therefore, securing to that language the undying interest and unstinting effort of all who would think or know.'

Bear in mind, readers, that a literature is "unapproachable save through its language." You ask for translations of Welsh literary efforts. Learn the language and translate them yourselves—that is in effect, the advice of a leading representative of the Established Church, not a representative of what has been till lately its leading policy, but a representative of the views of a minority represented, we may suppose, by such names as Gwallter Mechain and Silvan Evans.

D. I. D., himself formerly a teacher, makes an eloquent appeal to those with that calling and responsibilities—

Day school teachers of Wales! Your opportunity has arrived. You complain from time to time that you work hard for the nation, where no one sees your self-denying exertions which, it seems to you, are in danger of being too little appreciated. How has the Cymmrodorion Society treated you during the last year? Has it not supplied you all with a report of its preliminary inquiry? Has it not asked you, one by one, what you thought of their suggestions? Has it not printed a thousand copies of your replies and placed them in the hands of every Cymmrodor? Does it not suggest the formation of a society, with headquarters in the Principality, of which every one of you may become a member, and the action of which you will be able to guide and largely control by your superior knowledge of the practical bearings of the question it is to deal with? Will you hesitate to join in a national movement which, whatever may be its ultimate outcome, must elevate the position of the educators of Wales? Will you allow others to

take the place marked out for you? Will you follow when you
might lead; and blindly obey when you might help to frame the
word of command? I believe better things of you. You will
prove you are the hope of Young Wales, that longs to elevate
Welshmen by means of a thoroughly effective, because truly
national, system of education, and will not flinch from patriotic
work because it is going to give you some trouble at first. A nation
that now possesses for the first time the political power to obtain
an alternative Code for Welsh districts will not forget you, nor fail
to lessen your burden, if you will only with patient clearness show
it, why some of the present educational arrangements are too
hard to be borne. We appeal with equal confidence to non-Welsh-
speaking teachers as we do to the Welsh-speaking teachers. They
know well the aspiration of Young Wales is not for "Wales for the
Welsh." The policy of the rising Welsh party is not to ask
candidates for any office—Parliamentary or local—"Do you speak
Welsh?" but, "will you support a school system that will give
your children, grandchildren, and great-grandchildren opportunities for learning Welsh!" We do not wish to exclude Englishmen, Scotchmen, and Irishmen from Wales, but, when they are
settled in our midst, to include them and their good qualities in our
own national life.

How many teachers of Wales have read and considered
these words, "Will you follow when you might lead, and
blindly obey when you might help to form the word of command." Did not this man know what he was writing about?
Was he not perfectly well aware of much that constitutes the
life and work of a teacher in Wales? A large number of you
have confessed the need of an alteration, but how much have
you done "towards obtaining *a thoroughly effective, because
truly national, system of Education?*" Make that your watch-
word at all your district Association meetings for the next five
years. Don't quietly say, "Yes, very good, very good," fold your
hands complacently, and then discuss superannuation questions,

or anything but "patriotic work, because it is going to give you some trouble first."

If there are a few renegades or Saxons in your midst, who either will not or cannot understand that sense and reason demand a new and "thoroughly effective" system which gives proper consideration both to the existence of Welsh and to its educational value in elementary education, be satisfied that the time will come, if you persevere, when you will be able to demonstrate to them that their mountains are molehills, and that an enlightened public opinion supports you, and that practical results have amply justified your pains.

In addition to this series of letters there appeared another (consisting of eight in all) in the "*Baner ac Amserau Cymru,*" by the same author, which was reprinted in pamphlet form, under the title of "*Tair Miliwn o Gymry Dwyieithog yn* 1985." These letters have never appeared before the public in an English dress, and some of my readers may be interested with a summary of the leading points in each of them.

In Letter I., he apologizes for appearing before the Welsh public inasmuch as he could not recollect ever having written a Welsh article before, except one which he had just written for "*Y Geninen,*" and he had written but little for the English Press, his bent of mind having been principally towards mathematics and science.

The reader will, I hope, excuse me in endeavouring to offer translation of D.I.D.'s own words. To some, this and much that follows in the chapter may be uninteresting, I scarcely think, however, that it will be so to many who are engaged in Welsh Education and understand the important bearing of the subject. He says—

It is not a bard or a *littérateur* or an *eisteddfodwr* of the old school who addresses thee, but one who is quite content (*wrth fodd ei galon.*) when seeking to impress on the minds of Welsh children and the friends of education in our country the need of teaching English, science and art. My life has been devoted to the spread of these indispensable acquirements. This year I have turned out of my usual path on account of a strong conviction of the importance of this period, in our history as a nation, to speak a word as an educationalist, because no one who has enjoyed the same opportunities (of observation) is ready to address the Welsh on the subject which incites me to this employment, viz.: Would not the knowledge of two languages—English and Welsh—be very advantageous to the Welshman. I had better confess the following facts before going a step further :—

I. Though I have not been in any sense one of the family of "*Dic Sion Dafydd*" I formerly shared for a long time the feeling which is to be found commonly diffused that the extinction of the Welsh language would be, on the whole an advantage to the Welshman.

II. I do not believe very strongly in "*Oes y byd i'r iaith Gymraeg*," because as I shall try to shew further on, the attitude of many Welsh people to it, shews that they are entirely indifferent, if not antagonistic to its preservation.

III. Notwithstanding, I have not entirely lost hope, since Welsh appears to be increasing in strength and influence in these days, in spite of the neglect and opposition of those who ought to defend and uphold it. There is a need to spread information about the blessings which have come to us as a people through the old language, and about the possibility of receiving many other good things through its medium in the future.

He next notices the action of the Cymmrodorion Society, and gives an extract from the *Gaelic Journal*, published in Dublin, which says in reference to the almost national system of teaching children to read Welsh in those called Sunday schools.

Had the system of teaching Welsh children through the medium of English been persevered in during the last 150 years, as in the

100 years preceding the time of Griffith Jones of Llanddowror, the people of the Principality would now have been as low at least in respect of education as the people of Donegal and Connemara."

LETTER II. refers at large to the testimony of the eminent Charles o'r Bala, written perhaps about 1811, and from which I extract the following:—

More than 150 years ago, in Wales, the whole country was in a most deplorable state with regard to the acquisition of religious knowledge. For a long time previous, fashionable people had been trying to stamp out the language of the country, and to have the children taught altogether in English. Against these people, and against this state of universal ignorance, the Rev. Griffith Jones, of Llanddowror, was raised up. He asked:—"Should all our Welsh books, and our excellent version of the Bible, our Welsh preaching, and the stated worship of God in our language, be taken away, to bring us to a disuse of our tongue?" *So they are* in a manner in some places—the more our misery; and yet the people are not better scholars, any more than they are better Christians for it. Welsh is still the vulgar tongue—and not English. * * Sure I am, the Welsh charity schools do no way hinder to learn English, but do very much contribute towards it; and perhaps you will allow, Sir, that learning our language first is the most expeditious way to come to the knowledge of another; else why are not your youths in England, designed for scholars, set to Latin and Greek before they are taught English? . . . . Experience now proves beyond dispute, that if it ever be attempted to bring all the Welsh people to understand English, we cannot better pave the way for it than by teaching them to read their own language first. This method will conduce, more than any other I can think of, to assist whatever attempts may be made to spread the general knowledge of the English tongue in this country.

This is a contribution so the history of the status of Welsh in the seventeenth and eighteenth centuries, which brings us

T

face to face with an attempt to "stamp out the language," that
is still bearing fruit to-day.

In the early days of the Society of Friends in Wales many
of them were Merionethshire and Montgomeryshire people,
who emigrated to America from 1680 to 1700, and who have
left various letters and records behind them which are mostly
in English, even when written before their departure, though
in their new home the ministry at public worship was for some
time generally Welsh.

I have by me some early minute books of Monmouthshire
Friends beginning 1703, which are wholly English, except a
kind of introduction or compendium of rules placed at the
beginning in Welsh; but Thomas Story, when he visited Pontypool Friends, about 1717, mentions hearing ministry in Welsh
from a friend of that town. What I have seen of Merioneth and
Montgomery minute books *circ.* 1730 is of a similar character.

I think that we must place these cases parallel with that of
a Carnarvonshire or Cardiganshire youth, who writes home to
his parents in English, because the familiarity he has acquired
at school in writing that language seems to make it the easiest
thing to do, but *thinks* and *speaks* almost entirely in Welsh.

The conclusion then we arrive at is, that as early as the
seventeenth century English was the dominant language of
written communications even in Merionethshire, perhaps more
so than now, though far less universally understood.

The following appears to be an extract from an Irish writer:—

The parents in Wales were as much opposed to the teaching of
the Welsh language as the Irish parents have been to the teaching
of Irish; but they gave up the conceit at the persuasion of the
Rev. Thomas Charles, as he himself tells us in continuation:—

At first the strong prejudice, which universally prevailed against
teaching them to read Welsh first, and the idea assumed that they
could not learn English so well if previously instructed in the

language, proved a great stumbling-block in the way of parents to send their children to the Welsh schools; together with another conceit they had, that, if they could read English, they would soon learn of themselves to read Welsh. But now, these idle and groundless conceits are universally scouted. This change has been produced, not so much by disputing, as by the evident salutary effects of the schools, the great delight with which children attend them, and the great progress they make in acquisition of knowledge.

I take the liberty to republish these extracts, because it is rather comforting to a Welsh education reformer, to find that Thomas Charles had exactly the same difficulty to contend with in his day, as we have in our days, from the prejudices of ignorant parents, though the system he espoused was one which contributed greatly to the material advancement of Wales, and has lived through all opposition to become as before hinted to a large extent a national one. And though we still have the aforesaid prejudice to contend with, both from parents and from some who ought to know better, it is believed the time is at hand to EXTEND and PERFECT such a national, we might almost say utilitarian system, and relieve schools that are professedly devoted to religious purposes from the work that ought more properly to be performed in elementary day schools, viz., teaching boys and girls to read their mother-tongue, as well as write it, and that in a more thorough and efficient way than can be attained by comparatively untrained, amateur teachers.

LETTER III. alludes to a recent speech of A. J. Mundella's, at Sheffield, in which he said, after alluding to a conversation he (A.J.D.) had in Switzerland with a young shop-woman who spoke idiomatic English—

The story I was going to tell you was this:—I was in Switzerland, in the Engadine. At the door of the hotel was a shop, where all

kinds of *souvenirs*, for people to carry away with them, were sold—
whether they were Swiss carving, or some French, German, or
English articles. There was a bright clever young woman selling
all kinds of *souvenirs* for people to carry away with them when
they went home. A gentleman, very well known to English
people, was staying at the same hotel with me, and he said:—
"That's a very bright girl that keeps that shop. I recommend you
to go and buy something." So I made a pretext to buy some trifle,
and she addressed me in perfect idiomatic English. I asked her
where she learned English; and she replied, "At Lucerne." "You
speak excellently," I said, "and of course you speak French and
German, for they are your native languages?" "Of course I do,"
she answered. "Anything else?" I asked. "Oh, yes: Italian and
Dutch:" and she afterwards confessed she also knew a little
Spanish, and was studying it. I found, on making further enquiry,
that the girl was taught at Lucerne, and that it cost a franc a year—
that is, only tenpence—which was spent on paper and pencils.
. . . . The Director of Schools in that canton told me—"All
our schools are free—all our children attend school—every child,
however poor, masters two languages, French and German; and
those who go to the Secondary School must learn at least one
other.' I said, "Who pays for these things?" "The commune
city." "But don't they grumble?" "No: they know it is the
safety of the rich, and the best inheritance of the poor."

Ah! say some of my readers, there is more sense and reason
in teaching children for a second language—one spoken by
some great nation, such as the French or the German, which
may some day come in useful in the counting house, rather
than Welsh, which is nowhere so far as business is concerned.

In reply to such an objection, which is not unfrequently
heard, I would say that the possibility of effectively teaching
such a foreign language in elementary schools, either in Wales
or England, is a mere figment of the imagination which has
been "weighed in the balance and found wanting," with very

slight exceptions. I speak of the nineteenth century: what may be possible in the latter half of the twentieth, I do not venture to assert.

The advantages of some education in a second language, where it can be arranged, are frequently considerable. In England there is however no opportunity for introducing one. In the largest portion of Wales there is such an opening, even in districts partly Anglicized, where the children speak English among themselves, because they are so frequently brought in contact with this second language in one shape or another, that it is not a wholly foreign one to them, and the results of experiments appear to shew that it can be effectively and profitably introduced.

In the beginning of LETTER IV., D. I. D. remarked that when the history of Wales should be written with the necessary exactitude, he believed it would be shewn that English had sometimes lost ground after gaining it, and that Welsh had gained ground after losing it; instancing the testimony of William Rees (*Gwilym Hiraethog*), that Welsh had recovered part of Flint; he refers to his article (*"Cymru Ddwyieithog"*) in the *Geninen*, saying, that it would there appear that the English, Irish, and Scotch were learning Welsh by thousands. The article itself is of an interesting character, and I will endeavour to summarize some of the facts it contains.

As an Inspector of Schools, he says, he was daily surprised to find Welsh [speaking] children bearing English or Scotch names. He gives a list of 100 such names, as Grant, Whittaker, MacDonald, Puleston, Hamer, Frazer, Donovan, Randell, Frost, Dyke, etc. D. Roberts, of Wrexham, tells him that Scotchmen in that Anglicized town are to be heard teaching the children of Welsh parents on the first day ("Sunday") to pronounce the old language properly. "The superficial spread of English gives an English face to the

country to the face of an Englishman, and the travellers who
quickly travel through it. But the centre and heart of the
land is Welsh." The following statistics are worthy of being
preserved for their historical import, even if they are considered of no immediate interest.

Statistics of coal mine in Cwmsaerbren Farm, Treherbert, Glamorganshire: —

Number in the Pit	500
Welsh Workmen	353
Of other nations	147
Of the 147 able to speak Welsh well	80
Do. moderately well	40
Able to understand it when spoken by others	20
Unable to understand or speak Welsh	7

In Abermorlais School, Merthyr Tydfil, out of 510 children
in the Second Standard and above, the statistics were as under: —

Of the 510 able to speak Welsh	215
Understanding it but not speaking it	96
Unable to understand or speak, although of Welsh parents	100
English Children	99

I might extract more, but the following must suffice:—

If my words could reach the ears of the indifferent Welsh
people of Glamorganshire towns, I would say to them—one thing
is clear, the children of the West and North, the sons of Cardigan
and Merioneth are going to take appointments in your county
from your children on account of your neglecting Welsh.

Since those words were penned Merthyr has taken some
steps in the direction of reversing the old barbaric policy, and
as time goes on will be called on to take further ones.

To return to LETTER IV.,—he expressed his great surprise
at finding the daughter of a country squire near Cheltenham
able to speak Welsh, learning which had been a self-imposed

task, he adds—"Is there not here an example worthy to be followed by the great men of Wales. Why is their influence so small in comparison with what it might be?"

One reason of that is their neglect to the language of the people. As an illustration of the class of men alluded to by D. I. Davies, we will take the Lord Penrhyn, who died a few years ago, and who regretted on his death bed he had not been master of the language, so as to communicate more fully with those around him. But what has his successor in the title profited by such an experience?

Not one whit, so far as can be seen. He is now just as far from knowing Welsh, or intending to know it, defended and backed up in his cogitations and purposes by an immense pile of £ s. d., drawn from the bowels of the earth by the labours of Welsh quarrymen, than whom he would not easily find in England, a more intelligent or intellectual body of men in a similar condition in life.

D. I. D. goes on to say—

No system of education for Wales will be complete, if it does not give opportunities to learn it, to the children of those who have neglected Welsh.

In this way again it is possible to reunite our upper classes *(penaethiaid)* to the people of the country, and prevent the middle classes of the population from losing their influence on the mass which is one of the great dangers of democratic days.

Bear this in mind, you members of School Boards, teachers, sub-inspectors; these are the words of a practical Government Educationalist, they are the words, moreover, of a man about whom, after his lamented death, the Chief Inspector of Schools in Wales remarked in his 1889 report to the Imperial Government:—

I think it only right to say that by the death of Mr. Davies the Department has lost an able, a zealous, and a valuable officer, and his native country an enlightened educationalist, who strongly felt the loss arising from not utilising, to a far greater extent than has been done, the home language of Welsh-speaking children in cultivating their intelligence and in teaching them English in the elementary schools.

Note. He did not merely recommend utilizing the home language of Welsh-speaking children, but also the actual *teaching* of it afresh to those whose parents had neglected it, or neglected them.

In the same letter he proposes the insertion of six questions relative to language in the Census of 1891.

Judging by the way in which an actual attempt to take an account of language was carried out in that census by the officials, it is perhaps best that D. I. D.'s more minute proposals were let alone.

LETTER V. gives an anecdote told the author by Andrew Doyle, who for many years was an Inspector of Workhouses, and had in North Wales became acquainted with a German, a tutor in a private family. One day he started on a journey into a mountain parish, accompanied by his German friend, but found to his dismay that no one in the room where he conducted his business understood English, hence he was fain to send for an interpreter, when the young German offered himself for that office, and fulfilled its duties satisfactorily.

Coming in the course of a journey to Builth, a town almost, if not entirely Anglicised, D. I. D. quotes the almost astounding testimony of the manager of the National Provincial Bank there, viz., that there were 1,500 customers of the Bank who had rather do their business in Welsh than English.

In LETTER VI. we again find incidents of his journeyings, and consequent reflections. Carmarthenshire is now his central point, and he instances the testimony of Shadrach Pryce, M.A.,

Inspector of Schools,* that the knowledge of Welsh is not decreasing in that county—travels with the wife of a Welsh coal trimmer, who has learnt French, and relates the vicissitudes of the language in semi-Anglicised districts as follows:—

Ask the children of Gwent and Morganwg† in Standard V., what language they can speak best—Welsh or English. The answer you may expect is—English. They have been so accustomed to it in the day schools for years, that both children and teachers think Welsh is dead; but let two years go by, you meet with those boys again when they are fifteen. Ask them "what language do you like the best now?" "Welsh" is the answer. When they are eighteen other reasons may incline them to English; but when they are thirty, and settled in the world, they are members of Welsh causes. etc. Sometimes their inclination is Welsh sometimes English! In the long run the man will generally to be Welsh. How is it often now in Wales? Here are 300 people together, and none except 10, 20, or 50 of them, according to the nature of the meeting or the linguistic condition of the neighbourhood are ignorant of the Welsh:—The 290 must give way to the ten, and the business go forward in English. "Should not the ten learn Welsh for shame?" You say, is it not a serious consideration to think how many persons fall down on a footstool to the small minority?

It is very serious, if you choose to look at it from that comic standpoint. But the seriousness changes into disgust when we consider how much weakness to the nation is in this cringing spirit that rejoices in educational arrangements which do not give fair opportunities to the ten, and their children, to learn Welsh, so that there may be a way open to make use of one of the two languages, according to the taste of the teacher, without there being any cause to fear that any would misunderstand the addresses.

* The usual abbreviation H.M.I. is not used in this book, as it involves acquiescence in the term *His or Her Majesty*, applied to a frail, mortal creature.

† Monmouthshire and Glamorganshire—this paragraph would not be applicable to a large extent to Monmouthshire.

L

*   but let a position be given to the old language in the
day and evening schools, there it will be out of the quarrels of
political or religious parties. If it (the language) sets its feet
down there, it will remain in the Sabbath schools, as well as increase
in influence, there will be fewer English classes to be seen in Welsh
schools, and more Welsh classes in English schools.   In a bilingual
country that is how things ought to be.

Once more the lesson he would teach is, let English-speaking
children in Wales have opportunities to learn Welsh—such
a course is more than is generally supposed, *possible, practicable, profitable.*

LETTER VII. alludes to the fact that some Welsh people
speak at times as though giving up Welsh would be equivalent
to giving up poverty, and as though adopting English in its
place would be the same thing as entering into the possession
of fullness and plenty.   *   *   "Thousands are to be found
in Wales in these days who have gained nothing in either sense,
either temporally, morally, or spiritually, by changing Welsh
for English."

Turning to the East End of London, he mentions the Jews'
Free Schools, for over 3,200 children, in Spitalfields, where the
working hours are those of the School Board, except that
they work from nine to one, instead of nine to twelve, in order
to find time for an additional subject, namely—Hebrew.
Ninety percent. of the children are foreigners, but the 7th
Standard children are exactly thirteen times more numerous
in proportion, than those of the general schools in the
country.

This appears to be an exception to the rule that it is visionary
to attempt generally to teach a second language in English
schools; I account for this in two ways—

First, by heredity.

Secondly, by constant contact with the second language in the synagogue and at school.

In semi-Anglicized Wales, both the principles of heredity and "constant contact" come into play, but cannot of course be applied generally to the study of French and German in England.

The following incident is worthy of note:—

I have heard of an Englishman, an extensive landowner, going to a Welshman, who is known to his nation in every corner of the world, and who stands high in the estimation of every patriotic Welshman, and addressing him in the following manner, only the conversation was in English [D. I. D.'s version is, of course, in Welsh]:—"I should be very glad to be able to speak Welsh as well as you can: if you will give me instruction in your language I will pay you five hundred pounds when I can speak Welsh as well as you." "I cannot," was the reply, "other engagements *(goruchwyl-ion)* take up all my time, and they would take up more if I were master of it." "I am very sorry for that," said the other, "my parents (he spoke with a regretful feeling) made a great mistake in my early education. They paid hundreds, if not thousands of pounds to finish me in the Greek and Latin languages, which I have never had occasion to use, but they entirely neglected the language of the people, among whom they knew I should have to spend my lifetime." * * The Welshman who refused the £500 is my authority for this anecdote.

I am glad to be able to add that his friend, who is of English lineage, but with Welsh sympathies, can speak our old language fairly well to-day notwithstanding the mistake made by his parents in his early education.

In reading the foregoing narrative, we cannot help remembering the father, not of an Englishman, but of a Welshman, mentioned elsewhere in this book, who so neglected his education that his son, it is believed, even at the present day is unable to read the Welsh books or manuscripts which pass through his hands in the transactions of a well known publishing business, with an extensive sphere of operations in Wales, although it is probable that it was thought he received an "advanced education" before entering the family concern.*

D. I. D., after alluding to the desire to learn Welsh, which is common among English people in Wales, queries whether the present parents of Wales will learn a lesson from their mistakes? He quotes A. J. Mundella, M.P., as to the importance of learning languages, and the dislike of English boys and girls to speak a different one, alluding to Glamorgan as a favourable field for bringing up children as bilinguists.

LETTER VIII. alludes to the fact little recognized by the public, that everything taught in Elementary Schools is at the choice of the local managers, and is not compulsory, except reading, writing, arithmetic, spelling, and sewing. From this he draws the lesson, on the one hand, that it is not possible to introduce Welsh into a district against its will, and on the other hand, that though Erse and Gaelic are paid for in Ireland and Scotland, not a brass penny is paid for Welsh in Wales. This was in 1885.

He asks why Welsh papers should not be set at pupil teachers' examinations for Queen's scholarships?—Should there not soon be a change in that direction?—It would be easier to some Welsh youths and girls, who gain certificates after successful service as assistants to obtain an efficient education in Welsh than in Latin, French, or German.

"Do you want to teach Welsh in the English parts of Wales," says one of the doubting brethren? Since you pointed at our English Wales, we will try to show that a certain amount of Welsh could easily be taught there to the advantage of every one without distinction.

---

* "The ignorance of the ——— is a source of loss to themselves, and the nation." Extract from a letter from a well-known Welshman to the author received since the paragraph was written.

Queries why the Board Schools should read the English
Bible instead of the Welsh. There is no (legal) necessity for
this. He says it is the choice of the Board School itself to
give an ineffectual education in English to the children, instead
of giving an effectual religious education in Welsh. Alludes
to the desirability of Welsh Railway Companies having
bilingual officials, etc.

LETTER IX. "If the proposed scheme is accepted at Aberdare, it will take *years* in point of time, and a multitude of
opportunities to study the details of the changes which we
wish to see. The judgment of one man is not important in a
matter of this kind, but we must arrange to have what the
doctors of our country call a Collective Investigation Committee. The first place in the investigation belongs to Welsh
schoolmasters of every description, if they are patriotic enough
to take the trouble to explain the matter to the nation. We
firmly believe that they are lovers of their country and their
language, and that they will not allow others to stir themselves
in this matter without their cordial co-operation."

"On the other hand, since the reins *(awenau)* of authority in
country governing bodies have fallen at last into the hands of
Welshmen themselves, in the greater part of the thirteen
counties, which make up the Welsh [educational] division,
we believe they will not allow the school teachers of Wales
to suffer much longer from the heavy disadvantages of the
Educational Code, prepared by Englishmen for England, and
which is not on that account suitable in every respect for the
Welsh of Wales."   *   *

"The first hint of the importance of forming a National
Society to carry forward the movement, came from one of the
Cardigan J.P.'s, Mr. Henry T. Evans, of Neuadd Llanarth,
who wrote at once after the appearance of the abstract of my
paper in the *South Wales Daily News*, to thank me for what I

had done, and to say that the time for making a movement of the kind was at hand."

The above three paragraphs are translations or condensations of the original. Note the farsightedness of the man—years required to study details of changes—the necessity for the expression of judgment by a great many persons.

It is hoped that the present volume will in some degree supply the deficiency of the "Collective Investigation Committee," by presenting, after the lapse of a few years, evidence from various sources that has accumulated in the meantime.

D. I. D. also thanks his fellow workers under the Education Department, viz., W. Edwards, M.A., John Rees, and Gomer Jones, B.A., for the assistance they had rendered him. He quotes the words of the Marquis of Bute, "For a man to speak Welsh and willingly not to be able to read and write it is to confess himself a boor;" and goes on to say that on reading the above apothegm he felt as if a fire had fallen on his skin, and that he was aware that hundreds of thousands were speaking Welsh without ever trying to write it. On thinking of the matter, he says, he clearly saw that the fault lay with our system of education, and not with individuals in many instances, mentioning one of the most enterprising and successful Welshmen in the South Wales coal field, with whom he had recently conversed, who, with his wife and some of his children could speak Welsh, but never trusted "himself to write it for fear of making mistakes, but how easy it would be to remove this difficulty out of the way."

Very shortly after LETTER IX., which was the last of the series, had been written, a paragraph appeared in the *Globe*, of 8th mo., 1885, commenting on a speech made by the Lord Aberdare, in which he said that he felt sure that although undoubtedly English was making progress, Welsh was advancing, and that there were more people speaking Welsh than at any previous period.

Lord Aberdare. who ought to know, believes that there are now more Welsh-speaking people in Wales than there have ever been before. If he is right, as in all probability he is, it is mere affectation on the part of the Saxon to turn the Welshman's attachment to his ancient language into ridicule. It is far easier to make fun of Taffy's love for what ignorant people imagine to be consonants, than it is to seriously find fault with any man's preference for the tongue to which he has been born and nurtured. Of course, the practical importance of the matter lies in its connection with education; and Lord Aberdare struck an exceedingly suggestive point in pronouncing that a thorough and grammatical instruction in Welsh is better than the loose education that most of us have received in English. *English has this fatal defect, from an educational point of view—that it is a congeries of vague idioms and superfine distinctions, while a Celtic language can be learned with almost as good a mental result as Greek or Latin.* Moreover, a bilingual person, as a genuine Welshman is bound to be, has a distinct intellectual advantage at starting, over one who is nursed into the belief that there is only one language in the world, and that all other modes of speech are foreign jargons. Then, to the advantage of Welsh over Erse or Gaelic, it has a real and living literature—and a literary language is hard to kill. *We consider that it is not a mere matter of sentiment that Welshmen should be ambitious of learning English without prejudice to Welsh—indeed, to be disloyal to one's mother tongue is well-nigh equivalent to be false to one's father-land.* The narrower the spirit, the more intense; and we cannot afford in these days to lose much more of that local enthusiasm in which vapid cosmopolitanism find its best and most natural corrective."

How extremely hard it is to dislodge from the minds of Englishmen (this writer in the *Globe* was an exception), and I am sure it is from the minds of a large number of influential persons in

Wales, the idea that the bilingual education movement is a
sentimental one.   They see Welsh sentiment on the right hand
and on the left in *Eisteddfod* speeches, and the like, and they
imagine that bilingualism is propped up, or intended to be, on
the same foundation.   It would be quite idle to deny that
sentiment affects the matter, but if we eliminate its influence
entirely, and decide on what course to pursue from a solid, cold
matter of fact basis, I am justified in saying that right thinking
people will severely criticize and repudiate traditions of three
centuries of Welsh education, that they will not in a milk and
water way simply confine themselves to utilizing Welsh in
learning English, but that they will not be ashamed to make
provision for positively teaching it within safe limits, which
may be later indicated, to future artizans, labourers, domestic
servants, and tradespeople.

Vapid Cosmopolitanism expresses a state of mind to be met
with at Cardiff, Swansea, and elsewhere.   Cosmopolitanism
is essential to a man with an enlarged mental horizon and a
liberal mind, but the true sort goes hand-in-hand with the
development of those natural qualities and gifts with which
each nation, race, and individual is endowed, and it ultimately
tends to the well-being of the whole.

CHAPTER V.

IN the previous Chapter I omitted to state that the publication
of the foregoing letters, in the *Baner ac Amserau Cymru*,
preceded in point of time the formation of the Society for
Utilizing the Welsh Language in education, of which the
first general meeting was held at Cardiff in the autumn of
1885. For a summary of its avowed objects and principles, see
Appendix G. It almost immediately received a very encouraging
measure of support from Welshmen, in almost all parts of
Welsh-Wales, and aroused a spirit of discussion in part ven-
tilated in the columns of the *Western Mail*, which, as we have
already seen, opposed its aims.

The Vicar of Ruabon, in a communication to the same paper,
ably replied to a correspondent who had urged the superior
claims of French and German on Welsh children. He says—

The proposal, as I understood it, was to introduce Welsh, not as
a substitute for English, but as an optional specific subject, and to
say that a smattering of French or German that could be acquired
at an Elementary School would be preferable for Welsh-speaking
children to an accurate grammatical knowledge of their own
language would seem too absurd. It would probably be generally
admitted that accuracy and observation are the two most important
things to be aimed at in all mental training. And, regarded simply

x

as an educational instrument, what could there be for Welsh children that would be more likely to conduce to the formation and strengthening of these habits than their proper and systematic training in the grammatical laws and construction of the grand old language in which they think and speak? There can be no doubt a knowledge of the two languages adds very much to the intelligence of the Welsh children. But this knowledge taught grammatically, and, as your correspondent says, philologically, as far as such teaching could be made suitable for children, would make the advantage they already possess far greater. Your correspondent was wrong in saying that "every English or foreign scholar who has mastered the language says that the literature it contains, does not justify the time and labour of acquiring it." Mr. George Borrow, quoted in your article of the 18th inst., thought differently. The last time I met him, on a pilgrimage to the grave of Dr. Owain Pugh, at Nantglyn, some 25 years ago, I well remember his saying that he considered that even the writings of Hugh Morris and Goronwy Owain alone were quite sufficient to repay anyone for the study of the Welsh language. This, however, is quite another question to giving Welsh children the power of reading and writing their own language with accuracy and intelligence.

Perhaps my readers will pardon my making a short digression, to give some account of Geo. Borrow, although his book on *Wild Wales* is doubtless familiar to some of them. His father had a military appointment in Ireland, where the son learnt some Irish, and afterwards as a lawyer's clerk in one of the Eastern Counties of England, he took up the study of Welsh, being assisted by a Welsh groom, whose acquaintance he had formed.

As he was of Cornish descent on one side, he possessed a certain *ingenium* which I have no doubt much facilitated the acquisition of Celtic languages. However that may be, he was not content with a mere smattering of Welsh, but acquired a sufficiently extensive knowledge of it, to read almost anything

in the bards. How did he attain what many Welshmen themselves fall short of? By reading Dr. W. O. Pughe's "*Coll
Gwynfa*" ("Paradise Lost") twice side-by-side with the
original. Many years after he travelled in Spain and Portugal,
and gave to the world the records of his journeys in "The
Bible in Spain," but he never forgot his early love of Welsh;
and in 1854 went a walking expedition through the country.
His work is marred by the introduction of a good deal of
public-house chat, but it betrays an acquaintance with Welsh
literature far more extensive than is to be found in the works
of half-informed English tourists of an earlier date, whose
works are looked up to as standards, and in vain we search
Pennant and Nicholson, or such County Histories as Fenton's
and Coxe's for the kind of information we get here.

George Borrow did not go to gaze on half effaced effigies in
parish meeting houses, to describe the gables of manor
houses, or even so much the beautiful scenery of the country,
as he went to see the *people*, knowing not merely their language
but the character of their literature; not merely so, but
he was able to quote their poets from the stores of his powerful memory, *e.g.*, on the top of Snowdon, he repeats—

> Oer yw'r eira ar Eryri, –o ryw
> Ar awyr i rewi;
> Oer yw'r ia ar riw 'r ri,
> A'r Eira oer yw 'Ryri.

> O Ri y 'Ryri yw'r oera, —o'r ar
> Ar oror wir arwa;
> O'r awyr a yr Eira,
> O'i ryw i roi rew a'r ia.

and then relates how three or four English stood nigh
with "grinning scorn," and how he apostrophized a Welshman
who came forward and shook his hand. "I am not a Llydawan

[a Breton]. I wish I was, or anything but what I am, one of a nation amongst whom any knowledge save what relates to money-making and over-reaching is looked upon as a disgrace. I am ashamed to say that I am an Englishman.

Despite its blemishes Borrow's *Wild Wales* still remains the only book in the whole circle of English literature which illustrates fairly-well the literary side of the Welsh character, though he almost entirely omits mention of nineteenth century writers, nor can an introduction to this period suitable for English students be found anywhere at present.

Matthew Arnold a few years later called the attention of the English public to Welsh literature, but as he was unacquainted with the language he was naturally unable to take a comprehensive view of it.

I will now select another letter from a well known Welshman, which is valuable, because it is an unvarnished testimony to the result of these parents' prejudices, which, unhappily, appear to be given way to, if not fostered by some elementary teachers, if not school managers. Newspaper correspondence, as a rule, is not worth reproducing, but I cannot debar myself from using it on the present occasion, because it illustrates (1) the intellectual and social history of Wales, in a certain part of the nineteenth century, (2) the action of general principles, and is of assistance in forming conclusions, which the mere *ipse dixit* of the author would not warrant.

E. Roberts, of Pontypridd, wrote as follows:—

My good father, holding then the mistaken notion held by some still, that a knowledge of Welsh would retard my progress in learning English, forbade me to have anything to do with the Welsh language, and even went the length of forbidding me to attend a Welsh Sunday School. Submitting to the parental authority, I did not attend a Sunday School or attempt to learn Welsh until I was about sixteen years of age, although

I was practically a monoglot Welsh lad. My education up to that period, I can assure you, was anything but a pleasure, for the little I learnt was learnt mechanically: the intellect had nothing to do with it. When I thought of entering college I thought it high time that I should know something of what grammar really was. I therefore procured Mr. R. Davies's Welsh Grammar, and committed a great part of it to memory; but, this grammar being so erroneous in many parts, I had but an indistinct idea of what grammar really was, until I began to translate from Latin into English. Then my eyes were opened on the subject, and all that I had stored in my memory first became of any use to me. But what a drudgery I had passed through previous to this! And that simply because the familiar Welsh was not used as a medium for explaining matters to me. I have thus given my experiences at some length, because my own case is an illustration of the difficulty which a Welsh boy meets with in trying to learn English without the aid of his native tongue. It is my firm belief that if what this Society aims at doing had been done in my youthful days, I would have made a great deal more progress intellectually and educationally, in English and in Welsh, than I did. The sad experience of my youthful days makes me yearn for some method of teaching Welsh boys similarly circumstanced in a more intelligent and pleasurable way.

As a set off against this may be mentioned the opposing attitude to the movement, which was taken by Professor Vance Smith of Carmarthen Presbyterian College, although only a recent settler in the country, and ignorant of the language. He met an able antagonist in Beriah G. Evans, the master of the Llangadock Village School, but since attached to the staff of the *South Wales Daily News*. It is really surprising that a person who must have possessed some educational acquirements of an advanced character should have allowed his mind to be blinded by prejudice, as to oppose the removal of an antiquated and effete system of education replete with both social and intellectual disadvantages, but which still more or less leavens nearly all the educational institutions of Wales. "The artificial propping up of the Welsh language" was a phrase used by Vance Smith, which a real thinker should have scrupled to use. What is artificial, is to purposely neglect the ordinary medium of thought, for the expression of ideas until a sufficiently secure foundation for their reception has been obtained through the use of another medium.

I quote the following from B. G. Evans's reply:—

You will, I am sure, readily concede that, being yourself only a recent comer to Wales, you cannot be expected to understand Welsh questions so thoroughly as those who have spent their lifetime among the people do. More than this, not being yourself possessed of the key of the Welsh language, wherewith you might be enabled to open for your students the door to further knowledge, you are placed under a serious disadvantage for estimating its practical value as an educational medium. Were the objects of the Society is to cultivate Welsh at the expense of English, then there would be force in your reasoning. I would appeal to you, sir, to throw the great influence your position as principal of so important a training institution in Wales gives you to promote and not to obstruct a movement calculated to remove such disabilities, and which has already secured the adhesion of leading educationalists who have enjoyed a life-long practical acquaintance with the people, their language, and their needs.

In 1886, a Royal Commission was appointed to enquire into the working of the Education Acts, of which the late Henry Richard was a member. The subject of bilingualism would probably, as usual, have been ignored had not that veteran champion of Wales secured its insertion in the syllabus of the points of enquiry. As a consequence, various Welshmen interested in the subject, were asked to give evidence.* In the course of their examination it was clearly indicated that room

was open for the Government to make very considerable modification of these regulations as applied to Welsh schools. In
fact, scarcely anything but a Code devised specially for Wales
would have sufficed to remove all the legitimate objections
raised of the present course of Welsh Education.

The names of the witnesses who gave evidence on the
bilingual question were Ebenezer Morris, of Menai Bridge.
Beriah G. Evans, Dan Isaac Davies, B.Sc., Dr. Isambard
Owen, M.A., D. Lewis (Rector of Merthyr), Archdeacon
Griffiths, T. Marchant Williams, Prof. H. Jones, of Bangor,
and W. Williams. M.A. (Chief Welsh Inspector of Schools).

The evidence of these witnesses contains opinions or facts
nearly identical with some which are noticed elsewhere in this
book: but at the risk of being thought guilty of repeating
myself, I venture to give a digest of some of its more
salient features, which I believe will not be uninteresting to
future students of Welsh history, whether they be so now or not.

Among the disadvantages arising from the present† system
of ignoring Welsh, it was stated that—

It makes a child nervous and afraid to give expression to his
thoughts. Either he hates the language of his home or hates
the foreign language.   *Evans.*

Injury done is permanent. Majority leave school without
literary knowledge of either language.   *Do.*

Contributions to the Welsh press of a low order, through
inefficient instruction, tend to debase the native purity of
the language.   *Do.*

If a teacher followed a well-defined system he would have no
credit given him in the report.   *Do.*

---

* The evidence has been re-published from the *Blue Book* in a collected
form, under the title of *Bilingual Teaching in Welsh Elementary Schools.*
Price 1s. J. E Southall, Newport, Mon.

† I say at *present*, because nearly all these difficulties remain,
while only a few schools teach Welsh.

Does not give the language the status of honour and respect it should occupy in the child's mind.   *Evans.*.

"The Welsh Sunday School is over-weighted, and has not only to teach religion" but also reading.   *D. I. Davies.*

Parents in ignorance. Fancy a man cannot have two mother-tongues. Contradicts this from experience of his own family.   *Do.*

Reason why, "gentry of Wales" do not command the influence they ordinarily might, is that they give up the language before the people.   *Do.*

Omission of Welsh from pupil teachers' examinations a serious practical grievance. English girl from Cardiff to Bristol with a smattering of French gets marks for it. A Welsh girl who knows her own language far more thoroughly, gets no marks, and is shut out of her own college.   *Do.*

Had it not been for the Welsh "Sunday" school, very little real work would have been solidly done by our English schools.   *Griffiths.*

Experience as Inspector of Schools in London, and as a teacher is, that neither German or French can be taught satisfactorily in a public elementary school under existing circumstances for many years.   *M. Williams.*

Children often puzzled by anomalies in English Grammar, it would be a great advantage if Welsh grammar were taught.

                   Do.

If it were taught it would remove the shyness of Welshmen, and improve them intellectually.   *Do.*

Many teachers think teaching Welsh would involve a great deal of additional labour   *   *   I say, however, the teaching of Welsh systematically would be helpful to them in every sense.   *Do.*

Good of Wales dependent to a considerable extent on meeting the difficulty—no community ever improved except by developing the forces, intellectual and otherwise, that it possesses, and Wales will never be made richer by neglecting its language; nor do I think the English will be known better. For on the border counties where they do leave their Welsh, or have done so, and become English, there is a degradation of intelligence, because they do not really become English.

Prof. H. Jones.

Speaking of *parents*—the majority, especially the more intelligent, would see the importance of teaching Welsh.

Do.

[*re* Candidates for Training College]. The Welsh are very much handicapped by having to be examined in a language which is not their vernacular.　　　*Chief Inspector Williams.*

Believes English might be more thoroughly acquired by the use of Welsh.　　　*Do.*

Teaching Welsh as a special and class subject *may prove* a great blessing to the children. Has not quite made up his mind on the subject. Would like those who believe in it have a chance to try.　　　*E. Morris.*

"They only learn to read like parrots."　　　*Do.*

Thinks poetry should not be included in English. [Why could he not say, he would substitute Welsh poetry?]　　　*Do.*

Take number of chapels of four leading denominations, as 3511; of these 2853 are entirely Welsh, 898 English.

Evans.

English chapels as a rule small, and ill-attended. Welsh services often crowded.　　　*Do.*

"Sunday" school the great educating medium for the Welsh-speaking population here, they have obtained the only instruction in their own language they have ever had.

Do

Welsh literature made accessible to them by "Sunday" teachers.　　　*Do*

Y

Wide-spread taste among working classes for Welsh literature and composition; but absence of educational facilities to
attain a *grammatical* knowledge of language.   *Do.*

Better *enunciation* in reading found in Welsh schools than in
Gloucestershire.   *Davies.*

Took a bilingual parish in Brecknockshire; found people
could not read Welsh, but anxious to have sermons it it.
They have a fondness for the language—it is the language
of their inner soul, so to speak.   *Lewis.*

Neath very much Anglicized, people do their shopping in
English, but the people will go perhaps in scores to an English
chapel, but by hundreds to a Welsh one. No predecessor of
his [at Neath] could preach in Welsh with anything like
fluency for 50 years.   *Griffiths.*

Englishmen as colliers—"before they have been underground
six months they come out as Welshmen."   *Do.*

National virtues found to a greater extent in Llanelly than
in more Anglicized Swansea.   *Do.*

Circulation of 100,000 (Welsh) newspapers every week: 60
years ago not one.   *Do.*

The additional time and labour involved in carrying out our
suggestions would be trifling indeed.   *Williams.*

Modern Welsh poets frequently have more power than they
are able to manifest.   *Jones.*

Welsh treatise on the philosophy of Hegel, another text
book on Logic commended. Conducted lectures in Welsh on
Greek philosophy and on modern ethics at Bangor; and "more
admirable classes," chiefly of working men, he never had.
Did not know "any cultivated Welsh person" who did not
prefer to attend worship in the Welsh rather than in the
English language.   *Do.*

Archdeacon Griffiths introduced into his evidence the
utterances of an eminent Welsh scholar, Robert Williams,

a Vice-President of Lampeter, and of Bp. Thirlwall, which I
have reserved till last, so as not to break the continuity of the
summary. These authorities are quoted in the evidence
(abridged) as under:—

"I have often known people whose reading language was English,
but whose speaking language was almost exclusively Welsh. What
a confused medley of words and things must thus be produced in
their minds. How the eye of the intellect must be dimmed, and
its edge blunted, by the half caught gleams of ideas and tangled
mass of doubts thus presented, which it can neither see distinctly
nor decide with certainty. Can this be called education? or is it
giving the mind of our peasantry fair play?" Then another short
passage that I will read is this: "But what if, by our neglect of
Welsh, we are throwing away a great gift of Providence? Is there
any reason why a people should not learn and thoroughly understand a neighbouring language, without immediately smothering
their own?" Bishop Thirlwall held similar views and contended
that no Welsh child ought to be thrown entirely upon the contin-
gency that he may by the force of other circumstances than those
of school life acquire sufficient English to cultivate his mind by
the means which that language supplies, and that he ought not to
be debarred in the meantime by want of elementary education,
from the benefits that may be derived from books in Welsh. He
goes on to say. *   * "I am fully convinced that no maxims opposed
to these will bear the test of experience; and I rejoice to find that
they begin to be more generally appreciated, and seem likely to
exercise a greater influence on the system of popular education,
than they have hitherto done."

Six or seven weeks after this evidence was given, the
earthly hopes of a chief leader of the movement were shattered,
a severe cold contracted in London never left him, and Dan
Isaac Davies expired 5 mo. (May) 28, 1887.

Very seldom indeed in the history of Wales has any in
dividual risen so quickly from comparative obscurity to a

position of such prominent note, and seldom has there been
seen a funeral which manifested so much wide-spread feeling,
as well as sympathy with the national aspirations which he
represented.   To an outsider, Cardiff may appear to differ but
little from Hull and Sunderland; to such an one the loss of an
educationalist, however great he may be in his own peculiar
sphere, would scarcely be regarded as anything like a public
event.

On this occasion between two and three thousand people
were gathered from Swansea, Merthyr, the Rhondda Valley
and other places, forming a procession a mile in length.   I will
not here introduce any reports of the speeches delivered on
the occasion by various well-known Welshmen, some in Welsh
and some in English.   But enough has been said to shew that
there was an indication of a remarkable amount of national
feeling which would scarcely have been expected, and I think
it convincingly shewed that the principles he represented were
not simply the property of a few agitators or enthusiasts, but very
largely echoed by all classes in Wales—South Wales at least.

I venture, however, to give a short extract from "Morien"
on the event, which, although Morienic in its style, comes from
the pen of a ready writer—

In the scholastic circles of the Principality he had been long
known and admired; but at the time of his death, his name was
rapidly becoming a household one in the homes of his fellow-
countrymen generally.   His mind was not too much imbued with
"*awen*" to forget the practical in the imaginative.   While others
simply cried, "*Oes y byd i'r iaith Gymraeg.*"   Mr. Dan Isaac Davies
worked in the path of progress, and he fell, to rise no more, whilst
engaged in re-opening the national avenues of the native language
of the Welsh people.   We had hoped that Wales had, at last,
found in him one sufficiently able and earnest to restore the
Cymric tongue to its ancient dignity as one of the learned languages
of Europe, by making it the channel by which the youth of Wales

might reach quickly the vast treasures of knowledge contained to-day in the English tongue. It is perfectly true that Mr. Davies had two objects in view by his propaganda, namely, making use of the native language of the Welsh in the work of education, and thereby facilitating the progress of Welsh children in the paths of education, and also restoring its lost dignity among scholars, of the great language of the Cambro-British people. * * Poor Dan Isaac Davies! With tears we lament thy death; thy work is done, for, doubtless, thou wert, in the mysterious ways of Providence, only to inaugurate a movement which will be long associated with thy name. Thou wert only to utter the old cry. " *I'r lan â'r gaiu fauer goch!*" Thy early death seems to sanctify the movement! " *Gorphwys, frawd, mewn tangnefedd.*"

In 1887, Welsh education came very prominently before the Eisteddfod meeting of the Cymmrodorion, held in London, and in the course of one of the meetings a paper was read by W. Edwards, M.A., Government Inspector of Schools, Merthyr Tydfil district, which I venture to insert here nearly entire.

As a whole, it is far too good a production to be consigned to the oblivion of fugitive literature, such as is the fate of the large majority of papers read at congresses and meetings of various kinds, except those perhaps of a purely learned character, which mark stepping stones in the progress of any particular art or branch of science.

Perhaps I shall be found fault with for taking up so much space with matter which is not original. If so, I would say that one of the objects of this book is not to present any one man's opinions or views on subjects which so closely concern the educational future of Wales, but to collate expressions from witnesses of very different antecedents, education, and circumstances, so that from the whole a better judgment may be formed of the facts of the past, and of the requirements of the future. Indeed there is a need for it. Much has been said and written, and yet the subject is so far from being thrashed out that, it is still one on which a definite verdict is yet to come.

From the point of view of a Government Inspector we scarcely expect enthusiasm, but we have here something more necessary, viz., impartiality and penetration. In reading it, one can only feel regret that at present the enlightened standpoint of the author is far in advance of that of many managers of schools, and of many Welsh teachers. He says—

As one of the Inspectors charged with the administration of the Education Act, I beg to state that I regard the question of the utilization of Welsh purely as an educational one. It has no necessary relation to party or to sect. Nor do I appear here to join in any appeal for alteration in the present Code, which is probably elastic enough to admit of any change of practice that may be desired by the Society. What is really required now is a discussion on the principle, and in a matter of so much importance no one should stand aloof who can help the public to understand the principle and the reason why it is advocated. It is with many an incontrovertible axiom that the Welsh language is the bane of Wales, and that every friend should aim at its extinction. Others admit that a language spoken by only a thirtieth part of the population of these islands must essentially be a disadvantage, through the limitations of intercourse which it imposes, even although it were the most ancient and perfect language known to history. Let it be conceded, not absolutely, but for the sake of argument, that it would be beneficial for Wales if the native language were totally supplanted by English, the question remains as to the best means of arriving at this consummation. Now, there can be no doubt that the exclusion of Welsh from all the elementary schools, from all the grammar schools, and from all the colleges, is damaging to the vitality of the language. It operates in two ways: (1) directly by subtracting so many hours every day from the time that would otherwise have been spent in the practice of the native tongue; (2) by giving the Welsh a low-caste character.

Welsh suffers in prestige from being totally ignored, when other subjects are honoured, and a tendency will be formed in the case, at any rate, of some children to speak bad English in preference to good Welsh. I cannot, therefore, deny that the cumulative effects of what I may call the repressive system, acting through many ages, will eventually destroy the Welsh language, especially in combination with many other outside influences; such are set up by the social and commercial intercourse with England, and the immensely preponderating quantity of English literature.

But when this is agreed, how much time must be allowed for the completion of the process? It is dangerous to prophesy, but I do not fear to affirm that more than a hundred, perhaps two hundred, perhaps 500 years will be required to achieve the death of Welsh. For it must be remembered that a repressive policy, in order to gain its end with any degree of rapidity, must also be complete. It is not enough to exclude Welsh from the schools and colleges. You must also make it penal to speak Welsh at fairs and markets, to print Welsh newspapers and books, to preach Welsh sermons. If you cannot or dare not do this, the language will resist for centuries the effect of its banishment from education.

It is a plausible assertion that children who hear and speak and read only English at school, will become really familiar with that language, and discard the vernacular for the rest of their lives. But no account is here taken of the Welsh environment. Even while the child is attending school the outside intercourse counterbalances to a considerable extent the effect of school atmostphere. Nay at the school itself, during the time of recreation Welsh is the language of play, as I have had many opportunities of observing in my own district, which is far from the centre of Wales. It may be doubted whether the child is subjected to English influence for more than five hours in the day. He is probably more than double this time under the influence of purely Welsh surroundings. When his school career ends, at the early age of twelve or thirteen, the environment is wholly Welsh, and it is not merely antecedently probable, but a matter of experience that in parts of Cardiganshire,

Merionethshire, and even of Glamorganshire, away from the towns, the child frequently in a few months loses almost all his hold of English. Although therefore it may be admitted that the day schools do exercise a decidedly inimical effect upon the life of the Welsh language, it should at the same time be remembered that their influence operates only during the third part of the child's working day, and ceases altogether at a very early age.

If the schools were all boarding schools, so that the children might be withdrawn from all contact with the Welsh stock from which they sprang, the effect might conceivably be more measurable, but even on this hypothesis the Anglicizing influence would be incomplete, unless the children were confined to separate cells when not under instruction. The people who are sanguine of the speedy success of the present system do not realize the difficulty of killing a language, which at the present moment is very far from moribund, and may live as long as Dutch or Danish. The total neglect of Welsh will surely help to sap the vigour of the language, but what happens during the long era which must elapse before the end comes? A policy which gags the mouth of a child, stupidly ignores the habits and associations of home, and crushes every native sensibility, can only result in immense waste of energy, in the lowering of the tone of the nation, and in a paralysis of the intelligence of many generations of Welshmen. Is it fair that even a barbarous dialect should be so ignored in education as Welsh is at present? There is an outcry of sympathy if the children of Lapps and Poles are treated in this way, but nearer home there is a case of outrage upon nature and reason which is worthy of equal condemnation.

The blame rests upon the Welsh themselves for the continuance of this state of things, for the Department has not yet refused to grant any concession which has been asked for by the Society. * ⁜ Words may be read to almost an unlimited extent without the assimilation by the mind of the ideas to which they correspond. By the bilingual method the link between the English word and the idea is established. In the study of any other foreign language this is the method that would universally be adopted.

It has been urged that the best way to teach a child French is to send him to school in France, where he would hear no English. But the cases are not parallel. In one case the whole environment would be French, and the child must learn French, as a child is sometimes taught to swim, by being thrown into deep sea. You have not the struggle between the environment and the school, which creates the chief obstacle in Wales.

The advocates of bilingual teaching recommend that in districts where Welsh retains its hold as the common medium of intercourse, Welsh and English should be taught in connection. Welsh as well as English reading books should be used, the one set being idiomatic translations of the other. These books are not merely an instrument of interpretation, but also subject matter for a comparison of the grammar and idioms of the two languages. In some districts Welsh is weak, or divides the field equally with English. There, Welsh would be more advantageously taught as a specific subject to the highest standards for its purely educational value, while in the lower standards Welsh might occasionally be employed for purposes of illustration. In every town or village where any Welsh is spoken an opportunity should be afforded of learning to read and write Welsh correctly at some period of the school course. It is not proposed by the Society to agitate for the compulsory reading of Welsh, as it is feared by some. They wish to make the teaching simply permissive. There are many prejudices to be overcome on the part of school managers and teachers and parents before the movement in favour of bilingual teaching becomes general.

There are some persons, be it observed, who make it a reproach that Welsh is so seldom spoken correctly by the masses. Should it not rather be a matter of wonder[*] that the idiom is so purely maintained when the only instruction in Welsh is given in Sunday schools? But the same individuals inconsistently oppose the only

---

[*] How true this is, those who know Wales can vouch.

means by which the defects in the common speech can be cured.

As a matter of fact, the language of a Welsh peasant is far more correct than that of his compeers in England. The Marquis of Bute said at the Cardiff Eisteddfod, "For a man to speak Welsh, and willingly not to be able to read or write it, is to confess himself a boor." This is a noble sentiment; and it should put to shame those others who wish to keep down the Welsh as a nation of boors, rather than grant the instruction which would save them from the reproach. The bilingual idea is to be applied to schools of all grades. For there should be no division of classes.

What has done so much mischief in Wales in times past and present is the chasm existing between the English-speaking land-owner and gentry and the Welsh-speaking community. What separation of interests, material and spiritual, has resulted from this cause!

Let the opportunity, at all events, be given to the children of all classes to learn the rudiments of the language of the people. To a very numerous class, viz., to those who are to become the ministers, the lawyers, the doctors, and the teachers of Wales, instruction in Welsh will clearly be a professional advantage.

One strongly felt objection to the proposed Welsh-English instruction is that although the object primarily is merely to utilize Welsh to learn English better than to improve the general intelligence thereby, yet Welsh itself will at the same time be improved. This is to some people a great rock of offence. They are afraid that the longevity of Welsh will be favourably affected when it is systematically taught, even in a parallel line with English. Even if their fears are well founded, the objection cannot be listened to, if it is true that only by bilingual instruction can a Welsh child have an intelligent grasp of English. But I feel certain that the life of Welsh will not be appreciably prolonged by its recognition in schools. The status of the language will be raised, a more correct way of speaking will be in vogue, but it is the very essence of bilingual teaching that it makes the scholar facile in two languages. If Welsh will be strengthened, English will receive an accession of vigour.

You may have a bilingual nation for any length of time, if by bilingual nation is meant a nation, two sections of which speak different languages, but there is no instance on record of a nation of bilinguals. Switzerland is no example, for the bilingualism of Switzerland is only the overlapping of the French and German, and such a bilingualism is obligatory along every border. But when every Welshman knows English as well as he knows Welsh, and there is no nucleus of monoglots to act as a preservative, the weaker language will then rapidly die. But it will die a honourable death, instead of being strangled in disgrace. Welsh will have done its work. The continuity of the nation will have been preserved. The parents and the children will not have been made strangers by the premature forcing of an alien language. The children of the English resident will be brought into kindlier intimacy with the children of the Cymry. Finally, time will have been given for the transference of whatever is worthy in Welsh literature to the kindly keeping of that universal inheritor, the language of England, in which the genius of the Welsh will find a larger and more durable home.

What do you say, my readers, to having these lines written in gold on the portals of every school and every college in Wales.

The bilingual idea is to be applied to schools of all grades,

What say you to ousting, as ignorant or incapable, every school manager, be he a high and mighty cleric or a village grocer, who will not subscribe to this advice of the Inspector—" In every town or village where any Welsh is spoken an opportunity should be offered of learning to read and write Welsh correctly at some period of the school course."

"Every town or village," recollect, includes those partially populated by Somerset and Gloucester workmen, the presence

of whose children is supposed by some teachers to place an
obstacle in the development of the bilingual idea. Why
should the children of the soil for the supposed interests of
these strangers be deprived of such opportunities of reading
and writing their mother-tongue as *systematic* instruction in it
can afford them.

What are you going to do to help fill up this social "chasm"
that the Inspector speaks of (the very expression which was
running in the writer's mind many months ago), caused by a
portion of the people by habit, association, and preference,
speaking a language and reading a literature of which the
wealthy and influential are almost entirely ignorant? What
are you going to do to remove those prejudices of school
managers, teachers, and parents, which the same experienced
authority tells us must be overcome before the movement
becomes general?

One of the objects of the volume is to call the attention of
the Welsh people to these inconsistencies, and blots upon their
character as a practical people, to the errors made venerable by
the incrustations of centuries, to the need of greater educational
enlightenment, and to the desirability (I would here even
go further than Inspector Edwards), of not leaving the decision
of these matters, mainly in the hands of either managers,
teachers, or parents, who are frequently either from inexperience
or ignorance, not the fittest authorities to decide upon them.

Bear in mind, too, that the foregoing paper is not the
product of the brain of an impractical enthusiast, a mere theorist,
as some of the opposers of bilingualism in Wales are apt to
class its advocates; it is the expression of man who is pre-
eminently entitled to a hearing though we may differ from
him on minor points. For instance, he appears to the writer to
much under-rate the influence of bilingual instruction in pro-
longing the life of the language, but on the central point viz.,

the desirability of *bilingualism*, or *teaching* Welsh, not simply *allowing* its use in explanatory processes becoming universal where the language is spoken, and that it should be applied to schools of *all classes*, we agree.

If this had been done ten or fifteen years ago, we probably should not have had the pitiable spectacle, alluded to elsewhere, of a well-to-do Welsh publisher in Wales unable to read the books issuing from his own press, and having to depend on the judgment of others as to their character, if he form one.

In some other points also I am inclined to differ from the author, as for instance where he advocates Welsh and English reading books being the idiomatic translation of each other. To give an effective bilingual education, this should only be partially the case; some pieces, particularly poetry, should be inserted in each language and untranslated.

Second only in importance to the Inspector's paper was a short speech by the then Warden of Llandovery College, in which he said that education in Wales should be of a *distinct*, and *national*, and *Welsh character*: education was not merely putting a number of facts and figures into the pupil's head, but consisted also in the development of the mind: it was not creating, but fashioning and forming raw material: it was impossible to educate a Welsh-speaking Welshman unless a knowledge of the Welsh language were taken into account: although from one point of view it might be a mistake to devote two hours a week to teaching a boy Welsh, yet it would be found as a fact that he learnt Latin and French all the quicker for having that knowledge.

Observe that the warden used these adjectives in characterizing what education in Wales should be.

DISTINCT. NATIONAL. WELSH.

Distinct means that there should be a clear essential

distinction between education in Wales and that over the border, which there is not at present.

National means that it should be general throughout the country.

Welsh means that instruction in the Welsh language should form an integral part of such distinct and national education.

These two advocates of bilingualism may be regarded as representative men, both filling important educational positions, both having a claim on the confidence of their countrymen.

Take another practical witness—Owen Owen, head master of Oswestry High School in the Welsh portion of Shropshire. He was strongly in favour of leaving education in Wales entirely to Welsh men and Welsh women. They should aim at a "COMPLETE AND THOROUGH NATIONAL SYSTEM," leading step by step from the village school to the University. I suppose that he also would be considered both successful and practical in his profession.

In 1888 the Report of the Education Commissioners was issued, which shewed that although it was composed entirely of Englishmen, with the single exception of Henry Richard, they had been so thoroughly convinced of the reasonableness of the demands of the Utilization Society, that almost every point asked for was conceded to. They recommended—

> That schools in Welsh districts should be allowed to teach reading and writing of Welsh concurrently with English.
>
> Permission to use bilingual reading-books.
>
> Liberty to teach Welsh as a specific subject.
>
> To adopt an optional scheme for English as a class subject, founded on the principle of a graduated system of translation from Welsh into English for the present acquirement of English grammar.

To teach Welsh with English as a class subject.

To include Welsh among the languages in which Queen's scholarships and certificates of merit may be annexed.

The next step to which the friends of the movement turned their attention was to secure the adhesion of the Government to these recommendations, so that it might be possible to give them practical effect. In this work Sir John Puleston, M.P., himself of a North Wales family noted in these pages, took an active share, and repeatedly interviewed Sir W. Hart Dyke. the President of the Committee of Council on Education.

The result, as is well known, was regarded as a complete success for the principles of the Society; every recommendation of the Royal Commission being adopted by the Government. with the exception of the inclusion of Welsh in Queen's scholarship subjects for pupil teachers. This was a great omission, but it is hoped that it may be remedied before long.

As one of the South Wales papers pointed out, these concessions in effect, open the door for a thorough change in the whole system of Welsh elementary education, although little prominence indeed is actually given them in the Code; but besides embracing the afore-mentioned recommendations, in practice they give advantages not quite apparent to one not familiar with elementary school working, which are indicated by the following summary.

I. A grant of 4s. to be paid per head for each child passing in Welsh Grammar, as a specific in Standards V., VI. and VII.

II. A grant of 2s. per child in the average of the whole school for successful results in teaching English as a *class* subject by means of translation from Welsh to English.

III. In all standards, and in all subjects, bilingual reading-books may be used, and bilingual copybooks may be used in teaching writing.

IV. The geography of Wales may be taught up to Standard III., and the history of Wales may be taught throughout the whole school, by means of books partly Welsh and partly English, and a grant of 2s. per head on the average of the whole school may be earned for each of these subjects if the results of the examination are satisfactory.

V. Schools taking up the new method of teaching English as a class subject may also claim the right to substitute translation from Welsh to English for English composition in the elementary subjects, and thus reap a double benefit.

VI. Finally, the small village and country schools, so numerous in the Principality, may, for the purpose of class teaching re-arrange the standards into three groups. *e.g.*, Group 1, Standards I., II.; Group 2, Standards III.. IV.; Group 3, Standards V., VI., VIII. This will be a material relief to under-staffed schools.

In the Spring of 1889, after these concessions had been made known, a meeting of the Utilization Society was held at Aberystwith, the Earl of Lisburn taking the chair at the public meeting. At the previous members' meeting Principal Edwards in the course of an admirable speech remarked—

It appears to me a real danger to the intellectual and moral life of the Welsh people, this transition from Welsh to English. Whatever may be said about Welsh, it is a simple fact that Welsh is a literary language. It has been found amply sufficient to express the most abstract truths of ethics and religion. It is at once the symbol and the instrument of a civilization. To regard such a language as an encumbrance, and not a most potent ally, in the education of the people who think and worship in it, whose intellectual and moral life is fashioned by the ideas it has conveyed to their minds, is fatuous and guilty conduct. (Cheers.) To permit the people of Wales to lose their knowledge of literary Welsh, the language of the Welsh Bible, so that they will under-

stand no other Welsh than the mongrel *patois* of the streets, is to
abandon deliberately the creative influences of the past, to break
for ever with the enobling examples of our great men, to throw
away the heritage of many centuries, in order to start afresh
forsooth from the low intellectual and moral condition of savage
tribes. Let English come into Wales and take possession, if it can.
But let the intellectual and moral life of the future be the natural
development of the past. This it cannot be if we foolishly and
criminally neglect to teach literary Welsh until we have accomplished the task of teaching literary English. Hitherto, this most
important work has been done in Wales by Sunday schools. Putting
aside for the moment the spiritual interests of Wales, and regarding
the question only in its intellectual aspects, I do not hesitate to
avow my strong conviction that all sects and parties alike ought
to acknowledge their indebtedness to our Welsh Sunday schools and
to their peculiar characteristics, and to make a great effort to
maintain their efficiency. But they cannot adequately meet the
demands of the age. The people must be taught, not only to read
the Welsh of Bishop Morgan, but also the Welsh of Goronwy
Owain, and to feel in the very depth of their being the creative
influence of the past that should always be present, and of the dead
that never die.

What do you say, you lethargic officials and managers steeped
in the traditions of Whitehall? What do you say to these
words of a man whom Wales delights to honour? The *people*
must (it is in your hands very largely to make it a practical
MUST) be taught not only to read the Welsh of Bishop
Morgan, but also the Welsh of Goronwy, or if Goronwy is too
difficult, that of Islwyn and Hiraethog.

Time has amply justified the following:—

Having obtained all it asked from Government, the Society
must take into account the sluggishness of a considerable number
of school managers, in whom as in most officials, the *vis inertiae* is
strong. Not indeed that the country at large can be justly charged

AA

with apathy. An intelligent observer made the remark that
whereas the study of Irish is but the hobby of a few antiquaries
in Dublin, the entire people of Wales love their language and wish
it to live. At the same time, the Society will not find that all
School Boards have enough foresight to see the necessity for the
immediate and full adoption of the concessions made in the New
Code. Public opinion must be continually formed and maintained
on the question, until the use of Welsh in teaching English and
the teaching of Welsh as a literary language become universal in
Welsh speaking districts. But this will never be brought about
unless suitable text-books are provided.   A strong and
successful Society is an instrument for good which ought not to be
thrust aside too soon, and this Society will not perish, so long as it
adapts itself to the special wants of the time, and performs its work
with the same energy in the future as it has shown in the past.

Here again we have a man well known outside Wales, whom
some of his friends perchance, think too much of an Anglicizer,
often occupying English pulpits, yet not satisfied with the bare
" utilization of Welsh to learn English," but positively enforcing
it as an educational maxim, that the teaching of Welsh as a
literary language should become universal in Welsh-speaking
districts, and foreseeing that only by continued exertions can
the deleterious whims or caprices of local managers, and the
vis inertiae of schoolmasters be overcome.

At the same meeting at Aberystwyth, Morgan Owen,
Inspector of Board Schools, said that he was pleased to see
the interest many parents took in the subject. In South Wales
in many cases, though parents objected to see their children
doing home lessons in English subjects, they were very glad to
find a Welsh book brought home in their hands. This
apparently conflicts with other testimony as to parents' views.
I conclude that the true solution of the difficulty is, that in
districts where the parents fear that their children will grow up

monoglot Welsh, they are often opposed to any secular education in Welsh, but where there is a danger of the children growing up monoglot English they are glad of opportunities given at school to return to the old language.

Professor Roberts of Cardiff said—

The great and rapid success of the agitation indicated that the Welsh language was destined to render another signal service to the nation, in addition to its services in the past. During the past fifty years, in spite of the fact that much of the cultured opinion of the country was for relegating the language into neglect and decay, the body of the people and their trusted leaders adopted another course. They in fact "utilized" the language— not as a barrier to keep the people in darkness —but as the sole available means of educating and informing the nation by speech and in writing. By a flood of lectures and periodicals and other literature, the people had been so educated that in no part of the kingdom could the masses be said to be more intelligent and better informed on all general questions than in Wales. But while the people thus utilized their language to their great and permanent benefit— it was wholly neglected and ignored in the official system of education.

Yes, so wholly neglected and ignored that the " flood of [vernacular] lectures and periodicals" have, in certain districts, become almost things of the past, though the want of familiarity with the language in the rising generation, which would have been induced by a little education in it at school.

T. E. Williams, Aberystwith, comparing Radnor with Cardigan, said—

Radnor had lost its Welsh. By this time it had become English not only as far as language was concerned, but the English spoken in the county was about the poorest English they could get anywhere, and, educationally, it was one of the lowest counties, if not the lowest in Wales. On the other hand, let them take the county of Cardigan. There they had Welsh spoken, and, educationally, Cardigan was one of the highest counties in Wales.

Not merely so, he might have added, but Radnor and Cardigan resemble each other ethnologically, perhaps, as much as any two counties in Wales, if so, the inferiority of Radnor is not accounted for by difference of race.

Speaking at the public meeting, Professor Lloyd believed that the study of Welsh grammar afforded a better mental training than the study of French or German.

They also wanted to utilize Welsh literature. English literature was no literature to Welshmen who had grown up to mature years without a knowledge of the English language. He did not understand the associations—the subtle associations of the words; and he thought that was well illustrated by the fact that the one English poet whom Welshmen knew something of and appreciated was Milton, and the reason was that they understood the background of Milton.

This may be true, but in fact English literature is "no literature" to Englishmen who have grown up to mature years, without some previous literary training in the very language they are supposed to speak. To enjoy Milton, it is not simply necessary to be born in an English home, and to have learnt to read and write.

The literature of the newspaper is accessible, but scarcely that represented by more modern names, such as Cowper and Tennyson. Welshmen are often recommended to learn English, or to value it for the sake of the literature; but in point of fact the best English classics are not much read except by the professional or leisured classes, and even at this fag-end of the nineteenth century, perhaps less than ever, if we except cotemporary writers, whereas a Welshman has less mental labour to go through to appreciate writers of the same class and degree in his own language, than the Englishman has in

his; not that I am placing actual Welsh literature on a level
with English, but shewing its possibilities with regard to the
mass of the people.

In the meetings of the Society for the Utilization of the
Welsh Language there has been generally a studious avoidance
of praise of the language, doubtless lest its claim on the
public should be prejudiced by the introduction of sentiment,
but on this occasion it was reserved to a foreigner to Wales,
a Roman Catholic Priest (Hayde), of Cardiff, to fill up the
meed of admiration for the intrinsic beauties of the Welsh
language.—

Respecting the Welsh language, he might say that he had never
studied a language in which he had felt more interest, more pleasure
and more mental training. The idioms and the structure of the
language were so different from those of other languages that by
comparing them the student acquired strength of mind, and
that was the great end of education.   Welsh was not
only a most beautiful language, but would compare favourably with
Italian, Spanish, Portuguese, German and others with which he was
acquainted; and he said further that if Welsh had been developed
as German had been developed during the past one hundred years
by some of the greatest men who had ever lived, and as English
had been developed by the writings of Shakespeare and others.
Welsh to-day would have been looked upon as one of the most
perfect languages on the face of the earth.

He ended with a short address in Welsh, quoting—

Tra'r môr yn fur i'r bur hoff bau,
O bydded i'r hen iaith barhau.

So much for the utterances of public men and officials.
They are neither few in number nor deficient in sense and
quality. Supposing these expressions of opinion, these marks
of sympathy with a proposed public object, had been made
with a corresponding intensity in England, can we suppose for

a moment that the English character would have allowed the whole thing to sink into partial oblivion?

Certainly not.   There would either have been dissentient voices, strongly biasing public opinion in the other direction, or else those who had put their hands to the plough would not be satisfied, until with the sweat of their brow, success had crowned their patient and constant endeavours.

Welsh people are not always made of that sort of mettle. They are not very fond of facing wind and weather, and of actions as good and as sound as words.   I have spoken of public opinion; although a solution of this question will affect every family in Welsh Wales, and a great many in English Wales, it is not to be supposed that it is exactly one in which the mass of the population have a mature judgment, but it certainly deserves to be met with a distinctly active attitude, either of opposition or of positive countenance and co-operation by intelligent persons interested in the conduct of Welsh education.

So far as opposition goes, few movements spread over a large area have encountered less of an open and public kind. What then are the tangible results before us in Wales?   After the great exertions made by some friends of the new Society; after the lapse of six years in the work of practically reforming the system of elementary education, *directly* they amount to little more than the following, viz.:—

1. The publication of two small text books* for teaching Welsh as a specific subject, while the third advertised some years ago as "in preparation," is still, so far as the author's information goes, lying in the limbo of the future.

2. The introduction of Welsh as a specific subject into a few schools, mostly in semi-Anglicized districts.

---

* Welsh Stage I., 1887.   Welsh Stage II., 1889.   Simkin Marshall and Co., London; 6d. each.

It will thus be seen that at the end of six years the great majority of the rising generation is untouched, and unaffected by this incipient reformation.

This is at first sight discouraging. In reality, however, it is not quite so much so as may appear, although direct results are extremely meagre. Indirectly, there is reason to believe that the educational status of Welsh has been somewhat raised, and a further place assigned to it in developing the intelligence of children than previously. This cannot be however, thoroughly and efficiently done without the use of Text Books, partly printed in Welsh, in the actual course of instruction in elementary subjects.

The Bilingual Books which, in 1889, the Council of the Welsh Utilization Society was to issue "without delay," are still not forthcoming, and it is to be feared, notwithstanding the warm and zealous recognition of the Society's claims on Wales, there will be a danger unless more energetic and thoroughly systematic action is taken, of relapsing into a quiet and slavish acquiescence in the *status quo.*

Thus far, some sort of a soporific has prevented the elementary schoolmasters uniting, as they should do, and knocking at the door of the Society's Council Chamber demanding the speedy issue of these Bilingual Books, and it is to be feared that the apathy of the Department is partly responsible for this. After receiving the report of the Royal Commissioners, which most clearly shewed that various injuries were being inflicted on Wales, and a certain amount of educational power allowed to run waste through the present method being pursued; after the generous concessions made by the Government to the claims of Wales, how is English-Welsh, as a class subject, treated in the Code? Simply allowed a most insignificant place, just barely mentioned in a sort of note. How is it treated in the Departmental instructions to Inspectors for 1890? Surely

with all this weight of evidence, the permanent officials at
Whitehall would tell the Inspectors that it was their duty to
assist in inaugurating a radical reform in the education of
Wales, not in an authoritative way, but by suggestions to
school managers and teachers, and by recommendations that
they should endeavour, as soon as may be, to equip themselves
for a better system which promises to improve the knowledge
of English as well as of Welsh.   Did they thus call attention to the first steps necessary to break up the fallow ground?

No.   Not by a single word.   It was as if the said permanent
officials, or whosoever drafts out those instructions to the
Inspectors, was desirous of hushing the whole thing up, and
in all probability the chiefs—"My Lords," had too much to
think of, to notice such an apparently trifling omission.

It would, however, be injustice to Lord Cranbrook and
Sir W. Hart Dyke, to question the sincerity of the interest
they have taken in the matter, but we must come to the conclusion that if all the heads of the Department had recipro-
cated these sentiments, it would have been easy to have given
such additional force to the movement that every schoolmaster
and every manager in Welsh Wales would have felt a certain
amount of moral suasion to change tactics.

Beyond *vice voce* explanations &c., the work done has been
entirely confined to dealing with Welsh as a specific subject,
i.e., teaching it as a *foreign* language in the three higher
Standards only.   The uninformed reader may need to be told
that *specifics* are extra subjects, such as algebra, agriculture,
French, physiology and domestic economy, which are to a considerable extent at the option of the School Board or managers.
Success in these is paid for by a grant per head from the
Government.

It is practically found that specifics can only be attempted
in few schools, and many children leave school before entering

Standard V. The Utilization Society was quite aware that much more would be needed than the introduction of the specific, as they said in their memorial to the Royal Commission in 1886 : "We should however deeply deplore the restriction of concession to Welsh needs to the introduction of the specific subject only, as from the nature of the majority of the schools in Wales, such concession would benefit but comparatively few."

To Gelligaer School Board, bordering on Monmouthshire, belongs the honour of first introducing Welsh, viz., in 1885, before the issue of either of the Text Books. Some gleanings of the experience gained there and elsewhere will doubtless be interesting to the reader.

A Welsh schoolmaster thus commented upon the results of the first examination in the Gelligaer schools:—

Here we have one School Board alone, without adequate text books, and with a large admixture of English-speaking children among its pupils, passing over 82 per cent. in the first examination in Welsh as a specific subject, and adding thereby a sum of twenty-one pounds to the school fund in additional grants. In one instance 62 per cent. of the children examined spoke English habitually at home, and yet 92 per cent of these English-speaking children passed successfully in their first examination in Welsh! One purely English child—a girl—was reported as having attained the third highest place in percentage of marks for Welsh exercises.

One of the head masters under the Board evidently regarded the matter something as a fad, and simply allowed two pupils to stand, but later on came to see that it might be more useful and profitable than he had anticipated, and successfully passed a considerable number.

In the report to the Education Department (Blue Book of 1888), Inspector Edwards, of Merthyr, appears to be quoted as speaking favourably of the text books of the Society: and

Inspector Bancroft remarked on the fact that children in the *English* speaking parts of Pembrokeshire are often remarkably slow in answering one question in arithmetic.

The Chief Inspector in issuing the report, refers to the great slowness with which the teaching of Welsh was spreading, and alludes to parents and managers' objections, comprising the "popular delusion" spoken of in Chap. IV. He adds very much to the purpose. "Surely a movement which aims at improving what cannot now be considered satisfactory ought to have a fair trial, and to be pushed forward by enlightened educationalists, without waiting for a demand from the parents, most of whom naturally believe that the present system must be the best that can be devised."

Of course it ought. I am very glad such a man is in such a position, and has the good sense and boldness to make the remark. Ask the parents their opinion about the land laws and the Established Church, or the labour movement, and they have a right to be listened to, but it is a doctrine that should be most strongly protested against, that they should dictate a system of education to persons whose opportunities for forming a broad and liberal judgment are far more extensive than theirs.

Parents in general have but a limited idea of what education, even such an education as is possible and suitable for their circumstances in life, means: they need strong minds to direct: so do many school managers, and this narrowness of culture is one of the difficulties the Welsh has to contend against.

Inspector Pryce, of Carmarthenshire, in the same report, appears to depreciate teaching Welsh, which was entirely excluded as a specific from his district, but gives no reason except the unpopularity with parents,—not of the language, but of its introduction into secular education.

In the Welsh Division Report for 1890, published in 1891, the Chief Inspector alludes to the fact that "specific subjects are almost confined to higher-grade Elementary Schools," such as those established in large towns like Cardiff, where we should naturally expect to find not much *Welsh* attempted, and that ordinary schools find sufficient to do without, while teaching little more than "elementary, and two class subjects," an observation which accentuates the remark following, that the "full value of the movement will not be attained till bilingual reading books be used in the lower standards"; he even goes further than this, and says that his experience has strengthened his conviction that advantage would accrue from using "the child's knowledge of his own language in teaching not only English but other languages as well."

Although specifics are thus handicapped, after listening to the Chief Inspector, we will give some consideration to the reports of Inspectors.

The Carmarthen district Inspector says: "Welsh has not yet been chosen as a specific subject in any school in my district. This is, no doubt, partly owing to the children in the larger schools possessing a fair knowledge in English, especially in the higher standards." Now, in fact, if these children are bilingual, the reason assigned is a poor one. He admits to passing 408 in specific subjects; the boys in Algebra and animal physiology, and the girls in domestic economy. Algebra, it is true, would teach them to think, but so would Welsh, besides enlarging their powers of expression.

The Denbigh District Inspector says : " Welsh seems to be the popular specific subject in my district * * * in one school, strange to say, an English girl beat her Welsh fellows in this subject." This is simply the Gelligaer experience repeated. If popular in the Denbighshire district, which includes semi-Anglicized Ruabon, why not in Carmarthenshire, where a convenient knowledge of both languages co-exists to a large extent ? If the reason assigned is that the children in the latter know Welsh already, why not, on the same ground, say that they know English already in Llanelly and Carmarthen, and refuse to teach them English composition.

The Pembroke District Inspector remarks on most of his schools, being unable to go in for specific subjects, that Welsh would " probably be more popular as a class subject, as there are but few scholars above the 5th Standard."

The Merthyr District Inspector (W. Edwards) says : That as things are at present, Welsh is begun to be taught too late in a child's course, and that a boy cannot take kindly to the conjugation of Welsh verbs, and the declension of nouns, when he has not previously read a Welsh book, and become familiar with the written form of the language, which he only knows colloquially.

What is said from the Carnarvon district, the very headquarters of modern Welsh literature, and Welsh writers the classic ground of *llenorion a beirdd* now, and perhaps for a long period, in the future ? Absolutely nothing. The Inspector has an English name, and though he may possess a small knowledge of the language, it is believed that he rarely exercises it.

In bilingual districts the subject is more likely to be popular with parents, but the *ogre* of the English manager or member of a School Board, who thinks he knows what the children want, but wishes to checkmate Welsh, is still more likely to present itself. Perhaps he is a colliery or tin-plate manager, or even a tradesman from across the border, and it is not impossible that he will approach the subject with that dogmatic assurance of a " little knowledge" which is sufficient to be a "dangerous thing."

Mynyddislwyn School Board, for instance, took Welsh not long since. In the only school under that Board, with which I am acquainted, it was a success, the children were getting on well; but at the end of some five months, without assigning a reason they stopped it, under an Englishman as chairman, and one or more English members. It is true that one of the head-masters is also an Englishman, and I heard he makes fun of their language to his Welsh scholars. Perhaps the influence of the two combined, *i.e.*, of two or three ignorant persons who happened to be in positions of authority, was allowed to turn the judgment of the Board back from the course on which it had entered.

I made it my business, shortly before hearing this, to call at another Monmouthshire school where a different Board. though by no means warmly attached to the Welsh idea gave the master liberty to teach Welsh as a specific.

The sum of his testimony of the results of its introduction was:

1. That the children have a higher opinion of their language.

2. It is a success.

3. The children take an interest in it.

4. Their English is improved.

Now, if it is so in this school, why should it not be so in 1100 out of 1425 schools in Wales? Can anyone give a clear answer in the negative? I have read carefully, a good deal bearing on the subject during the last six years, and however much, invectives may be hurled, or contempt cast on those who work in the direction of bringing this about. nothing has yet been written or said which shews that the balance of evidence lies against the conclusion that this is about the proportion of schools in which Welsh can be used, either as a specific subject, or as a class subject side by side with English, or in the process of teaching elementary subjects, *i.e.* reading, writing and arithmetic.

Into the 325 remaining schools, perhaps it would be unwise to attempt to introduce anything of the sort at present, though with even where a minority of the population speak Welsh the Government concessions still make it possible to teach it.

A boy, John Smith, for instance, can read a page of a bilingual book in English, if he knows nothing of Welsh. The next boy, David Hughes, half a page in English and half in Welsh; perhaps with general benefit to the class.

The following table shews the progress of Welsh as a "specific" during four years :—

	1887	1888	1889	1890
No. of scholars examined in Welsh	192	369	403	450
Passed - -	140	253	285	271

We must not look on Welsh as a specific, simply as an arrangement for the benefit of Welsh children. English children learn the language readily in Welsh districts. Near the very Monmouthshire school above mentioned, I was told that English children learnt Welsh with their fellows, and *preferred* talking it.

Children like those don't know much about nationality and sentiment—the real pleasure, doubtless, arises from the second language awaking a hidden spring of mental power, which they are able to enjoy without much effort.

Putting specifics now for the moment aside, how does the current Report deal with other possible forms of teaching the language. Any thorough and widely extended system is, perhaps, not possible until the publication of the Text books, but in the meantime a little is possible in teaching English composition, in lieu of which translation from English into

Welsh is allowed. All teachers, and managers ought to know that this is now permissible, and does not necessarily require the use of specially prepared school books to carry it out.

What does the Chief Inspector say? Why, that he is "*surprised* and *disappointed*" to find so few teachers availing themselves of it, while he is fully persuaded that the results would be more valuable than an attempt at Composition.

The Cardigan Inspector, weary of the insipid monotony of some portions of his work, says, after speaking of certain teachers being not quite up to the mark in English grammar, that in some cases of the sort "Welsh might very well be attempted, for there are many teachers in the Welsh part of my district who could make the subject interesting and beneficial to their scholars. I should be glad if some tried it, only *for the sake of a little variety.*" [*i.e.* tried Welsh as a *class* subject].

Lastly, I will note the recommendation of the Merthyr Inspector, which, if carried into effect, would introduce Welsh into all standards and all schools, because that language would be incidental to the *compulsory* subject, reading. " It is, in my opinion, highly desirable that in all Welsh schools one of the reading books should be wholly or partly in the vernacular." He goes on to make the very sensible remark that parents are not capable judges of the merits of the change—is convinced that a Welsh child will not lose in a material sense, and will gain a great deal intellectually,—the bulk of teachers in his district could with very slight preparation qualify themselves for giving the bilingual instructions sanctioned by the Code of 1890.

Now, what meaning can we attach to this backwardness, when no less than 339 of them gave affirmative answers as to the desirability of the introduction of Welsh as a specific in

1885 ? In part we must put it down to the fact that some of them may be waiting the appearing of Text Books, and only a few are in a position to introduce a specific to their schools. To be honest, however, this leaves a large part of the problem unexplained.

I would venture on one hypothesis—they share that common inheritance of weak humanity, a reluctance to launch out into the unknown when the known presents a plausible amount of satisfaction and ease.

> Illi robur et aes triplex
> Circa pectus erat, qui fragilem truci
> Commisit pelago ratem
> Primus   *   *

I would figure them like those children whose first introduction to the sea is at one of those Welsh watering-places where fond mothers have succeeded in steeling their own hearts to commit them to the care of some weather-beaten mistress of a bathing-machine, to give the young hopefuls *willhe*, *nillhe*, a good sousing into the briny deep.

Now some teachers are just in the position to profit by such a good sousing metaphorically, but who will be able to play the part of *Gwragedd glan y mor?*

Of course, in view of the appearance of the long-looked for bilingual reading books, and the consequent introduction of Welsh into all the standards, much that I have written here may read like ancient history, before the present school generation has entirely left the benches. I must, nevertheless, treat the question as it is, and not as it may be in a short time : only thus can its bearings be grasped intellectually.

One cannot help strongly contrasting the extraordinary and popular demonstration at the death of the late D. I. Davies,

---

* Horace, Carm. Lib. I. iii.—Around his heart were fixed stout oak and threefold brass, who first to the wild ocean entrusted his frail skiff.

his being treated almost like a national hero, the long procession and the imposing array of influential names who either honoured his memory by their presence at the grave, or by written communications, with the small amount of actual pains which have been taken by such to spread the views which he so energetically and ably set forth, and to educate the country up to the necessary degree of discrimination in a matter—apparently a detail of education, but in reality one of great and unforeseen importance.

One cannot help, on the other hand, reflecting on the lethargy, shall I say boorishness, displayed by a large majority of school managers in the face of such clear representations as have been made in public, though they may not have troubled to direct their reading to the quarters where non-official statements would be likely to be found, or to the official representations made by persons such as D. I. Davies, Chief Inspector Williams, and W. Edwards, appointed by Government to superintend schools, and advise on any point which the powers of the Code allow.

It is not the duty of the Inspectors (officially) to go and argue with these managers, but has there not been a Society established for the express object, amongst others, of educating public opinion? If it has failed in taking proper steps to do that, and remained quiescent, whose fault is it? Have the admirers of D. I. Davies's educational principles nothing to say or do, and is the presence of an influential Englishman, or Anglicized Welshman on a School Board, to quash all enquiry and linguistic enterprise in a district? Wait a bit, and when the bilingual reading books are issued we shall again have an opportunity of seeing what mettle Welsh educationalists are made of.   .

To ponder, in an unreasoning way, over parents' objections is childish.   There are, however, some difficulties, one of the
cc

principal ones of which is the want of previous training on the part of many teachers. But most or all of them will gradually vanish in a few years, or be greatly minimized under the influence of a special Code for Wales, and special regulations for would-be teachers.

As the Chief Inspector has remarked, the movement has done good in inducing some Inspectors to pay more attention to the scholars understanding what they read in schools. This is good so far, but Wales needs more than this. The scholars should not only understand that which it is attempted to teach them in school, but also should have the advantage of systematic training in the language which is taught them at home, and which for many, will form their principal medium of communication for the remainder of their life. In short, the efforts of school authorities should be directed not merely to enable the scholars to understand English, but they should also not be afraid to T-E-A-C-H W-E-L-S-H.

I will close the chapter by an extract*from a paper by one of the few schoolmasters who has had this practical experience—

For the sake of our children, our chief care, who have so far been suffering wrong at our hands, inasmuch as an ignorant zeal has hindered their true progress, and we have taken from them the only means which they possessed of becoming intelligently instructed, to wit, their language—the only proper key to open the door of their minds—have slighted every thing that was dear and sacred in their eyes; have robbed them of the self-confidence which was necessary in order for them to grow up as men, and be men everywhere. Our cry for them is, make their path straight by giving their language the position it is worthy of in our educational system, that there may be more sympathy between the hearth and the day school, because the latter will be a "home from home" to the children, which it has not been in the past.

---

* Translated from "*Cymraeg yn yr Ysgolion Dyddiol*," gan T. Clement Thomas, in Y *Traethodydd Gor.* 1890.

CHAPTER VI.

IN the three preceding Chapters, we have dealt with Welsh principally as affected by school regulations. We will now endeavour to obtain a more general view of its present status and future prospects. In spite of the outcry in Wales, occasioned by the reports of the three Commissioners in 1847, English opinion, to a large extent, took its cue from them for several years. It was not, in fact, till eighteen years afterwards that any important portraiture of Wales calculated to reach English readers appeared.

In 1866, a series of fourteen letters was published in the *Morning and Evening Star*, written by a comparatively unknown London Welshman, who held the office of Secretary to the Peace Society, and whose father had been a somewhat eminent Congregational preacher in Cardiganshire. Mainly in consequence of these letters, HENRY RICHARD became a household name in Wales, mentioned with respect and affection: a seat in Parliament was open to him till the day of his death, and his work distinctly modified English opinion on the character of the Welsh people.

In his opening letter he alludes to the three young barristers, who, went "groping about in the dark for some means of

acquiring the information they were in search of, fell into the
hands of one class, who hoodwinked and misguided them in
every possible way." Of course, the "one class" was that of the
"*gwŷr mewn dillad duon*." I quote his words, but perhaps
they were a little one-sided.

A considerable portion of the letters was taken up with
matter bearing on the religious, moral and political character
of the people, the dereliction and apathy of the Established
Church in the past, the rise and popularity of Nonconformity,
the unwillingness of the early Nonconformists to engage
actively in politics, anomalies in political representations, evic-
tions for voting against the landlord's views, and a refutation
of the Commissioners' reports as regards the morality of the
country.

In reference to the latter he said —"I believe I can shew
that though falling lamentably below the standard of the
Divine law, it [Wales] has the right to claim credit for superior
purity as compared with most of the other parts of the
kingdom."

The two letters which principally require comment here are
those on the intellectual condition of the country, and the
political influence of the gentry.

In the former he expressed the belief that at no period had
"the people of Wales sunk into that utter mental torpidity
which marks" some portions of the English peasantry.

He speaks of national traditions being cherished with great
tenacity, and mentions that of *Brâd y Cyllyll Hirion* being
still current in his boyhood. This is somewhat remarkable,
the event happened somewhat near the Sixth century, and
though it is perhaps impossible to prove that the tradition
existed, not by means of concurrent manuscript testimony, but
purely by the force of oral relation right down to the Nineteenth
century, I am personally inclined to believe that this may be the

case, and that the story would have been preserved much as
we have it, independently of any literary evidences.

People living in towns, which principally owe their existence
to the industrial developments of modern civilization, and
which attract to themselves varied and mixed populations from
different districts and with different antecedents, have, I
believe, generally little idea of the force of tradition in some
Welsh country districts. I do not speak of legend (and
perhaps *Brâd y Cyllyll Hirion* is of that class), but of what
rests on reliable and historical foundations. We need not, however, confine reliable and ancient traditions to Wales. Careful
observers doubtless come across it repeatedly, in England.

For instance, a descendant of a certain family named
Prichard, which resided for some time close to Offa's Dyke,
in Herefordshire, related, not many years ago, the family
tradition that the Prichards had entertained the Black Prince.
Now, *Hallam's Constitutional History* records the fact that
a certain Picard did entertain that prince in London. Other
evidence exists that the family residing on this spot right
through the Norman and Plantagenet period was that of the
Pritchards, Picards, or Pytchards, and that one or more of
their number represented the county in Parliament. Hence,
prima facie it appears clearly to point to the identity of the
family tradition with the historical fact, and the former must
have been continued in complete ignorance of the existence of
the latter. I have also heard that the motto of this family
was "*Heb Ddnw heb ddim, a Duw a digon*," rendering it probable that though of Norman origin they became Welsh-
speaking.

Adverting to the current literature of the country, the
existence is noted of five quarterlies, twenty-five monthlies, and
eight weeklies, circulated among an estimated Welsh reading
and speaking population of 850,000. Concurrently with this,

there was a large circulation of English literature, which is still more the case to-day, even in districts where little but Welsh is heard at home.

After saying that only for some twenty years had the Welsh begun to have anything like a political literature, he records the early struggle of the *Amserau*, in the hands of *Gwilym Hiraethog*, who used to print it at Douglas, Isle of Man, to escape newspaper duty, but on the gentry and clergy of North Wales, calling the attention of the Government to the fact, it had to be removed thence. Contrary to the wish of its opponents it survived and lives to-day, incorporated with the *Baner* in the well-known *Baner ac Amserau Cymru*.

It is not surprising to find that Henry Richard devoted a letter to the political influence of the gentry. Although there are points of similarity, there are certain points of difference between the landed classes in Wales and England, which no Englishman, who lives in the country, and becomes one with the people, can fail to be struck with.

Few nations are more disposed to attach themselves to families than the Welsh. Witness their almost servile following of the Tudors, their loyalty to the unworthy Stuarts, and the prestige which several old houses in Wales still enjoy, not on account of what their members are in themselves, but from the consciousness that they have descended from ancient lords of the land.

Wales differs considerably from Ireland in this respect. There are very few estates, if any, which have the tradition of being property confiscated from native hands, and given into the hands of foreigners. Even the families with Norman names generally have some claim to represent an old Welsh stock, through intermarriage, and so far, there is a predisposition not to be over-critical, of the disposition and acts of the large landlords towards tenants.

Over-riding all this, however, there are opposing forces which in effect, place a considerable distance between the two classes, and which prevent their assimilation into an homogeneous whole, viz.:—

I. The deprivation which members of most of the county families have suffered through their early education, being wholly English, which prevents them from being fully qualified to be leaders of the people. About this defect, Henry Richard wrote as follows:—

Many of the former are ignorant of the language of the country. and are rather proud of their ignorance. while others, who have acquired a little smattering of colloquial Welsh, make no attempt to acquaint themselves with the current periodical literature, through which, in Wales as everywhere else, the national mind and heart and will, find expression. This is not a sentimental, but a very real and serious grievance; for the people among whom they dwell remain unknown to the upper classes, or rather, what is far worse, they are misknown, the impressions of them which they receive being conveyed through a false medium—the medium of minds coloured and distorted by interest or prejudice.

II. The difference of religion between the landed class and the mass of the people.

If the landowners are really conscientiously convinced that it is their duty to be Conformist to the ritual of the State Church, and so long as they believe that a Spiritual omnipresent Being requires such conformity, no one would deny their liberty to carry out their belief. It would, however, be doing them no injustice to say that a great many of their number could not strictly confess as much.

It seems moreover passing strange, that intelligent men, not only in Wales, but England, should so implicitly pin their faith to the doctrine and ecclesiastical arrangements made in the middle of the sixteenth century by a few men who had been mostly educated as Papists. Is it possible that they have never read the lesson of history, that the progress of error from the first century downwards, was continual and slow; until, if it had not been checked by the civil power, it would have culminated in the freehold of the country being handed over to ecclesiastics by the dying possessors of uneasy consciences and until the freeborn Briton himself would have had nothing left he could call his own ?

If the progress of error has been slow, why should not the return from error be slow too, and why stick fast by the framers of the *Book of Common Prayer*, in the middle of the sixteenth century, and not entertain the idea that possibly some who dissented from the use of that book, had juster and clearer views of the relation of man to the Supreme Being than its authors?

All this is *à propos*, because there are a large number of the privileged class who are not merely content with their own belief, but are very diligent by means of their Primrose League meetings, National Schools, favours to *eglwyswyr*, and slights to Nonconformists in endeavouring to prop up the now tottering establishment, which retains more of the rags of Rome than any denomination in the country. The time is coming, though not in the lifetime of the generation now on the scene of action, when not only the present supremacy of the reigning Sovereign (*i.e.* the Government), over a professedly religious body will be abolished, but in which there will be such a wide spread and conscientious acceptance of doctrines much more consistent with spiritual religion, that the present will be looked back to as a time of ignorance and darkness.

A third cause why the "gentry" command less influence than they might otherwise do, is the fact that in a number of instances they marry English women. This, combined with the sort of religious and secular education they receive, gives them somewhat the character of aliens, separated from the mass of the people by a great gulf.

Witness the present P————— of R ——, although descended from one of the fifteen Royal tribes, and his family has for hundreds of years lived in one of the most Welshy parts of Wales, he cannot speak "a word" of the language, which is not so much to be wondered at, as he comes from a stock that has now and again frowned fiercely upon dissent from the time of Richard Davies,* 1675, to the election of 1859. The representative of the family having gone to England for a wife, she has had the good sense to learn the language, and is credited with having moderated her husband's homage to the doctrine of the Divine right of kings and landlords to reign. Yet, the heir of the estate is monoglot English, notwithstanding, or rather is ignorant of Welsh, whatever he may know of foreign tongues.

It is, perhaps, justice to the class spoken of to say that to some extent the Welsh revival has affected them, and it is likely to affect them still more, if a Welsh University is established on a really National basis. To decide as to whether there is less intolerance now than a quarter of a century ago, I will leave to others. Certainly there is more civil liberty, and apparently a tendency to cultivate the Welsh language among some of the old families which did not exist then.

If this is properly fostered, it ought to end in Welsh-speaking nurses being engaged for their children, a policy which it is to be hoped many more middle-class families in Glamorganshire will carry out, than has been the case. Some years ago, a colliery proprietor at Brymbo, near Wrexham, attempted this, but the maid engaged for his family was so

---

* Richard Davies says that Colonel P. was not in the main a persecutor, but was put on by some "peevish clergymen, so called."—*Philadelphia Ed.*, p 125.

anxious to learn English that she neglected teaching her charge Welsh. This was, I suppose, about 1860; and though such cases would be less likely to occur now, it would be safer to engage a duoglot person.

To endeavour to present an accurate and faithful portraiture of the social, moral and mental forces which affect the use of the language in Wales, would necessitate the writing of some 200,000 family monographs, and the weaving of them into a complete whole. Perhaps a German specialist will in the dim future direct his mental camera in this direction, and present to the astonished world a complete delineation of the various shades of subjective and objective phenomena which the co-existence of the Welsh and English languages gives rise to. My work in this direction can hardly be otherwise than patchy, but if patchy, and unworthy the name of a monograph, it occupies ground to a large extent untraversed by English pens.

We will now examine another witness; this time it is neither a popular favourite—an ex-Dissenting preacher, nor an obscure Newport tradesman—it is an *Officirid* of the very mother Church that you of the wide-spreading acres and the rent rolls delight to honour. D. Williams, in the 1879 Episcopalian Congress, at Swansea, read a paper on the Welsh Church press, in the course of which he said—

Bishops and barons leading the van, with a motley crew of country squires and clerical expectants officiating in the rear, have expelled the Welsh language from their drawing-rooms; and she, with the true instinct of womanly revenge, has shut the heart of the nation against them, that they shall no longer be rulers of her people. There are very few parishes in Wales without a resident landlord, to whom the people look up with more or less expectation. These natural leaders of the people, because uneducated, and perversely ignorant of the language, have abdicated their proud position, and allowed the people to be led by those who had no business to be leaders of the people at all.*

This, my readers, is one side of the question given by the eloquent pen of a writer to whom, notwithstanding his facility in it, English was a foreign language; after describing how the nation is not led, he describes how it is led:—

It is the Welsh-speaking portion of the community, under the spell of their weekly and monthly periodicals, who wield the political power in the Principality ; and it is impossible to gain their confidence by ignoring their language.　There is one tenant-farmer in Welsh Wales, whom 1 know well, who wields a mightier political influence than the four Bishops, four Deans, and ten Archdeacons of Wales put together.　The united forces of the hierarchy cannot sway the will of the nation with the magic that this one Welsh tenant-farmer can.

In inserting the following paragraph I am reminded of the remark made to me by a young Lampeter man.　"Welsh does not pay.　The best livings are given to English preachers."　D. Williams, after alluding to the Welsh Encyclopaedia,† which, he says, in point of fulness, research and learning, need not shrink from comparison with similar works in England, says—

Our literature—our modern literature—is to a great extent peasant literature ; contributed and read by them ; and that almost every clergyman who was found guilty of any literary ability had to incur episcopal displeasure with its demoralising results ; 1 ask, is it a matter of wonder that the Church suffers from a decadence of literary ability, and that the people have become in the main a nation of Dissenters ?　The reading monoglot is a Dissenter.　There are clergy living amongst us at the present moment, of European fame as philologists, and of unimpeachable character, and most efficient as parish priests, coldly left in poor and obscure country

---

* Extract from report in *South Wales Daily News*, 10 mo., 11th, 1879.

† *Y Gwyddoniadur Gymraeg*, published by Gee Denbigh.

parishes, who, if they had produced in the English language the learned works they have in Welsh, would long ago have found a becoming recognition at the hands of the rulers of the Church. Justice demands that the same consideration should be shown to authors in the Welsh language.

Another who took part in the Congress spoke in high contempt of the idea that because English is generally understood, not much attention need be paid to the vernacular; he calls this a terrible argument when applied to the "Welsh Church," *i.e.* the Episcopalian body.

This is the policy which has thrust on us men, clever enough indeed to learn our tongue, but never to feel it, or for the people who speak it. Our tongue cannot be learned by a stranger, its fire burns only in the native breast.* This is why the Welsh, though a duoglot people, linger delightedly on the accents of a speaker, however halting, who addresses them in their own language, while the sublimest thoughts otherwise expressed fail to reach more than the ear, and leave the audience unimpressed.

The above extracts will be of some assistance in elucidating the position of what are called the upper classes towards the Welsh language. So far from being themselves, as in former ages, the literateurs of the country, and leaders in thought as well as in action, they are obliged, to a considerable extent, to take a secondary position, which is in part the result of democratic influences common to England and Wales, and, in part, the outcome of the legislation of Henry VIII.

We should do well, moreover, to bear in mind that up to within recent years Wales can scarcely be said to have had a middle class. The backbone of a nation in such times as ours is the existence of an intelligent and conscientious *bourgeoisie*. It was the *bourgeoisie* which enabled England to shake off the

---

* But then the "native breast" is sometimes found the other side Offa's Dyke.

yoke of the Stuarts, and it was just the absence of that class which placed Wales in an antagonistic position to the Parliamentary powers in 1645. Even at the present day we cannot go into some English towns without being reminded that their burghers three or four centuries ago were capable of great things, and that in point of material accommodations and social intelligence, they must have been considerably in advance of the working country population.

The middle class in Wales, such as it is, has largely been created by the industrial developments of the Nineteenth century. The fathers and grandfathers of most of the well-to-do tradesmen, merchants, and professional men, at least in South Wales, were to be found in very different spheres of life. I believe that this is one of the factors, which accounts for the undefinable social differences met with by a person who has lived in Bristol, Gloucester, or Hereford, when he comes to make his home in Wales.

The absence of a middle class has operated in this way: socially and intellectually, the people have been left very much to carve out their own path. This has resulted in the establishment of a certain standard of native culture, particularly in North Wales, but it has also had the effect of throwing a very much larger proportion of influence into the hands of the preachers of the various nonconforming denominations than they would otherwise have possessed owing to the fact of their being almost the only educated persons representing popular aspirations. I am speaking, of course, of a state of things which is passing away, but one which for many years to come, will leave its stamp on the character of Wales.

In South Wales, notwithstanding the spread of English, there is still far too much isolation of the mining population from outside influences which certainly would not be the case had these populations grown up for one or two generations

surrounded by such a middle class as they would naturally
look up to with confidence. The new middle class in Wales
represents two distinct lines of influence, the one distinctly
Welsh, the other Anglicized or entirely English; I shall,
however, illustrate my meaning better by saying that in Wales
there are in reality two social and intellectual worlds; the one
is practically unapproachable from the outside, except through
a familiarity with the Welsh language, either in its colloquial
or literary forms, or both; the other is simply a provincialized
aspect of English life and thought.

The first class of persons move in both those spheres, the
second move in the latter only. There are Englishmen who
have been living in Wales for years, entering into the relations
of every-day life with its people, following the course of events
as recorded in English papers published in Wales, who, notwithstanding they may be on terms of familiarity with their
neighbours, are still *foreigners*. They may think they know
Wales, but they do not, and cannot in the same sense, as
those who understand the national literature, or the Dual
character of a Duoglot people.

No doubt there are, notwithstanding what has been said,
many Englishmen, as well as many Welshmen, who feel that this
is not satisfactory. The best practical remedy, it appears
to me, is not to attempt to hasten the decay and
death of Welsh, but to introduce it into the curriculum of
middle class schools. Until, however, a Welsh University is
founded this will be exceedingly difficult to any great extent,
because middle class schools aim at adapting their course to
English University examinations, where Welsh is not taken
into account at all, and because the conventional ideas attached
to the word "education," in Wales, create a barrier in the way.

The University of London has had, I believe, at least two
appeals to make room for Welsh as an optional subject at their

matriculation, but hitherto without effect. I was indeed told, some years ago, by no less an authority than the late D. I. Davies, that the Senate feared a desire for Home Rule for Wales lay behind one of these appeals, but found out their mistake when too late to alter their decision. Meanwhile time goes on, and an increasing number of the well-to-do middle classes enter on the battle of life unequipped by such a desirable addition to their acquirements, as a moderate literary knowledge of the language, if not an efficient colloquial one, would give them, and this remark need not be withdrawn, even in some cases where English is the prevailing language.

There is no doubt that one important factor in lessening the influence of the Welsh language on the middle classes is just that which has hastened the decay of Manx,* viz., not only English in the concerns of every-day life, and the flood of English literature, which necessarily biasses the mental action, but also what we call *"respectability,"* and perhaps I might say a false standard of it. This is what a vernacular paper (*Y Goleuad*) says on the subject—

There is not a word in the Welsh language corresponding with the English word " respectability," — Neither does Wales require it whilst it retains its native characteristics. It is a foreign term, representing foreign habits ; but the misfortune is that there are many among us who try to imitate the foreigner. There is no class of persons whom we despise and hate more than the " respectables." There is too much of it in religious circles. Persons are appointed deacons because they are respectable, and others are turned aside because of their poverty. Nonconformity stands in serious danger on account of the spread of respectability.

* I once asked Professor Rhys if he could account for this decay of Manx ; like nearly every one who is asked a similar question about Wales in districts where English gains ground, he was somewhat at a loss to reply, but narrated how, when a friend of his, who is a competent Manx scholar, was about preaching in that tongue on a certain occasion, one of the better-to-do of the congregation got up and walked out,

Be careful about "despising and hating," otherwise we will say—*Da iawn, Golenad golenrdig!*

The middle class, however, is every day growing larger and more wealthy in Wales, in fact the very Methodism of the 18th Century has tended to create a middle class, though very much handicapped till recently, through the scarcity of any means of obtaining more than a very elementary education.

As to the Third class, constituting the mass of the population, and who make up Wales in a more complete sense than the corresponding class make up England: I would include in it for the present purpose, all persons whose secular education has been principally or wholly derived from the Elementary Schools. The word education must of course be understood in a popular, rather than in a precise sense.

In Welsh Wales few things strike a stranger more than the literary activity manifested by those who would be called "uneducated people" in England, and not merely that, but we find also originality of mind, though taking a different turn from that we generally meet with in the poor. Take for instance Dic Aberdaron, in station little better than a labourer, but the compiler of a Welsh-Greek-Hebrew Dictionary, whose character was, however, more eccentric than useful.

Then again, Iolo Morganwg, the son of a stone-cutter, in Glamorganshire, one of the men who assisted in bringing to light portions of Welsh literature of the middle ages, till then lying in manuscript, and which publication gave an impetus to the study of Welsh literature, that has never quite spent its force. Iolo was a man of ideas, and a man of principles, too; he refused a "windfall" several years before his death because it had been acquired by means of slavery.

An English memoir of him by Elijah Waring is long since

out of print. In the appendix is given a strikingly fine elegy on the occasion of his death, by Gwallter Mechain, beginning—

> O Gweddw ddawn, ei ddawn a ddwg,
> Mawr gwynion bro Morganwg.

I know personally a (Monmouthshire) Welshman, of quite humble birth, who was brought up in a village where the language was nearly extinct, but was taught Welsh by his mother, and has since acquired a literary knowledge of nearly every important European tongue. including modern Greek and Russian, besides the classical and one or two Semitic ones, while he is reported to speak Italian "like a native." All this is without ever going to any school beyond the village one, without any apparent aim or ambition to "rise in life," and with scarcely travelling outside the limits of his native county. *Anglo Saxon* he leaves out of his list, telling me he cannot bring his mind to tackle it—the language of Hengist, and of the holders of the *Cyllyll hirion*.

Such persons have frequently a strong sense of racial affinity. "I have," said he "visited Bristol, Exeter, and Oxford, but I could not live at either place. I have only to cross the Bristol Channel and I am among foreigners." Last summer he visited County Down, in the North of Ireland, there, said he, "I feel at home at once. I could live there, if necessary, the population is mixed, but much like that we have at home, and what we see come into Newport from the Western Valleys." His remark probably implied that he found himself in the presence of a Celtic, mixed with a partly Celticized Teutonic population.

From Anglicized-Wales we will go to Welsh-Wales, to another acquaintance of the author's, in quite unpretentious circumstances in the world, living in a village where little English is spoken, and where I presume he received his education. His

EE

English is good, and not satisfied with that, he is also a French
reader, and possesses a number of books, including several
volumes of *La Revue Celtique*, and one or two philosophical
works, besides being a contributor to the Welsh Press.   If he
had been an Oxfordshire villager in similar circumstances,
what would his library have contained? Perhaps a Veterinary
Handbook, an English Dictionary, and a few Dissenting or
Episcopalian publications, as the case may be.

Let Englishmen who sigh for the day when the echoes of
the last word of native Welsh will expire amid the craggy
heights of Snowdon, and let half ignorant Welshmen, who
profess to believe that Welsh culture is an incubus, listen to
the testimony of Anna Thomas, an Englishwoman, living at
Bethesda vicarage, near Bangor—

There is no English in church or chapel for miles round.   We
are, however, in full communication by rail with the outer world,
and our people are in no way behind in civilisation, being exceptionally refined and intelligent.   More English there certainly is
within my knowledge of the district during fourteen years, much
more English, but not one whit less Welsh.   Both English and
Welsh newspapers are largely bought, and English literature is
studied to an extent that would put to shame many an educated
Englishman.   The two languages flourish side by side, doing each
other no wrong, but much good to their duoglott possessors.   We
have a large class for the study of English literature, and the
masterly way in which English is there turned into Welsh and
vice versa would convince the greatest enemy of Welsh that the
two languages are better than one, if only for the intellectual
training in exactness of expression and grasp of idea.*

Once again—this time it is George Borrow making comparison between "a Welshman and an Englishman of the
lower class."   He had been talking to a country miller's man,

---

* *Western Mail*, 1885.

who understood and translated verses from Taliesin, repeated
by G. B., and informed him of the whereabouts of the place
(Pont y meibion) where Huw Morris had lived. This called
forth the remark : " What would a Suffolk miller's swain have
said, if I had repeated to him verses out of Beowulf or even
Chaucer, and had asked him about the residence of Skelton?"*

I have on two or three occasions heard working men or
small tradesmen lament the fact that they were ignorant of
Welsh.   During a journey, in the course of which some of the
information given in this book was collected, I called at
Knighton (Tref y Clawdd), situate on Offa's Dyke, and where
for perhaps one hundred years, no indigenous Welsh has been
spoken. At the Railway Station, on leaving, I entered into
conversation with an intelligent man (keeper of a coffee-house
in the town) who came from the central part of Radnorshire
(at or near Llanbadarn Fynydd). He lamented being cut off
from a knowledge of Welsh, and spoke of it, while praising
the language, as a "great intellectual loss."   I have also an
acquaintance, a shoemaker, in a small town in the Eastern
Valleys of Monmouthshire, whose circle of reading includes
Charles Lamb and Coleridge. The latter he expressed great
admiration for, and gave me a commission to procure him,
second hand, George Fox's Journal, for which he was prepared
to go to double the sum I first suggested.

How had he come to hear of George Fox? He had read
about him, and was there not a description of a Quaker's
meeting in Charles Lamb's writings,† a volume of which was
produced.

Canst thou speak Welsh? I said.

No, I wish I could.

---

* John Skelton, a Fifteenth century English poet.
† See "Essays of Elia."

How is that; wast thou not taught it when thou wast young?

No, I was brought up an Episcopalian, and my father was quite under the parson, who brought pressure to bear, and told him that he should not teach his children to learn Welsh, and now I am the sufferer. I would give fifty pounds to know it. My mother is a Welsh woman, and can speak it well.

I remarked that such writers as Coleridge had culture of thought, but they had not such a complete power of expression as the Welsh language affords.

To this he agreed, adding, "sometimes a word in Welsh has an indescribable meaning, and it makes me elated—the very thought of it."

I am strongly inclined to suspect that the parson above alluded to was one of the heroes of 1847, and belonged to that class of Episcopalians who appear to have regarded the extirpation of the Welsh language as one of their peculiar missions, and who are even now represented in the country. In the district where my friend the shoemaker lives, success has nearly crowned their efforts or their wishes, or both.

Not long ago I was travelling near Ebbw Vale in a compartment with some working men, on the day of the flower-show. One of them, a strong powerfully built man, of middle age, was talking with equal facility in Welsh and English, and spoke the latter, if I recollect right, much more free from the local accent than is usual. On enquiry I found he was of English parentage, one parent being from Wiltshire and one from Bristol. English was his mother tongue. He *preferred* Welsh to English, but his physique was English, not Welsh.

Now under the present so-called enlightened system of education in Monmouthshire, an English child, such as this man was some thirty years ago, would not have the chance of

becoming bilingual, that is, the Welsh element in the district
of Aberbeeg is not now sufficiently strong to spread in English
families which it might do to some extent, were Welsh introduced into all standards by means of Bilingual reading books.
This would give many such children indirectly a wider range
of ideas, and a greater command even over their own language
without much extra labour on the part of the teachers,
especially if the character of the text books obviated the
necessity of trying to get a dull English boy to read Welsh.

This man is, I believe, only a sample of many more either in
this county or Glamorgan, where a large amount of English
blood exists in persons speaking the Welsh language, from
parents who have come to Wales in the last 60 or 70 years. I
was struck with this lately at Mountain Ash, on one of the
colliers' idle days, when little but Welsh was heard in their
conversation, but the signs of English descent, if I mistake
not, were numerous. It is important for the welfare of Wales
that the children of the foreign settlers who have arrived
more recently, should be engrafted into the national life, for
which purpose the day schools must be brought into requisition,
and now there are so many facilities for travelling and cheap
reading, bilingualism should not be left to the chances of
learning by the ear only.

The English immigration between 1830 and 1850 has probably
Anglicized the country far less than that between 1870 and
1890, for the following reasons: In 1830—1850, the new
comers were absorbed with greater readiness into the Welsh
speaking population, because the influence of daily contact
with the latter was not so much neutralized by a one-sided
system of education which was at that period extremely loose
and ineffective, and sufficient time had not elapsed to build
many English meeting houses ; consequently in many cases the
children of English people attended Welsh Bible classes ; they

learned there to read the language, and to some extent this process is going on to-day. Lastly, the English Press had not learned to cater for the masses, and pour forth such a flood of penny weeklies, good, bad, and indifferent, as now seek admittance in the homes of working people, as well as others.

I hope to show before this work is finished, that all that does not necessarily imply the extinction of Welsh, or of its cultivation as a literary language, if only school facilities for bilingualism are created, but I think we have evidence that where such facilities are denied in districts such as I have described, not only does the power to read and write Welsh cease, but the English reading of the population is of a lower tone, and denotes lower culture than it otherwise might, and that it becomes more difficult for them to rise in the social scale.

A short time since I called on the publisher of the leading Welsh paper in the colliery districts of East Glamorgan, and asked him what was his experience as to its circulation. "To give you my humble opinion," said he, "the old generation who have learnt Welsh in the Sunday school is dying out, and their places are not being filled up."

It may not be fair to bring this forward as a test case : if the aforesaid paper was in the hands of a man of literary ability, who not merely knew Wales, but had known how to make use of the literary power to be found in his district, and printed his paper well, I believe the circulation would soon rise, and permeate a higher stratum than before, with a correspondingly increased value in the advertisements, and that, in spite of its socialistic and democratic tendencies. If his observation implied that there were fewer Welsh readers in the district than twenty years ago, I think he was wrong, as in the Rhondda Valleys the Welsh Independents alone, in 1890, numbered eleven more edifices than in 1877, the numbers being sixteen for 1877, and twenty-seven for 1890, while the edifices of the English section increased by six ; the amounts collected from Welsh congregations amounted for the total period to £84,470, from the English to £12,720.

From the above it appears that, taking the Independents' statistics as samples of others, that there has been a very considerable increase in the number of persons coming under Welsh influences, accompanied with indications that a considerable proportion of the younger part of such population is not sufficiently familiar with the language to read its secular literature freely, although members of Welsh Bible classes, which would in part account for the falling off the publisher of the ———— complained of.

From North Wales, however, we learn a different tale.

In 1890 I conversed with one of the leading Welsh publishers, who assured me "we sell more Welsh books now than ever we did," and in 1876 with another well known publisher, who made a similar remark. Similar evidence as regards his own paper was collected from the mouth of a leading North Welsh newspaper proprietor in 1890.

The rationale of this undoubtedly appears to be, that, though Welsh is spoken over a slightly decreasing area, and, notwithstanding the partial disuse of the literary language in some industrial districts of South Wales, the actual amount of current Welsh literature has rather increased within the last twenty years.

This last phenomenon is partly accounted for by the more general spread of education, but I think there can be no doubt that in South Wales the presence of a large foreign element in the population, whose children are denied the opportunity in the day schools of becoming Welshmen, exercises a paralyzing influence on the development of Welsh literature. This will come under notice later on.

The most formidable resistance offered to the culture and

use of the Welsh springs from the widely current idea, not
confined to the ex-Lampeter cleric, that "Welsh does not
pay." How far this is so, in regard to persons of his class,[*]
others are more competent to judge than myself, but I would
say, (1) that this difficulty is much exaggerated in the
minds of many people : (2) the residuum of truth there is
in the saying is accounted for partly by arbitrary and artificial
causes, which are removable, and partly by natural causes (if
we may call them so), which are unremovable, except by a very
unlikely sequence of events. That is to say, that if Welsh does
not pay, to a certain extent this is accounted for by social
and educational influences which are within the power of the
people to alter or modify, so as to make it "*pay*," while
there will be continually, on the other hand, a counter influence arising from the power of association and close intimacy
with England, commercially if in no other direction, tending
to the use of English ; yet to regard this exclusively would
be folly.

Not merely are the linguistic and mental problems which
the existence of two languages in Wales presents somewhat
intricate, but when intelligently considered they yield no little
interest—to myself both interest and astonishment.

The ordinary Welshman takes the existing state of things to
which his father and his grandfather has been more or less
used all their lives, as a matter of course, and sees little
peculiar about the circumstances and vitality, either of the
colloquial or literary language.

The ordinary Englishman in Wales also sees nothing peculiar
about the present use of the language, which he complacently
believes to be quietly dying out, and which in the interim must
be patiently suffered, as a temporary anomaly.

---

* How sordid and repugnant to Christianity is the idea of studying to
preach with a view of its "*paying*."

I cannot, however, help believing that an intelligent stranger, were it possible for him to enter the scene free from previous associations or knowledge of Wales from any source, would find much here to call forth his wonder.

In the first place he could not fail to be struck by the contradictions inherent in the Celtic nature, and he would have to face apparent contradictions at almost every turn of the road, whether he looks back to the Fifteenth century and recalls the bitter hatred of England then existing, and the uprising which, had it been successful, would have ended (so contemporaries thought) in the extinction of the English language, and then remembers the tendency in the Sixteenth, to forget everything distinctly Welsh, or whether, on the other hand, he regards the zealous resentment with which every apparent slight rendered their language is visited by the natives, who then turn round, and give the slight themselves, or neglect to provide for its preservation ; he will recollect, too, the vast amount of pabulum for national pride, supplied by the Eisteddfod, the loud pretensions of its supporters as to its encouraging the literature of the country, and yet with scarce a murmuring voice the same persons will allow their birthright to be steadily, stealthily and surely stolen from their children without any approach to a practical protest : he will see bardic daggers drawn about trivialities, and then when Time has ended all, for one of the combatants there will be the glowing *Cwynau coll Enwogion* (Elegies for the illustrious dead).

All this is a matter of course to—I was going to say, the naturalized Welshmen.

It is in itself a strange thing to see one of the nations making up the British nation, speaking a language what has ceased to be the officially recognized for three centuries and a half; while not merely has such recognition been wanting in matters of civil

FF

administration which may be said to concern every householder
if not every individual, but the education of rich and poor,
with unimportant exceptions, has been conducted on a basis
which simply treats the Welsh language as non-existing,
although, as we have seen, its use as a medium of verbal conversation between teacher and scholar is occasionally absolutely
necessary.

Again, leaving out of sight students at theological colleges,
it would not be far from the mark to draw the corollary from
the above, and say that every scrap of literary knowledge of
Welsh possessed for centuries by high and low, as well as the
ability to communicate their ideas through its medium in
writing has been obtained, quite outside what school* or
College training they may have had.   It has indeed, I believe,
not unfrequently been the case that ambitious parents, wishing
a professional career for their children, have studiously barred
their way from becoming proficient in Welsh, so that they
might the more readily satisfy a board of examiners, or obtain
appointments : or, perhaps, if a youth is intended to appear
as an Episcopalian preacher, he comes forth as a half-fledged
Welshman, with just sufficient of Rowland's grammar in his
brain to take a "cure" and disarm opposition, but with
nothing like a colloquial or literary mastery of the language.

So long as the syllabus of subjects in public examinations
excludes Welsh, this state of things must continue, for Welshmen come out apparently inferior to others, whom they might
otherwise excel (if judged by some mental-strength testing-
machine), because they have had to learn in the course of their
lives one more language than their competitors, which the
arbitrary standard of the examiner does not give them credit
for.

---

* The term school is used in reference   recognized secular education.

Long custom has so thoroughly ingrained into the minds of the people the idea that *education* implies casting Welsh to the winds, and to rise in life they must not only *learn* English, but English must also be, if possible, the sole medium of instruction, as well as of legal administration, that the net result has undoubtedly been a dwarfing of their ability as accurate thinkers and speakers.

Such an education bears resemblance to the antiquated and monkish education of the middle ages, when, as we have seen, English boys were taught to construe into French—the language of the barons, of Parliament and the law courts, *i.e.*, they were not simply taught French, but were taught it in a way involving a great waste of mental labour, English being apparently excluded from the schoolroom.

In a similar way Latin was taught later on—Latin, the *lingua franca* of the learned of Europe, and the base of a large portion of our language, taught if I mistake not, by means of books which excluded the home language from the view of the scholar. Perhaps circumstances rendered it defensible then, but who would dream of teaching it thus now.

It is somewhat striking that Forster's Education Act, passed under the rigid scrutiny of Parliament, in 1870, and framed, no doubt, under the cognizance of men specially conversant with Elementary Education in the British Isles, should have entirely ignored the existence of the Welsh language. This seems to indicate a hope at headquarters that the teaching of English to every Welsh child, and fostering the old mediaeval idea of excluding the mother tongue, either as a subject of instruction, or as a written medium of instruction, would soon be the means of sounding its death-knell.

Now the real aim of a National Education Department should be primarily neither to compass the extension of a language nor to introduce another as a medium of social intercourse.

It should be rather to educate—draw out—expand the mental powers of the children under its care, and to store their memories with useful facts, by the simplest, most economical and effective means within their reach, partly with reference to the exterior conditions of life in which the children are placed, and in which the large majority are likely to pass their lives, and partly without such a reference, to strengthen their command of thought and language, their faculties of observation and reasoning, ever consistently with the exercise of the moral sense and judgment.

There is a great want of appreciation of what education really is among some teachers, who, like the parents, think of it too much as a mechanical implement for earning so much hard cash; in the first place, as it affects their own pockets; in the next, as it affects their scholars in after life. I am satisfied that too narrow and contracted a view on their part prevails in Wales. Much is said about the advantages of technical education, and rightly so; but if the public imagine that it is the duty or in the power of day schools to teach boys and girls handicrafts whereby they may earn their living in after life, they are much mistaken. Even in this technical education cry, there is too little of the educational and too much of the hard cash idea.

What is wanted, and what will shortly be accomplished, is greater attention to the simultaneous* training of the eye and hand with the intellect. It is doubtful if any system of Government grants and trained teachers will do much towards teaching a competent practice of any particular handicraft or

---

* *Simultaneous* refers to such training being combined in making up part of the school course; not necessarily to the combination taking place at a given moment of instruction.

profession. What they can do is to prepare the minds of pupils the more readily, thoroughly, and quickly to master their work when it comes on them in the future, by the intelligent application of general principles.

In some branches, however, of technical or semi-techinical work, day schools, apart from evening classes, may be of considerable service to the nation, for instance, by teaching chemistry and botany, as applied to the theory of agriculture; or by teaching the use of carpenter's tools, on such a system as the Swedish *sloyd*, which means, doubtless, work spread over EXTRA HOURS, if efficiency in other respects is maintained. But extra hours will well pay for themselves, without much danger of overstrain, in so far as they are spent over manual rather than brain work.

Much is said also about the great desirability of learning French and German to prepare for commercial life, and to compete with foreign clerks. What I am about to say has reference rather to intermediate than elementary education, though French is pressed into service now in "technical" evening classes. The outcry about French and German brings us in contact with the hard cash idea. As a matter of fact German is not of much use to Englishmen as a commercial language; an employer could probably procure a German clerk by advertising in the *Daily Telegraph* cheaper than an English one, and even if he prefers the latter there are very few openings in South Wales for the commercial use of German. If an importer, for instance, wishes to write to a German firm, probably they would be glad to write back in English. Then, as to French, there are a few vacancies in South Wales now and then for French correspondents, but very few in comparison with the number of middle-class youths every year let loose from the trammels of school. The language which is commercially used in South Wales next frequently to French, and which affords far more prospect than German of possible use in the future, either at home or abroad, as a commercial language, is Spanish, and yet this is generally acquired by self study, or aided by tuition to only a small extent.

Do I advocate dropping French and German out of the middle-class curriculums? No, because the effort to acquire them is itself educative: because it broadens the sympathies and widens the mental horizon; and because their literature in any one branch of Science is a mine of wealth. It is a favourite idea with some schoolmasters that French and German are to be studied on account of the remains of their classical writers. Practically that comes to little, beyond, I fear, a perusal of writers who had better be left unread.

With reference, however, to French as a subject of "technical" instruction, we may believe that if the young men who wish to learn it, had first a year's drilling in Welsh grammar and composition (where Welsh is spoken) before tackling French at all, that they would ultimately make better progress: consequently such a course would *pay* better than the present, notwithstanding the contemptuous cry of "waste of time" which would probably be raised.

In the town in which I write, a Young Men's Friendly Society has been formed, with evening classes. I was informed by the teacher connected with it, that when it was left to the option of the youths offering themselves, which language they would be taught, each of them with a Welsh patronymic, without exception, chose *Welsh*. None of them, so far as is known, could speak it.

So far as I have been able to read Welsh life, those who really stand the best chance of taking a lead in Wales, are the sons of small farmers or shopkeepers in the thoroughly Welsh parts of Wales, where little else is heard round the fireside, and who think during their early years entirely in Welsh, although later on they may have to think in English, and undergo some humiliations in surmounting the difficulties of acquiring it.

Not unfrequently the doctor or the lawyer are Welsh in sympathy, but unused to Welsh as a literary weapon, while the class above alluded to, produce some of the writers whose names are known up and down the country to a larger extent than is the case with their compeers in England, than whom not only are they of more literary habits, but often able to command a greater range of ideas, in spite of all that is said about the narrowness of a Welshman's vision. The real truth is that in attempting to analyze the phenomena of Welsh life we are continually confronted with paradoxes, and with contradictory assertions, both of which have some element of truth in them, whether we make enquiries either into the national character, the use of the language colloquially, the extent of the literature, or even the attitude of the people towards such an institution as the Established Church.

The following will serve as a partial illustration of my meaning, and in any case it may be taken as a fairly typical illustration of the conflicting linguistic and social elements in Wales at the present day, although it is now twelve years since the incident happened.

In the autumn of 1879, a person named James Shaw, whether English or Scotch is not quite clear, wrote to the *Times* newspapers, from Taibach, near Swansea, bitterly complaining of what he called the bilingual misfortune of Wales, and giving that as a reason why "Welsh industry is scarcely keeping abreast of the day, and culture and learning seem to have no home here."

Oh what a hornet's nest that letter stirred up; what correspondence in the *Western Mail* and *South Wales Daily News* extending over some eight weeks. I query much

whether anything of the sort has created an equal sensation in
South Wales since the days of the famous " *Brad y llyfran
gleision*," of 1847, affecting, as it did, the moral character of
the people.

I will give some extracts from writers who took part in this
controversy: the first is from the letter of James Shaw himself, to the London *Times* :—

In this valley from which I write there are about 7,000 people.
Let me at once say that we have no bards, no curious antiquarian
lovers of Welsh traditions, no learned enthusiasts seeking to preserve the continuity of Welsh legends or Cymric philology ; and I
have never heard of or seen these worthies except at Eisteddfods,
where they generally managed to be conspicuous by their eccentri-
city. Our people here have to earn their daily bread. and in
this matter of language are the mere creatures of a custom which
they are not encouraged to throw off, but which they feel to be a
constant disadvantage. The whole population of this valley speaks
Welsh ; but the curious thing is that, although we have 1,600
children at school, not a word of Welsh is taught there. The
children speak Welsh at home, the little which they do read is in
Welsh, and they attend Welsh services on Sunday, They are
doing only what their fathers and grandfathers before them have
done in this valley. Not one of them can speak Welsh grammatically, because they have never been taught it. You may imagine
the difficulties under which such children labour in acquiring the
English education which we give them; in nine cases out of ten
it ends in complete failure. Our children leave the schools at 13
or 14 years of age with the elementary smattering of English
which they have with difficulty been taught, they go into the
collieries or the ironworks, and in four or five years you would
never believe that one of them had ever entered an English school.
A few who are made pupil teachers or clerks in the offices are
the only exceptions. Welshmen are deploring the low state of
intermediate and higher education in Wales : but there can be no

love of education in a people placed so disadvantageously. A people educated in this way are neither able to enjoy the language they speak nor the language they acquire; and until Wales has made its choice it will remain, what I believe it now is, the worst educated nation in Europe. The great mass of the people are at present losing the advantage which a good and sound knowledge of even one language would give them. The result is that they read no literature and devote themselves to music, which is universal, and in which they excel.

Now Shaw overlooked two questions which materially affect a practical judgment on the linguistic state of Wales :—

First—Is the genius of the Welsh people, independently of language, likely to present to the world the Faradays, the Watts, and the Arkwrights, whose absence he called upon them, in his reply to his critics, to mourn? If not, he was making a bugbear that would not stand the strain of careful examination.

Second—Supposing the Welsh are badly educated, whatever proof is there that their language is the cause? I am, however, inclined to think that if the managers of Elementary Schools and their teachers were really well educated (where no Party or Ecclesiastical prejudice came in the way), they would frequently see the importance of introducing Welsh into their classes, and try to do away with at least some part of the reproach thrown out by Jas. Shaw, "A people educated in this way are neither able to enjoy the language they speak nor the language they acquire." There is really far more truth in this statement as applied to many districts in South Wales than has been generally supposed, and so far, we must credit him with good sound sense. He speaks of it being a "curious thing" that there were 1,600 children at school, but not one word of Welsh was taught there, yet appeared scarcely willing to *directly* admit that this was an irrational and harmful thing.

GG

Of course several of the correspondents who replied to his communication recognised the fact that he did not really know Wales, after only two years residence, though it seems very difficult to convince intelligent hard-headed Englishmen, who have only seen one side of the medal, that they haven't seen the obverse. No doubt J. S., after such a short time, had not had time or opportunity to become acquainted with the literary history of Wales and its self-taught men, or to form a fair estimate of the amount of general intelligence and literary ability displayed even in remote parts of the country.

Let the reader note the remark about the mass of the people "losing the advantage which a good and sound knowledge of even one language would give them:" we find this illustrated in South Wales, where a good and sound knowledge of Welsh is more lacking than in North Wales, and where, at the same time, there is a deficiency in attaining a good and sound knowledge of English, which, as mentioned elsewhere, is difficult even to an *English* working man. If Jas. Shaw really believed what he said, why did he not advocate teaching Welsh?

There is, also, some residuum of truth in the accusation that they read no literature, and devote themselves to music, because if elementary education were conducted on more rational principles, instructive English literature would be better appreciated, as well as Welsh, and less time would be wasted on music. How far the remark that they "read no literature" can be accepted as applying generally to Wales, the reader will be able to judge, after reading the subsequent chapter on the Welsh language and literature. Extracts from the correspondence which ensued, follow here:—

"Gwyliedydd" says—

It is a recognized fact that no person can carry on business in

Wales with any success unless he can speak, read, and write
English. All the business men in Wales are keen enough to see
that, and all those self-made men that are to be seen in every
locality are doing their utmost to give English education to their
children. But who can convince them that the old language is not
worth maintaining, and that it is losing ground? Nobody; therefore it would be wise on our part to wait patiently until time
will proclaim the fate of the beautiful old language that has lived
over two thousand years. In connection with Mr. Shaw's remarks
about the children, the truth is that there are few workmen
working under Mr. Shaw that are not able to read, write, and
speak the English language quite as well as many clerks or the
officials, and who were kept in school only until they reached
twelve or thirteen years old. As to the statement "That they
read no literature," the English and Welsh publishers will vouch
to the contrary. Mr Shaw doesn't know that there is an encyclo-
pædia published in Welsh, worth £5 to £6, and that the Welsh
people have a "Gazetteer of the World," another of Wales, that
the "Travels of Dr. Livingstone" has been published in Welsh in
two editions (one a pocket edition and the other a large one), with
thousands of volumes, and no trash scarcely.

"Abergwilian," in the service of the G.W.R. Co., says he
hardly understood one word of English when he went to the
day school, challenges James Shaw to read a few verses in the
Greek Testament with him, and adds:—

I cannot conceive why Englishmen should persist in weighing a
Welshman's general knowledge by the amount of English he may
understand, more than a Welshman, Frenchman, or German should
test his by their languages. Is it not a fact that a Frenchman
can be as efficient in general knowledge as the Englishman that
can only speak one language? Then, if so, neither the English
nor any other one language is a test.

"Bilinguist" says—

Out with such notions as to expect a whole nation to speak

grammatically.   It is sheer nonsense to think of it, at the present
time whatever.   Greater nonsense still to think one of a nation
whom Mr. Dickens says are so very guilty of "exasperating their
h's and murdering their g's" should take the liberty of teaching
another nation their duties, when most likely he has not taken the
trouble of learning the Welsh alphabet yet.

D. E. Lewis says—

That a knowledge of the Welsh language is not only unattended
with any embarrassment in the training of the intellect, but
that it forms a substantial aid –though it be an adventitious
one — to its highest development.   *   *   *   *   A
language is mightier far than any number of books which
may have been written in it :* for such productions, great though
they be, at best embody what was in the hearts and minds of
individual men : but language, on the other hand, is the impress
and life of a nation.   "The Iliad is great, yet not so great in
strength, or power, or beauty as the Greek language."

Beriah G. Evans says—

Mr Shaw is evidently either totally ignorant of, or wilfully
ignores, the fact that there are abundant materials for a work on
"Self-made Welshmen," materials for a work which, in the hands
of a skilful artist, could rival in interest with, and illustrate as
wonderful turns in fortune's wheel, as Smiles's "Self Help."

Herefordiensis [the author of this]—

I will not now enter into details, but express the opinion that
an unprejudiced observer will see that the phenomena presented in
connection with the use of the Welsh language and its deep hold
on the people are not to be explained by reference to love of the
past, however much of that there may be co-existing.   The reason

---

* This is a remark worth remembering, the power of the English
language is not measured by the genius of Milton, but by its adaptability
to express the thoughts and feelings of the people who use it; so with
Welsh.   In fact such a sentiment is the key note of much that the author
of this book has written about the latter.

for these facts lies far deeper, and it will not be elucidated by men
who do not take the trouble to assure themselves of the truth of
their statements, or to view the question beyond the region of
their own limited horizon.

It is singular that none of these answers discussed the
education question, but they did show that there was a much
larger amount of intellectual culture, and more instances of
men who had risen among the Welsh-speaking people than
James Shaw knew of, though they did not admit what
I have called the residuum of truth in some of the facts which
he erroneously supposed to be caused by the language rather
than by a defective system of education, which ignored it.
There is no hint at any remedy to increase the ability of the
people to " enjoy," as well as write the language they acquire.

Again it may be said, that if this bilingualism was really a
drawback, we should not find Welshmen who have become
proficient in reading or writing their language after they have
settled in England, and so often ready to keep it up. For instance, some years ago I knew a Monmouthshire Welshman who
told me that there was more Welsh spoken at Witton Park,
near Stockton-on-Tees, than at Tredegar, and his brother's
family, though born in England, were yet brought up to speak
Welsh. Another Monmouthshire Welshman, who cannot speak
Welsh well, has been some years in London, but when I saw
him last he habitually attended Welsh preaching in that city.
So that speaking Welsh, or listening to Welsh, is sometimes a
matter of choice, in the face of difficulties, and not, as
frequently implied, necessitated by circumstances.

In a long letter, replying to his critics, published in the
Western Mail, 11th mo. (Nov.) 11, 1879, Jas. Shaw gave
back a little of his ground, and said, " It is the deficiency of
a higher intellectual standard above and beyond this [the

culture of the working classes], without disparaging the intelligence of the Welsh masses, which I, in common with others, deplore."

Now here he much more nearly hit the nail on the head, but, as elsewhere stated, Wales is only just begining to have an important "middle-class," and consequently any considerable call for "higher education;" yet even now, when the future professional men of the principality are brought up in middle-class schools, in ignorance of the grammatical structure or power of the language, which many of them are familiar with colloquially, is it to be wondered at that a large proportion of them should either grow up wanting in habits of precision and exact thought, or else separated by an impassable chasm of language from freely participating in the intellectual life of the nation.

The main point lies not in the existence of the language, but in an educational system conducted generation after generation after English models, to satisfy an artificial standard not really adapted to national requirements.

So long as Wales is without a national University this is likely more or less to continue, and so long as it does, *Education*, in the mind of an average Welshman, will too much mean, not simply mental cultivation abreast of the civilization of the Nineteenth century, but ability to compete with Englishmen on the ground chosen by English judges, to wit, directly or indirectly the governing bodies of English or Scotch Universities.

For instance, if thirteen Englishmen compete with thirteen Welshmen for prizes or scholarships at Aberystwith College, and each of the former is ahead of each of the latter (*i.e.* Welsh-speaking youths) it does not necessarily follow that either of the English are better educated, or possess more ability than any one of the Welshmen, though there is a certain amount of presumption, even considering the present state of intermediate education, that it would be so. But if there were thrown into the scales a paper testing ability in Welsh composition, or translation from English into Welsh, and the Englishmen still excelled, there would be little room to doubt that they were both more highly educated and were mentally more capable than their competitors.

No one really desirous of the welfare of Wales will cry "Wales for the Welsh," but it is quite another thing to materially modify the curriculum of Colleges, so as to make room for what would be found a good mental exercise, though it might be of no more *direct* benefit than the making of "hexers" and "pens," so much in vogue not many years ago, and doubtless still practised in various classical schools or colleges.

Few persons will be found who would wish generally to exclude those of English birth from the benefit of the scholar-ships offered at Welsh University Colleges, but let the test of merit for the possession of the scholarship stand on a broader and more liberal basis, and provide in a much larger number of such examinations than is the case at present for the exercise of ability, *both* in translating from Welsh into good, pure and idiomatic English, and from English into good, pure idiomatic Welsh.

Let us see for a moment, from their Syllabus for Scholar-ships, what Welsh Colleges are doing with the funds at their disposal.

ABERYSTWITH, in Sessions 1891-92, offers ten Open and five Closed Scholarships or Exhibitions to new comers. In competing for these a candidate must choose three elementary subjects (out of fourteen), and two advanced subjects—one of the latter *may* be Welsh.

The Cynddelw Scholarship is not included in the above list,

and will be competed for in the Autumn of 1892 : it *necessitates*, among other things, the production of a Welsh Essay, a knowledge of systematic Welsh Grammar, and of the History of Welsh literature.   This is a scholarship provided for by the Cynddelw Memorial Fund.

BANGOR offers nine General Scholarships and Exhibitions, besides special ones for Technical and Agricultural candidates, Teachers, and girls.   For all the Entrance Scholarship examinations candidates may chose Welsh as one out of a maximum of five subjects.

CARDIFF offers twenty-three Entrance Scholarships and Exhibitions, besides five Exhibitions for intending Teachers. In these Welsh is an *optional* subject in the more elementary part of the examinations, but an English Essay paper is *necessary*.   The D. I. Davies Scholarship for proficiency in Welsh is in reality a prize of £12 offered annually on the results of the Sessional Examination.

Now a little reflection will show that these scholarships and examinations may be tests of the preparedness of the candidates to enter on the prescribed courses of study for the different examinations preparatory to London degrees, but they are not tests either of education in the abstract or of comparative ability, *i.e.*, they are not tests of units of intellectual development or of intellectual strength.   It is impossible, in fact, they should be absolutely so, but if a knowledge of both Welsh and English were presupposed in *all* candidates as the basis of examination, they would be efficient in that direction to a larger extent than at present.

The *optional* use of Welsh probably counts for little in the case of Welsh-speaking candidates, because the course of their previous education at school has left them unacquainted with its use in those phrases and turns of expression which help to make up a successful examination, and their memory on the subjects chosen has been chiefly exercised in English, while in addition to this they have had to spend a certain number of hours of their short life in acquiring the English which they thus practically need as a medium of communication in the course of the examination, as well as in that very important subject—"English" itself, which is provided for in most preparatory courses.

Now it may be impracticable to put the English and Welsh candidates for exhibitions at these Welsh Colleges on equal terms; there must be a slight advantage given to the foreigner, or the monoglot Anglo-Welshman, but it can be minimized by requiring from all candidates a knowledge both of English grammar and composition, *also* of Welsh grammar and composition. At present both subjects are nominally *optional*, and in reality English grammar and composition are needed, as I have just remarked, for the execution of an answer; but Welsh grammar and composition are not needed, and probably only a few even of the very Welshy candidates come prepared to face an examination in the latter. What is required is not to make them both wanted equally, but to make WELSH WANTED A LITTLE BY ALL, and much by some if they choose. Were this system carried out, there should be no grumbling if all the scholarships fell to Englishmen; no cry of Wales for the Welsh; no "exclusive patriotism,"* rather let the strangers take away all our scholarships if they can, but in the act of allowing this, let us by an act of "inclusive patriotism" brand them as, in some small degree at least, naturalized, and able to play their part as men of Wales, understanding the country, and forming a part of the Welsh unity.

It is very easy to say, "require from all candidates for

---

* The *Western Mail* recently said of the *South Wales Star* that it was more in touch with the exclusive patriotism of the Welsh people than the ordinary English papers.

exhibitions at Welsh Colleges a knowledge of &c., &c.," but
every one who knows the A B C of these things is quite well
aware such an independent course would be in a high degree
both impractical and impossible for either of these Colleges
now to adopt.

But the future, what of that? It largely depends upon the
constitution of the new Welsh University, which will probably
be shortly an accomplished fact, and upon the temper of its
governing body.

If that governing body were to say : We think it expedient
that a slight knowledge of the grammatical structure of the
Welsh language, its idioms and its vocabulary should be the
common property of all persons receiving an advanced national
education, irrespective both of sect or party, and with that
view we require all candidates at our matriculation examinations to be prepared with an elementary knowledge of Welsh—
even if nothing further was said on the subject in the legal,
medical, or science courses, such a resolution would go further
to revolutionize education in Wales from tip to toe as regards
its attitude to the language than years of agitation or yards of
speeches could do in the ordinary way.

What would be the effect of such an apparently trifling
measure ? In the first place, probably, a good deal of grumbling,
snorting, and growling in the newspapers and other mediums
of publicity : in the second place, middle-class schools and
County Council Intermediate schools (if in existence) would
turn right-about-face, call for Welsh grammars and reading
books, and coach up their pupils to sufficient proficiency in
Welsh to meet the standard ; besides which Normal Colleges
would find it suit their purpose to introduce Welsh in the
education of would-be teachers preparing for University examinations.

What would be the ultimate results ? Simply this, that no

professional man with a Welsh University degree would be quite ignorant of the language, and inferentially such would in general be more in sympathy with the people that speak it; many more elementary teachers would have had systematic training in it, and be consequently prepared to frame the education of their more advanced pupils for the intermediate schools. There would be these results and many more besides. The whole nation would then be unified as never before in the last three hundred years.

Be it observed that I do not advocate any very large expenditure of time to be spent by youths of average intelligence in attaining the Welsh standard for their entrance examination, tests of superior efficiency might be made optional further on, but I am sure that many in after life, even if they went no further in the study, would be glad they had an initiation in it. Another point of supposed advantage which has been insisted on by a late writer to the *Baner*, is that Welsh would specialize the University training, and thus indirectly give a greater value to a degree.

The following is a specimen of the kind of opposition called forth by this movement for a Welsh University. It is a "*Welsh Rector*" pouring his grief into the ear of the Editor of the *Western Mail*, who had enough worldly wisdom to drop no comments :—

Dissenting youths of the lower and lower-middle classes would be attracted thitherwards, as is the case at present with Aberystwith and Cardiff, while the upper middle and more cultured would seek their degrees elsewhere, from centres free from the taint of vulgarity and political sectarianism. Call it what you like, it will soon drift into the most sectarian Dissenting seminary.

As he is entrusted with the "cure" of souls, or rather believes he is, we could advise him, and such as he, if at any

time they feel disposed to sniffle about the precincts of the
Colleges in search of the "taint of vulgarity," to fortify themselves with the quintessence of Eau de Cologne, or Eau de Lampeter, lest they should unconsciously carry any infection home
to the flock.

Having thus disposed of the subject of Welsh in relation to
the social and educational life of the country, we will now enter
on some consideration of the study of the language itself,
and the character of its literature.

CHAPTER VII.

IT is not an uncommon thing for English boys and girls
entering, for the first time, upon the study of German to
find that it has a strange fascination for them. There is
something in German which seems to call forth a deeper
response from the inner nature than French, and the young
student traces with delight the words conveying homely ideas,
which are nearly alike in both languages, and feels as he pro-
gresses, as if there was an element cramped in his mother
tongue, which he unexpectedly finds has shot up into a luxuriant
and vigorous growth in German, so that on the whole it commands more enthusiasm both in school and college, than does
any classical or modern language commonly studied there.

So much for the language of the great Empire of Central
Europe, but what if I affirm about Welsh that it too has the
power of awakening the sympathies and the enthusiasm of a
large number of English students in an equal and, perhaps, in
a much greater degree than German? True, it does not open
out so much pleasure as does the latter in the exhibition of
such close relations between many familiar household words,
but then there is the response from the inner nature which is
called forth by the sound of the words themselves, the con-

struction of the sentences, and the general rhythm of the language.

Are Englishmen susceptible to the impressions from these sources, which so mightily stir the minds of many Welshmen?

I believe a large number, especially of those living in the western half of England are, and that on the other hand there are a number more, especially those living in the eastern half, who would regard them with indifference, even if they would not positively nauseate under them; and I further believe that were the practical test of ability in learning Welsh applied under equal conditions to a representative collection of youths from the western half, and to another from the eastern half, that the palm for facility in acquiring it would have to be given undoubtedly to the western-half youths. That is to say, youths from Cumberland would beat those from Lincoln, and youths from Devonshire those from Sussex.

Whether or not this theory is perfectly worthless, remains for my readers who are competent to do so, to judge. It is, however, given here under the belief that there is a foundation for it in the facts. Another deduction therefrom is quite clear, viz., that if Welsh were taught to the English-speaking youth of Wales, it would in general be much more readily acquired than in many parts of England.

In any case, it is a fact that there is a considerable inclination on the part of many of the better-educated English-speaking inhabitants of Wales to learn Welsh, which is partly evidenced by the readiness with which a little book of phrases, &c., with the misleading title,* "How to learn Welsh," has sold, if I may judge from the information given from W. II.

---

* I say misleading, because the contents consist of little else than phrases and the meanings of words.

Smith's bookstall at Newport, and by other symptoms of interest.

There are four reasons for this inclination :—

I. The wish to mix on equal terms with those who know both languages, sometimes for business reasons, sometimes for curiosity or social reasons, and to understand better the phenomena of their daily life.

II. The inner penchant alluded to.

III. For the sake of philological and archæological investigations.

IV. For the sake of reading the literature.

However, whatever inducements it may offer, the study of Welsh can naturally be considered from two chief standpoints :—

First—That of the philologist, the archæologist, and the pure *littérateur*, the bookworm or the university man.

Secondly—As a living language spoken in the Nineteenth century, and as part of the social and intellectual life of the 900,000 or 1,000,000 who habitually use it, or listen to it from the lips of preachers.

In this chapter I purpose to consider the language and its literature chiefly from the latter standpoint, viz., that of everyday life, or rather as it concerns the many and not the few.

This study has not yet found its level at Oxford and Cambridge, nor in the examinations of London University. The time, however, is coming when it will do so, and this is a fact perhaps generally recognized. Its future as a scientific study may safely be left in the hands of Professor Rhys, and others who shall follow him.

What is not so generally recognized, is that it may still find a level in Wales itself, side by side with English in almost every department of national life, and it is with a view to facilitate such a result, or rather to arouse Welshmen to

consider what is involved in it, that the writer has chiefly
been inclined to enter on this work.

Now, as this book will probably fall into the hands of some
who are only English-speaking, they may wish to be told the
best method of procedure in learning Welsh.   Bearing in
mind the very different degrees of previous culture, age and
stamp of mind which form factors in the case, it is impossible
to give any general rule which will best apply to all would-be,
self-taught students.

The first step in almost any case, is to get the key to the
pronunciation and accent ; though anything like perfection in
these respects would require years of practice, to a person
reared in the heart of England, at the same time I do not
know that the difficulties are in themselves any greater than
in French pronunciation.   For a foreigner (a Londoner, for
instance) a passable facility is not nearly so difficult to attain
as is generally imagined ; if, for instance, the student reads the
directions in his grammar, and then gets some acquaintance to
read a few verses in the Testament, or some stanzas of poetry ;
if he really has an ear for the language, two or three hours
divided into small periods for every occasion will set him on
his legs, and he will have a better foundation to go forward
on, than the German I heard of at Aberystwith some years
ago, who attempted to speak to the people there the Welsh
he had learnt in Germany, but was a " barbarian" unto them.

The next step, if he has had previous experience in learning
languages, would be to go roughly and quickly through a
grammar, say Spurrell's, published at Carmarthen, learning off
most of the prepositions and other particles by heart, but not
attempting to burden his memory with much besides, and
then thoroughly to go through the grammar a second time carefully noting the inflections and verbal constructions, while at
the same time using daily, say for fifteen minutes only, a

bilingual book, or the English and Welsh Testaments used together, which will increase his vocabulary without wasting his time searching a dictionary, and he will find that in such a course many difficulties gradually vanish, and a familiarity with the language is induced.   I would also recommend him to supplement this by committing to memory some stanzas of poetry, even if he is not able entirely to translate them; such a simple piece for instance as Mynyddog's "Gwelais Johnny bach yn myn'd i'r ysgol." This will tend to initiate him into the genius of the language perhaps as much as any means at his disposal.

To still further increase his vocabulary he must resort to considerable dictionary work in translating, say from periodicals such as *Y Traethodydd*, or *Y Geninen*, or *Cymru*.   A further advance still will be made when the student is able to read the *Cywyddau* and *Englynion* of modern poets, to say nothing of ancient ones, which many Welshmen themselves find beyond them.   I mention these two metres, because in them, as well as in others governed by the laws of *Cynghanedd*,* he will find a larger proportion of uncommon words than in works in the free metres.

To attain a more thorough grammatical knowledge, especially of Welsh syntax, there is not a better work to be had than Rowlands' Welsh Grammar, supplemented by a volume of Exercises by the same author, which will assist in *speaking* and writing the language, though not abrogate the necessity of *practice* in order to a colloquial use of it.

To quite a young person, and one who is unacquainted with a foreign tongue, I would recommend "Welsh as a specific subject," Stages I. and II.† Stage III. is not published, but may be, soon after this book is in my readers' hands.

---

* *Cynghanedd* generally involves alliteration. It is a term not easily Englished.   † Simpkin, Marshall and Co., London, 6d. each.

II

The initial mutations, or changes of some of the initial
consonants, under certain conditions, doubtless have frightened
some people who have commenced the study of the language ;
in reality, however, this is a far less obstacle when properly
encountered than may be supposed, so far as reading the
language is concerned, though it is a more difficult matter
to obtain absolute correctness in writing and speaking it.

Before quite leaving the question of grammars, our ideal
student will, after learning to read the language, find it worth
while to look at one of the various grammars written in Welsh,
such as "*Gramadeg Hwr Tegai;*"* or "*Gramadeg Caledfryn;*"
not that there is much philological science to be gleaned from
them, but they sometimes touch on various matters such as
the rules of poetry and prose, not strictly belonging to an
English-Welsh grammar, and therefore may not improbably be
intended for the use of country people and others who wish
to compete in literary meetings with compositions of their own.

The number of native Welsh Grammars is a singular feature
in the modern literature of Wales. A vernacular writer in
Yr Adolygydd† has commented on it, and I take the liberty of
freely translating an extract from his article.

We should recollect that we cannot on every occasion draw
comparisons between the Welsh and the English. We have no
Royal, princely, nor aristocratic families among us to influence
our customs. The few rich ones who live in the country are
strangers to the people as regards language, and foreigners in
respect of religion. We do not possess such an extensive and
wealthy middle-class as exists in England, but we are, as a nation,
composed of farmers, small shopkeepers, and working men. Under
these circumstances it is clear that the influences which govern
the mass must arise from themselves. This truth appears more
clear, when we recollect that the preachers of Wales spring from

---

* Published by Humphreys, Carnarvon.   † Cyf. ii. 176.

the ranks, and that the priests who belong to the moneyed class have but little influence on their fellow countrymen. Perhaps the history of the world does not present a parallel case. When the nation saw that the *boneddigion** were forgetting and despising their language, they devoted themselves to its culture. When they saw that their shepherds only cared for the flock on shearing day they chose for themselves teachers. When they understood that there was no longer any vision in the old mass houses (*cyssegroedd*) they stirred themselves to build new worship houses, and they can listen complacently to the Bishop of Llandaff† recounting their success. "The priest of Glyn Taff took me," said he, "to a place at the side of his house where eleven chapels could be seen, and only one church." Many another priest, besides an old renegade from the Nonconformists, could have done the same thing with the Bishop.

The Welsh were obliged to do this, or sink into barbarism. After all care about them, either from the Government or the higher classes had ceased, they were obliged to care for themselves, or to die of neglect. The Irishman resolved to die ? linguistically , the Welshman resolved to live, and the different effects of the two conclusions are easily to be seen in the present condition of the two nations. The Welshman threw himself on God and himself, and the consequence is that the nation, as a nation, is moral, intelligent, and religious. A proof of the truth of what we have been saying is the great number of Grammars that are continually being published, and a remarkable fact is, that some of them are composed by persons who only enjoyed but few literary advantages. Having studied their language themselves, they present the fruit of their labours to the care and notice of their fellow countrymen, and although some of the teachers of the people frown on things like this, yet we gather from them an unshaken assurance that the Welsh will not allow themselves to be uneducated.

Perhaps it will not be out of place for the writer to give

---

* Gentlemen.　　　† (?) Bishop Oliphant.

some outlines of his personal experience with regard to learning Welsh. I was, perhaps, nine years of age when a warm attachment sprang up in my mind towards Wales, kindled by what cause I scarcely know, unless by some small portion of Gray's fine poem, "The Bard," given in "Little Arthur's History of England." Some of my readers may be familiar with the opening stanza, addressed by the bard to Edward I.—

> Ruin seize thee, ruthless King,
> Confusion on thy banners wait.
> Though fanned by conquest's crimson wing,
> They mock the air in idle state ;
> Helm nor Hauberk's twisted mail.
> Nor e'en thy virtues, tyrant, shall avail
> To save thy soul from mighty fears,
> From Cambria's curse, from Cambria's tears.

It was not, however, till years after that I read the whole poem, one of the finest lyrics in the English language, and had the allusions explained.

This attachment was perhaps the more singular as one of my early governesses, although belonging to an old North Welsh family, and a descendant of Owain Glyndwr, was English by education, an Episcopalian by religion, and antagonistic or indifferent to anything distinctively Welsh, nor was there anything in family connections or bias that appeared likely to incline any member of it to "eat the leek." I had, however, heard my father mention in company that he should like to know Welsh, mainly, I suppose, for conversational purposes.

When about twelve years of age I had the enjoyment of visiting Welsh-Wales, and carried home a trophy in the shape of a copy of "*Yr Herald Cymraeg*," without, of course, being able to read it, and recollect, moreover, how astonished I felt, being told at one of the Cambrian Railway Company's stations, that the Welsh still called themselves *Cymry*. These then, I thought to myself, are the identical people that allied themselves to the Teutons, and sacked Rome under Brennus, 490 B.C., an event which had been well impressed on my mind by means of a "Child's History of Rome," and how extraordinary that nearly the same name should have been preserved!

Two or three more years passed, and I accompanied my father to a Friends' Quarterly Meeting, at Neath. One of the *notabilia* of the visit was seeing a Welsh notice in some neighbouring grounds headed *Rhybudd;* on returning to school, at York, I took the liberty to write *Rhybudd* on a notice pasted upon one of the school doors, an act which, as might be expected, met with scorn. However, on returning from Neath, by the Neath and Brecon line, and hearing Welsh spoken in the carriage, I secretly made up my mind to learn it, being of a contrary mind to a certain English tradesman of my acquaintance, who almost felt himself insulted by some people speaking Welsh at Gloucester Station. Think what a "positive nuisance" it is to an Englishman to be in the company of persons whose speech he doesn't understand!

The course of education I was then pursuing did not leave me leisure to commence Welsh, but during the next vacation I bought dictionaries, and in the course of the subsequent half-year wrote to the Professor of Welsh, at Lampeter, to ask his advice as to books for reading. I think he recommended a bilingual booklet, published by the "S.P.C.K.," also *Y Cyfaill Eglwysig*, and as an advanced book, "*Drych y Prif oesoedd*," and he added that he should be glad to hear from me again.

It came to the knowledge of the headmaster that I

had been so impertinent as to venture to trouble such a person to spend his time writing to a boy like myself, and consequently I had to stand a reproof, though I suspect he somewhat chuckled at the idea, but I have no doubt that the Professor was really pleased to be called on to give the information, and that he would not have taken it amiss had I reported myself to him after he became Bishop of "St." Asaph.

After leaving school came a time of leisure, in which Spurrell's grammar and the Welsh-English Testament were my frequent companions, supplemented at first by the S.P.C.K. book alluded to, and, I think, a simple biography of Dafydd Lloyd, a cottager, in Welsh and English, with a number of the *Cyfaill Eglwysig*, followed by *Caneuon Mynyddog*. For pronunciation I had about ten days in Wales, in the month called "August," followed by a similar period in "October," during which I found myself for once at least a member of a Welsh "Sunday School" class, and got the old Town Crier of Aberystwith to read Glan Geirionydd's "Morfa Rhuddlan," which convinced me that there were certain poetic possibilities in the language which are beyond the reach of English. It was not long before I committed the whole of that remarkable piece to memory, and although it is too much at variance with Quaker peace principles to afford the same pleasure as formerly, some further notice is given of the poem a few pages further on.

During the winter succeeding, and for some years after, the requirements of business and other considerations, rendered it advisable to pretty much shelve this attractive study, in which, to the present day, I am far from attaining any high degree of proficiency. To intending students I would, however, say that two things will very much conduce to attaining a mastery of the language when its colloquial use is not easy : first, the committal of short pieces of poetry to memory, which familiarize the mind with the genius and rhythm of the language: second, the practice of turning English into Welsh mentally, by means say of first rendering a verse in the Testament into any sort of Welsh that comes to the mind, and then referring to the correct version.

There is one very striking line of difference between English and Welsh, and one which is very inadequately noticed either by Welshmen or Englishmen. For several centuries English has lost (or nearly lost) the power of forming new words from roots contained in the original Anglo-Saxon stock, and has been obliged to borrow a very large proportion of words expressing abstract ideas, as well as nearly all scientific terms, directly or indirectly, from Greek or Latin sources.

In considering this we must bear in mind that up to within a comparatively late period of the middle ages English was the language of serfs, and not that of culture, although it must have been all along the vernacular of a great majority of the nation. Now the result of all this appears to have been a sort of unconscious mental compromise—when French could no longer be sustained, the writers of the transition period gradually learned to take English as their base language, and to modify, as well as amplify it, first by the introduction of many Norman-French words, and afterwards by words direct from the Latin. I am aware that the latter movement had effect chiefly in Henry VIII.'s time, and subsequently, but believe it to be explained by the Norman-French influence having so effectually nipped the growth of " English undefiled," that it came most natural to subsequent writers to recur to draw their materials for the expression of new ideas from classical ground.

Perhaps the most popular book of the day, in the latter end of the Fourteenth century, and during the first half of the Fifteenth, was Sir John Mandeville's Travels, written by a Hertfordshire man. He did not, however, choose English for his first medium of publicity, the book was written in French (about 1370), and afterwards translated into English, just as Stanley's Travels might be first published in English to secure the larger and more influential circle of readers, afterwards in Welsh to make the information it contained more completely general.

Now, if English had been the sole language of the nation for two hundred years, I don't think the writers of the Sixteenth century would have dared to introduce so many words of foreign origin, any more than Luther and his coadjutors did in Germany during the same period. As the matter stands, it would be a simple piece of affectation now for any English writer to attempt to substitute for them those expressions, which we are well warranted in supposing the genius of the Anglo-Saxon language would have developed, if left to itself. It is rather the fashion to extol the purity of a writer or speaker's diction, while ascribing his influence to the use of Saxon terms, but such statements, when examined, have but little worth, except as comparisons between one writer or speaker and another. It is a simple fact that a man cannot express himself now in English concisely, or in an effective style, he can neither generalize nor specialize, without freely drawing into use words originating from extraneous sources. The day for an Anglo-Saxon development has in reality long ago passed, but at the same time a heavy, artificial, Johnsonian style is as repugnant to an ordinary Englishman as one from which classical words were excluded, would be either pointless or obscure.

Now, in Wales the case stands differently; Norman-French influence made itself strongly felt there, and tinctured the vocabulary of the time, especially with military terms, but it is doubtful if it ever was so much the language of the ruling classes as in England, and consequently its traces on the

Welsh of to-day are much fainter than correspondingly in English.

When we come to words, the occasion for the use of which has arisen in modern times, the difference is still more striking: instead of the continual influx of foreign synonyms, there is a continued tendency in Welsh to draw upon its own stores. I call it a tendency because it has only partially had effect, on account of the oft-mentioned condition of secular education. Of course English words have become incorporated in Welsh, some of them during the period under notice, say 1500, to the present time, most of them previously, but considering the peculiar circumstances in which Welsh has been placed, they are far fewer than might have been expected. In addition to these there are a large number of foreign words knocking at the door for permanent incorporation in the language—words frequently used in conversation, and by writers, who do not profess an elevated style or pure diction, and which so far have knocked in vain, because they have rivals bred and born on the soil used by the most gifted pens of the nation, and which refuse to die. If only the literary cultivation of the language, nay, if only reading aloud in Welsh, and Welsh grammar are introduced into schools, these rivals will not merely live, but they will flourish, and lift their heads above the foreigners, who may not die, it is true, but have a more circumscribed existence.

It is this fact of a vocabulary adapted to the civilization of the Nineteenth century being to a large extent self-contained in his language which helps a Welshman the more easily to attain a certain standard of literary culture than an Englishman *ceteris paribus*, (which they are not), and this, be it remembered, constitutes in itself a powerful argument for introducing the language into a system of Welsh national education.

KK

What idea does the word *Electricity* convey to an English child? Absolutely nothing until, perhaps, he is a grown lad, when he learns that it has something to do with the telegraph wires, even then he may not be quite sure whether or no a lost umbrella can be sent by telegraph.   He knows nothing of *amber*, and still less that *elektron* was a Greek word referring to the properties of amber.   Now, *Trydaniaeth*, to the Welsh child is not an empirical collection of sounds, like electricity is to the English one; true it does not convey in itself a knowledge of the nature of electricity (and who knows that?), but it puts him in the track at once, and in grasping the idea of electricity, so far as communicable, he has a less distance to go than his English brother.

Look then at *astronomy*, here is another empirical word, expressive enough when it is understood, but quite foreign in its radical components, to English home life ; the Welsh have a ready key to it in SERYDDIAETH ; so with DAEARYDDIAETH for *geography*.   Take *science* again, how many vague phases of meaning are attached to that word in the mind of an English middle-class boy before he arrives at the general and popular acceptation of the term.   The Welsh boy may have some difficulty, but far less of its kind when he hears of GWYDDOR.

Now, how does a Welsh schoolmaster deal with words like this.   He is supposed to e-duc-ate, lead out the mind in the shortest possible time and most efficient manner, with reference to the requirements of after life ; yet he does one of two things, either he absolutely ignores the Welsh terms, and confines himself to the empirical, hardly understood English ones if he has occasion to use any, or else he limits the use of Welsh ones entirely to word of mouth explanations, in the same way as if Welsh were a sacred language, as in the days of the Druids, to be spoken but not written, and NOT to be brought before their pupils by the evidence of the eye as well as the ear.

The Department would doubtless have altered this long ago but for two things, viz., ignorance, and a *fear* that if such a course were pursued the children would be LEARNING WELSH.

This feature of the adaptability of the language to education is remarkably little noticed by native writers, and many intelligent Welshmen of the present day seem scarcely alive to its existence, but the author of " Echoes from the Welsh Hills " has a few lines to the point.   An extract from that work is given in the appendix.

Much is said in Wales about the importance of teaching English, but I suspect that, while there is no controversy about the great importance of it, many who enunciate those platitudes are unaware how imperfectly the working and lower middle-classes in England are acquainted with their own language, far more imperfectly probably than the corresponding classes in Germany, where the difference between the literary and spoken language is less than in England. Of course English must be taught, but the generality of such advisers do not realize on the one hand, how difficult it is to teach English thoroughly, even where Welsh has long been extinct, nor how powerful an adjunct to education Welsh may be made.

One of the excellencies of Welsh consists in the number and force of the plural terminations which are in some degree classified according to the nature of idea expressed in the words.   For instance, the plural of names of animals and birds generally ends in *od*, those of abstract nouns in *au*, trees and some natural objects in *i*, plurals and objects conveying an idea of immensity or vastness or power most frequently end in *oedd*, which is in itself a more powerful plural termination

than any found in English; there are other terminations,
such as *ion* and *ydd*, besides the modification of the vowel,
which sometimes takes place.

It is a popular delusion to suppose that Welsh is a language
abounding in consonantal sounds. In fact, it is said to be
less so than English, but its peculiar strength and expressive-
ness is in part the result of its possessing three sounds not
found in English, viz., those represented by the signs *ch, ll, rh*,
to which might perhaps be added *ng*, which is slightly more
nasal than in English, and in part owing to the long vowel
sounds being longer than with us—prominent among these is the
a sound in *cast*. There are, it is true, some features in the syntax
which detract from conciseness, such as the construction of
dependent verbal clauses, and the reduplication of personal
and possessive pronouns, but on the other hand the language
gains in its appositional power.

The question is sometimes asked, "What is the use of
learning Welsh? It has no literature, and everyone can speak
English." I will not now attempt to discuss the practical
utility of the subject, but shall endeavour within a short compass to give a general view of the extent of Welsh poetical
literature in the past, followed by notices of some of the chief
bards of the Nineteenth century, after which will come some
reference first to Welsh prose and the literature of Wales not
strictly Welsh, secondly, to periodical and fugitive literature.
This is necessarily a partial method of treatment, when the
matter might well be expanded into a good sized book;
under the circumstances, however, I do not know of a better.

There is one thing, that a study of the Welsh language and
its current literature does for a stranger, it opens his eyes to
the existence of a little world which he has previously known
only by report. I have already alluded to this, and to the
fact that a mere residence in the country is not sufficient

to understand it; this will hold good so long as the
Welsh language forms an integral part of the social life,
and is the "natural exponent" of the religious convictions
of any considerable proportion of its population, or even
so long as its literature becomes an influential factor in
their life, although in many other respects such individuals
may appear to be Anglicized. I think this explains
the anxiety of many servants of what is usually called
"the Church" to substitute an English monolingual for a
bilingual condition of the country, on account of the fact that
their chief support arises from a monolingual minority, backed
up by prestige, who pull one way, while the *gwerin* (the
commonalty) pulls the other.

There are others of them who much doubt if this is the
correct course to pursue. Certainly the English Government
has proved that it does so, by its recent Episcopal appointments. Whether, however, that policy will be allowed so far
to prevail as to permit the National Schools to become
centres for the spread of the bilingual idea, or whether any
disposition to yield in this direction is simply a sop for
Cerberus, which will be snatched away as soon as he shews a
disposition not to bark, remains to be seen by the generation
that is just coming on the scene of action.

Of course my remark about Anglicized persons, not really
knowing the country, applies all round, without distinction of
rank or party, and is true both with respect to the industrial
districts of Glamorganshire as well as the retired valleys of
North ; of any John Smith, of Tre'r Estron, as well as of the
inheritor of the estate and twentieth descendant in the direct
line of some Hywel ap Gwyddno ap Elidr fras, who cannot converse in the home language of his tenants, much less read the
odes in praise of his ancestors.

Another thing which strikes a stranger is the amount of

contradictory testimony offered by Welshmen themselves as to the extent and calibre of the native literature.   Compare the following :—

WELSHMEN'S TESTIMONY.

One need only read the Welsh publications to be con-convinced of the non-utility of the language for any practical purpose whatever. – *Incumbent of Trevethin*, p. 97.

ENGLISHMEN'S TESTIMONY.

I come to the conclusion that the English language cannot answer the same purpose as the national language, and that the preservation of Welsh is the only hope for the Welsh nation to develop itself on its own lines.* — *T. Darlington, M.A., Iaith a Chenedlaetholdeb.*

The Welsh language has no valuable writings, either in prose or poetry. — *Rector of Llanhil-leth*, p. 96.

He [Geo. Borrow] considered that even the writings of Huw Morris and Goronwy Owain alone were quite sufficient to repay anyone for the study of the Welsh language. — *Verbal expression of G. B.; quoted by the Vicar of Ruabon, in 1885.*

The testimonies of the two Welshmen are samples of what may be met with in our midst, though fear operates to keep such uninformed views from finding much public vent, while on the other hand we may add those of two more, and "*pob un yn llym gyfreithiwr.*"

He read more Welsh now than he had ever done before in the whole course of his life. He supposed he might consider himself as having arrived at years of discretion—at all events, he had reached that time of life when people were able to judge some-what of the literary character of an essay or the beauty of a poem, and all he could say was that when he turned back, not only to

* T. Darlington has learnt Welsh, and I translate from an address of his in that language.

the old Welsh poems, but to some of the later ones, he found them
the most beautiful things he had ever read in any language in his
life. There were Welsh poets now who wrote most lovely things,
and if they could only get them published, they would have the
effect of elevating men's minds.—*Report of Speech by Judge Gwilym
Williams, 9th mo., 1891.*

The surpassing loveliness of the Celtic language, and the inesti-
mable value of the literature of the Cymry, were revealing themselves to the very people who not long since treated the one with
supercilious irreverence, and the other with unmeasured contempt.

* he contended that their poetry generally contained a
subtle refinement of expression wedded to beautiful thought. -
T. Marchant Williams, in 1888.

I will assume that the depreciators of Welsh literature are
qualified to speak ; that being the case, and they are not few
in number, it is evident that doctors disagree, and the student
must decide for himself as to the value of their allegations.

At the outset, I would advise him to broadly distinguish
between language and literature. Quite true, the difference is
self-evident, but let it be also known that the value of a
language does not necessarily depend upon the literature
preserved in that language either as respects quantity or
quality.

It is possible that a language may be wanting in precision
and powers of expression, that is to say, of course, that it
possesses radical deficiencies as an instrument for the communication of ideas and mental impressions, but at the same
time it may possess a valuable literature. Another language
may have a most meagre literature, and yet be one of the most
perfect exponents in existence of the language of the human
mind in a state of civilization. It is a mistake to assume that
for any but colloquial purposes a language should be studied
mainly on account of its literature. In some cases this is true,

in others, and Welsh is notably an exception to such a rule,
however extensive the literature may be, the power possessed
by the language *per se*, is in itself a means of mental development, which might in the abstract justify the study of it.

Dismissing for a time this matter of language *per se*, we will
suppose the idea student to have climbed to the top of the
hill of difficulty in the way of acquiring a passable facility in
reading modern Welsh, what is the nature of the prospect
before him ?

The remains of the oldest poets, whose works are extant, are
supposed to date back to not long after the time when the
Roman forces were withdrawn from our island, but it is not
till the Eleventh century that we have any indication of a
considerable body of native literature existing.

From that time down to the accession of Henry VII., the
names of a large number of writers are handed down, some of
their works have been printed, but many more are lying in
manuscript, either at the British Museum or in private
libraries.   The works of very few poets up to the Seventeenth
century have been printed in a separate form.   One exception
is in the case of Lewis Glyn Cothi, a writer during the wars of
the Roses: a considerable body of mediæval poetry exists in
the *Myfyrian Archæology*, published by T. Gee, Denbigh, and
in *Gorchestion y Beirdd*, by Humphreys, Carnarvon.

The chief interest of by far the larger portion of these is
antiquarian, from their throwing light on the character of the
times in which they lived, incidentally rather than otherwise, as
much of the matter is taken up with the praise of the princes
or chiefs who patronized them, or with the recital of of deeds
of arms.

One of them, Dafydd ap Gwilym, stands out pre-eminently
as an amatory poet, as well as in descriptions of nature, and
is still considered to hold the chief rank in that and succeed-

ing ages. He was one of the earliest writers who conformed to the laws of *cynghanedd*.

Few people have any idea of the immense amount of manuscript literature which must be existing in Wales, the production of which is largely fostered by the Eisteddfod system. A few of the poems and essays are published, and a large number are consigned to oblivion, not always because they have no merit, but because the writers have not the means, or the desire to risk loss by publication.

Poems written in the twenty-four measures, such as the *Odlau*, for which chair prizes are awarded, are more difficult for the general public to read without a certain amount of training and a facility in the literary language which many Welshmen, especially in South Wales, are deficient in. I believe this to be one reason why so many compositions are allowed by their authors to lie dormant.

In the poetic department of literature it is surprising at a first glance, out of such a large number of volumes and booklets published during the present century, how small a proportion is now accessible to the public. This is mainly due to reasons which I will refer to further on. Notwithstanding these deductions the body of printed poetry which remains is quite considerable for the size of the country.

"Wrtydyn" is publishing, in *Y Geninen*, a complete list, so far as known, of all Welsh poetical publications printed since the commencement of the century to the present time; it is unfinished,* but I gather that the total number of works is likely to prove not less than 1,000. Some few of these are reprints, but the great majority are original publications.

Much that has been published is of a character so different, both in manner and in form, to what we find in English, that

---

* The editor seems to set slight store by this valuable list, as the publication of it has only gone on at intervals for nearly five years.

it amply repays examination ; though my own acquaintance
with this great mass of Welsh poetry is slight enough, it is
perhaps sufficiently general to be utilized in remarks that may
interest my readers, though not satisfy them.

At the outset we do well to bear in mind that there appears
to be strong reason to believe that *rhyme* was first cradled
among the Celts,* and from them it crept into the Romance
languages, then into the Teutonic and Scandinavian ones.
We have no classical Latin rhymes, no Anglo-Saxon rhymes,
but we find rhymes existing among the *gogynfeirdd* (the most
ancient Welsh poets), Taliesin and Aneurin. Such a circum-
stance might prepare us to expect special developments of the
poetic art among the descendants of the Britons.

So far as the Welsh are concerned we are not disappointed,
and even in this Nineteenth century, with its superabundance
of material energy, their language exists as one of the most
harmonious of modern Europe, with a poetical literature which
is absolutely inapproachable, so far as the relation of sound to
ideas is concerned, by any Continental tongue. I am not
saying that Welsh has produced greater poets than any other
nation, but I say this, that there will be more poetry in the
works of a Welshman, bracketed equal in ability with a
foreigner, than in the works of the latter, simply by dint of the
Welshman having superior material to hand. German is
effective, but heavy ; Italian, emasculated, lacking in force ;
Spanish, grand, but wanting in flexibility ; French, in range
of sound and emphasis, is deficient ; while English is more
unemotional, and does not readily lend itself to rhyme, as
compared with the Cymric tongue, which again is superior
to its sisters, the Cornish and Breton.

Probably among other reasons why, when Welshmen wish to

* The subject has been discussed by Schultz, in a Prize Essay some
years since.

write poetry, it is almost invariably performed in Welsh, is the one that even presupposing an equal familiarity with both languages, they feel they could not do themselves justice in English: but if they want to write prose it is more likely to become a simple question as to whether what they wrote would find a market if in Welsh, and whether they could sufficiently reach the classes intended, by confining themselves to the latter: so that frequently considerations of name, money, and sometimes of greater usefulness, incline them to English, as a vehicle for prose compositions, but seldom for poetical ones.

However, that may be, it is a fact that a cultivated style of Welsh prose has received but scant attention. No one can point to a master of Welsh prose in the same sense that we can point to Froude or Ruskin, as masters of English.

When we deal with poetry the case is different. If it be true that the powers of the language are as yet comparatively undeveloped in prose, it is far otherwise in poetry. For hundreds of years past there has been such attention paid to this department of literature, and such intricate rules have been formed for the guidance of candidates, into what are considered its classic paths, that the effect has been extraordinary in preserving in use a large vocabulary, although, at the same time, gratifying a taste for sound at the expense of *original thought*.

What I term its classic paths, are guarded by the *Llyffetheir-iau* (the shackles) of *cynghanedd*. In the early poetry of Wales this appears to have not existed at all, or only to a limited extent, but, as a writer has observed, after the independence of the country was gone, it was no longer the clash of arms, but the jingle of consonants—resonance, if we use a more respectful term, which attracted the bards' attention. Certain new bardic rules sprang up, but in the confusion

incident to the outbreak of Owen Glyndwr, and the bitter
hostility of the English Government to the bards, these rules
appear to have got into an unsettled state ; in part to remedy
this an Eisteddfod was called at Carmarthen, in 1451, under
the presidency of Gruffydd ap Nicholas (ancestor of Lord
Dynevor), when a bard of the north, Dafydd ap Edmwnt, a
landowner of some position, won the chief prize by compositions in the twenty-four measures, which bear his name—
constituting what is called the *Dosparth Gwynedd.*

The bards of Gwent and Morganwg were not willing to
concede superiority to these measures, and continued a system
of their own, differing but slightly from the other, and which
is known as *Dosbarth Morganwg.* All these metres contain
cynghanedd, i.e., a regular sequence of consonants, and no
Chair prize at any modern National Eisteddfod is awarded to
a composition in free metres, but in their published works
nearly all the bards now use both the free metres, in which we
find a considerable variety as well as beauty, and also the
mesuran caethion (the restricted metres).

Of the latter, one of the most striking to an Englishman is
the englyn, of which there are three kinds, the commonest
being the *Englyn Unodl Union.* There have been repeated
attempts to exemplify this in English. It is, however, quite
unsuited to our language, and generally falls flat on the ear.

By means of the englyn a great deal can be said in a short
space. Hence it is peculiarly suited for epigrams or for short
descriptions of men or things.

The englyn must contain the above-mentioned alliteration in
each line. The syllables runs 10-6-7-7. One last word of the
third or fourth lines must be of one syllable ; each of the
three last lines must rhyme with the word preceding the dash
in the first line ; the word or words succeeding the dash in the
first line must alliterate with the second line.

The following is an example of an English englyn, followed by one of Ceiriog's, taken from his poem, "*Y Daran*" (Thunder)

> " Wake sweet Harp! Why warp in woe —why linger.
> 　In languishing sorrow?
> Let no rough and bluff wind blow
> Thy wailings on the willow."

> Y*n* y ddu e*n*yd, *n*aw*dd* i anian—*nid* oe*d*
> 　O*nd Du*w noddwr pobman ;
> A *Hw*n*w* ddaeth ei *hu*n*an*
> I'*n* b*yd d*u mewn e*n*b*yd* dan.

The latter exhibits an example of *gynghanedd groes* (cross consonancy); the former of *cynghanedd sain*, or consonancy of sound, which involves either a sequence of final consonants, or finals combined with one or more in the first syllable of the succeeding word. The letters printed in italics indicate the *cynghanedd* in the Welsh stanza. Note that *nd D* in the second line correspond with *nd d* after the dash in the first line, and that the syllable *an* rhymes in all four lines.

That this style of composition is by no means extinct may be inferred by the fact that no less than 110 englynion by as many competitors, were sent to the adjudicators at the Swansea Eisteddfodd, 1891, for the £1 prize offered there.

Another pretty metre is the *hypynt hir*, consisting of two triplets, each with syllables 4-4-8; the last syllable of the fourth and sixth lines rhyming, also their fourth syllables rhyming with each of the other lines, e.g.—

> Ysgrifenydd
> Myg areithydd
> Deg areilydd—digwerylon
> Hynafiaethydd
> A chyfieithydd
> Iawn gyweirydd—Enwog wron.

To discuss Welsh prosody at length, is both beyond my scope and abilities, while asking my readers to accept *cum grano salis*, the declamations by a certain class about the poverty of the literature until they feel able to form a judgment of their own.   If there is one thing more than another, noticeable about Welsh poetry from a general point of view, that is, its realistic power.   Under its influences the sky lowers more darkly, the lightning flashes more vividly, the thunder rolls more heavily, the tempest tossed ocean dashes itself against the rugged rocks more awfully and more grandly, the brook murmurs more sweetly, the lark 'pours forth a clearer note, and springs up to the heavens more lightly, the peaceful and the calm of nature, the light and the shade, the stupendous and the vast, as well as the minute and the insignificant seem to be brought out in bolder relief, and in language that is at once more expressive and harmonious 'than we are accustomed to in English.

Whether the bard describes the lily or the rose, a drop of dew, or a dashing waterfall, spring-time or winter, the effect of the wild wind of the mountains, or the soft breezes of summer, and whether he is talented or not, a very genius, or common place, his language almost invariably lends an intangible charm to his subject.   When he deals with humanity, when he goes to the house of mourning, or calls for the exercise of other emotions in which the human breast is participant, the heart beats quicker, and the sympathies are more readily enlisted, so far as it is in the power of language to affect them.   Read " Elen Wynn," by Mynyddog : or " Bedd y dyn Tylawd," and ask thyself reader, whether Wordsworth, a Pen-fardd Lloegr, has written anything to match either of them.

But what about the weaknesses of Welsh poetry ?   One of them is certainly the excessive amount of personal praise lavished by the bards upon their friends, either living or dead.

One would think to read the effusions poured forth in various newspapers or periodicals, that Wales was simply a land of prodigies, faultless characters, extraordinary geniuses ; in fact, that the common-place was rather the exception than the rule.

It is highly probable that the rules of *Cynghanedd* have fostered a disposition to write *couleur de rose* descriptions of men and things by the introduction of words implying more than the reality, but which came in convenient for poetic requirements, until the habit has become firmly engrained. I say this, making all due allowance for a poet's license, to convey his thoughts in metaphorical or even hyperbolical language, and with regard to these personal poems, we must make further allowance for a people whose affections are warm, and whose habits are strongly sociable : notwithstanding a real evil exists in this direction, which urgently calls for reformation.

These habits are by no means of recent growth, part of the profession of the ancient bards being the compositions of *Cywyddau Moliant* (odes of praise) to their patrons or friends, as well as elegies on their departure. Call to mind the well-known incident of Gruffydd Gryg and Dafydd ap Gwilym, fourteenth century bards. In the midst of a poetic quarrel several retaliatory poems passed between them, and Gruffydd plumed himself that he was made of different metal to Rhys Meigen, who has fallen dead on the spot, stung by D. ap Gwilym's biting retorts.

In order to alter this disgraceful state of things, the monks of Woollos Priory (?), on the site of the Austin Friars' Timber Yard, Newport, resorted to a " pious" fraud.* They spread in North Wales a report of the death of Dafydd ap Gwilym, and in South Wales a report of the death of Gruffydd Gryg. This resulted in each expressing their grief in such mournful

---

* See Wilkins's History of Wales, p. 48, and Hanes Llenyddiaeth Gymreig, p. 148.

and affectionate elegies, that when the *ruse* was discovered a
warm friendship was begun that lasted to the end.

Personally, I consider another weakness of Welsh poetry, is
the prize system, which causes many poems to be written
under artificial promptings. Of course it does not follow that
all prize poems are necessarily much damaged by continually
looking to the opinions of a committee of judges, and by
being on fixed subjects, and there is no doubt that the volume
of literature is vastly increased by this system, but it must
detract from originality of treatment.

My preceding remarks must not be understood as altogether
condemning or depreciating *cynghanedd*; it is simply a further
extension and elaboration of one of the main principles of
rhyme. If it has shackles on the one hand, it has power in
the other, when used by a master : nor do I not think it will
disappear even with the Twentieth century, the strife of
tongues, the din of mental or physical battle. The *awdl* may
remain, plain rhyme may remain, but the poetry of abstract
thought will more than hitherto be expressed in *blank* verse.

Without attempting to criticise or even offer a fair resumé
of the scope and character of modern Welsh poetry, the
following pages will give the general reader, especially the
English reader, some further ideas in the subject than he can
glean elsewhere, while not feeling myself precluded from giving
short extracts from the originals, which cannot in justice be
served up in translations. The following are notices of the
works of bards which are chiefly still in print.

Modern Welsh poetry, so far as it is published, may be
almost said to begin with Huw Morris, of Pontymeibion,
the " Eos Ceiriog," whose works were re-printed at Wrexham,
in 1823. He lived from 1622 to 1709, and his language is
nearly as intelligible as the Welsh of the present day. Just
as in English, we find a great gap between the language of the

Fifteenth century and that of the Sixteenth and Seventeenth, so we do in Welsh. Lewis Glyn Cothi, who died about 1490, is difficult, few Welshmen could read him at first sight with pleasure. Huw Morris is as intelligible as Bunyan, and is considered one of the best writers of his time.

The latter, as regards melody of verse, may be called the Spenser of Wales, however much he was unlike him in other respects. Spenser made extensive use of the Alexandrine stanza of Tasso, one which is seldom or never used now, though graceful and effective. Huw Morris wrote a good deal in a metre which is perhaps peculiar to Wales, and more striking to the ear than Spenser's; very few have handled it since, the most notable being Edward Richard, of Ystrad Meurig. Its peculiarity lies principally in the last line, which to be effective must be read with two pauses, the previous three with one only, in the centre. The following is an example :—

> Dyn anghall dan 'wingo, ni fyn mo'r gorphwyso,
> Lle gallai fo wreiddio, a llwyddo ar wellhâd ;
> Rhoi serch ar gymdeithion, ac ofer chwareuon,
> Yw perion arferion ei fwriad.*

GORONWY OWAIN, born 1722, is one of the most remarkable poets Wales has produced. The son of very poor parents, means were procured through the generosity of a friend to send him to Oxford, and hence his introduction into the Established Church. It is reported as a proof of his readiness in acquiring knowledge that he was only three months learning Arabic, and that Greek, Latin, and Hebrew were at his fingers' ends. His *cywydd* on the "Last Judgment" is esteemed a masterpiece, but not easy for a beginner. It is included in his works sold by I. Ffoulkes, and the notes in that edition are by his friend Lewis Morris (*Llewellyn Ddu*).

---

* Carol Cyngor in Cyf. ii. 123. Wrexham Ed.

Goronwy Owain has dazzled men by his genius, and the lofty flights of his imagination. Contemporary with him was another writer, who shortly before had been, like himself, a curate in the Established Church ; the one wrote for the few in the language of the learned, and the other met rich and poor on a common platform, and influenced men's hearts as very few writers have done before or since : hence it is that WILLIAM WILLIAMS, of Pantycelyn, is still read, and his name still honoured wherever the Welsh language is spoken. Almost as a matter of course he is called the *per-ganiedlydd*, the sweet singer, and, in fact, the extraordinary facility, though not always the polish of his pen, both in Welsh and English verse, warrants the term.

The last edition of his works (nearly complete) is quite recent. Vol. I. is published by Evans, Holywell ; Vol. II. by W. Jones, Newport, Mon., 1891.

In his "Theomemphus," and other writings, we are brought in contact with an allegorical Eighteenth century style of treatment, not altogether in accordance with present-day taste, *e.g.*, in "Theomemphus," a poem of some 1,500 stanzas, no less than thirty-eight personages, such as Philocritus, Orthocephalus, Seducus, and Boanerges, mostly with Latinized names, are introduced, but the author, in his preface, says that it cannot be called an allegory, as the persons are real men, sins, graces, temptations, and other inward and outward enemies. It is principally by his hymns that Williams, Pantycelyn, will be remembered; some of them are superficial, but with regard to others, few Welsh hymn writers have surpassed him in depth of feeling.

I have mentioned Goronwy Owain, because he seemed to follow nearer to Huw Morris in the point of time, but presuming that I am now writing principally for readers who wish Welsh literature introduced to their notice, rather in the

order in which it is easiest followed and understood, and as
there is not any set scheme of treating the subject historically,
the name next to be introduced is one of our own day.

ISLWYN (1832-1877?) lived within a few miles of Newport,
near Ynysddu Station ; he wrote both descriptive and reflec-
tive pieces. There is a slightly Germanic vein in his writings.
Common consent gives him one of the first places among the
bards of the latter half of this century, but only a small portion
of his works are published, others of them still lie in MSS.
under the care of a relative at Ynysddu. The following is from
his description of Bala Lake, in "Cader Idris" :—

　　　Ardderchog Lyn y Bala,
　　　A llên o arian rydd
　　　Amrywiaeth hoff i'r oror
　　　Lle 'r egyr dôr y dydd.
　　　Ac fel angylaidd ddringfa
　　　I fynu 'r wybren fry
　　　Mynyddau 'r Aran welir,
　　　Pob gris yn fynydd sy'.
　　　A chadwen faith y Ferwyn
　　　Sydd yn canllawio llwybr
　　　I yspryd yr ystorom
　　　I rodio tros yr wybr.
　　　Morgilfach Aberteifi,
　　　Fel gwerddlas fythol waen,
　　　Yn mhell i'r gorllewinbwnc,
　　　Ymegyr oll o'n blaen :

OSSIAN GWENT.—Close on 100 short poems of this writer
are published by Hughes, of Wrexham. They contain some
exquisite touches of external nature—the lark, the nightingale,
the swallow, the wren, the redbreast, the lake, the moon, the
sea, frost and snow, the winter's wind, the lily and the
primrose, all form subjects of separate treatment. A
good many are well within the grasp of children. One

short poem of this class, full of pathos, begins thus :—

Fe syrth y ddeilen olaf	The last leaf will wither
Cyn bo hir,	Before long,
Mae'r oeraidd drwst y gauaf	The cold blast of winter
Yn y tir.	Now has come.

How is it that children in elementary schools are compelled to continue grinding away to commit to memory such poems as "Casabianca," while others much more suited to develop their powers of expression are close at hand, in the works of writers of their own country. Such a one in particular is that fine lyric of Islwyn's "Gyrwch Wyntoedd," which in form somewhat recalls Schiller's "Lied der Glocke." It begins,—

Gyrwch wyntoedd,	Rush wild winds on
Ar eich hyntoedd.	Your wanderings,
Dros y llyn,	O'er the lake.
Dros y glyn,	O'er the vale,
Dros y bryn,	O'er the hill.
A thros lawer Alpfor gwyn.	O'er mountain seas of white snow.

Ossian is still living at Rhymney, in Monmouthshire.

IEUAN G. GEIRIONYDD.—I have already alluded to his "Morfa Rhuddlan," which furnishes a style of poetry equally with the peculiarly melodious metre used by Huw Morris, scarcely to be found in England.

The poet is standing near the Marsh of Rhuddlan; as he looks to the west the sun is slowly sinking down behind the majestic mountains of Carnarvonshire, the shades of night gradually creep over the landscape, while the subdued roar of the distant waves meet his ear, and his heart beats fast while he thinks of how the blood of Wales was spilt at the very spot he stands on. He seems in the twilight, to see the indistinct glimmer of the shields, and hears the clatter of warlike missiles projected against it, the hissing of the arrows, and feels the very trembling of the earth, while above all,

Caradawg's voice is heard sharp and loud. He goes on describing the conflict, and the anxiety felt in all Wales as to the issue. All of a sudden a bitter shaft of sorrow strikes him, while he hears the harsh rejoicing cry of the enemy. The original is deeply realistic—

> Troswyf daeth, fel rhyw saeth, alaeth, a dychryn.
> Och! rhag bost, bloeddiau, tost ymffrost y gelyn.

Then in consternation and confusion those who were awaiting the issue at their doors, flee to the hills, while the rocks, the vales, and the hills participate in their mournful cries, which reach even to Eryri (Snowdon).

> Bryn a phant, cwm a nant, llanwant a'u hoergri
> Traidd y floedd draw, i g'oedd, gymoedd Eryri.

The effectiveness of this piece is due to no small extent to the wonderful adaptation of the metre to the subject : in each couplet, there are no less than eight rhyming words, and yet the matter flows so naturally, that a reader is all but unconscious of the fact.

I believe that those of my readers who are able to judge, will agree with me that from the study of this single poem alone, we may conclude that a field of poetry is open before us, into which the English language cannot enter as a competitor. Were the whole body of Welsh literature struck out of existence but this one piece, it would of itself give a stamp to the character of the language which would warrant such a conclusion, as to its almost unequalled power.

While we search English literature in vain for a poem wherewith to make a comparison with "Cyflafan Morfa Rhuddlan;" in point of metrical structure, we shall not be altogether at a loss to find one in Monkish Latin; to wit, the source of some devotional pieces familiar to English ears,

such as " Brief life is here our portion," and " Jerusalem
the Golden." The original, some of my readers may recollect,
commences,

Hora novissima, tempora pessima sunt vigilemus,
Ecce minaciter, imminet arbiter ille supremus.

Only a portion of the poem, "*De contemptu mundi,*" from
which it is taken is, so far as I know, published in England;
in each couplet there are six rhyming words, and the
author, Bernard de Morlaix, judging from his name, appears
to have been a Breton—if so a Celtic language was probably
his mother tongue.

The "*Awdl ar Orlifiad Cantre'r Gwaelod*" (ode on the
inundation of the Lowland Hundred), and "*Ymdrech Serch
a Rheswm*" (the contest between affection and reason), illustrate further Glan Geirionydd's extraordinary powers.

WATCYN WYN, headmaster of a private school at Amman-
ford, Carmarthenshire, is a living bard; one of his prize poems
on "Bywyd" (Life), was published at Merthyr, 1882. It
is a *campuswaith* easy to read, and although composed
in a free metre, with eleven or twelve syllable couplets,
it is distinctly Welsh in its character. Like hundreds of
other Welsh publications, it is probably very little known.
Ossian Gwent wrote a beautiful poem on "Solitude"
(*Unigedd*); Watcyn Wyn follows him with one on "Silence"
(*Dystawrwydd*); though not written in such a sweet metre
as Ossian's, it is full of matter, and great thoughts not
fully developed. The following is an extract:—

Dy ddwfn dawelwch, O! mor ddwfn fyfyriol,
Terfynau dy fwynhad mor annherfynol;
Yr enaid yn ymgolli 'n dy gyfeillach,
I'th fynwes fawr yn gwasgu, dynach, dynach.

*   *   *   *

O anherfynol fawredd diddechreuad,
Rhyw annibynol ddim o ran dy haniad :
Dy lanw dystaw ar ei dônau llyfnion,
A nofia'r enaid i fôr mawr dy swynion.

Towards the end of the poem a few stanzas are introduced in a different measure.

One of the writers holding a chief place, both in poetry and prose, is the late GWILYM HIRAETHOG, of Liverpool, where his works are still to be obtained. Hiraethog is not merely known in Wales, but in Germany, as may be seen by the following extract from the letter of a Welsh Elementary school-master, who had studied abroad, to the late D. I. Davies :—

When I was settled down comfortably in my lodgings at Leipzig Dr. Loth, Dr. Tegner, Dr. Erdmann, and Dr. Lögler called on me wishing me to read Welsh with them. I need not tell you that I was very glad to comply with their request, and we commenced our work in earnest. I showed them my little library of Welsh books, and gave the loan of them to them until they procured their own. The plan they adopted was the following :—They read carefully through Spurrell's Grammar, and commenced with a very easy prose writer : they then mastered Rowland's Grammar and commenced " Emmanuel." I ought to mention that Dr. Tegner was very well versed in the comparative philology of the Semitic languages, and Dr. Erdmann in the comparative philology of the Aryan languages. In reading Welsh they traced every Welsh word to a similar word either in the Semitic or Aryan group of languages. By doing so they were able to remember the meaning of the word when it occurred again in their reading. In about six weeks they were able to read the " Emmanuel " of HIRAETHOG with ease and account for all the idioms. When I returned to Cambridge, I received a letter from Dr. Erdmann, written in a very good Welsh style, which is a proof that the Welsh language can be mastered in a very short time by anyone who is well versed in the comparative philology of the Aryan languages.

Some fifty years ago it was the opinion of persons competent
to judge, that DAFYDD IONAWR (died 1827), the author of
" Cywydd y Drindod," was one of the greatest poets of his
time.   This poem is composed in the *Mesur carth*,
called *Cywydd denair hirion*, and consists of 11,005 lines,
being nearly 500 lines longer than " Paradise Lost," and is
said in the plan of its arrangement to resemble Pollok's
" Course of Time."   The *cywydd* is, I am sure, too monotonous a measure to make a long poem popular, though it
may be used with good effect on pieces of a moderate length.
It is made up of heptasyllabic couplets, the final word of one
line *must* be a monosyllable, the final word in the other line
constituting the couplet *must* consist of two or more
syllables, consequently the accent falls alternately on the
last, and on the last syllable but one in each line, which gives
a pleasing effect.

Daniel Ddu o Geredigion spoke thus highly of Cywydd
y Drindod as " a masterly performance, of equal merit with
Paradise Lost.   The spirit which it breathes is truly
religious, and the poetry of it is beautiful beyond comparison.
I have perused it, I think, *fifty times*, and the more frequently
I do so, the more am I pleased and gratified."*

Dafydd Ionawr was a scholar of Ystrad Meurig Grammar
School, under Edward Richards, one of the chief bards of that
day, and there, in order to test the power of his *awen*, before
commencing his great poem, " Cywydd y Drindod," he composed a *cywydd* on "The Thunder."   One of his Welsh
reviewers, Ieuan Gwynydd, alludes to this in language which
I am disposed to give a translation or paraphrase of here, as
the style is eminently rhetorical and Welsh, though it necessarily somewhat loses its force in a translation.

" Look at his mental efforts (*ddirdyniadan*),† as he was

---

* " Character of the Welsh as a nation," p. 88.   † Writhings.

trying to find a subject to measure his strength with (*ymaflyd codwrn ag ef*).* He thought of the pleasant dales, but that would not do. He heard the birds singing, but that would not do. He looked on the bright flowing waters of the Dysyni, but the *awen* did not flow in accord with them. The evening breeze gently sighed, but it did not move the strings of his harp. The flocks of sheep pastured on the hills, but their bleatings did not raise the sympathy of the great genius which was about to manifest itself. The wind whistled wildly, there was a little movement: the ocean roared, and the breast of the bard heaved back responsive (*rhuai yr eigion, ac adruai mynwes y bardd*); the cloud grew dark, and the tumultuous torrent of his heart was pent up; the thunder burst, and the flood-gate of the genius which was to deluge the literature of his country with glory, was removed. The thunder touched the spring of his soul. He had within a divine consciousness of very great strength."

More than that, Ieuan might have added that he looked upon the writing of Cywydd y Drindod as a kind of fulfilment of a Divine mission, to which his heart had been turned from boyhood.

Dafydd Ionawr occupied various situations as under master or usher, and after a love disappointment he made up his mind never to fall in love again. His poem on "Y Drindod" being finished, he asked his father for assistance to publish it, but was indignantly refused. Means were, however, obtained from a Thomas Jones, of Ynysfaig, on condition of his sacrificing his patrimony, but of being kept during his life by the said Thomas Jones : with him he lived, except seven years passed as teacher in Dolgelly, till his death, in 1827. During his residence at Dolgelly, he is described as running about, leaping, clapping his hands, and

---

* Wrestle with.

NN

throwing his hat into the air with the greatest delight.   If the Education Commissioner of 1847 had been able to predate his visit to the time when Dafydd Ionawr taught the free school there, what kind of a report would he have given? especially if he had heard that the clapping of hands and laughing some-times continued through the night.   We need not be sur-prised to learn that not everyone at Dolgelly was convinced of his being in a state of sanity.   So it is, great genius often borders on the debatable limits between the sane and *unsane*.

Jones, author of "Character of the Welsh as a Nation," says that D. I. was "one of the greatest contributors that Wales has ever produced to the poetical department of its literature;" whether he will ever be brought prominently again under public notice, time will show, but in these days the eccentric, though gifted and religious author of "Cywydd y Drindod" is but little known.

The following is from Cywydd y Daran, and will give the reader, who has some initiation into the language, an idea of the style of a *cywydd* generally :—

> Y daran o'i du oror
> Mal berwawg derfysgawg fôr.
> Wybrendwrf, braw drwy 'r bryndir,
> A dychryn drwy 'r dyffryn dir.

The following is from C. y Drindod, where Eve is relating to Adam a frightful dream or vision she had had, presaging the fall :—

> *Poen swrth*, mewn cwsg *pan syrthiais*,
> Gwae fi, yr oedd gwayw i f' ais.
> Tywyllwch tewdrwch a'm todd.
> Caddug anferth a'm cuddiodd.
> Chwyrn iawn yr awn ar unwaith
> I lawr i ddyfnder mawr maith.

Note the *Cynghanedd* italicized in the first line.

Perhaps a more popular poet than any of those above-
mentioned is CEIRIOG, who though formerly a stationmaster
on the Mid-Wales Railway, is considered the chief lyric poet
of modern times. Then there is Mynyddog, full of pathos and
humour; Eben Fardd, of Carnarvonshire; and Dewi Wyn o
Essyllt, of Glamorganshire, all deceased, who would require
special notice, were this volume a history of Welsh literature.

There is one more poetical composition which I will allude
to now, namely, the version of " Paradise Lost," by DR. W. O.
PUGHE (*Idrison*). Some sixty years ago George Borrow made
that his war charger on which to ride victoriously through the
difficulties that beset an understanding of the language used
in mediæval Welsh poetry,* and I do not think that a *private*
student will even now find much more efficient assistance in
any other book, which arises from the simple fact that a great
many uncommon words are used in its composition, which are
easily explained by reference to the English original. From
the point of view of some Welsh critics this translation of the
" *Coll Gwynfa*" has the unpardonable fault of containing forms
of Welsh which are never used elsewhere,† and are the product
of Idrison's inventive faculty, but the man who has no criterion
to judge by, but the language of the poem itself, acknowledges
that it is a truly grand performance, superior to a subsequent

---

* G. B. tells us that at the expiration of his clerkship, in East Anglia,
he was able to read not only Welsh prose, but " what was infinitely more
difficult, Welsh poetry in any of the four-and-twenty measures, and was
well versed in the composition of various old Welsh bards," especially
those of Dafydd ap Gwilym, whom he always considered as the greatest
poetical genius that has appeared in Europe since the revival of
literature.

† Since writing the above my friend, Michael D. Jones has supplied the
following remark : —" Dr. Owen [Pughe used to say that he did not use
any word in ' *Coll Gwynfa*' that was not used in some part of Wales in
his day. I collected hundreds of these words for Daniel Lâs (Daniel
Sylvan Evans). There are many unrecorded now, and used by the
inhabitants of localities."

attempt by I. D. Ffraid, to put Milton into a more generally
readable form. The Welsh language free from the shackles of
Cynghanedd, rises in the blank verse of Pughe to the height
of the subject, sound and sense combining together in majestic
concordance, and seeming to dispel the idea of a translation.

W. O. Pughe was one of a small band of London Welshmen
who, at the beginning of the century, united together to
rescue a large number of old MSS. from oblivion, and
published considerable selections from them in three volumes,
under the title of the "Myvyrian Archæology of Wales,"
named from "Myfyr," the *nom de plume* of Owen Jones, one
of the three who issued the work. Up to the present time, a
reprint of this, forms the principal source accessible to the
public, of Welsh poetry written from the Sixth to the Fifteenth
centuries, except in the case of a few authors whose works
have been printed, while a considerable number of productions still lie in manuscript, either in the British Museum or
elsewhere, where it is difficult, though perhaps not impossible,
to make their acquaintance. Another very much smaller
publication called "Gorchestion y Beirdd," containing similar
productions, and which is a reprint of a work published in
1773, is to be obtained at Carnarvon..

In a paper entitled, "A Short Review of the Present State
of Welsh Manuscripts," inserted in the "Myfyrian Archæology,"
and written probably by W. O. Pughe or Iolo Morganwg, the
extensive character of Welsh verse, up to the Fourteenth
century, is thus alluded to—

Our system includes not only all the varieties of verse that have
yet been produced in all known languages, and in all known ages,
but also a number equally great of such constructed verses as we
have neither seen nor heard of in any country or in any tongue,
and yet these latter are by far the most beautiful and musical that
we have.

As time goes on the number of unpublished MSS will be gradually diminished, through their being transcribed for the printer. The Welsh MSS Society has done some work in that direction, which was commenced in 1840, two years after the publication, by private enterprise, of "The Mabinogion," by Lady Charlotte Guest, with an English translation of her own. This is a mediaeval work, consisting largely of Arthurian romances and children's tales. Quite lately a new edition, and one, I understand, in first-rate style, has been published under the care of J. Gwenogfryn Evans, of Oxford.

Before dismissing the subject of Welsh poetry, we may notice a great deficiency, viz., the absence of any good anthology. From all the vast store of modern poetry, printed and manuscript, there are scarcely any pieces collated in a representative collection worthy of the name. Is it because Welsh publishers are only half asleep and half awake, fattening on their gains?

Blackie and Son, Edinburgh, did, it is true, publish "*Ceinion Llenyddiaeth Gymreig*" (Beauties of Welsh Literature), some time since, in six parts, at 2s. each, but they introduced hardly any pieces belonging to the Nineteenth century. If the principals of that firm had known Welsh, and the whereabouts of the literature, as well as they knew English, I incline to think they would have taught a lesson to some of the native publishers, though they had, it is true, a Welshman as editor.

In the Department of Welsh prose, though the publications are numerous, the number of leading names is but small. The late Lewis Edwards, of Bala (father of Principal T. C. Edwards), Gwilym Hiraethog, Gwallter Mechain, and Brutus, are among the principal belonging to the present century, among a multitude of theological writers. The three first will be mentioned again.

Brutus (1794-1866) was for many years editor of " *Yr*

Haul," an Episcopalian monthly, where his pungent easy style, made his name known far and wide.

This is what one of his friends, Titus Lewis, F.S.A., said of him—*

Yr Haul became not a periodical, but a classic. The dialogues of Brutus were considered not only a triumphant embodiment of Church principles, but there was also offered in them, month after month, such food for thought, full of renewed beauty and freshness, vigour, and grand creation, such force of expression and flashing wit, such gorgeousness of imagination, almost pictorial, as will destine them to live as long as the Welsh language is a vehicle for thought. Well, it may be objected. " What more do you want? have we more in favoured England?" Alas! with all its beauty, freshness, and wit, the writings of Brutus were cast in a mould of bitterness. It might be said, " he knew not of what spirit he was." Classical as the writings of Brutus must be regarded, powerful though they had been, and will be, yet there was underlying them all a vein of scathing satire, and such a burning sarcasm, that Brutus came to be regarded by his opponents, the Dissenters, as a walking vial of wrath, a quenchless wildfire, a corrosive sublimate. ° * ° Brutus had under-currents of the most kindly and genial disposition, and the great depths of his grand human heart were brimful of charity and humane feeling, but for that, his ferocious lashings and merciless invective and satire served to keep his good traits concealed, and men knew not of them.

One of Brutus' works, " Wil brydydd y Coed" (Will, the poet of the Wood), is still in print at Carmarthen. Another entitled "Christmasia," is to be had at Liverpool ; the latter is biographical, and contains little or no satire.

Perhaps he did not more than equal a much less known writer, *Siluriad,* in *Y Geninen,* for 1885, and again in 1890,

* At the Swansea Episcopalian Congress, 1879, as reported in the *S. W.D. News.*

whose trenchant article, "Denominational Philistinism of Wales," excited considerable attention at the time—but I fear less reformation. "Siluriad" attacks in vivid satire the degeneracy of the lectures and literary meetings, and then makes the denominations one by one feel his lashes, while the impartial reader has to admit that much may be well deserved, and that the writer himself is rather a reformer than a misanthrope.

A new school of Welsh prose is now arising, which aims at reproducing as literature the *llafar gwlad* (common talk), or rather, I might say, as combining some colloquial methods of expression with what has hitherto been the standard of literary Welsh.

Owen Edwards—the editor of *Cymru*, and some of his University friends, are considered representatives of this innovation. Not long ago a bookseller known to the writer offered *Cymru* to a massive old Welshman, himself a literary character, and an admirer of his native language. It was returned, after being taken home, with the remark, " *Cymerwch e'yn ol, nid wyf fi yn leicio Cymraeg bechgyn Rhydychain 'na*" (Take it back, I don't like the Welsh of those Oxford boys). Notwithstanding this remark of my old friend's, the style of O. E., although very much *sui generis*, is very readable, and therefore popular, being a stepping stone from the colloquial to the more abstruse literary language, which is sometimes in the South called " *deep Welsh*," *i.e.*, beyond the speaker's capacity. While popular, it is neither slipshod nor boorish, being historical and picturesque, investing even small details with interest.

Speaking generally of Welsh prose, the rhythm is distinctly different from that of English : when it is idiomatic, and the words are well chosen, the effect is very pleasing, yet it cannot be denied that, except for periodicals, it is likely to be continued, on a small scale only, in the future, unless systematic instruction in Welsh become more general.

Welsh is pre-eminently the language of *cumulative effects*; in Welsh writing as well as in public speaking (though I am but little familiar with the latter) ; adjective is piled upon adjective, antithesis upon antithesis, one apt illustration follows another, until the rivulet becomes a strong current, and the *hwyl* of forgetfulness carries away both teacher and listener ;—just as *cynghanedd* of sound forms one of the chief charms of Welsh verse to many critical ears, so Welsh prose of the class I allude to, possesses an almost unconscious, invisible *cynghanedd* of sense, representative of the people and of the country.

Any of my readers who wish to obtain further information on the subject of Welsh literature have a choice of the following books, which will carry them at least to the end of the Eighteenth century.

1. Stephens' "Literature of the Cymry," which embraces the period from 1080 to 1322, but is now out of print.

2. " Hanes Llenyddiaeth Gymreig," by the late Gweirydd ap Rhys, of Holyhead, an essay which won the £100 prize in the National Eisteddfod of 1883, and is published by Foulkes, of Liverpool, price 10s 6d, demy 8vo., 488 pp. This is a history of Welsh literature from 1300—1650, and is likely to be a standard work of reference for some years to come.

3. " History of the Literature of Wales, from the year 1300 to the year 1650," by Charles Wilkins. Ph.D., published by D. Owen, Cardiff, 1884. This is not quite so complete as the former work, but it is very readable, and in English, though anyone capable of following them would prefer extracts from the originals rather than translations.

4. " Llyfryddiaeth y Cymry " (sold by Humphreys, of Carnarvon), is a Bibliography of all printed books in Welsh, or relating to Wales, down to 1800, interspersed with short

biographical notices of many of the authors, and incidental information which much heightens its value.

This work, by a Wesleyan preacher (Gwilym Lleyn), gives evidence of an immense amount of labour and research, existing over a long number of years, and was published in 1869, by John Pryse, Llanidloes, under the editorship of the learned D. Silvan Evans ; it is still one of the standard books of reference, without which a student of the literature of Wales can scarcely consider his library complete. When and by whom will the Bibliography of this century be executed?

The first person who subscribed for "Llyfryddiaeth y Cymry" was a Monmouthshire collier, but not many collier's sons in this county, under the present system of education and present surroundings, have the chance of growing up with the capacity to appreciate such a work.

Three out of the four Bishops were subscribers—Llandaff being the exception—doubtless the influence of Silvan Evans gave prestige to the book in clerical circles—among others we find the Lady Llanover, Earls Vane and Powis, Judge Johnes, Andreas o Fôn, Idrisyn, and a number of persons who evidently belonged to the class of small shopkeepers or working men.

A fifth work, by Charles Ashton, a Merionethshire policeman, carrying forward the history* of the literature from 1650-1850, which received a prize at the Swansea Eisteddfod, of 1891, is still lying in manuscript, with a probability of its being shortly published. Whatever the character of this work is, it is beyond the bounds of reasonable probability to suppose that one man can give anything like exhaustive treatment to the subject for this period. It may break up the fallow ground, but will no doubt leave ample room for another work

---

* This (in Welsh) is a companion volume to *Hanes Llenyddiaeth Gymreig*, and not a Bibliography, such as *Llyf. y C.*

going over the same ground, provided sufficient buyers can be found.

There are other books belonging rather to the literature of Wales than strictly to *Welsh* literature, which may claim our attention, inasmuch as they illustrate in some shape or other " Wales and her Language."

One of these is Dr. John David Rhys's " Cambrobritannicae Cymricaeve linguae Institutiones," a Welsh Grammar written in Latin, and published in 1592. The author is principally known in Wales by this work, written after returning from a residence in Italy, during which he had issued a book in Latin, on the " Pronunciation of Italian."

In the Latin title to the former, it is expressly stated that these " Rules and Rudiments" were " not less necessary than useful in order to understand the Bible, which had lately been idiomatically and elegantly translated into the Cambrobritish language." To these he added explications of the rules and varieties of Welsh poetry.

In the Welsh introduction he speaks of a little " improvement and cultivation" of late given to the language by some good and learned men, " principally for the purpose of translating the Bible into our own language." He then alludes to the general diffusion of classical knowledge among the nations who have paid particular attention to their own languages, and hints at the tendency to denationalization which accompanied the era of the Union :—

But we may observe that many of our own countrymen have become so vain, so proud, so conceited, so affected, and so negligent of everything that is patriotic, and so ignorant of their own language, and so attached to everything that is foreign and exotic, and consequently so different from most other nations, that if they have been but a short time out of their own country they pretend to have forgotten their native language, and if they condescend to make an attempt to speak, they do so in so conceited and affected a manner that their former acquaintances are astonished to hear them, and feel quite ashamed of them.*

Speaking of the MSS. of his time, he says :—

I was at last in a manner compelled to do what I could for my nation and country, in order to draw the attention of the learned to the many beauties of our own mother tongue, and the many curious remains still concealed in numerous Welsh MSS., now fast hastening to decay in the chests and libraries of those who do not seem disposed to publish, or to permit others to peruse and examine them.

Of the whole work 1,250 copies were printed in London, and published at the expense of Sir E. Stradling, of Glamorganshire, a scion of an old Norman family. The reader is referred to " *Llyfryddiaeth y Cymry* " for further details, both about the author and his Grammar.

Only one copy of it has ever come under my notice. When a youth, some twenty years ago, this was exposed for sale in a bookseller's shop in Bristol, bound in vellum, and with the name of Stradling inside, perhaps in the handwriting of Sir E. Stradling himself. I was quite unaware at the time of its unique character, but the cursory glances bestowed on it gave such results that very shortly Stradling got mixed up in my dreams. The only Nineteenth century Stradling I can distinctly call to mind, is a working man, whose name occurred in the pay-sheet of a Glamorganshire colliery, near Caerphilly.

The next book, which it is within my compass to refer to, is one well known to Celtic philologists at home and abroad, viz., the "Archæologia Britannica," of E. Lhuyd, a native, it is generally supposed, of that corner of Shropshire which belongs to Welsh Wales.

---

* Wilkins' Literature of Wales, p. 167.

For the purpose of obtaining information about the Celtic languages, he engaged in long and expensive journeys in Ireland, Cornwall, and Brittany, if not the Highlands, towards the cost of which he received considerable assistance from various subscribers, and in rendering an historical account of the status of the Welsh language, it may not be out of place to examine the subscription list, prefixed to the great work published in 1707, which contained some of the results of his investigations. This included those who assisted towards the expenses, receiving apparently a copy of the book, and others who contributed without subscribing, altogether about 210 names.

Sir Thomas Mansel, of Margam, appears to have been one of his chief supporters. The list includes several Englishmen of high position, including Prime Minister Harley, the Earl of Clarendon, Lord Spencer, the Marquis of Powis, and Trelawney, Bishop of Worcester, the same Trelawney of Tower of London note, in James II.'s time, whose Cornish lineage is sufficiently indicated by the refrain,

" And shall Trelawney die, and shall Trelawney die?
And twenty thousand Cornishmen shall know the reason why."

It is not impossible that Trelawney's father or grandfather were Cornish-speaking, which would naturally the more incline him to patronize E. Lhuyd.

Among members or connections of well-known Welsh families we find Sir J. Aubrey, Henry Somerset Duke of Beaufort ; R. Foulks, E. Brereton, Sir W. Glyn, Sir Jeffrey Jeffrey, Sir C. Kemyes, Sir R. Middleton, Sir R. Mostyn, Sir R. Puleston, Sir E. Stradling, Sir J. Wyn, Powel, of Nanteos ; Price, of Gogerddan ; Salisbury, of Rug : and Vaughan, of Corsygedol.

The introduction of his "British Etymologicon"* is addressed to a man he calls, in a style extremely offensive to right feeling, the "Right Reverend Father in God, Humphrey, Bishop of Hereford." Bishop Humphrey was no novice in Welsh, as amply appears by this address, and elsewhere. Possibly he was the last Welsh-speaking Bishop of Hereford, for the Hanoverian dynasty, which shortly became paramount, is not credited with any favour towards Welsh ecclesiastics.

E. Lhuyd's preface itself is worth reading, if only to shew the difficulties such a man had to encounter. It is followed by a curious set of congratulatory verses, in Irish, Gaelic, Latin and Welsh, and these again by a Welsh preface, "At y Cymry."

To the Cornish Grammar he prefixed a Cornish preface of his own, the first piece ever printed in that language, and to his Irish-English Dictionary, an Irish preface. As a philological authority, Lhuyd has been long superseded, but his book is still not without interest.

Another work, but not occupying such original ground as either of the two preceding, was Thomas Richards' "Welsh-English Dictionary," published in 1753, based probably upon the "Welsh-Latin Dictionary" of Dr. Davies, of Mallwyd, published in 1682.

Somewhat singularly, R. Raikes, of Gloucester, was one of the vendors whose name appears at the foot of the title page. Why a Gloucester bookseller should make a speciality of selling a Welsh Dictionary we cannot easily understand, unless it were with a view to secure Herefordshire or Monmouthshire customers. W. Williams, bookseller, Monmouth, takes twenty-five copies—it is questionable if it would be safe

---

* This was a short vocabulary of about twenty pages, containing English words, with their equivalents either in Welsh or some other language, forming the 8th part of the work.

for anyone there now to take two.   This large number of
twenty-five copies can hardly be understood, but as an indication that East Monmouth and South-west Herefordshire contained at that time country squires who were either able to
read or took an intelligent interest in the language.   Raikes,
however, only appears to have subscribed for one copy.

Other subscribers include Sir T. Mostyn, M.P. for Flintshire,
W. Morgan, of Tredegar, and Capel Hanbury, of Pontypool,
M.Ps. for Monmouthshire; Herbert Mackworth, M.P. for
Cardiff; John Lloyd, of Peterwell, M.P. for Cardiganshire;
and Sir T. Salusbury (sic), Knt. ; nearly all these names represent
families existing at the present day, and I strongly incline to
believe that they were Welsh-speaking. When "Llyfryddiaeth
y Cymry" appeared the Mackworths and the Hanburys had
become too much Anglicized to be likely subscribers ; the
Morgans, not quite Anglicized in sentiment, but out of the
circle of Welsh letters ; on the other hand three of the Salis-
burys and Sir Piers Mostyn appear in the list.

PERIODICALS AND NEWSPAPERS.

In the course of compiling this volume, I entertained the
idea of giving a tolerably complete list of EXTINCT PERIODI-
CALS, but have since had to abandon it ; the difficulties of
procuring even a passable list are great, and very few Welshmen are equal to the task of furnishing one.

What I have seen of these convinces me that along with much
rubbish, along with much of merely a transient interest, there is
a good deal stowed away in their pages, illustrating the religious,
social, and literary history of Wales. A man who has the scent
of a trained book-hunter developed in him, will not however, be
long before he picks up various copies on dusty shelves in
small booksellers' shops, or on bookstalls, say in Cardiff,
Swansea, Bristol, or Chester.

The following is an attempt to present, more or less completely, a list of all Welsh periodicals and newspapers published in 1892, at the time of writing:—

CYLCHGRAWNAU (PERIODICALS).

NAME.	CHARACTER.	PLACE OF PUBLICATION.	WHEN ISSUED.
Athraw, Yr...	... Baptist ...	... Llangollen...	... Monthly, 1d.
Baner y Plant	... Independent	... Corwen ...	... Weekly, 1d.
Caniedydd y Plant	Children's Singer...	Briton Ferry	... Parts, 4d.
Cennad Hedd, Y	... Independent	... Merthyr ...	... Monthly, 2d.
Cerddor, Y ...	... Musical ...	... Wrexham ...	... Monthly, 2d.
Cerddor y Cymry ...	Ditto ...	... Llanelly ...	... Weekly, 1d.
Cronicl, Y ...	... Independent	... Bangor ...	... Monthly, 2d.
Cyfaill Eglwysig ...	Episcopalian	... Carmarthen	... Monthly, 1d.
Cyfaill yr Aelwyd...	Family Undenom'l	Llanelly ...	... Monthly, 3d.
Cymru ...	... Undenominational	Carnarvon...	... Monthly, 6d.
Cymru y Plant	... Children's Paper ...	Ditto	... Monthly, 1d.
Cwrs y byd...	... Independent	... Ystalyfera	... Monthly, 1d.
Diwygiwr ...	... Independent	... Llanelly	... Monthly, 3d.
Dysgedydd, Y	... Independent	... Dolgellau ...	... Monthly, 4d.
Dysgedydd y Plant	Ditto ...	Ditto ...	... Monthly, 1d.
Drysorfa, Y	... Calv. Methodist	... Holywell ...	... Monthly, 4d.
Trysorfa'r Plant...	Ditto, Children's ...	Ditto ...	... Monthly, 1d.
Eurgrawn Wesley-			
aidd, Yr ...	... Wesleyan ...	... Bangor ...	... Monthly, 6d.
[Frythones, Y	... Girls' Periodical ...	Llanelly ...	... Monthly, 2d.
	(Now emerged with Cyfaill yr Aelwyd).]		
-Geninen, Y	.. Undenominational	Carnarvon...	... Quarterly, 1s.
	(Two extra numbers yearly).		
Greal, Y ...	... Baptist ...	... Llangollen...	... Monthly, 3d.
Haul, Yr ...	... Episcopalian	... Carmarthen	... Monthly. 3d.
Lladmerydd, Y	... Calv. Methodist	... Dolgellau ...	... Monthly, 2d.
Llusern, Y ...	... Ditto	... Carnarvon...	... Monthly, 1d.
Newyddion da	... Missionary	... Newport, Mon.	... Monthly, 1d.
Pregethwr, Y			
Trysorfa'r Adroddwr	Recit. and Singing	Briton Ferry	... Quarterly, 3d.
Tlws Cerddorol	... "Singer's Jewel"...	Briton Ferry	... Six parts, 3d.
Traethodydd,Y	... Undenominational	Carnarvon...	... Bi-monthly, 1s.
Tywysydd ...	... Indep'nt Children's	Llanelly ...	... Monthly, 1d·

NEWYDDIADURON (Newspapers).

NAME.	CHARACTER.	PLACE OF PUBLICATION.	WHEN ISSUED.
Baner ac Amserau Cymru	Liberal	Denbigh	Bi-weekly, 2d. & 1d
Brython, Ye	Unionist	Lampeter	Weekly, ½d.
Celt, Y	Independent	Bangor	Weekly, 1d.
Cenhadwr, Y	Ditto	New York	
Columbia	American Welsh	Chicago	Weekly.
Clorianydd, Y	Episcopalian	Llangefni	
Cymro, Y	Welsh Socialist	Liverpool	Weekly, 1d
Dravod, Y	Welsh Colonial	Patagonia	Weekly, 1d.
Drych, Y	American Welsh	Utica, N.Y.	Weekly.
Genedl Gymreig, Y	Welsh Nationalist	Carnarvon	Weekly, 1d
Goleuad, Y	Calv. Methodist	Dolgelly	Weekly, 2d.
Gwalia	Conservative	Bangor	Weekly, 1d.
Gwyliedydd, Y	Wesleyan	Rhyl	Weekly, 1d.
Herald Gymreig, Yr	Liberal	Carnarvon	Weekly, 1d.
Llan a'r Dywysogaeth, Y	Episcopalian	Merthyr	Weekly, 1d.
Rhedegydd, Y	Labour	Festiniog	Weekly, 1d.
Seren, Y	Local	Bala	Weekly, ½d.
Seren Cymru	Baptist	Carmarthen	Weekly, 1d.
Tyst a'r Dydd, Y	Independent	Merthyr	Weekly, 1½d
Tarian y Gweithiwr	Workmen's Organ	Aberdare	Weekly, 1d.
Udgorn Rhyddid	Nationalist	Pwllheli	Weekly, ½d.
Werin, Y	Labour Nationalist	Carnarvon	Weekly, ½d.
Wythnos, Yr	Local	Corwen	Weekly, 1d.

ENGLISH NEWSPAPERS with Welsh Reading.

News of the Week	Cardiff.
South Wales Star	Cadoxton.
Cambrian News	Aberystwyth.
The Observer	Ditto.
The Journal	Carmarthen.
Glamorgan Free Press	Pontypridd.
Merthyr Express	Merthyr.
Merthyr and Dowlais Times	Dowlais.
Pontypridd Chronicle	Pontypridd.
Central Glamorgan Gazette	Bridgend.
Bridgend Chronicle	Ditto.
Cardiff Times	Cardiff.
Herald of Wales	Swansea.
Industrial World	Ditto.

The history of early periodical literature is mainly denominational; three of the earliest, viz., *Y Eurgrawn Wesleyaidd*, *Y Dysgedydd*, and *Y Drysorfa*, each of them backed by powerful and religious bodies, exist at the present day. *Seren Gomer* was another early periodical, edited by a Baptist, (Jos. Harries), which has long been extinct.

Of course periodical literature in England is very largely the product of the present century, and in Wales it may be said to be more entirely so. The first magazine issued was a threepenny fortnightly, in 1770—*Yr Eurgrawn Cymreig*, which existed just over three months. The second, the *Cylchgrawn Cymreig*, started at Trevecca, 1793, was a quarterly, of which only five numbers appeared, and bore the same subtitle, viz., *Trysorfa Gwybodaeth* (Treasury of Knowledge) as its predecessor. For an interesting account of these ventures see the "*Traethodau Llenyddol*," of L. Edwards. When the Nineteenth century dawned on Wales not a single vernacular periodical existed, nor for some years until *Yr Eurgrawn Wesleyaidd* appeared.

In 1828 John Blackwell, speaking at Denbigh, alluded to the fact of fourteen periodicals rising from the monthly press, and to the anomaly that the peasantry were almost the only contributors to their Welsh pages.* It remains a fact to-day, that contributors to the Welsh Press, both periodical and newspaper, are not unfrequently persons from whom similar contributions would be much unexpected in England, but it is perhaps less so as regards periodicals than in Blackwell's day ; on the other hand a stranger can hardly fail to be struck with the number of writers who have received an advanced education, some of whom have distinguished themselves in English examinations, who not only write freely in their own language, but retain (comparatively) a pleasing purity of diction in it,

---

* " Llyfryddiaeth y Cymry "—Publisher's preface viii.

although, as hinted previously, the educational disabilities of the language (if I may use the term) have prevented Welsh prose reaching that perfection it otherwise might.

The three undenominational organs, exercising the widest spheres of influence at the present day, are *Y Traethodydd*, now in its forty-eighth volume : *Y Geninen*, established 1883 ; and *Cymru*, 1891. Neither of these three are exactly paralleled in English periodical literature. All of them, though pursuing different lines, are miscellaneous in the character of their contents. "Y Traethodydd" being the most metaphysical and philosophical; "Y Geninen," controversial, political and literary ; "Cymru," historical and educational—all of them biographical and poetical. "Cymru" is strongly tinctured with the personality of the editor, who moreover understands the value of good printing, and illustrates his matter copiously by engravings : within a very few months the circulation of this new offspring of Celtic enterprise has gone up to about 5,000.

Probably the highest circulation of any of the periodicals belongs to Trysorfa'r Plant, about 37,000 monthly ; of the newspapers, Y Genedl Gymreig may have about 23,000 weekly.

Though the fact is not clearly brought out by the foregoing lists, an immense preponderance of the circulation of periodical and newspaper literature belongs to North Wales and Cardiganshire, comprising half the total Welsh-speaking population who read considerably more than the other half residing in the remainder of South Wales. At any rate, east of Llanelly the South does not seem able to develop such a vigorous literary life as finds its centre in the historic district of Carnarvon.

FUGITIVE LITERATURE. — Properly speaking we should class newspapers under this heading, they have, however, been enumerated above, and do not call for much comment, as a whole, being inferior in general worth to the periodi-

cals : it is to the latter that strangers must principally look for
illustrations of Welsh thought.

Almanacs furnish other specimens of fugitive literature—
here is an extract from the frontispiece of one for 1890,
published at Cardigan :—

> John Jones a John Bull sydd gym'dogion
>   Ond faint o gyfeillion nis gwn ;
> John Bull sydd o lynach y Saeson,—
>   A gwr tra pheryglus yw hwn ;
> John Jones sydd yn Gymro tra gwledig,
>   Ond gwir wr boneddig yw ef,
> Nid ydyw o duedd derfysglyd.
>   **D**ros heddwch y cyfyd ei lef.

How exceedingly grotesque to an Englishman this appears—
the next stanza begins—

> John Bull sydd o duedd ymyrgar.
> Gwr gwaedlyd o'i febyd y bu.

of the third I will English the first four lines, thus—

> Bull's coffers are crammed full of riches.
> Altho' he has a big debt in hand.
> O'er the ocean his wide estate stretches.
> But the monster has stolen all his land.

the fourth begins—

> Bull wthia ei iaith ar y bobloedd,
> A chais Seisnigeiddio pob lle.

The English reader will better understand the piece when I
say that it is about two neighbours—John Bull (hereinafter
called Bull) and John Jones.   John Jones is represented as a
person who, although admittedly countrified. is of superior
birth, of quiet habits, and ranges himself on the side of
"peace and order."   Bull, on the other hand, is a dangerous
character, of a quarrelsome, fierce disposition from his youth

upwards ; he has abundance of money, also landed property in
foreign countries, but to tell the truth, he is at the same
time heavily in debt, and has acquired the said property by
very questionable means. This does not exhaust all Bull's
failings ; he has a disagreeable way of thrusting his language
down other people's throats, and trying to *anglefy* every
place he can. The almanac winds up by alluding to a
league between John Jones a rather more distant neighbour called *Pat*, and another called the *Albaner*, who hails
from Caledonia, by means of which they hope to keep Bull
more within bounds, and, in fact, the author prophecies that
the latter will get the worst of it. Poor John Jones, I fear,
thy alliance is a *mésalliance*.

Not very far from the place where this publication was issued
is an institution commonly called *St. David's College, Lampeter*, where some of the young Joneses go to be trained up in
what Bull calls his Church. The managers have a peculiar
knack of fitting the students for their after life by entirely
excluding Welsh sermons from the College pulpit, except on
one day of the year, although, as a matter of fact, the great
majority will be placed in parishes where Welsh largely pre-
ponderates as the home language ; some of them where it is
almost exclusively used.

Whether they think that Welsh does not pay, and the
more pay the more souls "cured," or " cared for ;" or whether
they hold the view of a certain mitred personage, that
Wales is only a "geographical expression," they do not make
bold to say. However that may be, a troublesome newspaper
man from the North, named Gee, publishes in the banished
language some very provoking letters written to his paper
from Cardiganshire about Bull's Church, and actually goes
the length of calling the said Church *Yr Estrones* — the
Strangeress (to coin a word), which repeatedly forms a head-

ing in this paper.　As a reward for his trouble, he is reported
to be the best hated man in Wales.

Another specimen of a very different class came from the
pen of a medical student at Thomas' Hospital, when waiting
for the lecture.　I only give a portion to avoid prolixity.
Eben Fardd's translation is, it will be seen by Welsh readers,
inferior to the original in freshness and simplicity :—

> Tra crwydro'r wyf a chalon brudd
> > Ar hyd y nos.
>
> Heirdd heolydd Tref Caerludd.
> > Ar hyd y nos.
>
> Llais hiraethlawn a ddyweda,
> Pell yw gwlad yr iach fynydda,
> Dinas estron yw hon yma.
> > Ar hyd y nos.
>
> 　　*　　　　*　　　　*
>
> Yng Nghymru anian wena'n beraidd.
> > Ar hyd y nos.
>
> Pant a bryn sydd baradwysaidd,
> > Ar hyd y nos :
>
> Pyncia'r adar rhwng man frigau.
> Y dyffryn chwardd gan frithlon flodau,
> Peroriaeth ydyw swn ei ffrydiau,
> > Ar hyd y nos.

EBEN FARDD'S TRANSLATION.

> Whilst with heavy heart I roam.
> > Ar hyd y nos.
>
> O'er London streets far, far from home,
> > Ar hyd y nos :
>
> The whispers of sweet longing tell.
> Far are the mountains that excel
> This City where but strangers dwell,
> > Ar hyd y nos.

　　　　*　　　　　*

Simple nature smiles in Wales.

> Ar hyd y nos:

Glory crowns her hills and dales,

> Ar hyd y nos;

Sweet the sounds of her cascades

Music all her woods pervades.

The valley's verdure hardly fades,

> Ar hyd y nos.*

The student was the late Dr. John Pughe, of Aberdovey (Ioan ap Hu Feddyg).

One more reference to fugitive literature: I was walking with a well-known Welshman, while he was speaking to me of the persecutions endured by Dissenters within comparatively recent times in the neighbourhood where we were, and remarked, as near as I can recollect, " there is a power greater than the landlord's."

What does he mean? thought I to myself.

"It is that of the satirist. If anything particularly bad happened, there were generally two or three young men who went home and wrote a piece on the subject."

Somewhat singularly the last editor of Williams, Pantycelyn, confirms this view in his prefatory biographical notice, where he supposes that Williams may have escaped the fierce persecution which fell to the lot of some of his contemporaries, through the fact of his being a bard, and remarks that the "proud squire or the boorish priest would rather pay the heaviest fines, or go to prison for a year, than be 'immortalized' in a *tuchangerdd*, or made public [*ystrydebu*] in an interlude" [such as the productions of Twm o'r Nant, or Jonathan Hughes]. The satirical poem is a *tuchangerdd*,

---

* It must be borne in mind that the y of *hyd*, and the o of *nos*, are both long. "Up to night-time" would destroy the cadence, though preserve the number of syllables.

WELSH PUBLISHERS.—We cannot compare the state of Welsh literature with that of English without reference to the publishers. An overwhelming proportion of English works are published in London. Edinburgh secures a gradually lessening share as a prime centre, and it is seldom that any work intended for general circulation appears in the provinces without the name of a London firm appearing on the title page.

London is the great, and the the only great centre for book distribution in England. It is so, partly for purely economical reasons. Country booksellers frequently make contracts for the conveyance of London parcels, and carriage being up to a certain limit, a fixed standing expense, is not necessarily increased by the inclusion of a new book, of which the carriage, if it came from Birmingham or Glasgow, would eat into a large proportion of the profits, if not annihilate them; independently of this, the fact of a dozen different publishing houses being near each other, and being able to supply a dozen different books which are perhaps required by an agent, to make one parcel for the country trade, tends of itself to economy. London publishers are usually not printers, they are simply mediums of publicity and distribution, relying upon the retail trade of the whole kingdom as their constituency.

Now modern Welsh literature had its beginning principally in books of a religious character, which naturally called into existence a set of publishers relying for patronage on one or the other of the leading denominations of Wales.

The publishers of such books stood little or no risk, their principal profit lying in the printing, further responsibility being shouldered by the denomination or individuals with an extensive interest or acquaintance therein. To this class of business was attached one of a more purely literary character, which in one or two cases has spread into considerable dimensions, travellers are employed, and their productions have come to be pretty widely known, but probably in comparatively few cases does the copyright belong to the publishers.

To put the matter in brief, Welsh, as compared with English, is handicapped by the following *technical* reasons : (1) the increased difficulty of distribution ; (2) the fact that there is no centre in which a miscellaneous order can be collected by an agent ; (3) a considerable portion of the total literary output has been entrusted to small printers, who either do not understand how to bring their productions before the public at large, or have no particular incentive to do so.

Now I would suggest a plan whereby the whole current literature may be centralized, viz., by all the printers of Wales selecting a representative, say in Bangor or Cardiff, or in both places, and agreeing to send to such a one a few copies, *on sale*, of every work issued by them, on condition of the agent printing, and sending out at his own expense, a certain number of catalogues embracing *all* such works in stock.

By the adoption of a similar plan to the above, any person in a remote district wishing to know exactly what was in the market, could send for the catalogue and order from it. Of course this would necessitate the payment of commission on orders which might otherwise have come first hand, but I feel sure that the sale of Welsh books would be increased, and that it would eventually pay the printers, besides possibly bringing some obscure but worthy authors into notice. If the printers decline to co-operate, why could not such a society as the Cymmrodorion arrange for a repository of Welsh literature. Some such idea was mooted years ago by the late D. I. Davies.

Out of a considerable number of Welsh printers and publishers five may be mentioned more particularly :—

H. HUMPHREYS, Carnarvon, is remarkable for issuing

ninety-six small penny publications, all of a miscellaneous character, such as the "History of the Huguenots," "Napoleon," "William Penn," "John Penry," "Christopher Columbus," "Translators of the Welsh Bible," which are to be had bound in two volumes at 5s. 6d. each; also "Llyfryddiaeth y Cymry," printed some twenty-two years ago, at Llanidloes, which is now offered at the reduced price of 10s. 6d.

T. GEE AND SON, Denbigh: Newspaper publishing is undoubtedly the backbone of this firm, but they publish the following among other works:—Welsh Encyclopaedia, in 10 vols., £7 10s., in boards; Myvyrian Archaeology, with a translation of the laws of Howell Dda, £2; English-Welsh Dictionary, by D. Silvan Evans, £2; and Dr. Pughe's Welsh-English Dictionary, £1 10s.; the latter will be perhaps the best Welsh-English dictionary obtainable until the completion of that in course of compilation by D. Silvan Evans; Hiraethog's "Emmanuel," in two parts, 5s. and 4s., are to be obtained here, also others of his works. Hiraethog was scarcely less noted as a prose writer than as a chief bard of modern times. A selection of his prose works, price 16s., is to be obtained from

I. FOULKES, Brunswick Street, Liverpool, who is issuing a new edition of the "Iolo MSS." in prose and verse, at 21s. His present list includes "Enwogion Cymru (The Notables of Wales), at 21s.; the "Mabinogion," 17s.; and a shilling series called "Cyfres y Ceinion," one of which is the poetical works of Goronwy Owain: other two each contain 1,000 selected *englynion* by a large number of authors.

W. SPURRELL AND SON, is the only important Welsh book firm in South Wales. Their list includes the late William Spurrell's Dictionaries and Welsh Grammar.

The works of Gwallter Mechain, now out of print, were published over twenty years ago, by W. S, three vols., 24s.: the first volume is principally Welsh prose on archæological and literary subjects, the second Welsh poetry, the third English prose, lectures, addresses, and letters.

The Welsh-English Dictionary, by D. Silvan Evans, of which two parts are already issued, will, if nothing prevent its completion, be by far the most important work hitherto published by W. Spurrell and Son, this will not merely be an elaborate dictionary, but will, from the amplitude of its quotations, be such a repository of literature as to make its appearance almost a national event. The English Government might, in fact, do much worse than subsidize such an undertaking.

T. Jones, of Treherbert, has Islwyn's "Awdl ar y Nefoedd;" "Caniadau" by Euryfryn; also a booklet of Mynyddog's, at popular prices.

Hughes and Son, of Wrexham, are the most extensive book publishers in the Principality, among their works are "Cofiant John Jones, Talsarn," by the late Owen Thomas, 10s. 6d., considered a masterpiece of biography; Works of Ceiriog, 7s. 6d.; Theological and Literary Essays, by the late Lewis Edwards, of Bala, 7s. 6d. each vol.; the Literary Essays (*Traethodau Llenyddol*) constitute one of the standard volumes of Welsh prose, not of an immediately theological character; they are principally reprints from "Y Traethodydd," and embrace, among others, articles on "Coll Gwynfa" (Paradise Lost), "Kant's Philosophy," and "the Writings of Morgan Llwyd," "Welsh poetry" and "Logic." Mynyddog's Works, Hugh Morris (*Eos Ceiriog*), and Canwyll y Cymry,* 5s. each; Rowland's Grammar and Exercises, 4s. 6d. each; Dafydd Ionawr, for 3s. 6d., Gramadeg Caledfryn and Gramadeg Dewi Mon, 2s. each., besides a considerable number of other works, principally theological and poetical are to be obtained here.

---

* A cheaper edition of "Canwyll y Cymry" is published by W. Jones, Newport, Mon.

In South Wales there is a considerable falling off in the purchases of Hughes and Son's books. Really this is not much to be wondered at, they appear willing to run scarcely any risk, although probably a wealthy firm, nor do they attempt to introduce any new ideas into the trade, nothing even similar to the " Cyfres y Ceinion," of I. Foulkes, or the little penny publications of Humphreys, nor anything got out in better style altogether, to parallel, say Cassell's 3d. vols. in English literature, with, of course, less matter to meet the necessary smaller circulation in such a limited area.

The popular demand may be insufficient, but has any serious attempt been made to develop or create one?

There is at present but little published in Wales as a stepping stone between the ability which is possessed by thousands of young people in South Wales to read a little Welsh, and the ability to read with sustained interest any standard book, such as even " Drych y Prif Oesoedd " (out of date though that be). This stepping stone is practically taken in English, so far as many in England and Wales are concerned, by means of unmitigated rubbish. London comic papers, cheap novelettes, and the like, sold at railway book-stalls and elsewhere. In Welsh, it is partly supplied by "Cymru," and would be further by the publication of such a series as " Llyfrau 'r Bala," began sometime since by Owen Edwards. How much more food for reflection or useful information is there in such a book as " O'r Bala i Geneva," than in a publication like "Snap Shots," and a whole tribe of unmentionables, whose names shall not disgrace the pages of this book, and yet the language of this series (" Llyfrau'r Bala ") is within the reach of any ordinary youth or maiden of eighteen in Welsh Wales, and would be more so if the elementary schools developed the foundation knowledge gained out of school on a systematic basis.

In fact there is still room for an enterprising publishing firm to help fill up this gap to really assist in educating the taste of the nation, and familiarize the young people with the language they already know in part.

Have any of the larger Welsh publishers warmly promoted Welsh day school education ? With one exception (T. Gee), strange to say, although the adoption of such a course would almost infallibly strengthen their trade and improve both the quantity and quality of the vernacular literature, they stand to one side, not perhaps apathetically, but to say the least, as though it was a matter not worth their while to spend a penny on an effort to provide for the literary future of the nation, in which either they or their successors will be so much interested pecuniarily. If English becomes the prevailing language, they will cease to be publishers to any considerable extent, while the distribution of literature, will still more than at present be made from London.

By far the larger part of the 1,000 poetical works estimated to have been issued during this century have been put in the hands of small printers, perhaps local friends of the authors, who have trusted to their own immediate circle for the sale of their works. The result has been a low bill for inferior workmanship, poor paper, and poor ink, and a very limited circulation : they would like to get at all Wales, instead of half a county, but how to do it they know not, and perhaps after a few years the remainder of their stock is destroyed, or sold for waste paper. In fact the "remainder" of the first edition of *Cywydd y Drindod*, was burnt by the author.

Be that as it may, the number of rare books in Wales is excessively large, none of the officials of public institutions appearing to have even the ghost of an idea of making collections of their own local literature. Ask the public librarians at Swansea, Cardiff, and Newport, or the local secretaries at

most of the working men's clubs in Wales, if they aim at
securing copies of all works published by authors residing
within or on the borders of their county. Can they furnish fair
samples of the local train of thought, which will enable a
future historian to see what was said, and how it was said,
by men of the period? No, their managing committees would
feel like fish out of water, or else targets of ignorant ridicule
if they attempted such a thing, and then the said librarians
might think themselves ill-used if they were expected to be
au fait in unearthing half forgotten *odlau*, or even some plain
cofiant of a local worthy.

Does Newport Library possess anything of Islwyn's ; Cardiff
any of the Rhondda booklets ; Swansea any of the Swansea
Vale and East Carmarthen poets? The two latter libraries may
possess a few gifts of comparatively well-known works, but
that is a very different thing to having a comprehensive collection, such as a few sixpences and shillings spent every quarter
of a year would have brought together.

The idea of a Welsh museum has been mooted again and
again, but has taken little root, possibly because the popular
idea of a museum is rather confined to fossils, skeletons,
stuffed birds, and that ilk. It is, however, a matter that
certainly deserves to be brought before the public again, though
in a few generations it will be a much more difficult and
expensive matter to obtain a fairly perfect collection of Welsh
literature than at present.

Gwilym Lleyn advocated more than twenty years ago a
Welsh museum, where a copy of every Welsh book, or
relating to Wales, might be preserved. He says, in reference
to the need of such a place containing fugitive literature, that
an Elegy, Association Circular, or Almanac, may give more information than would be supposed on first thoughts, and that
complete sets of the periodicals ought to be obtained,—

Y mae Marwnad, Llythyr Cymanfa, Cerdd neu Almanac weithian
yn rhoddi mwy o wybodaeth nag a feddylid ar y dybiaeth gyntaf
ac heb law hyny gwelid yn angenrheidiol meddu holl gyfnodolion
Cymreig pob oes yn llawn.—Llyf y C. preface xxii:

Although the fact is not clearly brought out in the preceding
pages, present day Welsh literature may be looked upon as
being the result of two somewhat distinct historical currents,
which are necessarily more or less mingled.

There is a literature in a line of continuity with that
possessed by Wales in the middle ages, which may be described
as national, and largely unique in its character, yet always the
property of the few, rather than of the nation at large.

We have, first of all, the old bards, and the elaborate versi-
fication settled in the Fifteenth century : then, a small but
almost unbroken succession of those who were initiated into
the system during the three succeeding centuries down to
Goronwy Owain, while the Grammar of J. D. Rhys, the
Dictionary of Dr. Davies, and the "Archaeologia Britannica,"
successively paved the way, both for the systematic study of
Welsh or kindred languages, and for increased attention being
given to the records of the past, which otherwise might have
remained in oblivion : in the same line again we have the
" Myfyrian Archaeology," the labours of Iolo Morganwg, and
subsequent publication of the " Iolo MSS.," Gwallter
Mechain's works the " Mabinogion," and other works.

Turning now to the other current, to which we are principally indebted for the existence of an extensive and *popular*
Welsh literature in the Nineteenth century, we place its
source with the works of Wm. Salesbury, and the translation
of the Welsh Bible, in the Sixteenth century, " Canwyll y
Cymry," and other religious works, in the Seventeenth ; while
its great expansion is due indirectly to the Methodist revival
of the Eighteenth, and the general practice which arose shortly

after of teaching young and old in Dissenting congregations to
read their own tongue. To the ability to read, writing was
frequently added as a SELF-TAUGHT art, then the additional
acquirement of literary composition, contributions to the
Denominational magazines, and the coming forward as a local
poet or essayist.

If it had not been for this religious movement (which in
reality included secular instruction), the literature of Wales in
the Nineteenth century would be within much more contracted
limits than it actually is, and we should not be able to record
the phenomenon of (roundly) 1,000 poetical publications being
issued during that period.

We must, however, also consider that the mental energy of
the people once stimulated, has caused the popular current to
run somewhat alongside that other and more classical one,
though we see, especially in some places in South Wales, that
the process of Anglicization has so far absorbed that energy,
that a development in either direction is dwarfed.

We have in our own day the *chair awdl* and more popular
englyn, or the continuation of the style of the old literature,
as well as the study of the literature itself, side by side with the
language as an academical subject, though only to a very
small and limited extent ; and we have on the other hand the
simple *pryddest*, or poem, the literature adapted to the
capacities of the people, which may or may not yet become
invigorated with fresh life and firmness, in accordance with
the course followed by the leaders of the national education.
If that is the case, the division between the esoteric and
and exoteric, the inner and outer circles will become less and
less sharply defined—what more, let the Twentieth century
tell.

Enough has been said in the preceding pages, to indicate
that in the Welsh language itself we have an instrument

remarkably adapted for popular culture, and by a certain obtuse-
ness of insight or by prejudice on the part of the governing
powers almost as remarkably neglected : a language not merely
adapted for the imparting of ordinary and necessary knowledge, as well as applicable to many of the material exigencies
of modern life, but in a high degree nervous, refined, and
capable of calling forth the emotions, as well as educating the
perceptive faculties : a language moreover certainly worthy
the attention of Welshmen, and one affording to Englishmen
an excellent and bracing mental exercise, far more so, in fact,
than either French or German.

Then as to literature, the civilized world will probably never
turn to Welsh, to find expositions of the latest solutions of
biological or physical problems, or even of the most press-
ing social questions, what however it will expect to find, is
word-painting of a high order, vivid portraitures, life-like
sketches of men and things which may if handled aright, be
of service to mankind.   Welsh literature moreover, is a living
literature ever seeking expansion, but ever being cribbed,
confined, and weakened by the peculiar and adverse circumstances which it has to face.

In the concluding chapter we will refer again both to the
signs of vitality, and signs of decay exhibited in the principality
at large, with regard both to the spoken and written language.

CHAPTER VIII.

WHAT constitutes a nationality? Authorities may echo a few stereotyped answers to this question, but I much question whether, if they attempted truly to analyze these mental conceptions, the judgment of each would not be found to differ in some point from that of his brother authority.

We do not attempt to call the peoples of British India a nationality; though they are united under one Government, we have to admit that they include several nationalities, yet the essentials as to what constitutes a nation cannot be brought exactly to book, they are of too subtle and indefinable a character.

We may however, admit the term *nation*, as applied to the Welsh, because they naturally speak of themselves as *y Genedl Gymreig* (the Welsh nation), in preference to *y Bobl Gymreig* (the Welsh people), and because there is ground to believe that such a distinction is natural and historical, and not artificial, *i.e.*, not forced by some attempt to *manufacture* patriotic sentiment, and that what a nation calls itself under these circumstances is *prima facie* evidence that we shall not be transgressing the laws of language (even of the English

language) by literally translating the word.   In the same way,
supposing the Poles or Hungarians habitually use a corresponding term of themselves, it is alike entitled to respect and
acknowledgment.

On the one hand we see a million people more or less
acquainted with what is to us English folk a foreign tongue,
a large number of whom carry on their mental operations in
it ; and on the other hand half a million living in the same
country who are strange to the said tongue.   Can we roughly
draw the line, as the census draws it, between those
with an exclusive knowledge of English, and those with a
knowledge of Welsh ?   Perhaps we can from some points of
view, because many of the half million look upon themselves
as belonging to no other *nation* than the English, but in
reality, apart from the rough and ready linguistic test,
NATIONALITY is much more indefinable, though it is not complete without the sense of *corporate existence*.   Such a state
has been denied to Wales for many hundreds of years.

Modern life is supposed to tend to break down all the
barriers of nationality of race and even language. and to weld
the nations of the earth into one mighty mass.   That something like this may not be witnessed in a future stage of the
world's history I am not prepared to deny.   It may by way of
confirmation be justly affirmed that in a state of savagery
and barbarism distinctions rapidly accumulate, separations
become intensified, and languages but of yesterday bearing
the closest resemblances. become in a few years mutually
unintelligible ; so that the whole tendency of civilization
appears opposed to the perpetuation of local distinctions of
blood and speech.

When, however, we come to examine more closely into the
working of the laws which govern the mental habits of the
population of the United Kingdom. we shall find that side by

side with the levelling tendency which annihilates distinctions
and which would have one law, one language, one cosmopolitan character throughout the land, that there is a
counter tendency of a natural and involuntary character constantly emphasizing distinctions and building up local differences, tending even to make languages, and that it leaves
tangible phenomena in almost every town we may visit, which
are in fact the offspring of these two divergent forces—the
CENTRIPETAL and the CENTRIFUGAL of the human mind,
as manifested in language.

Take, for instance, the heart of civilization, London itself,
perhaps none of my readers need be told that the London accent
is strongly noticeable in a large proportion of its inhabitants :
and more than that, the wealthier classes, who would by all
means eschew the accent, have a certain style of speech,
which is a differentiation of language in embryo. Just a
similar remark might be passed about the two classes of society
in Bristol, viz., the well-to-do or the highly educated and the
artizan classes, each of them manifest a tendency to divergence
in language which is continually checked by the centripetal
force of outside association.

Nearly all the great English towns have peculiar features,
quite *sui generis* in speech or habits of thought and mental
characteristics. Manchester has the Manchester man; Liverpool
is reported to possess the Liverpool gentleman ; the great Mercian capital, Birmingham, has a character peculiarly its own (I
am not, of course, alluding principally to physical features) ; so
has Leeds ; so has Newcastle.

It does not require much insight into the nature of language,
to affirm, that if it were possible to isolate any of these great
centres from the rest of the world, that they would rapidly
without a literature, and slowly with one, pass into a stage
wherein their populations would become foreigners in mind,

and unintelligible to other Englishmen in language. The great point is this:—that this tendency to incipient nationality manifests itself even in such leading English towns, in this busy wide-awake Nineteenth Century.

If there is one great town in Great Britain more than another that possesses no distinctive type of character, that town is Cardiff; there is really nothing about Cardiff men to set them off distinctively as Cardiffians.

The probability is that this arises from Cardiff being a new town, the home of foreigners, of settlers from various parts of the country, that in a hundred years time there will be no occasion for such a remark, and that there will be a Cardiff type as distinct as that of a Bristolian. I venture to surmise a further probability, viz., that the type will be found in the main to possess Welsh characteristics, and that the process of assimilation will be much accelerated by the foundation of a Welsh University. Not that I am so foolish as to suppose that there is an inherent force in any particular course of literary education which will produce results exactly analogous with the illustrations already brought forward, which are largely affected by the peculiarities of individuals who lived a thousand years ago or more, transmitted to descendants, and modified or developed by various local circumstances affecting the mental habit directly or indirectly mainly through the bodily organism, while all the heterogenous elements introduced into such a community from time to time have failed to destroy a certain residual homogeneity of character: but I rather affirm that the needs of Wales call for a distinct character of literary education, which will in its turn eventually *assist* in determining the complexion of the mental habits and tendencies of the population at large, though it may not mainly decide it.

How absurd, some of my readers may say, how ridiculous to suppose that the grandsons or great-grandsons of wealthy

Cardiff merchants are ever likely to reflect physically and mentally their proximity to a people whose language and distinctive features are rapidly being swallowed up in the ever-advancing tide of English influence.

To this I reply, there is, it is true, a tide of English influence, which is the absolutely necessary concomitant of recent developments of the resources of Wales, of the influx of English-speaking populations, and the necessity of acquiring much information through the medium of their language, but this by no means precludes the possibility of a contemporaneous tide of Welsh influence giving a strong flavour of the soil to the immediately succeeding generation, and fusing all the differing elements of Welsh society into a more homogeneous mass, both linguistically and socially.

Whether this be so or not, whence come the middle-class of Co. Waterford, of Co. Dublin, and other parts of Ireland, who from their speech and habits are put down at once as unmistakably Irish, and who are Irish too, in patriotic* sentiment? To a large extent it is English and Welsh, not Irish blood that runs in their veins, and yet in the course of a few generations these families have been leavened with the Irish-Celtic character, not such an unmixed one, it is true, as is found in the West, but one which markedly differentiates them from Englishmen.

The Anglo-Normans of the Twelfth century settled down within the "Pale," but they speedily became Irish in speech and habits.

Cromwell's soldiers, and other English colonists of the Seventeenth century, came to live among a people terribly decimated by the sword, but in the course of a few generations

---

* By patriotic I must be understood as *not* using the term in its usually accepted political sense—love of country exists apart from any ideas as to form of government.

their descendants became redolent of the soil, and par-
takers of a character which, whether the term is defensible on
ethnological grounds or not, we call *Irish*. Even in the
North, where the work of depopulation had advanced to a
greater extent, and the sturdy Scot stepped in, keeping almost
unchanged the religion of the Kirk, he has not escaped, (as
far as my observation goes) losing some of his previous
national characteristics and nolens-volens, adopting some of
those of the land of Patrick. What has taken place in Ireland
has also taken place in Wales on a smaller scale, and will
probably continue to do so, in perhaps a less marked way in
the future.

Not merely do we see these two tendencies in England, but
also on the Continent. There, the Greek language is purifying
itself from Turkish idioms or phrases, Norwegian casting off
Danish influence, Flemish asserting itself and recognized in
the scheme of elementary instruction, and on the whole we
may say that a small nation has a better chance of living in
the Nineteenth Century, than in the Seventeenth.

So much for what I may call the general principle of the
spontaneous growth of nationality. Now let us see it applied
to the modern racial affinities of the Welsh, without going so
far back as to disentangle Gael and Cymry, Iberian, Pict and
Brython.

A very striking feature to a traveller in some parts of South
Wales, who is alive to racial characteristics, is the number of
Welsh-speaking persons he meets with whose physiognomy
indicates that they are much more nearly related to the
"*hiliogaeth Hengist*" than to Caradawg or King Arthur;
to the Saxon than the Briton.

There are three or four common types of physique and of
countenance seen in Wales, which may be in popular parlance
put down as *Celtic*, that is, they are worn by persons repre-

senting peoples who have spoken Welsh, or a Celtic tongue, for some 1.500 years : these types predominate still in Wales, especially in North Wales, but individuals are frequently met with, of recognized English types, speaking Welsh, and, in addition, with Welsh habits of mind, more or less. Some of these are from families quite lately introduced, and bearing Scotch or English names, a fact which was commented on by the late D. I. Davies, in the course of his examination before the Education Commission. Such families soon learn the pretty twirl at the end of a sentence, which is common to North and South Walians when speaking English—on this Alexander Ellis, president of the Philological Society, remarked in a paper on the " Delimitation of the Welsh and English Languages,"* published in *Y Cymmrodor*.

Some years ago Dr. Beddoe, of Clifton, wrote a prize Eisteddfodic essay† bearing on the Ethnology of England, shewing that except in the case of Ipswich and Hull, (two towns where foreign influence doubtless affected the result,) the *average* colour of the hair deepens in colour as we proceed further westward, until it reaches its maximum in the black haired peoples of Wales and Cornwall.

He did, however, carefully guard from the assumption that the colour of the hair of an individual was proof of his ethnological relations, illustrating his position by the case of the Jews, who are a dark haired nation, though there are light haired Jews in every nation under the sun.

---

* " The peculiar intonation, or rising inflexion spoken of at the end of the Extract [from a communication by Dr. I. Owen] is a very trustworthy mark of a Welshman speaking English. It is sometimes very pretty　*　* but it is decidedly un-English at all times." [D. I. O. quotes Warner of Bath, in 1798,] " all the children of Flintshire speak English very well, and were it not for a little curl or elevation of the voice at the conclusion of the sentence (which has a pleasing effect) one should perceive no difference in this respect between the North Walians, and the natives of England."

† This was never published.

Speaking of Cardiganshire, he remarked on the traces of
Flemish blood by the banks of the Teivi. This is another
instance of absorption into the body of Welsh nationality. In
South Pembrokeshire and Gower the Flemings remained distinct,* but in Cardiganshire they failed to do so, though they
left behind them a memorial of their existence in the name of
a spot still called *Verwig*, the *wig* being the *wick* we get in
Berwick, and they have, I incline to suspect, left a permanent
impress of their character upon the men of Cardiganshire—the
"red Cardies," as they are proverbially called, but so far as I am
aware their language has left no traces in the vernacular of
the district. Flemish blood is also mixed in that of the Welsh
speaking district of Llandudoch (Pembroke).

Just as in the case of England, Welsh nationality is not
based upon unity of ethnic relations, though it is generally
believed, and probably with some foundation of truth, that
there is less mixture of blood in Wales than in any considerable district in England; however that may be, a
NATIONAL CHARACTER has been developed, containing points
common to both North and South Wales, and which may in its
entirety be taken as coming nearer the French type of character
than it does to the English, this is especially the case in South
Wales; not merely is it so with the people themselves,
but there is an assimilation in the pronunciation of certain
words derived from the Latin, which the English tongue has
treated very differently, c.f., *gras Duw*,† and *grace Dieu ;* also
the aforementioned *Dwfr* and *Douvres*, which we have
lengthened into Dover.

Again, there is far more similarity between the physique of
Englishmen and Norwegians, and Frenchmen and Welshmen,

---

* The English language which differed but little from Flemish
survived, Saxons being probably mixed with the Flemings.

† This is pronounced nearly as in French.

on the one hand, than between Englishmen and Welshmen on the other: that is to say, notwithstanding all the
anomalous or unlooked for types that may be found in these
nations, there is a certain average standard which may be
taken as the basis of comparison.

In the Fifteenth century Welsh nationality, which had been
weakened 300 years before by the establishment of the semi-
independent Norman Lordships, and again rudely shaken by
the conquests of Edward I., was still a tolerably compact, and
perhaps a growing force, supported by a comparatively
abundant literature, but without the keystone of responsible
government, with no centralization, no ground of political
unity.

The Sixteenth century saw begun what we have before
noticed as the process of "denationalization and deodorization," which was partially averted by the publication of the
Welsh Bible, but ruled more or less till the middle of the
Eighteenth century. It is to the Methodist revival that Wales
owes much of what she possesses in the way of a national
spirit.

This unprecedented movement—not to speak now of its
religious aspect—did two things for Wales, it trained the
people in habits of association and organization, and it gave a
lasting impetus to efforts which had been previously made to
teach the people to read in their own tongue.

Episcopalianism has accomplished neither of these results to
anything like the same degree, hence it is by no means uncommon to find an Episcopalian who is able to speak the language
colloquially, but was never taught to read it. And on the
other hand such is the influence of Welsh in dissenting congregations, that there are at the present day thousands of young
people, and some older ones, who can read Welsh (imperfectly),
and listen *habitually* to Welsh sermons, but who cannot speak
ss

it, or at least, are more masters of English. This is a silent, but convincing proof of the power and vitality of the language, and should disprove the idea that Welsh preaching in large towns, is almost exclusively arranged for those who *think* in that language. It can easily be seen in which class the national sentiment is likely to be most consciously felt—whether among those who can read the language or those who cannot.

So much for the historical aspects of the question, we will now make some attempt to discuss the Welsh mental constitution ; or rather some of the peculiar aptitudes and disabilities of the people.

It has been long the fashion to cast the blame of a Welshman's non-success in practical life upon his language. This is an unphilosophic way of putting it. The real drawback, viz., ignorance of English, is another matter about which every year less and less can be said, and even that by no means covers the whole ground.

Such objectors appear to forget the influence of national characteristics in determining the aptitude of individuals for particular lines of work ; for instance, if every Welshman were to wake up to-morrow, as entirely English in speech as a Kentish farmer, while the whole of his past knowledge of Welsh had passed into the limbo of forgetfulness, have we any right to suppose that such a condition would further the material advancement of Wales, and that her sons and daughters would be at the top of the tree in every useful art ?

Certainly not : I much doubt if there would be, on the whole, a superiority to what exists at the present time in any one calling or trade in consequence, beyond that acquired by increasing familiarity with English technical trade literature, and such as would be consistent with a more thoroughly Duoglot state than Wales has yet attained ; then, as now, England would lead in the mechanical arts and sciences.

Wales has produced respectable mechanical engineers, and will do so again, but for the same reasons that the largest engineering firms are principally found in parts of England where Scandinavian blood is most abundant, (not even always in the neighbourhood of coal, as the names of Robey, Marshall, Hornsby, Ransome will testify,) in preference to those parts where Celtic blood is more largely found, we may well suppose that Welsh mental characteristics are not pre-eminently favourable to excellence in practical mechanics. I am pretty well satisfied that it would be found that those men whose names are connected with useful mechanical inventions, as well as triumphs of heavy engineering, much more largely represent Eastern, especially North-Eastern families, than Western or Southern.

We cannot, however, draw any hard and fast line, such a one does not exist in nature ; for instance, the son of Taliesin ap Iolo lately died as manager of the large concern of Bolckow, Vaughan and Co., of Middlesborough : he was, I presume, a Welsh-speaking Welshman. The lesson I wish inferred from the above remarks, is that the mental activity of the nation, quite independently of whichever language is spoken, does not chiefly find its outlet in the direction of the mechanical arts, but in ways which do not lead to so much result from a pecuniary point of view.

In poetical genius and powers of oratory, we have to yield the palm to the Welsh, and in making the comparison, the standard should not be what poets and orators can one country muster, with a population at various periods from ten to eighteen times to that of the other, with all the advantages furnished by colleges and schools of long standing, over against the poets and orators of the smaller country, the language of which has for nearly 400 years ceased to be that recognized by the civil power, and whose education in it has been carried on out of school; we must rather compare the average mind of the one with the average mind of the other, as well as look at living examples.

As an illustration of Welsh oratorical powers of speech, I insert the following, which relates to the late Owen Thomas, of Liverpool, himself a highly educated man, and author of some Welsh works, such as "Cofiant John Jones, Talysarn."

"An Englishman even, not understanding the Welsh language, could not fail to be rivetted as Dr. Thomas would be heard reasoning with his audience, now in argument, now in tones of warning, now in earnest appeal. His clear, ringing voice, his distinct articulation, his crisp sentences, his varied tones, the thoroughness with which he threw his whole soul into his preaching, could not fail to fasten the attention even of one who might not understand a word he said. It is recorded that Charles Dickens one day stood in amazement as he heard him preaching at Bangor at an Association to a crowd of 15,000 people, keeping his hearers spellbound. How much more would it be thus with one who understood all he said."[*]

Recollect reader, that it by no means follows, that because a certain gifted preacher had such extraordinary power, as has frequently been exercised by native Welshmen, both literate and illiterate, that therefore there is any true divinity about it *i.e.* that *his words were inspired from above.*

The possession of these oratorical powers, is often a great snare, both to people and speaker, almost as much as when the grand swelling chords, the awe-inspiring music of Handel, combined with scripture words, fills them with the delusion that they are either offering some service to the Almighty, or are on the borders of doing so. When the standard of preaching is generally acknowledged, as it will in a future day, to be nothing short of an immediate exercise of Divine

* "Monthly Tidings," vol. viii, p. 162.

power, apart from mere natural gifts ; then not only will priest-
craft of all shades and descriptions fall utterly, but the
miserable substitutes for Divine music in the soul found in
so-called "sacred" concerts, cantatas, and oratorios, the darling
idols of the Welsh people, will be thrown to "the moles and the
bats." There will then, it is true, be found a place for oratory,
but a very different and more subordinate one to that it now
occupies.

What about Celtic influence on the character of English
authors and statesmen? Three great men of the Seventeenth
century were of Welsh descent, on one side or the other,
Oliver Cromwell, William Penn, and John Milton. Englishmen may smile incredulously when spoken to about the
Welsh blood that flowed in Milton's veins; personally I do
not think the idea at all ridiculous, that it materially
influenced his genius and assisted him to take a foremost
place in English literature.

So with Robert Burns: it is not impossible that he may
be called a Strath Clyde Briton, with a Celtic-speaking
ancestry, dating not many centuries back. Macaulay's genius
and style was certainly a Celtic one, notwithstanding his
unreasonable prejudices against Highlanders and Quakers,
himself descended from a family of the former on his father's
side, and from the latter on his mother's side.

John Bright seems to us a typical Englishman, and I confess
I cannot from a superficial glance see much of the Celt about
him, but have little doubt that a lineal ancestor of his was a
Brit, *i.e.*, a Celtic Briton, just as the Lollard Walter Brut, of
Herefordshire, appears to have been a Welshman of the
Black Mountain district.

The average Lancashire man has a good strain of Celtic
blood, and I think we must give him credit for superior commercial abilities, power of organization, and grasp of detail.

Few elementary schoolmasters are unapprised of the existence of the house of John Heywood, the head of which is now
the third of that name, founded some fifty years ago, by a
poor man, whose features remind one in some degree of a
Northwalian. As an instance of the extraordinary powers of
John Heywood II., it is said that of the *thirty thousand* or so
of accounts opened in his books, there was not one of which
he was not personally cognizant and completely informed.
Perhaps few men could say as much of a tenth of that number. Query, was this power of memory derived in an intensified form from some of the subjects of that British "king" of
Strathclyde (which includes Lancashire), who rowed King
Edgar on the Dee, circ. 961?

In the drapery business, a Welshman's sense of form, colour,
and harmony generally assist him, in fact drapery is one of
those callings in which Welshmen who go up to London are
peculiarly successful. Some years ago I knew a Monmouthshire man whose father was English, but who had Welsh pro-
clivities, and had taught himself the language by going to a
Bible class, and making use of such opportunities as he could
lay hold of, attending a Welsh congregation, both when in
London and when I knew him in Bristol. When wanting a
situation in London from a drapery house, previous to my
acquaintance with him, he contrived to secure a berth in the
mantle department, of which he knew little or nothing, by
concealing his ignorance, and, what is more, worked it successfully, by using the "*naws*"* with which nature had endowed
him. In his case a knowledge of Welsh proved a stepping
stone to French.

It is not an uncommon error for English people to imagine
that they can well afford to leave the Welsh language or

---

* I use this word in its Herefordshire sense of "tact" (low English=
gumption), which differs somewhat from the Welsh meaning.

Welsh nationality out of their reckoning, in regard to social and political questions, because English is generally understood.

This is illustrated by a comparison of the career of the two Cardiff dailies, one of which echoes the popular voice, and on financial or economical questions frequently adopts sounder views than the other paper, which opposes the sentiment of the majority of Welsh people on political and ecclesiastical questions, tooth and nail, in season and out of season. Yet, strange to say, its circulation probably comes near, if it does not exceed that of its rival. One reason for this I believe to be, that it has on its staff men who understand Wales, not from a distant standpoint, but as themselves part and parcel of the nation knowing intimately its weakness, and better able to judge of its strength than strangers, knowing its history and language more or less sufficiently well to enable them the better to understand the Wales of to-day from the Wales of yesterday, so that, although an article may sometimes appear bitterly ridiculing the national idea, it may be followed by another manifesting an undercurrent of sympathy, or perhaps by a biographical sketch of a deceased person, which Welshmen instinctively feel could not have been written by a non-naturalized *alien*.

Not long since I was in a railway carriage in Mid-Wales, where some English persons, one of them a settler in Merioneth-shire, were discussing the proprietor of an English newspaper published in Wales. "It is no use," said one in reference to this proprietor's attitude, "ignoring the Welsh language. It is a fact and you must recognize it.' He could not speak it himself, but I understood that his family were being brought up to do so.

Let no one suppose, that because I take occasion in this volume to speak of the extraordinary beauty of some portions of Welsh literature, of the power of the language, of the ease with which it can be adapted as an instrument of education

in the abstract, and view it (conjoined to English) as conducive
to a participation in the civilization of the Nineteenth Century,
that therefore I am crying up the Celt against the Saxon.   No!
I am too much of a Saxon myself to do that, and while I
admit that such a people as the Welsh, have possibilities
within their reach, which the English will never be able to
aspire to, I admit, once and for all, that the latter have
national qualities, which to a far larger extent go hand in hand,
with material progress.   From the commercial point of view
the Welsh language comes but insignificantly into sight, and
we are correspondingly tempted to assign a minimum quantity
of the existence of Nationality, nevertheless it exists, as a
solid fact.

In the face of the steam engines and the telegraphs of our
age, we are brought in contact with characteristics, modified
it is true, and perhaps almost transfigured, but at the root the
legitimate lineal representatives of those which predominated
in the Gaul, long before he had bowed his neck to the Roman
yoke, and characteristics on the other hand the ancestry of
which we find in the manners and habits of thought of rude
and simple dwellers by the Elbe.   That is to say, the Englishmen and Welshmen of to-day exhibit in their own persons,
effects of causes which operated at the very dawn of history.

It is well-known that were every man to trace his ancestry
back to the Norman Conquest, several lines of descent would
be found to unite in one individual, and back in the Eleventh
Century the ancestors of every Englishman now living must
have been very numerous, while there is probably in no case
a line of independent descent: or, in other words, that
distant cousins have married of very necessity, otherwise the
ancestors of the English would immensely outnumber what
we know to have been the maximum population of our island
at any time under the Norman Kings.

Now, bearing this in mind, let us set ourselves theoretically to analyze the blood of the average Englishman. Of course we are not saying that an individual specimen anywhere exists, any more than an average ear of corn exists in a wheat field, they may be all above or below the average. We will suppose, as a preliminary, that the influence of each parent is equally divided in the offspring.

Proceeding on these bases, perhaps it would not be far from the mark to assign influences in the average English mental constitution to the sources and in the proportion following :—

SAXON AND ANGLIAN	15
CELTIC	30
DANISH ...	15
DANO-NORMAN	5
FRENCH, JEWISH, ROMAN, &c. ...	5

Celtic ancestry must be understood not in a strictly scientific way, but to relate to persons speaking a Celtic language. French includes Huguenot ancestry. Roman blood is partly derived from the Imperial occupation of the country, and partly through indirect sources.

Attempting to analyze Welsh blood the same way, we might say,

CELTIC	70
SAXON AND ANGLIAN ...	15
DANISH ...	5
NORMAN AND ROMAN	5
FLEMISH, &c. ...	5

Turning to the mediæval history of Scotland, we find a Celtic house reigning over a Teutonic-speaking population in the South-east, and also over different Celtic-speaking populations in the remaining parts of the country.

Just as in the case of Wales,—there are considerable

TT

differences of blood, but at the same time a distinct feeling of Nationality.

But the parallel between Wales and Scotland does not go much further. The feeling of Scotch nationality, it is true, has reference to the past history of Scotch independence, but it is kept up in this work-a-day period of ours, if not largely based upon the existence of various distinct institutions of Civil government. Foremost among these is the Scotch system of Elementary Education, capped by the four Scotch Universities, adapted to persons of very slender or moderate means : besides which there are various small differences in legal matters, which help to remind a man if ever he crosses the border, that he was brought up a Scotchman.

Their national system of religion, will it is hoped, be soon abolished, though the effects of the attitude of the nation towards the reformation, will be, and are perpetuated in the general character of the free Churches of the country. Under the present system of the state recognizing Presbyterianism only, as soon as the Queen's railway carriage has conveyed her across the border the fiction is assumed of her ceasing to be an Episcopalian, and becoming a Presbyterian : as soon as she returns to England, she lapses back again to Episcopalianism i.e. a few shades nearer the unreformed Popish religion.

Welsh nationality differs from Scotch also in the fact that it exists apart from legislative enactments. It draws upon the history of the past undoubtedly, it loves to dwell on the time when national independence was realized, though haltingly, and it treasures up store of the memory of men whose deeds have been handed down with approbation, as links in the chain of national progress ; but in reality the great backbone to these feelings, is the existence of the Welsh language; not but what Welshmen are very willing to put it aside and not refer to it, while they take their part as British citizens,—but it is there underneath the surface, the key to the entrances of what I have called the "inner circle" of Welsh life ; even where Anglicization has done its work, and the knowledge of the language is lost, nationality may remain, but the former is felt to be the missing link, which would very gladly be purchased at some cost, were it practicable.

Quite recently I had an interview with an Englishman or a Scotchman, who conducts a paper at Swansea. He complained a good deal of the language question, said that it divided the town into two halves, that the Welsh preachers did not take any part in public affairs, and felt like he should do, if he were in a *French* town. It must be undoubtedly vexing to him, as to other English persons engaged in literary enterprises in the country, not to be able to understand the district as easily and thoroughly as if they were to settle down in Sunderland or in Brighton ; although he appeared rather opposed to the existence of Welsh, his evidence confirmed me in the view that a much more general spread of bilingual instead of exclusively English education even in such a district as Swansea, would do something towards consolidating and improving social feeling, let alone its educational value.

It was not surprising to hear that my informant depreciated the Welsh language (which he was ignorant of) as a civilizing agency, and could scarcely believe me, when I informed him that *ceteris paribus*, it was easier to attain a literary education in Welsh than in English.

The next day, I was in the company of a sober, intelligent working man, who was, a short time since, employed as a porter by the Great Western Railway Co., at Swansea station ; he was of Welsh parentage, could understand a little Welsh, but could not speak it. "It is a great mistake" he said, in

reference to the matter of language "for us to have allowed
the English to have had the monopoly over us : our present
educational system is responsible, and will be so, until it is
reversed." This is the substance of his remarks, so far as recollected. Now here is a man, not an isolated mountaineer,
but used to every day contact with modern civilization, re-
gretting his want of acquaintance with the language of his
fathers, and advocating in his own way a national system of
Education. I am sure that this feeling is far more common
in Semi-Anglicized Wales, than is generally supposed.

We cannot conclude these somewhat discursive jottings on
Welsh nationality without some reference to the moral standpoint.
This is a far more difficult matter to handle than the literature,
and I must confess to a smaller admiration of the Welsh
moral character, than of the tender pathos, the grace, and the
descriptive power of their poetry. It lacks intrepidity, a
disregard of consequences, and the fine sense of honour which
commands respect even from a foe. Wales is not so much the
place for individuality as England, but public sentiment moves
much more *en masse*, owing to the gregarious habits of the
people —a people who go in flocks. yet who are not united.
How far these phenomena are due to the warmth of tempera-
ment which characterizes them, how far they are the effects of
historical or other causes, I will not venture to decide— for in
such matters,—

"Fools will rush in, where angels will not dare to tread."

Wales has produced men of genius, and men who could
hold the magician's wand and entrance the multitude; men
whose works even the learned could read with bated breath,
who could cast a halo of fascination over almost any subject
they touched with their pens, but what Wales wants more than
men of genius is men of character, who will live above the
varying plaudits of an unthinking crowd, strike out new paths

in the moral and social world, and give ample evidence that it is not the sweets of life they are seeking, but the stern, undeviating path of *duty* —duty first and duty last, though fire and water lie between.

The lack of a middle class in the past has thrown the mass of the people on their own resources, and not without good records; now wealth and education are accessible to an extent previously unthought of, and accompanying them are certain subtle tendencies to deterioration of character, which, in reality, form a very poor exchange for the more Spartan simplicity of earlier days.

Seventy years ago, who was one of the most influential men of Wales? Christmas Evans: and yet for twenty years after his settlement in Anglesea his salary was only £17, and for 18 years more only £21, out of which he spared a guinea to the Bible Society, and a guinea to the Missionary Society. Whatever errors there may have been in his theological views, he must have exhibited both consistency of character, and convictions of essential Truths, to have commanded the influence which accompanied him during life, and which surrounds his name after death.

Summing up the evidence as to Welsh Nationality, we arrive at this—

I. Welsh Nationality is not a family matter. Community of blood is *not* mainly the bond that gives a national character to the people, though it probably does to a larger extent, than in the case of the English, popularly known as an Anglo-Saxon people, just as the Welsh are known as a *Cymric* one.

II. That notwithstanding the mixture and existing differences, as between North and South, there are still special mental characteristics and habits common to all Wales.

III. That an inner sense of nationality has been produced, and is now maintained.

IV. That from whatever source it springs, it is a diffusive, expansive, ethereal force, subtlely propagating itself, but severely checked —though not checkmated— by adverse circumstances.

V. That it is partly the result of the consciousness of historical facts : partly the result of the community of mental habits ; partly the presence of a language, the formation of which is in unison with such habits and characteristics ; partly the result of an extensive vernacular literature.

VI. It has not the strength of such a recent political unity, as has existed in the case of Poland, whose fate it has been that "Russia, Prussia, Austria, have parted her in three;" in the case of Wales we have to go back six centuries instead of one.

VII. It has to contend with all the interlacing and inter-blending of English material interests, which late years have developed, in combination with the very powerful influence caused by the pretty thorough system of ignoring Welsh Nationality, in the administration of civil government for many generations.

VIII. That not merely the national idea, but the unconscious development of nationality itself, is probably a living force to-day, which is simply hidden from sight by the more manifest counterforce tending to uniformity.

IX. That where properly regulated, this tendency to national development is the best calculated to foster individual development, which cannot reach its maximum under the exclusive dominance of the counter-force.

X. That such influences, tending to check individual development, are prejudicial to moral stamina, independence of thought, and action.

XI. Speaking generally, so long as, and where the Welsh language exists, Nationality asserts itself often in a hidden, almost invisible way, in the consciousness of a community of interest, and a common understanding of one another from *Caergybi* to *Caerdydd** as the stock phrase goes, and the real Englishman is looked upon more or less as a foreigner, one who does not quite understand the why and the wherefore of the mental attitude of the people.

Such, then, is Welsh Nationality—it is not complete unity of race; it is not formed on political independence : it is an intangible somewhat and something more than either, heavily pressed down and yet existing,—existing now, and destined to exist and to exert an influence in the future.

---

* From Holyhead to Cardiff.

CHAPTER IX.

THE EXTREME BOUNDARIES OF WELSH DESCRIBED, WITH PERSONAL
EXPERIENCES AND SELECTIONS FROM COMMUNICATIONS OF COR-
RESPONDENTS — THE MAP — THE 60 PER CENT. BOUNDARY AND
THE CENSUS — OFFA'S DYKE - PATAGONIA — CLASSIFICATION OF
POPULATION.

WE will now give some attention to the geographical limits
of Welsh as a living language, *i.e.*, if I may borrow a
term, the extreme boundaries of *indigenous* Welsh, as distinguished from the Welsh spoken by settlers in England. In
order to do this it will be most convenient to take each county
which exhibits such a boundary separately.

FLINTSHIRE. — The extreme north-eastern boundary of
Welsh commences, about two miles west of Connah's Quay,
and about nine from Chester, thence to Northop; Northop to
Bistre, which is about four miles from Hawarden: Bistre to
Padeswood, some two miles east of Llong, where I was
informed at the station that "*pob ddyn onest*" spoke Welsh;
from Padeswood the linguistic line nearly follows the Wrexham, Mold, and Connah's Quay railway to Caergwrle.

Caergwrle, by the way = *Caer y gawr lleon.* Chester in
Welsh is *Caerlleon gawr,* both meaning the Camp of the Great
Legion.

DENBIGHSHIRE.—From Caergwrle to Wrexham, thence to
Ruabon and Chirk, pretty well alongside the Great Western
Railway. I have no information of its existence east of that
line. From Chirk the line run to Gobowen and crosses into
Shropshire.

SHROPSHIRE.—From Gobowen to Oswestry, Trefonen,
Llanyblodwel, Llanymynech.

The linguistic condition of Oswestry presents some rather remarkable features to the enquirer. Here is a country town in an English county, *east* of Offa's Dyke, without large industries or collieries to attract workmen from a distance, and yet I was informed by an English youth in the street that he thought half the people in the town spoke Welsh. I regarded this as an exaggeration, but on learning shortly after that there were no less than five Welsh meeting houses, all well attended, inclined to believe that this rough estimate is not far from the mark.

In Shropshire the boundary cannot have varied much for centuries, and although so many people speak Welsh in Oswestry I cannot learn that it is spoken at all east of that town.

MONTGOMERYSHIRE.—From Llanymynech to Four Crosses, Arddleen, and Welshpool thence through Berriew to Newtown.

Montgomery, it will be observed, is left out in the wholly English portion of the county, so are Llanllwchaiarn and Kerry.

Why Kerry an obscure, out of the way town, some miles from the English border, should be wholly English, and Oswestry something like half Welsh, is a problem which appears not easily solved.

The exact boundary south of Newtown is somewhere between Kerry and Llangurig.

RADNORSHIRE.—I place the boundary thus : "St." Harmon, thence straight to Rhayader, thence to Disserth,* thence to the Wye or west of Aberedw, thence two or three miles east of the Wye to Boughwood and Erwood. Rhayader, numbering

---

* I was informed by an old woman, a native of Llandinam, but long resident in Radnorshire, that some natives of the district at Disserth (near Newbridge) could still speak Welsh.

EU

only 800 inhabitants, is one of the principal towns of Radnorshire, in a wild district, 17 miles from the English border,
and about as far from Offa's Dyke, yet very little Welsh is
spoken there. A correspondent, well-known in Radnorshire,
says :—

Welsh seems to have steadily died out in Radnorshire ; and the
reason, unless it were the ill-success of the Calvinistic Methodists
here—the Baptists seem to have been generally English,—is
difficult to ascertain. Kerry, I suppose, fell away from its
proximity to Radnorshire.

In this parish, *Nantmel*, there are two Welsh-speaking people
just above me ; but *both* originally came from Llangurig in Mont-
gomeryshire. There *may* be a very few on the other side of (S.)
Harmon parish by Sychnant-fawr (marked in your map) and
Waun-cilgwyn, and there are perhaps a dozen old people in
Rhayader who prefer Welsh, and many others in trade who can
speak to the Breconshire, Cardigansh, Montgomerysh, and Cwmdauddwr (top part) parish, Radnorshire (right bank of the Wye),
Market people.   *   There *may* be a very little *occasional*
Welsh preaching in Sychnant Calvinistic Methodist Chapel, but
people come there from Llandinam and Llangurig parishes in
Montgomeryshire somewhat. * * * Even on the right bank of
the Wye all the way down Welsh is only *understood*, not preferred
or generally spoken on the side of the hills nearest the river.
Until 10 years ago perhaps Welsh was generally spoken all over
the upper or western parts of the parishes of Cwmdauddwr, Radnorshire, and Llanwrthwl, Breconshire, but now even there
English is prevalent. About five years ago the last purely Welsh
(Baptist) minister of the last place of worship in Radnorshire
where only Welsh was preached, resigned, and his place was filled
by one half Welsh and half English, and hard by there is an old
Episcopalian chapel—Capel Nantgwyllt * * where the service
has long been half and half. The Methodists have occasional
purely Welsh worship and preaching at a farmhouse higher up.

It is somewhat singular that at a Baptist Association meeting at Rhayader, five summers ago, preaching was carried on in Welsh to some five thousand people, many of whom were no doubt from Welsh parts, but many more cannot have understood a word. Among the latter was a poor man whom I heard talking to his mate the next day and expressing his admiration of the language.

The authority above referred to, S. C. Evans-Williams, of Bryntirion, Rhayader, gave an interesting address at Knighton, bearing on the question of the Welsh language in Radnorshire, in the spring of 1891, from which the following is extracted—

A thought which occurred to him in connection with the Welsh character of the eisteddfod - that was the decay of the Welsh language in the county of Radnor. Few, perhaps, realised the fact how short a time ago, there in this town of Knighton and neighbourhood, it was since Welsh was the vernacular language. He had lately been getting up a little of the subject, and he found that in the year 1730, in the neighbouring parish of Beguildy which they knew was close on the Shropshire border -the Welsh language was used for Divine service once a month in the parish church. That showed that, down the very border, the Welsh language was at any rate used nearly half and half with the English. The next period they had any information with regard to the subject, which he had been able to find, was in an account of a lawyer who went from Bridgnorth to Llandrindod Wells just at the middle of the last century. He said, in his written account, that after leaving Knighton the whole way to Llandrindod he crossed commons or waste lands, and was not understood by the natives—neither did they understand him -so it was impossible for him to ask his way. A Mr. Lewis Morris in 1794 "?] paid a visit to Radnorshire and described that visit. He spoke of the Welsh tongue being used at that time in every parish church [!!] in the county, and he further said that in Penybont at that time the Welsh language and the English were spoken equally by the

people. The people talked better Welsh and far better English
than their neighbours in Montgomeryshire. At the same time in
Glasewin both languages were spoken, and in New Radnor Welsh
was the prevailing language. That was 1747. So that the Welsh
language appeared to have died out very gradually, travelling
towards the west. In the parish of "St." Harmons only 50 years ago
Welsh was divided with the English as the language which was
used in Divine worship. He had pretty well worked out a theory
that the Welsh had gone out to the west as the English advanced;
but lately he had received a pamphlet by Mr. Ivor James, of the
Cardiff College, in which he seemed to say that he believed the
English prevailed in the Principality 200 years ago more than the
Welsh language. It thus appeared that the Welsh language had
rather driven out the English, after the Civil Wars, from the
country which previously it had generally possessed. Mr. James
gave Radnorshire as one of the principal instances, and said that
the cause of the prevalence of English in Radnorshire—which was
so marked among the counties of Wales—was that the English
language had never really been driven out by the Welsh in the 17th
century, during the beginning and to the middle of which the English
language prevailed in Wales more generally than was supposed.

Ivor James' explanation of the prevalence of English in
Radnorshire may be correct, but it does not quite commend
itself to my mind. It is scarcely likely that English and
Welsh existed side by side for so long amid a very scant
population without literary culture, when probably most were
unable to read. My friend, S.C.E.W., says himself that the
reason is very difficult to ascertain.

The result of personal enquiries at Penybont has been quite
fruitless as to any person with even a traditional knowledge of
Welsh-speaking villagers there. In the south-west of the
county, I learn from a native that Welsh still lingers in the
neighbourhood of Boughwod and Erwood, but is extinct on
the east of the Wye at Aberedw.

Several years ago I was acquainted with an old Radnorshire woman from Abbey Cwmhir, whose recollections extended back to, say, 1810. In her youth the parish was evidently a bilingual one, and farm-house preaching was partly English and partly Welsh. One of the verses used in the neighbourhood began thus—

> Sôn am farw, sôn am farw,
> Clywir yma, daew draw.

Another was an English doggerel,

> How many miles, how many,
> Is it from Leominster to Llanllieni?

Llanllieni, it may be recollected, is the Welsh name for Leominster, which was for many years the Metropolis in which Radnorshire folk disposed of their salt butter at the annual fair.

BRECONSHIRE.—I include the whole of the north-west of the county within the linguistic border, which I take to enter the county about Llyswen, near Three Cocks, thence to Talgarth, and thence it skirts the northern slopes of the Black Mountain to Olchon in Herefordshire. In fact, nearly the whole of Breconshire is thus included, though not much is spoken between Brecon and Talgarth, and none, so far as my information goes, between Talgarth and Hay, though in 1878 one or two old people at Glasbury, I believe, spoke Welsh.

HEREFORDSHIRE.—On making enquiries from a person resident near Longtown, I was positively informed in writing that Welsh was *understood* only, by a proportion of the population in Olchon, Longtown, and Pandy—apparently my correspondent had written *one-third*. Wishing to satisfy myself, a personal visit was resolved upon—not to wild Wales this time, but just to the east of the towering, dignified Black mountain that I had so often gazed at in childhood and youth,

covered in the distance with a hazy mantle, which only
brought to view its dim, gaunt outline against the South-
western sky.   Pandy station, on the borders of Herefordshire,
being my terminus, I commenced operations in the County of
Monmouth.   The first old man on the road conversed with
me a little in Welsh, but Radnorshire was his native place,
and he had learnt Welsh at Rhymney about 1850.   I was,
however, assured by John Davies, F.S.A., that native Welsh
was not quite extinct in that parish.

At *Longtown*, in Herefordshire, an Episcopalian preacher
informed me that at Newton, near Pontrilas, the children at
the Board School were taught Welsh songs.*   In the village,
of Longtown, however, I failed to meet a single native who
could converse in that language, but was told that "some sort
of Welsh" was spoken there about 30 years ago.

Still further to the North lies Olchon House, where a farm
servant was found, about 40 years of age, who said he could
understand and speak a little, and that a few people higher
up could do the same.   Strange to say, in that out-of-the-way
place, a Cardiganshire youth was working and assisting the
man with the sheep ; he had come there to learn English.

"Sixty years ago you might go into a house by chance and
hear nothing but Welsh," was the testimony of an old farmer
north of Longtown.   "They did not teach the children Welsh;
I should like very much to have learnt Welsh."

Now, how is it that the last flickering flames of a knowledge of Welsh still lingers in South-west Herefordshire, while
at Presteign, perhaps, we may say, no one has ever known any
one (a native) who ever knew any one—to put it genealogi-
cally—who could speak the language.   One answer to that
question is that it was for long years a place that nourished
dissent.

---

* This is, of course, were taught to sing in a Foreign language.

Go back to the fourteenth century, and take note of Walter Brute, a reformer before the Reformation from this very district; remember the Lollard's "chapel" in Deerfold forest some twenty miles to the north, and Sion Cent, the Lollard monk-bard, going in and out of the halls of the Scudamores, a few miles to the south; remember, again, that in the 17th century one of the very earliest Welsh Baptist congregations was formed at Olchon, that in 1794 the Cymanfa Ddeheuol was held there,* and issued their circular letter, and even as late as 1875 or thereabouts one Morgan Lewis occasionally preached there in Welsh.

The valley of the Olchon, and that of the Honddu both belonged to the Wales of the Welsh Bible, and perhaps of Canwyll y Cymry, but they have never belonged to modern Wales—to the Wales of Y Traethodydd, Y Drysorfa, and Y Dysgedydd, of Gwilym Hiraethog, and of Brutus, nor even, to that of William Williams, Pantycelyn.

As I left the spot the sun still lighted the top of the grand natural barrier which towered up in majestic dignity on my right, while to my left lay the fertile vales of Herefordshire—a rare junction of the wild and the stern with the fruitful and the mild, of the mountain with the lowland.

At Clydach, on the way back, an intelligent old peasant, John Gwilym, told me that his grandmother could speak Welsh. She was born, say, in 1767, so that about 1790 children at Clydach and Longtown were beginning to be monoglot English. Now Clydach lies close to the border, but there is a much more remarkable case than that of Welsh speaking in Herefordshire. Some years ago I knew a Welsh-man in Newport, who assured me that about 1835 he had conversed in Welsh with the mistress of a farmhouse at Yazor,

* Llyfryddiaeth y Cymry, 1794. No. 23.

on the north bank of the Wye, 8 miles from Hereford, who assured him that in her childhood the children generally spoke Welsh there.

On first thoughts from a comparison of these facts, especially when we learn that in the city of Hereford* in 1642 many people spoke Welsh as a native language, it would seem that the history of the language was that of gradual, though constant retrocession to the West. There is some truth in this, but, on the other hand, there is reason to believe that the Saxons early settled at Withington and Ashperton, within some 12 miles of Hereford, and that Thinghill represented the meeting-place of their local council. This cannot have been much later than the ninth Century—if so, the exterior boundary of the English must have continued nearly constant for several centuries. We can understand a Welsh district in a county keeping up its characteristics for a certain time (as probably in the case of the Peak country, Derbyshire), but how it should have done so to such an extent as at Yazor, where the children must have grown up Welsh-speaking for nearly 1000 years after the Saxons had approached within some twenty miles is a marvel, especially when we recollect that the palace of the great King Offa at Sutton, lay near Hereford.

South of the Wye, in the districts of Ewyas (Euas) and Archenfield *(Erging)* around Ross, the population in the middle of the fifteenth century must have been nearly solidly Welsh speaking. It was during that period that Lewis Glyn Cothi addressed an adulatory ode to a squire named *Winston*, at Whitney-on-Wye, near Hay, in which he speaks of him as a patron of the Welsh language.

As late as circ. 1707 we find E. Lhuyd speaking of Eirinwg (Herefordshire) as an habitat of the Gwenhwysaeg dialect of Welsh.

---

* Diocesan History of Hereford, S.P.C.K. series.

I shall have a little to say about present day Welsh in a detached portion of Herefordshire, under the following heading :—

MONMOUTHSHIRE.—The linguistic boundary enters the county between Pandy and Llanfihangel stations, on the Hereford and Newport railway, thence to Llangattock Lingoed, Llanfihangel Ystern Llewern, a few miles North-west of Monmouth, thence to Clytha and Trostrey into Newchurch parish, and as far South as Llanmartin, thence nearly due West to Ponthir, thence to Newport, but not including Caerleon, thence to the mouth of the Usk, the west bank of which may still be considered to be Welsh speaking.

The valley of the Torvaen, from Pontypool to Ponthir, is inhabited largely by newcomers or their descendants to the third generation. Native Welsh is, however, not quite extinct in it, although there is no Welsh preaching between Pontypool and Newport. In Goytre and Llanover, between Pontypool and Abergavenny, Welsh is generally understood by a considerable proportion of the inhabitants. In fact, at the latter place, it appears that the children can mostly speak it, to judge by the testimony of Coedmoelfa, a North Walian residing there,—

" Mewn attebiad i'th ofyniad ynghylch iaith y plant yn Llanover, Cymry yw y rhan fwyaf a Chymraeg a siaradant."

How is it that here remains an island of green not yet swallowed up by the advancing tide of red? The answer is not far to seek, and is found largely, if not wholly, in the influence of Llanover Court ; supposing an English squire had settled there 60 years ago and introduced English stewards and English servants into the district, what would have been its linguistic fate? Of course, it is well-known, that under the rule of *Gwenynyn Gwent* (the Lady Llanover), the very contrary has been the case, and that the village school of

XX

Llanover was for many years the only one in all Wales where Welsh was being systematically taught.

At the beginning of this century, I believe that Welsh was generally understood over the whole of Monmouthshire, except in Monmouth, Chepstow, and a part of the Caldicot level. It was not, however, quite extinct in Monmouth, as I have spoken to a botanist, born, possibly in 1800, whose mother was the last person in that town who could speak it.

The Saxons had possession of part of the Caldicot level before the Norman Conquest. Perhaps the names of Roggiett, Redwick, and Ifton, all in the lowland between the Wye and the Usk, are relics of that time, but if it be true that their language has prevailed there ever since, it must have been only over a very limited area and near Chepstow.

The following is from the pen of Colonel J. A. Bradney, of Talycoed Court, 7 miles from Monmouth, than whom there are few, if any, better qualified to speak on the linguistic condition of the east of the County. Besides being a Welsh speaker he is a Welsh reader :—

I, myself, learnt Welsh from a native of Llangattock-juxta-Usk, who is still alive, and lives close by here, working on this place every day. He has a thorough knowledge of the language, although he is absolutely uneducated. Around Llangattock-juxta-Usk, I believe that all the old native people have a knowledge of Welsh. In Llangattock Vibon Avel there are no Welsh-speaking people left, though several of the old ones have a slight knowledge, being able to understand ordinary simple sentences; but a clergy-man tells me that 25 years ago, when he was curate of Llangattock Vibon Avel, he found that the aged people in the village of Llanfaenor (in the parish of Llangattock Vibon Avel) had an imperfect knowledge of English, and that he went to the trouble of getting some Welsh devotional books for them, which they much appreciated.

In Llantilio Crossenny the older generation of natives, though not able to converse much, can understand a certain amount, and they will complain that their parents used to talk Welsh to one another, and English to their children. These remarks apply to all these parishes around here—Penrose, Tregaer, Llanvihangel Ystern Llewern, Dingestow, etc. Llanarth was Welsh-speaking till quite lately. An old woman there, who talks Welsh, a native of the Pitt, near Clytha, tells me that all the inhabitants at the Pitt used to talk Welsh habitually in the days of her childhood. At Llanvapley an occasional Welsh service is held in the chapel. and at Llanddewi Rhydderch chapel a Welsh service is often held. In the chapel at Talycoed an occasional Welsh service is held.

But during the last twenty years the population of all this country has changed to an extraordinary extent —immigrants have come from all parts and the natives have been migrating elsewhere. To such an extent has this happened in this parish of Llanvihangel Ystern Llewern, that there is *only one* middle-aged native in it. All the other inhabitants (except, of course, the children) were born elsewhere. The same thing has taken place in the surrounding parishes to a greater or less degree. So that when one looks about for an aged or middle-aged native, who can tell one something of what used to go on in days gone by, one has a difficulty to find such a person. Of course, among the many immigrants who have come are many Welsh-speaking people, most of whom keep their language up, and help to keep it up in the mouths of those who are already here, and I, myself, am one of those who, whether rightly or wrongly, do everything to encourage the language, and persuade the people to converse to their children in that language instead of in English.

Of the Welsh-speaking people in my employment, I have three natives of Monmouthshire —one from Llangattock-juxta, Usk, one born in Llanddewi Fach, but reared in Llangibby, another born in Llanover.

This evidence as to the change of population is interesting; it may be partly accounted for by the natives flocking to the

iron works thirty or forty years ago, and leaving Glo'ster and
Somerset people to come in to work the land, but many other
factors besides this tendency must be considered. The only
possible way its effects on the language can be counteracted is
by stringent measures enforcing its use in elementary schools,
where the local vitality is sufficient to warrant such a step.
The same change of population is happening in South Glamorgan, and is alluded to in *Cymru* Vol. 1. p. 216.

In the Wye Valley, till at least 1830, Welsh was spoken at
Llandogo, close on the border of Gloucestershire,—such, I am
informed, is the testimony of W. P. Price, formerly M.P. for
Gloucester, and a native of the place.

In the extreme North-east of the County is a very long,
narrow, secluded valley, shut off from Herefordshire on the
east, and bordered by a detached portion of Herefordshire,
called the Ffwddog, and by Breconshire on the west. Wishing
to have further evidence as to whether Herefordshire really
was a Welsh-speaking county, I recently visited the district.
At Cwmyoy Welsh is nearly extinct. The old innkeeper
remarked, "Yr oedd bacat yn siarad Cymraeg deugain mlynedd
yn ol a rhai o'r plant."

At Llanthony, some three miles higher up, I was told that
most natives above 50 could speak Welsh. I conversed with
an old woman, who at first answered in English, but said that
there was "bacat yn y Ffwddog"* who could speak Welsh.
Crossing over into the Ffwddog I took farewell of Llanthony
Abbey, eloquent relics of a byegone age but not of a byegone
spirit. Those grey walls and high vaulted roofs, the fruit of
so much labour and pains, were built for men who imagined
as some do now, that the Most High dwelt in temples made

---

* Ffawyddog is the correct Welsh spelling : one of the old Welsh names
of Hereford is Caerffawydd, has this anything to do with its belonging to
Herefordshire, while entirely detached from it ?

by men's hands and that His Spirit could be coerced or cajoled by architectural magnificence to give them the smile of His favour, or that they were thus in some way likely to be nearer heaven than the poor Welsh goatherds or shepherds, who climbed the mountain side and braved the blasts of winter in pursuance of their duty. Llanthony disappears, and a few minutes hard walking brings me to the top of the ridge, surrounded by the heather and the mountain breeze, far away from the screech of an engine or the smoke of furnaces, while the face of external nature is nearly the same, minus the goats and deer, as it was six centuries ago, when the monks told out their beads in the valley below.

Slightly to the right rises the Skirrid (yr Ysgyryd) while to the west and south-west near and distant mountains meet the eye. In connection with one of these—Pen-y-Fâl, a landmark for many miles into England, and called by the Saxons the "Sugar Loaf,"* Gwallter Mechain wrote a fine *awdl* (ode) for the anniversary of the Abergavenny Cymreigyddion, in 1837. Poetry and history are here blended together, as he alludes to the different features of the magnificent prospect before him,—

> A dangos mor glos yw Gwlad
> *Mynwyson :*
>
> Edrychaf o'm deutu, ar *Loegr* a *Chymru*,
> A ddichon neb gredu mor wiwgu mae'r wedd ?
> Rhaid gweled i goelio, mi geisa 'u darlunio,
> Cyn yr elwyf fi heno i'm hannedd.

Far in the distance is Gloucester, nearer to hand Llantarnam, the ancient residence of Ioan ap Rosser, then he notices Goodrich Castle, the home of a Welshman, Samuel Meyrick, Llanover

---

* Think of introducing the ideas of a grocer's shop in connection with such an object, grand in itself and grand in its surroundings.

then Hereford, and the Malvern Hills. Over the Severn he sees Somersetshire and Devonshire, and would see Cornwall if fair weather and the rays of the western sun combined. Nearer Varteg, Blaenavon, the three Monmouthshire rivers and Raglan Castle, where instead of "moethus Gloddesta" (dainty feasting).

> O heno ! gwelir gwahaniad—ceir *cân*
> *Dylluan* yn gwawdio y lleuad !
> Neu greg Frân anniddan ei nad—liw dydd,
> Ar ei gilydd yn rhuo galwad !

The Brecon and Carmarthenshire beacons are not missed—

> Acw y *Bannau*
> Teir-fforchiadau ;
> Hwyntau'r *Mynnau*, dasau dwysir
> Cestyll rhuddion
> Haeniau cysson
> Saerniaeth lon, argoel ion gwir.

This ode does not follow the rules of Dafydd ap Edmwnt, but rather those of Glamorganshire. Perhaps it is not nearly the best piece Gwallter Mechain wrote, but to those who know the district it is not only of interest, but there is nothing in English to approach it as a lyric of the hills ; yet how many young men in the neighbourhood of Abergavenny or Newport to whom Pen y Fâl is a familiar natural object, can read it ?

GLAMORGAN.—The extreme boundary of Welsh only occurs in Glamorganshire, in the Gower Peninsula, between Penclawdd and a little north of the Mumbles.

CARMARTHEN AND PEMBROKE.—Carmarthenshire is wholly within the Welsh speaking area, excepting a very small portion in the extreme South-Western corner, between Laugharne and Amroth. It will be observed that the exclusively English part of Pembrokeshire, runs slightly to the north of Lampeter Velfrey, Lanhawden and Spital—the extreme boundary, both in Pembrokeshire and Gower, cannot have altered very much for a considerable period.

For the purpose of illustrating these linguistic boundaries, as also to shew the Welsh names of places alongside the English, where any particular difference is observable; and as an historical monument for the future, I have compiled the Map, which faces the Title page of this book. The boundary just discussed is that between the RED and the BLUE on the Map in the case of Wales; and between the RED and WHITE in the case of England. The term Wales includes Monmouthshire. The second boundary between the RED and the GREEN defines the limits where 60 per cent of the adult population are estimated to speak Welsh.

To acquire the necessary information for this purpose, it has been necessary to enter on some correspondence with persons possessing special opportunities of information, and as well as to visit certain districts myself.

The fact of a person residing on a spot is by no means a guarantee that he knows the linguistic condition of the population, e.g. "Colonel Byrde of Pentre Goytre, near Abergavenny, giving evidence in an enquiry held by the Bishop of Llandaff, in 1887, as to the necessity of appointing a Welsh-speaking person to the living, said he had lived in the parish for 28 years, and did not suppose there were a dozen persons who did understand English properly, and they were Nonconformists." Mary Evans, the next witness, gave her evidence in Welsh, and Colonel Byrde interposed, saying he had never heard the woman speak Welsh before, though he had had business relations with her for 25 years. Abraham Williams at the same enquiry, said he had lived 60 years at Goytre, and that three-fourths of the people understood Welsh.

This is a fair illustration of the way in which people can be

neighbours in Wales, and yet for one class to know but little
of the circumstances of the other as to their language. I
believe that very few County councillors of Monmouthshire,
have much accurate knowledge of the distribution of the
language in the County.

The 60 per cent. boundary is naturally one which must be
rendered theoretically, there being no precise data on which to
work, I take it to be generally within ten miles of the extreme
boundary, until it enters the valley of the Usk, near Brecon ;
it expands to a width of fifteen or twenty miles in Monmouthshire.

It will be observed that a considerable portion of the South
of Glamorganshire comes within this limit, but it is comparatively contracted near Swansea and in Pembrokeshire,
had I constructed an 80 per cent. limit it would in reality have
differed very little from the 60 per cent., but it would have
cut off most of the rest of Monmouthshire, (except the Nanty-
bwlch corner,) the Merthyr, Aberdare and Rhondda Valleys,
and South Glamorgan, with two or three towns, such as Carmarthen, Neath, and perhaps Aberystwith.

Llandovery is well within the 80 per cent. limit, and probably
will continue within the 60 per cent. for some generations, or
at least 60 per cent. of its population will be included in
classes I.-VI. (see a few pages further on) but I find that the
amount of Welsh literature sold there, has much fallen off
during the last ten or twelve years. In fact, English is
stealthily and surely eating its way into the heart of Wales in
that direction, and conversational Welsh will soon be a small
factor in the social life of the district. Whether this is due to
the influence of country Squires, who delight to rouse the
country, to see dumb animals ridden round and round a given
course of ground, or not, I will not attempt to determine.

Space does not permit me to minutely discuss these bound-

aries, the boundaries of the past, nor the present condition of
some places which offer features of interest. If however I
was asked the question—where would be the outlines of a map
drawn up in a similar plan for 1485, at the accession of Henry
VII, I might reply that the green portion would have come as
far east as Oswestry, but am doubtful if it would have covered
Hawarden (*Penarlag**) in Flintshire. It would have included
Clun Forest in the south-west of Shropshire, and nearly the
whole of Herefordshire west of the Wye, and north and east
of the Wye from Yazor to Leintwardine, and some part of
the Forest of Dean (*Cantref Coch*). As for the red it was
probably very narrow in Cheshire and Shropshire, but more
extended in Herefordshire and Gloucestershire, reaching nearly,
if not quite to Gloucester Bridge.

I omitted to state under head Monmouthshire, that the
results of my visit to the Ffwddog (Heref) established the fact
that native Welsh exists there, although I heard of no children
who can speak it.

OFFA's DYKE.—What schoolboy has not heard of Offa and
his Dyke? What grown-up person of culture has not met
allusions to it in books? But who has seen it? The tourist
on the Cambrian or the Central Wales, or on either of the
West Midland branches of the Great Western? In the great
majority of instances, the same negative answer would have to
be given as if passengers on the North Western or Midland
or North Eastern expresses to Scotland were asked if they
noticed Hadrian's wall or that of Antonine lying across their
line of route.

To tell the truth, Offa's Dyke—where it is not entirely
obliterated—is generally not particularly noticeable. Perhaps
the very best and most complete portion extant is situated

---

* In the map Penarth halawg (= the salty headland) but Penarlag is the
usual name.

about 1½ miles south of Knighton, some little distance away
from the main road. With a monoglot English-Welshman as my
guide, the identical man who had some time before lamented
his ignorance of the vernacular, I climbed the slope of an
eminence leading to the spot, and before long reached what
my companion considered to be traces of the dyke, which
simply formed a broad basis to the hedge, about three feet
wide, and barely raised above the level of the ground. "I
must see something more convincing than this," thought I.
There was not long much room for doubt; a little further on
was a deep towering bank, some twenty feet above the bottom
of what still bore the character of a trench or hollow on the
western side.

Here my companion left me, I sat down, and thought of
the time, as hazy to the mental view, as the western hills
facing me, when instead of a carpet of green grass mingled
with the dry stalks of last season's herbage, nought but bare
freshly-turned soil would have met the view.

Then, again, who were the labourers—were they defenders
of their own lately gotten soil, or were they forging against
their own liberties the chains of a foreign yoke?

They have perished; history is silent, but numbers them in
the band of the great unknown, the work of their hands yet
remains, that of their hearts we know not.

They have perished; and so have the armoured knights
who crossed and recrossed this very dyke, sometimes in league
with the Norman-English, sometimes with the Cymric Princes
of the soil. And, then, what of the mothers' sons who lay
weltering in their blood, whose sighs and groans were wafted
by the wind to their comrades in combat. What of those
who crossed never to return?

Such considerations as these were present on my mind,
while nature round whispered peace. Freedom and industry

are now allowed a dwelling-place in the land, but the dark passions of humanity have not changed, covetousness and cruelty have found other refuges than the donjon and the keep. Never before, too, had I realized the magnitude of the undertaking; even with the appliances of the nineteenth century, it would be no child's play to construct such an earthwork from the Dee to the Wye, if the bank near Knighton is a fair sample.

About one mile further on, the dyke assumes comparatively insignificant proportions, as it crosses the main road between Presteign and Knighton.

Now, who was this Offa, who caused the dyke to be made?—He was a King of the Mercian Saxons or Angles, who had married a daughter of Charlemagne: but he was also a murderer, and a violator of the rights of hospitality. Under the persuasion of his queen Quendrida he murdered Ethelbert King of the East Angles, who had come as a guest to demand his daughter Adelfrida in marriage, and afterwards conquered his country. The Pope promised security from punishment on *condition of his being liberal to Churches and Monasteries.*

What did he do to atone for such a black crime?—He became one of the chief pillars on which rests the legal claim of the most numerous religious sect of this country, to Tithes. To atone for this murder, he gave away a tenth part of the produce of the labours of unborn men, *i.e.*, to compensate for one wrong, he thought to buy the favour of heaven by committing another wrong, in its ultimate effects and tendency far worse than the first. Don't misunderstand me, the murder he confessed and knew was a horrid crime; the giving away of tithes was an act done in the name of religion which tended to spread a false idea of what religion is.

Who has any right to devote any portion of the result of the labours of unborn generations to any such purpose? What

body can truly and honestly call this their property, and give
the name of spoilers and robbers to men who seek to divert
such income into the National treasury?

Offa's Dyke is shewn on the map as far south as Almeley,
thence, I should estimate its course approximately through
Vowchurch and Kenderchurch, crossing the Wye a second
time at Lydbrook, near the boundary of Herefordshire, thence
through the Forest of Dean to Beachley near Chepstow.

THE CENSUS.—A material help towards elucidating the
geographical distribution of Welsh in Wales, and the proportion of inhabitants speaking it, would have been afforded by the
Census of 1891, had the resolution of the British House of
Commons, which virtually required a return of all persons in
the principality who spoke the language, been carried into
effect. Instead of honestly endeavouring to ascertain this by
sending Census papers with the column to be filled up with
the required information, *to every household* in the principality,
the authorities took upon themselves, to some extent, to decide
where to send papers with this column : such a course did much
if not entirely vitiate in some bilingual districts the trust-
worthiness of the returns which at the moment of writing, are
not yet published. In Newport, Mon., for instance, a batch of
papers were actually sent to the First day ("Sunday") school
of a Welsh Congregation, for this column to be filled in there;
whereas it is manifest that many Welsh speaking persons
would not be in attendance, and one woman was threatened
with a fine of £5 if she did not take an English paper,
in other parts of South Wales, similar inefficiency was observable. Whether the bungling that attended the Welsh Census
was the result of ignorance, or whether the authorities were un-
willing that the total number of persons who might fairly be
credited with ability to speak Welsh should be known, I will
not attempt to decide.

PATAGONIA. Welsh has been spoken in the New World, probably ever since William Penn left the shores of our country on his first visit to the infant colony, which justly gave in his eyes and those of his friends a bright promise for the future. Many of the first settlers of Pennsylvania, were Welshmen, seeking a peaceful asylum from the harassing outrages of informers, evilly disposed justices and clerics in their native country: some of them were of the poor and obscure of this world, others came of families of local note and position, who notwithstanding their Quaker convictions preserved genealogies for a succeeding age.* Traces of the nationality of these settlers are to be found in Pennsylvania, in such names as Merion, Brynmawr, Uwchlan, and Radnor, some, or all of which, are situated in what used to be known as the "Welsh track." The Welsh of the United States, is however, now spoken by much more recent comers, or their descendants, and is principally to be found in the iron districts of Pennsylvania, Ohio, and New York, and among agricultural populations in certain parts of the Western States.

Where, however, the language appears likely to find a more permanent home is in the valley of the Camwy,† in Patagonia. A hundred and fifty Welsh settlers were landed there in the middle of winter 1865. Without sustenance from the Argentine Government, the enterprise would probably have many years ago been added to the list of unsuccessful colonizations, as for a considerable period the colonists had to endure at times, hardships, privations and losses, until they not merely discovered that irrigation would be the secret of success, but found means to carry it into operation. In 1886, a canal forty miles long was made, and in 1889, a railroad the same distance;

---

* Dr. J. J. Levick, of Philadelphia, among others, has interested himself in these matters, and has published some of the records of early settlers.

† Chupat river.

in the same year wheat from the Colony gained a gold medal
in the Paris Exhibition, the amount raised yearly, being no
less than ten thousand tons.

When we consider that the total population is only three
thousand souls, and their wealth was estimated in 1890, at one
million sterling, it may be anticipated that they have a future
before them.   The proceedings of the local council are carried
forward in Welsh, which is taught in seven out of eight schools,
the other being a Spanish school, and now that a printing
press is established in the Colony, it is to be hoped that the
deficiency in Welsh educational works suitable to elementary
education, will be in some way supplied.

Continued ill success, naturally was the means some years
ago, of spreading black reports about the country : the following written by a Welsh traveller, gives another side to the
picture,—

" I have seen as many lands as it is almost possible for one of my
age to have done, yet truly none yet please me as well in every
respect as an ' Andine Wladfa.' New Zealand and Southern Chili
come nearest in beauty of scenery and natural excellence generally,
but in neither of these can we hope to hear the old language
amidst surroundings so natural to it. Streams, rivers, cascades
cataracts, falls, and lakes meet the eye in all directions, the whole
combining to form a most romantic picture."*

Having in an earlier portion of this work noticed the position of the different social classes in Wales, with regard to
the language and having now dealt with its geographical
distribution ; we will proceed to consider a classification of
the general population into those sub-divisions which the
presence of two languages induces under the natural laws of
association and thought, as well as under conventional influences ; such as classification will in the particular case of

* From the *South Wales Weekly News.*

Wales, enable us the more easily to appreciate the forces at work.

The linguistic classes, form in fact, the nett resultant of a variety of forces, foremost among which are two antagonistic ones, viz. :—that occasioned by the support given to a foreign language, by governments past and present, and the *vis vitae* of the vernacular in the hearts and minds of the people. In thus dividing the total population, *i.e.* that is those who have passed through school life, into linguistic classes, I do not assert that such hard and fast distinctions actually exist : individual cases may for instance exemplify more than one division, and between each division there are as many gradations as shades of colour in the material world.

We find then in Wales the following :—

I. Monoglot Welsh—able to read the language : from this class have come some writers whose names are treasured in the archives of modern Welsh literature. They are very fast disappearing, just as the class of Monoglot Welsh unable to read the language, is now nearly extinct, therefore hardly worth mentioning.

II. Semi-Monoglot—able to read Welsh well, also able to transact ordinary affairs in English, which they can read a little, they are to be found in every county in Wales, and form part of the amateur Literary Staff, which creates and supports current Welsh literature.

III. Bilingual Welsh—who not merely can read the language well, and have a greater literary mastery of it than any other class in Wales, but also are familiar with literary English, and who with almost equal readiness read or speak both languages. With the spread of education and the establishment of National Colleges, this class has considerably increased of late years, and its members have a vantage ground *ceteris paribus* in acquiring the lead in professional and political life, not merely

and thoroughly Welsh districts, but also in others partially
anglicized.   Owing however to the unthinking, ignorant way
in which middle-class education has been conducted, they have
to be recruited principally from West Wales, and from the
midst of *res angustae domi*; I don't like to say *poor homes*
for that might appear to cast a slight on poverty, especially
when we bear in mind that their proficiency in literary Welsh,
and sometimes in other subjects is largely the result of self-
culture.   Of course, were a national system of education in
force, young men from such districts as the Merthyr and
Rhondda Valleys, would stand a better chance of receiving
those bilingual appointments which occasionally fall vacant.
I recollect a Government official in a responsible position in
South Wales, remarking to me, "I owe this to my father:
when I came back from school he spoke to me in Welsh, while
I answered in English," implying that thereby he had picked
up sufficient Welsh to qualify him for his post.   It will easily
be seen that under the present system at school and college
every nerve may be strained in thinking, speaking, and writing
English, while any knowledge of Welsh that might have been
acquired in early life lies dormant.

IV.   Bilingual Welsh—who read and speak both languages,
but whose reading knowledge of Welsh is rusty, though not
so much so in denominational literature, this is a large class in
South Wales.

V.   Bilingual Welsh—who only speak a little and cannot
command a free flow of expression in that language, these are
sometimes to be found among the upper classes (so-called) as
well as among the poor.   I would include among them those
who speak the language but cannot read it, the latter are
mostly Episcopalians.

VI.   Monoglot English Welsh—who can read the language
more or less perfectly, but cannot speak it, though they may

understand a little of it when spoken, these are principally to be found among Dissenters in large towns, such as Swansea, Cardiff, Liverpool and London.

VII. Monoglot English and English-Welsh—who can neither speak nor rea l. Some neither know it, nor care to know, others would give many pounds for a facility which might have been acquired in the golden age of childhood.

In spite of all that may be said as to the rapid Anglicization of Wales, its having a dying language and the like, few things since my connection with the country have struck me more than the extraordinary vitality of the language, in the face of such adverse circumstances. This vitality is indeed wonderful but it cannot stand before the mental pressure of an exclusively English education and association, in the industrial districts. It may exist, perhaps for many generations even there, but in a dwarfed, cramped, unassertive way not as an important factor in the life of the people. In the counties bordering the Irish Sea, however, the case may be different, it is possible that the native education will sufficiently counterbalance the English education to preserve a really bilingual people, able to avail themselves of the information found in English books as well as in their own. If however the educational system is "reversed" the results both in east and west Wales, will soon give a very severe check to the process of entire anglicization, and an additional impetus to the numbers of the above class III.

I can scarcely be expected to close this chapter without reference to the number of persons to whom Welsh is more or less familiar, Sir T. Phillips in 1847 reckoned it at 800,000! After the Census of 1871, Ravenstein calculated that the number of persons *habitually speaking* Welsh was 1,006,100 out of 1,426, 514 in Wales* and Monmouthshire. I believe

---

* Report of Intermediate and Higher Education Committee, 1881, p. xlvii.

ZZ

that since that period, there has been a decrease of the number
of persons who *habitually* speak Welsh, but an increase of
those who either can speak it, or habitually listen to it in connection with the different denominations. Some years ago
Sir H. H. Vivian stated that 870,220 (including children under
ten) used Welsh among the Nonconformists alone, and when
we add to these the Episcopalians and the Welshmen attending
" English Causes," who draw upon themselves the bitter irony*
of some of their Countrymen, and those who go "nowhere,"
I think the number would be in excess of Ravenstein's estimate
even now. In reality however, Welsh has reached a crisis, it
is tottering in a state of uncertainty whether to go backward
or forward. Without such reasonable extraneous help as is
afforded every day to the competing language, there is scarcely
a doubt that it will have to succumb in extensive and populous
districts though not entirely there for some generations, and
perhaps not in West Wales for centuries.

There is every reason to believe that there are portions of
Wales where the Welsh language assumes an aggressive
attitude at the present day ; that is to say, where it is becoming
the mother tongue of families of English origin, and bearing
English names. I believe this is generally an easier process
than it otherwise would be on account of a large proportion of
the new comers belonging to the west of England, where Celtic
blood is more abundant than in the east, for instance, Welsh
has spread to some extent among the Cornish settlers at Llantrisant. Somerset and Devon supply a considerable proportion
of the English element.

I do not consider it at all the part of patriotism for Welshmen to disparage or to obstruct the influx of new blood ; pro-

---

* Ond y mae clywed ambell i Gymro uniaith yn y wlad yn dweyd mai
i'r " Inglis côs jabel " y bydd ef yn myned, yn ein gwnend i'w gashau â
chas cyfiawn [?]—but unreasonably intemperate—*Essyllt in Y Cymro.*

vided only that they take reasonable and proper care that their language receives equal treatment to that of the strangers, the new blood will then tend to the advancement of the nation.

Principal Reichel, of Bangor, alluded some time ago in an educational pamphlet to the difficulty of getting Welsh youths to think in English, as though that was one of the aims and objects of his mission in Wales.

Now it is probable that educationalists of the future will not quite conform to this model; what Wales really wants is educated men who know a little Welsh, but think in English ; and also educated men who are familiar with English, but think in Welsh, and express themselves freely and idiomatically in that language. When this is realized, there will no longer be any need for the complaint as to illiteracy at the close of the following quotation. It is a translation from an article in Y Geninen Vol. IX. p. 226. on "the difficulties of Welsh patriotism"—

Look at a boy in a day school, he is made an Englishman without knowing it. His tender mind is moulded on an English model, and an English bias is given to his self-consciousness. He is taught to respect England and not Wales. He is taught in the language of England. He does not hear a word of Welsh from the mouth of his teacher. * * The language of his father and mother is banished from the school. A foreign language is introduced instead of that of the hearth. * * They are taught to know what is a noun, a verb, and an adjective, and to form English sentences. They do not know what is an *caw*, a *berf*, nor an *ansoddair*, they are not taught to pronounce nor to form Welsh sentences. An unavoidable consequence is serious ignorance of the language. Only a few Welsh people can write their language correctly. Nothing surprises anyone connected with the Welsh press, more than the incorrectness of the written productions of our ministers and public men.

Notwithstanding the above, it is singular how much Welsh people talk about their language, and yet how little is said about the only available means to render it a common inheritance, viz.—its introduction into school life. Here is an example taken from the report (Adroddiad) of a Welsh congregation at Tredegar, (Mon.) for 1891, which shews an *increase* not a decrease of members—

"We strongly feel that disadvantages as to language form a great hindrance which militates against the prosperity of the Church. This is caused by neglecting to teach Welsh by the family hearth. We recommend the advice of Mynyddog. ' Whateveryou are doing, do everything in Welsh.' "*

Tredegar is inserted in the GREEN portion of the map, though I am somewhat doubtful of the propriety of doing so. Out of twenty-six meeting houses in the district, (including the Episcopalians') Welsh is only preached in thirteen; but probably these thirteen contain the largest accommodation. There are three Primitive methodist places. A traveller when he passes any of these in Wales, may be pretty sure that an English population has been imported from the Midland Counties or elsewhere.

It may be mentioned that the western boundary of Monmouthshire, runs nearly straight from outside Rhymney to near Machen, just west of that town.

---

* Teimlwn yn gryf mai un rhwystr mawr ag sydd yn milwrio yn erbyn llwyddiant yr eglwys ydyw anfanteision iaith. Achosir hyn gan ddiffyg dysgu'r Gymraeg ar yr aelwyd gartref. Cymeradwywn gyngor Mynyddog:—"Beth bynag fo'ch chwi yn wneuthur, gwnewch bobpeth yn Gymraeg."

CHAPTER X.

A REVIEW of the decline of the ancient Cornish has
directly nothing to do with " Wales and her Language,"
but it is introduced here, as affording a sidelight on the
position of the Welsh, and both to shew how far the history
of the two languages runs parallel, and how far important
differences exist, which must materially affect an estimate of
the future of Welsh, based on the history of the sister tongue.

Celtic scholars, who are well acquainted with the slender
materials which exist for such a digest as I am about to make,
will, I am sure, excuse a repetition, for the sake of the less
well-informed. In rendering this, I shall principally rely for
assistance upon information given in Jago's " Glossary of the
Cornish Dialect."

We have already seen that in Wales, at the time of the
accession of the first Tudor Kings, there was a large amount of
manuscript literature existing, apparently more in proportion
to the population than was the case in England, and there is
a probability the language was spoken both by feudal lords,
small freeholders, and serfs, over the whole of Wales (except
portions where alien colonies had settled,) and in parts of
Herefordshire and Shropshire. At the same period it is
probable that Cornish was spoken a few miles over the Devonshire border, (Devon-Cornish appears to have existed in
Queen Elizabeth's time), and that the whole country west of

the Tamar—the river dividing the counties—was nearly solidly Cornish.

From the nature of the trade carried on by the inhabitants, there was considerable intercourse with England in connection with fishing and mining pursuits, and though there is no evidence that English was anywhere generally spoken in the county before the art of Printing was introduced into England, the vocabulary was gradually becoming less and less representative of a pure Celtic tongue, something like the colloquial Monmouthshire Welsh of our day, which is interlarded with English words.

However, this may be, no English was used in the old parish masshouses before 1547, when the Vicar of Menheniot taught his parishioners the creed, the Lord's Prayer, and the Ten Commandments in English.

Now, it is very remarkable that within the very short space of 60 years not merely did it come to pass that English was generally spoken, but Carew, in his "Survey of Cornwall," published in 1602 said, "Of the inhabitants, most can speak no word of Cornish." About 1610, another Cornish writer says : " It seemeth, however, that in a few years the Cornish will be, by little and little, abandoned." By 1640, Cornish appears to have been excluded from all the parish meeting-houses but two, viz., Feock and Landewednack.

Though such extreme rapidity at first astounds a person who has only been accustomed to deal with the retrocession of the Welsh-speaking border, which at one point—Oswestry—can scarcely be said to have moved three miles in a century, on further consideration of the facts, the difficulties partially disappear.

In the first place, Cornwall is not known to have had a national literature. There was no Iolo Goch or Glyn Cothi or Dafydd ap Gwilym; no Triads, no Cyfreithiau Hywel Dda, no Mabinogion to be read in the halls of the country squires. In the next place, there was no translation of the Bible, and no religious literature beyond the so-called sacred dramas, which were meant to be performed rather than read. In the third place it was disused as a medium of communication in public worship, at first apparently, because the people could understand English, rather than because they could not understand Cornish. As to the real facts of the case—historians are at variance : Whitaker author of the "ancient Cathedral of Cornwall," affirming that the tyranny of England forced the language on the Cornish, by whom it was not desired : Borlase on the contrary says,—" that when the liturgy was appointed instead of the mass, the Cornish desired it to be in English."

Now the truth probably is that a small minority of the people, represented by such as the Vicar of Menheniot, desired the change of language, and that a certain amount of coercion was used to effect the purpose desired, which was remarkably successful owing to the combined effect of banishment from the Episcopal worship and the absence of printed literature, though a much longer period was required than from 1540-1640 before the conversational use of the language entirely ceased.

The last Cornish sermon preached noticed in history, was preached in 1678. In 1701 E. Lhuyd noticed the language being retained in fourteen parishes, along the sea shore from the Lands End to near the Lizard, by some of the inhabitants only. E. Lhuyd managed to acquire sufficient knowledge of the language to write a Cornish preface to his book. In 1746 a Cornishman was found who could converse with Bretons. In 1758 the language had nearly ceased in ordinary conversation. In 1788 Dolly Pentreath the last person whose mother tongue was Cornish died, although there were others alive then who could converse in it more or less.

We have just seen that there were surrounding conditions

in the face of which no language could be expected to live ;
nor the population speaking it, to partake of the civilization
of modern Europe.   In a state of savagery, its preservation
might have been possible ; but Wales and Cornwall have some
1600 years passed that stage of development.   External circumstances, then possibly accented by the policy of the Tudor
governments, starved Cornish to death.

Welsh still lives under differing external circumstances, and
is likely to do so for hundreds of years to come, as the starving
process has only been partially applied.   It is one of the
objects of this book to shew that such circumstances may be
so modified as to ensure it a natural, rather than an artificial
death ; or else to indefinitely prolong its life.

The following is two verses of the First chapter of Genesis
in old Cornish :—

Yn dalleth Dew a wrûg nêf ha'n nôr.

Hag ydh esé an nôr heb composter ha gwâg; ha tew olgow esé
war enep an downder, ha Spyrys Dew rûg gwaya war enep an
dowrow.

The following is modern Cornish followed by the corresponding Welsh (see Arch Brit p. 251)—

Bedhez guesgyz diueth ken gueskal enueth, rag hedna yu an
guelha point a skians oll.*

Bydd drawedig ddwywaith cyn taro unwaith, canys honno yw 'r
gamp synwyrolaf oll.

Breton the remaining sister tongue is more akin to Cornish
than to Welsh.   I have no precise date as to the population
speaking it—probably 900,000 would be near the mark.

Many people talk about a language as though it was simply
a matter of choice with the people which they spoke.   This is

---

* " Be struck twice before striking once, for that is the wisest achieve-
ment of all."   This occurs in a curious old story, containing the adventures
of a Cornishman, fished up by E. Lhuyd.

not so altogether. The amount of the actual use of a language is in reality, the resultant of several forces, the operations of which if they were capable of being weighed and measured could be expressed by an exact mathematical formula : as however, we can never reduce metaphysics into a branch of physics, we will not make the attempt.

Though we can never arrive at an exact conclusion, we may still take into consideration, the adaptability of the sounds and structure of a language to the mental constitution of the people who speak it, in other words how far a given language is an adequate representation of the feelings, ideas and mental powers of those who speak and write it.

The relation therefore which a language bears to the minds of those to whom it is a mother tongue, is indicated by what may be called its NATURAL OR SUBSTANTIAL VITALITY. The effect produced by laws, custom and education considered in themselves as exterior forces acting upon the use of the language, may be called the ARTIFICIAL OR ACCIDENTAL VITALITY.

The use of language is not a matter of choice with the generality of people, simply because it is not an end, but only a means to an end. That end is to express a wish, or communicate an impression to a fellow being with the least possible trouble and leaving aside the action of the baser emotions, such as pride, a person chooses that language to communicate in, of which the natural vitality combined with the artificial vitality enables him most freely to express his mind, and consequently produce the results aimed at, with the least mental effort.

Suppose for instance a nation with a language which possesses a certain correspondence with the expression of their own mental habits comes in contact with another language possessing a less correspondence, we might say that the natural vitality of the first language was greater than that of the second.

AAA

and up to a certain point notwithstanding the concurrent use
of the second, the speakers fall most naturally back upon the
first.   It is possible however that the use of the second may
through external or artificial causes so exclusively predominate,
that it takes root like the graft of a tree, the balance turns
the other way, the first occupies a secondary place, or it gradually
dies and its natural vitality is then only expressed by a tendency
of mind, to what naturalists would call "reversion," which
waits sufficiently favourable circumstances to assert itself.

The science of language has of late years received considerable additions—the history of languages, their growth and
decay, have been laid open to dissection as never before, but
the *philosophy* of language, the reason why one man in some
cases uses a different word to express the same idea as his
neighbour, and in other cases uses the same word, but sounds
it so differently that it is scarcely recognizable, the reason why
the collocation of ideas in the form of a sentence is so different in the mouths of one nation compared with that of
another, is still involved in obscurity.

For instance, what were the causes which induced the old
Greeks long ages ago to adopt v-d-r, the Saxons v-t-r, the Cymry
d-v-r, as their base for *water*?   Why are the English so afraid
of the guttural *ch* sound that they pronounce *night* as *nite*,
and Vaughan (*W* = Vychan) as *vawn*?   And why have the
Cymry a dislike to either the flat or sharp *j* sound, so that
Johnny becomes Shôni, while their brethren, the later Cornish
adopted it and *hir* (long) became *cheer*, a cliff now called the
"Chair ladder" in reality yr hir lethr.   How is it that we say
nothing but Edward for a man's name, but a person speaking
with a strong "Welshy" accent utters a quite appreciable
approximation to the French *Edouard*, only with a sharp *t*
sounded at the end?

Comparative Philology has brought to light many important

facts, it has taught us much of the relations of sounds, has traced obscure relationships in the words themselves, and has classified differences under the operation of laws, but it has a vanishing point. Just as biology under the guidance and appliances of modern science can deal with the most abstruse phenomena of life, but it can never fathom their well spring, so before the student of philology as well as that of biology there is always a curtain drawn, which he cannot lift: in other words he is still in the field of secondary phenomena not in that of origins.

Applying this to the matter in hand, we may have a key to the great vitality of the Welsh language, and shall be justified in at least being cautious before endeavouring to compass its artificial extinction, assuredly the time-honoured methods of the schools and colleges are artificial.

IRISH.

It is reported of Thor the Scandinavian mythological hero, that he set out from Asgard* for Jotenheim, the home of giants, the weird land of frost and snow : in the course of his wanderings he arrived at Utgard, where he was introduced into an immense banqueting hall: there around the table on stone thrones were gravely seated giants who were determined on taking the self-conceit out of him, and making light of his prowess, proposed that his capacities should be tested. At one of the experiments whereby this was done, he was handed a cup full of liquor which he was requested to empty ; after twice attempting to drain it by moderate draughts, Thor was surprised and vexed to find that scarcely any impression was made on the surface ; fiercely applying himself a third time he just succeeded in reducing the liquor a little below the rim.

Now a student entering on the study of Irish if he thinks to

---

* The home of the reputed gods.

master it by the same means, and with no more trouble than he would pick up most other European languages, would be very likely to share such feelings as the Scandinavian folk attributed to Thor after his capacious draughts out of the drinking cup, albeit, they apologize for him by saying, that the bottom of it reached the ocean, and the ebbing and flowing of the tides are the visible signs left of his mighty draughts.

The initial difficulty in Irish is caused by the great discrepancy between the spelling and the pronunciation: I defy anyone to acquire an approximately correct Irish pronunciation from such grammars as are at present published. A mastery too of the constructions, and the use of the particles is by no means child's play even to a person tolerably familiar with Welsh. Speaking of difficulties, a friend of the author's may be mentioned, whose business took him into every district in Ireland; being an intelligent man he wished to acquire the language, but was obliged to desist from the attempt, and I have heard him enunciate a theory that the superfluous consonants which constitute a worse bugbear than the initial mutations in Welsh, were inserted by the Monks in order to keep the people in ignorance, this is ingenious, but certainly unsupported by evidence.

We have already seen the disadvantages under which Welsh education has laboured, on account of the exclusion of the language from the course of elementary instruction. Up to within 1877 or thereabouts, the position of the Irish language in the course of government education was almost precisely similar to that of Welsh; there was however this important difference in the status of the two languages; for many generations Irish had been going down; it existed it is true, as a fireside tongue in the homes of the people, but it possessed no modern literature to speak of, and was rapidly becoming less and less used.

There was it is true, and is now, a professor of Irish at

Dublin University, and perhaps a little might be read there of the extensive Mediaeval literature of the past, but the persons up and down the country who could read the language were but few and far between.

Under these circumstances a society was brought into existence, called the "society for the preservation of the Irish language," the reader should bear in mind that its promoters were not afraid of the word PRESERVATION. This society held a congress in Dublin, in 1882, in which a considerable number of facts were elicited, which helped to throw up in relief the question of bilingual education in Welsh schools, in some matters there is a striking parallel between Wales and Ireland, in others quite as striking a contrast: I may also observe that this society does not timidly confine its aims to Irish-speaking children, but also that teaching the language may be extended to English-speaking children in Ireland. What have they done? They have sold 100,495 books,* among which are the first, second and third Irish books giving elementary instruction in that language, and 6,225 copybooks, with headings in Irish. The following table shows the progress made in the national schools :—

No of Pupils who passed in Irish.

1881	1882	1883	1884	1885	1886	1887	1888	1889	1890	1891
12	17	25	93	161	321	371	443	512	531	515

For 1891, the returns were made up seventeen days before the expiration of a full twelve months.

The passes in Irish, in the Intermediate programme rise from 43 in 1883, to 244 in 1891. These figures are taken from the last annual report. These reports usually contain interesting selections from correspondence with teachers and others, an example which the Welsh society might well follow.

---

* Of these 53,951 were the first Irish book.

Some of the reports from national school teachers, point
to exactly the difficulty with parents that has been experienced
in Wales, *e.g.* Parents of the boys disincline to allow their
children to learn, in some instances are found to have warned
them against speaking Irish, or admitting that they could,
(Ennis); children regard the language ashamedly, encouraged to
do so by their parents (Sligo). The difficulty of securing qualified teachers has also hampered the work of this society.
The total number of persons speaking Irish in 1881, in Ireland,
was given by the census as 949,937, but in 1731 the Irish-
speaking population was 1,340,808, in 1851 1,524,286; whether
or no the efforts of this society will ever lead to a recovery of
the figures of 1851, we may not venture to say.

Since the end of last century, we see then, that the Welsh-
speaking population has increased, the Irish decreased.

At the 1882 meeting, Marcus J. Ward, of Belfast, said—

I value the national language, while it lives, because it is the
key which alone can furnish a means of knowing completely the
Celtic genius of our countrymen. It is the only way to the hearts
and minds of our Irish-speaking population, in whom we may trace
unerringly what are the characteristics, the bent, and the tendency
of the nationality to which we belong, and on what stock have been
grafted the successive immigrations to this our land.

A very singular monument to the religious zeal of the ancient
Irish, before the fangs of popery were fully closed on the Island
is to be found at this day in Vienna, in *Die Schottische strasse*,
the Irishmen's street, so-called from its connection with the
Scoto-Irish missionaries of the early middle ages. These very
missionaries left manuscript remains to which it may be said
we are indebted for that monument of German industry and
difficult research, the "Grammatica Celtica" of I. C. Zeuss,
which has been for several years the chief authority among
scholars on Celtic grammar.

Although Irish Gaelic possesses scarcely any modern literature in the usual acceptation of the term, the Scotch Gaelic is rather differently situated. Mary Macpherson, a professional nurse, seventy years old, is a recent poetess, whose works have attracted some attention, yet strange to say, she can read, but cannot write her own compositions, of which a volume containing between eight and nine thousand lines taken down from her own recitation, was published at Inverness, in 1891, for five shillings.

The Gaelic speaking population of Scotland, is about 400,000 that of the Isle of Man, whose dialect by the way, appears far easier to master than Irish, my own small experience may be trusted, perhaps does not exceed a few score.

CHAPTER XI.

THE Welsh language has now passed under review in many different aspects.

We have seen the interest attaching to it as unlocking some of the facts of English, or rather British history exemplified in the names of places, and even as helping to modify the structure, and enlarging the vocabulary of the English language itself.

Looking back on the middle ages as they slowly matured to introduce the period of modern history, ushered in by the reformation and the invention of printing, we see this language and literature asserting themselves, in spite of the rude shock which the extinction of the national sentiments received by the extinction of the political independence of the country. We have seen how the Tudor period witnessed a tendency, fostered on both sides, towards the obliteration of all lines of demarcation between Wales and England, and how a participation in the national literature became gradually the inheritance of but few, while the general intelligence such as it was, developed independently of it, and then how a movement arose and spread, which put it within the power of nearly every individual in Welsh Wales to read his own language, and how it naturally largely increased the number of Welsh writers.

We have seen how concurrently with this a foreign language has not only had the pre-eminence in every department of civil life, but this wonderful, rejuvenescent, native idiom has been almost as universally excluded, from any contact with the government agencies either in law or education.

We have seen how with the peculiarly contradictory nature which is distinctive of the Celt, though ready warmly to defend his country and language on certain occasions, he has passively acquiesced in this state of things, partly under mistaken impressions as to material gain resulting from it, partly because he believes that "the thing which has been, shall be."

We have seen however, that the disadvantages of the present educational system are by no means slight, that it has been condemned by inspectors, by teachers, by prominent Welshmen, and that its supporters are but a feeble folk, scarcely able to give a reason for the belief that is in them, but that the tremendous momentum which long established usage and precedent has given to mono-lingual ideas keeps it still on its feet; that it is a fact supported by a mass of ignorance and prejudice among school board officers, and among clerical managers of national schools, but we have seen on the other hand, that a considerable mass of latent public opinion exists, which simply waits a favouring breeze to fan it into flame, and perchance to take full advantage of the very reasonable and generous concessions offered by Sir W. Hart Dyke, while somewhat remarkably this advanced public opinion is more manifest in some of the partially anglicized districts, than in entirely Welsh parts.

We have seen moreover, an undesirable social chasm created by the legal monopoly of English, in fact the reign of democracy hastened in Wales, by the indirect effects of the legislation of Henry VIII.

We have contemplated the phenomenon of a large part of the nation teaching itself to read the national language without so much as an hour's assistance from the government, until

BBB

it has become almost a second nature to them, not to ask for
or expect any such assistance; although we have noticed on
the other hand the almost enthusiastic welcome with which the
outset of a society having this object in view, was greeted
in Glamorganshire, and the triumph which crowned their
efforts, whereby it has become possible where local authorities
assent, to teach Welsh, not simply as now to a few upper boys,
but in all standards and in all classes.

We have seen that even with imperfect opportunities for its
development at their disposal, the vernacular press has issued
on the whole an increasing rather than decreasing amount of
literature, while at the same time less Welsh is read in some
localities, than ten or twelve years ago, which is partly accounted
for by the deficiency of bilingual instruction in day schools.

We have moreover become acquainted with the representative forces of three distinct eras inimical to the national
language—

The era of the union, and the legislation of Henry VIII.

The era of Hanoverian Bishops.

The era of modern immigration, from England, of Forster's
education Act and of cheap printing, which for mechanical
reasons gives a large circle of [English] readers an advantage
in price, over a small [Welsh] one.

We have seen how the tendencies of these periods, considered by themselves, have been met by counter tendencies,
irrefragably demonstrating the obstinate vitality of the language
they undermined.

The next question is, what will happen if the *status quo* is
maintained, if indirect efforts are still made to exile the
language from playing a part in the advance of practical life and
civilization? Simply this, that in a few years it will cease to
be representative of the Welsh nation, it will become a less
and less important factor to be dealt with, the deluge of

English will nearly obliterate it from the populous districts of Glamorganshire, Monmouthshire, and Denbighshire. But for a long time to come those very undesirable lines of demarcation caused by one part of the community, being quite ignorant of the home language of the other, will be felt in west Wales. It will become a provincial and rustic, rather than a national characteristic. But even if the *status quo* is maintained, even if, as is the case, whole districts become inclined very much to leave Welsh literature which they cannot understand, for the English rubbish, as well as English thought of the day, the volume of Welsh literature may have a season of future expansion before it begins to contract, and when it contracts it will be (as a whole) slowly and almost imperceptibly: quite as slowly, perhaps more so, a reduction may be effected in the numbers of attenders at Welsh causes, for nothing but positive ignorance of the language or a change of attitude with regard to religious matters is likely to bring that about. Did not a Professor of one of the University Colleges say that he did not "know an educated Welshman, so far as he remembered, who does not prefer the Welsh service."[*]

This, I take it, will be something like the future, if the present state of things is continued, but what if it is not? I think an unprejudiced person can hardly rise from the evidence on the school question, without feeling that in the teeth of so much testimony against the old system, far too much play is left to the whims and caprices of local authorities, and that the principle of local option is carried too far. The educational department undoubtedly recognizes *compulsion* in making the three R's, an essential in all their elementary schools. We simply want the principle further extended in Wales, that as English children *must* be taught to read and write English, Welsh children (within the limits of the GREEN at least) should

[*] " Bilingual Teaching," Newport ed., *vide* Evidence of Prof. H. Jones.

be taught to read and write both languages, which would be
effected probably with less effort to the teachers, than at
present, (if they had the advantage of some preparation which
the government ought to insist upon) excepting only the schools
in such towns as Merthyr, where the proportion of English children is large, but even there, more bilingual teaching
in a modified form might be insisted on, in the lower standards,
than at present. In the RED portion of Wales one or two
schools might be selected out of each board district for
experiment.

Within a few years we shall probably see the establishment
of a Welsh University: if the entrance examination *necessitated*
a slight knowledge of Welsh, not as an *optional* subject mind,
no supporter of the bilingual idea need trouble himself to put
the slightest pressure on the Preparatory, Intermediate or
Collegiate schools, they would face the inevitable, some with
undisguised satisfaction, others with philosophical resignation
a very few perhaps with uneasy murmurings.

We should then have—

I.   Bilingual teaching, *i.e.* reading and writing in both
languages made compulsory in the greater part of Wales, and
definitely encouraged in other parts where practicable.

II.   A compulsory course of Welsh at normal colleges.

III.   A compulsory course of Welsh, preparatory to taking
a University degree of any description.

Perhaps another desideratum is to make illiteracy in Welsh,
a positive bar to the acceptance of the office of J. P. for
the counties throughout the whole of Wales, except in the
BLUE portions. The parents or guardians of heirs of estates
would naturally make provision to meet the requirements of
such a law, which might also prove a wholesome medicine to
the Vaughan-Campbells, the Vane-Tempests, and the Pennants
of the rising generation.

These are simple regulations, but what would their ultimate effect probably be? Why that nearly every man, woman and child in Welsh Wales, and a large proportion of those in some semi-anglicized parts would have the common bond of an elementary knowledge of the language. And every professional man whether legal, medical or literary, with a Welsh university diploma would carry a guarantee of the same. The results on the Welsh press would in a few years be very noticeable, there would be an improvement both in quality (*i.e.* so far as style and language go) and in quantity. Whether this would materially retard the disappearance of Welsh, as a conversational language in the industrial districts, I am not prepared to say, perhaps not, but it would probably be spoken with greater accuracy and purity.

It may be well here to summarize the reasons which justify such a course, in a more compact form than hitherto. Bilingual teaching in Welsh-Wales—

I.　Educates the faculties by comparison.

II.　Forms a foundation or stepping stone for the study of European languages.

III.　Tends to more precise and correct methods of thinking and writing among Welsh people, than at present.

IV.　Cultivates the ability to appreciate a higher class of literary matter.

V.　Can be effected where proper methods are applied, with very little (if any) extra strain on teachers, and without the expenditure of more time than at present,* except in the case of districts where monoglot-English families are numerous. The Welsh code should frame regulations to meet that difficulty.

VI.　Will foster a common social bond up and down the country.

---

* Perhaps this remark will only hold good if applied barely to *reading* and *writing*.

VII.   Will tend to abrogate the protective bonus to English, created by competitive examinations, which now ignore the old language.

VIII.   Will give to young Wales a clearer view and understanding of the Wales of the past, and of the Wales of the present.

IX.   Will be a boon to many English children, some of whom as we have heard (chap. iv. p. 116) "speak it on every possible occasion," and others who after they have grown up, will be glad to have an opportunity to do so.

X.   Offers the Teacher, apart from any abstract possibilities of its effect on the future of a boy's course, a method of much improving the reading of the scholars: it offers him a chance not of teaching reading only, but also elocution.

As a comment on the way in which reading and grammar are taught in English schools, where there is no second language to be "utilized." The following is condensed from Inspectors' reports:—

Expressive and intelligent reading seldom met with.

A child can rarely say what he is reading about.

Reading—The worst taught subject in most of the schools.

Grammar is almost uniformly poor, the one subject which enables us to test the real intelligence of the children.

Notwithstanding, reading and grammar are so indifferently taught at present in England, and probably Wales is no exception to the rule (the complex character of the English language alluded to elsewhere, being partly responsible for this) teachers have made no united move to secure the adoption of a method which would, so far as reading goes, almost certainly guarantee improved enunciation. In fact, I think this would be the case with English boys in many districts, were a bilingual reader put in their hands, even if they could not entirely follow the matter.

In all probability few teachers realize the great importance of the subject. As an employer I have had many English boys pass through my hands, but on no occasion do I recollect meeting with a really good reader fresh from an elementary school—perhaps the best was a bilingual boy from North Wales, who *thought* in Welsh.

Now supposing these changes be desirable, how can they be brought about ? A more feasible plan than that of administration from English centres appears to lie in the idea of a

WELSH NATIONAL EDUCATION BOARD

partly self-elective, and partly representative of various public bodies who at present are connected with education, with power to control all the state aided Elementary, Intermediate and Collegiate education.

Under such a board appointing its own inspectors, regulating the subjects taught, and ruled by men having the confidence of the country, is it too much to hope for educational progress of the right sort, not merely in the way of utilizing the language to secure a maximum of the development of intelligence with a minimum of effort, but also in the higher walks of morality. to teach endurance, patience, generosity, self-control, the sinews of character, which it is true have only been indirectly within the sphere of influence of the elementary schoolmaster, but which the heads of more advanced institutions, have more frequent opportunities both to inculcate and to practise themselves as a means of personal influence on those under their care ? Such a board is already contemplated by some of the leading educationalists of the country, and if established, may it take no narrow or sordid view of what education really is.

My work is now nearly at a conclusion. I might, it is true, have given further consideration to various subjects which could be suggested by the title this work bears, such as—the Eisteddfod, a comparison of the Welsh and English character, the great injustice connected with the language and the administration of the law in civil and criminal courts, the constitution of the proposed Welsh University, and the vexed question as to the introduction of a theological faculty. Most of these matters are brought before the public from time to time, and could not be adequately treated without unduly swelling the size of this book, nor perhaps at all by the present writer. He now takes his leave of the subject and of his readers, once more impressing upon such of the latter as are, or may be connected with the educational machinery of Wales, the need of united, thorough and decisive action, in order that the mistakes of the past may be avoided and that the natural development of the future (so far as any system of secular education can influence it) may be in accordance with the right use of the peculiar gifts and opportunities which Providence has seen meet to already put in the way of the nation, or which are within its power to acquire.

THE END.

APPENDIX.

❖┄❖❖┄❖

A. GAVEL KIND.

Was a Celtic custom, whereby if a man died without a will his real property was divided equally among his children.

Relics of this still survive in Kent. Copyhold and freehold lands Monmouth, Usk and Trelleck, descend equally among Male descendants. Those of Archenfield, Herefordshire, among the Males and in default among the Females.—*See Stone's*, *Norway in June*, *p.* 58.

(?) Does Gavel = Gaffael.

B. WELSH PERSONAL NAMES, PRINCIPALLY BELONGING TO THE EARLY MIDDLE AGES.

NAMES OF MEN.

Aiddan	Ceri	Gwestl	Nefydd
Aneurin	Cyfeiliog	Gwytherin	
Alun	Cadfan	Gwyndaf	Parain
Arthur	Cynon	Gwyddno	Padarn
	Coel	Geraint	Peris
Bryneich	Cynddylan	Gwrthegon	
Buan	Cadwallawn		Rhystyd
Baglan	Caradoc	Hychan	Rhun
Beuno	Cadwgan	Hywel	Rhufawr
			Rhidian
Cybi	Dyfan	Ilid	Rhydderch
Cynidr	Doged	Idris	Rhys
Cynog	Derfel	Illtyd	
Caredig	Dyfrig	Ithel	Silin
Ceitho		Idloes	Senor
Cranog	Edeyrn	Ifor	Seisyllt
Cynllo	Eilian		
Cadoc	Eurgrad	Llywarch	Twrog
Cawrdaf	Egwad	Lluchaiarn	Tyssilio
Cenych	Ellyw	Llywelyn	Tyfrydog
Collin	Einion		Tyfnelog
Crwst	Egryn	Meugan	Tegwy
Cadwaladr	Erbin	Meurig	Teilo
Cedwyn		Madoc	Trillo
Crallo	Gwynlliw	Mabon	Tanawg
Cynfant	Gwalchmai	Morien	Tegid
Cadivor	Gwynio		Taliesin

NAMES OF WOMEN.

Arianrod	Eilineth	Gwenhwyfar	Nevyn
Arianwen	Eigen	Gwenllian	Nest
Arddun	Elian		
	Erfyl	Honn	Onnen

(*Continued p.* 386.)

CCC

Cathin	Eurgain	Myllen	Olwen
Ceindrych	Envail	Maches	
Ceinwen	Enid	Madrud	Rhuddlad
		Morfudd	Rhiengar
Denys*	Gwladys	Myfanwy	
	Gwen		Tybie
			Tydfil

Most of the above are names of so-called Saints, many of them are to
to be found in "Bonedd y Saint." I only give a selection, more might be
added.

C. "THE WELSH NOTE."

The idea is that if you shut Welsh out of the schoolroom and the playground, you are in that way likely to teach English better. There is a
plan by which if a boy is heard to speak a word of Welsh, a piece of stick
or board, about a finger's length, is taken out of the master's desk, with
the letters W.N. on it, meaning "Welsh Note." This is handed to the
child, if he has it in his possession at the close of the school, is to be
punished. This child is not now thinking of his lesson; he is very
anxious to find somebody who speaks Welsh, in order to hand the W.N.
on to him.—Dan. I. Davies' evidence before Education Commission, 1886,
Newport Ed., p. 19.

[The custom is nearly, if not quite obsolete.—J. E. S.]

D. TEACHERS' REPLIES.

Tabulated Statement of Teacher's Replies, in 1885, to the question.—
"Do you consider that advantage would result from the introduction of
the Welsh language as a 'specific subject' into the course of elementary
education in Wales?

County.			Affirmative.		Negative.		Neutral.		Total.
Anglesey	...	...	20	...	10	...	3		33
Carnarvon	...	...	38	..	30	...	2		70
Denbigh	...	...	19	...	18	...	3	...	40
Flint	...	...	8	...	13	...	1	...	22
Merioneth	...		29	...	12	...	2	...	43
Montgomery	...		19	...	17	...	—	...	36
Cardigan			33	...	18	...	—	...	51
Radnor	...		4	...	4	...	1	...	9
Brecknock	...	...	10	...	10	...	1	...	21
Pembroke	...	...	18	...	21	...	6	...	45
Carmarthen	...	...	34	...	25	...	3	...	62
Glamorgan	...	...	77	...	48	...	7	...	132
Monmouth	...	...	27	...	23	...	3	...	53
Oswestry district	...		1	...	5	...	3	...	6
Anonymous	...	...	2	...	3	...	—	...	5
Total	...	...	339	...	257	...	32	...	628
	Affirmative majority					...	...	82	

* Dinas Powis—should be Denys Powis—Denys was a Princess of Powis. "The Llafar
gwlad is right and the bookmen are wrong" says a Monmouthshire friend of mine.

It must be borne in mind that some teachers were on the negative side, evidently as a result of the system whereby the Government has ignored education in Welsh at the Training Colleges, and that they felt themselves incompetent to teach it.

E. WELSH IN MONMOUTHSHIRE.

The following indicates the number of Meeting houses in Monmouthshire where Welsh is regularly preached, at least once a week.—

Baptist	52
Congregational	37
Calvinistic Methodist	37
Wesleyan	7
Episcopalian	5

In all probability there are more members and attendants in connection with these, the hindermost tail (*geographically*) of Welsh Ecclesiasticism than there are Quakers in all Great Britain. I may not be absolutely correct to one or two units, the real discrepancy, if any, is but small.

F. THE CENSUS OF 1891—POPULATION OF WELSH COUNTIES.

(Returns as to Language not yet published).

Anglesey	50,379	Glamorganshire	687,147
Brecknockshire	57,031	Merionethshire	49,204
Cardiganshire	62,596	Monmouthshire	252,260
Carmarthenshire	130,574	Montgomeryshire	58,003
Carnarvonshire	118,225	Pembrokeshire	89,125
Denbighshire	117,950	Radnorshire	21,791
Flintshire	77,189		
		Total	1,771,174

G. WELSH URBAN SANITARY DISTRICTS, 1891.

Aberavon	6,281	Bridgend	4,759
Aberdare	38,513	Briton Ferry	5,778
Abergavenny	7,640	Brynmawr	6,330
Abergele and Pensarn	1,981		
Abersychan	15,296	Caerleon	1,411
Abertillery	9,138	Cardiff	128,849
Aberystwith	6,696	Cardigan	3,447
		Carmarthen	10,338
Bala	1,622	Carnarvon	9,804
Bangor	9,892	Chepstow	3,378
Barmouth	2,045	Colwyn Bay & Colwyn	4,750
Barry and Cadoxton	13,268	Conway	3,467
Beaumaris	2,202	Cowbridge	1,377
Bethesda	5,799	Criccieth	1,410
Blaenavon	11,451		
Brecknock	5,794	Denbigh	6,412

Ebbw Vale	...	17,025	Neath	...	11,157
			Newport	... ...	54,695
Festiniog	... ...	11,073	New Quay	... ...	1,284
Flint	... ...	5,247	Newtown and Llanllw-		
			chaiarn	... ...	6,610
Haverfordwest	...	6,179			
Hay	... ...	1,830	Oswestry (Salop)	...	8,496
Holyhead	... ...	8,726	Oystermouth	...	3,598
Holywell	... ...	3,018			
			Panteg	...	5,763
Kidwelly	...	2,732	Pembroke	...	14,978
Knighton	...	1,650	Penarth	...	12,422
			Penmaenmawr		2,710
Lampeter	... ...	1,569	Pontypool	...	5,842
Llandilo	... ...	1,714	Pontypridd	...	19,971
Llandovery	... ...	1,742	Presteigne	...	1,360
Llandudno	... ...	7,300	Pwllheli	...	3,232
Llanelly	... ...	23,937			
Llanfairfechan	...	2,407	Rhyl	... ...	6,491
Llanfrechfa, Upper	...	2,780	Rhymney	... ...	7,733
Llanfyllin	... ...	1,753	Risca	... ...	7,780
Llangefni	... ...	1,624	Ruthin	... ...	2,760
Llangollen	... ...	3,225			
Llanidloes	... ...	2,574	Swansea		90,423
Llantarnam	... ...	4,905			
			Tenby	... ...	4,542
Maesteg	... ...	9,417	Towyn	... ...	3,294
Margam	... ...	6,274	Tredegar	... ...	17,484
Menai Bridge	..	1,679	Trefonen (Radnorshire)		784
Merthyr Tydfil	...	58,080			
Milford	... ...	4,070	Usk	...	1,417
Mold	... ...	4,457			
Monmouth	...	5,470	Welshpool	...	6,489
Montgomery	...	1,098	Wrexham	...	12,552
Mountain Ash	...	17,495			
			Ynyscynhaiarn		5,224
Nantyglo and Blaina		12,360	Ystradyfodwg		88,350

II. PROPORTION OF VOWELS AND CONSONANTS IN WELSH AND

ENGLISH.—(*See p.* 260)

We judge that what makes Welsh *Cynghanedd* possible, is the near proportion between the number of consonants and vowels in the formation of
the words, together with the fact, that their proper sound is given to both
classes of letters. In English, Irish, Gaelic and French, there are a great
number of unsounded consonants * * But there is a notable proportion
in Welsh, as may be seen from the following examples—Out of 657 Welsh
letters contained in eighteen lines of a book opened at random, 331 were

vowels and 325 consonants, only a difference of five: out of the same
number of English letters, 264 were vowels, 393 consonants, a difference
of 129. Again in twelve lines of a Welsh *Cywydd*, there were found 115
vowels, and 113 consonants, while in the English, out of the same number
there were 95 vowels, and 133 consonants: under these conditions, [in the
case of English] it is clear *Cynghanedd* is impossible.
(Translated from Yr Adolygydd, Cyf. II. t. 418.)

I. THE "COLUMBIA" (AMERICAN) ON WELSH LITERATURE.

" Even in the Nineteenth Century," (so says a writer in the American
journal *Columbia*) " Wales has produced poets who, in real poetic inspir-
ation, in exalted imagination, in charming simplicity and beauty of style,
are scarcely inferior to the world's master poets. The Welsh mind is
original, and there is in her literature a wealth of literary treasure of
which now the Welsh language is the sole repository.—*From a Cardiff
Paper.*

J. " ECHOES FROM THE WELSH HILLS."

The inhabitants of Wales have clung so tenaciously to their language,
that during the last fifty years they have formed a new literature in their
own tongue. This, when we consider its youth, bears no mean comparison
for insight, beauty and force with the religious literature—for the literature
of Wales is essentially religious—of any modern nation.

The inconvenience consequent on the motley character of the English
language, as it regards the education and instruction of the English
language, is beyond belief to those who have carefully considered the
matter.

* * * * * *

It is a great advantage to have in common use a language that is self-
included, and that cannot fail to be understood in any of its combinations
and compounds, even to the full extent of modern discoveries, by the mass
of the people. To revert to the word "Omniscience," is there a Welsh
beggar-woman ninety years of age who could by any considerable possibility, misunderstand it ? " *Hollwybodaeth*"—there it is patently and infallibly comprehended by all men of our nation. And so on, *ad infinitum.*—
(*Extracted from p.p.* 179, 180, 183)

[It is surprising how few Welsh writers have realized this, it is in fact
only to be realized by comparisons which many of them have not had full
opportunities to make.]—J. E. S.

LIST OF SUBSCRIBERS' NAMES.

M.P. here denotes Membership in the Parliament sitting in the Spring of 1892.

Allen, E. G., 28 Henrietta Street, Covent Garden
Anthony, D., 39 " St." Mary Street, Cardiff

Ballinger, J., Chief Librarian, Cardiff Free Library
Bevan, Canon, Hay, R.S.O.
Beynon, Theophilus, Newport
Bedlington, R., Gadlys House, Aberdare
Bonaparte, Prince, Lucien (deceased)
Bowen, D., Abercarn
Bowen, T., 38 Miskin Street, Cardiff
Bowen, James Bevan, Llwyngwair, Crymmych, R.S.O., Pembrokeshire
Bowen, Rowlands, W. Q.C., M.P., 33 Belsize Park, London, N.W.
Bradney, J. A., Col., Talycoed, Llanfihangel Ystern Llewern, near Monmouth

Carter, J. Corrie, J.P., Cefnfaes, Rhayader
Cambridge Free Library, Guildhall, Cambridge
Chambers, W., Wallesley Grange, Birkenhead
Chance, F., Burleigh House, Sydenham Hill, London, S.E.
Cartwright, J., Printer, Dowlais
"Coedmoelfa," J., Llanover, Abergavenny
Corbett, John, M.P., Impney, Droitwich
Cotterell, S. A., Grainnrhyd, Mold.
Cripps, C. L., 70 King Edward Street, Newgate Street, London
Crispin, W., 3 Victoria Terrace, Jarrow-on-Tyne

Daniel, E. Rice, Cwmgelly, Swansea
Darlington, T., M.A., Queen's College, Taunton
Davies, Aaron, Pontlottyn, Cardiff
Davies, D., J.P., Aberceri, Newcastle, Emlyn
Davies, D., Castle Flemish, Tregaron, Cardiganshire
Davies, D. E., (*Dewi Mabon*) Colliery Manager, Cwmaman, Aberdare, Glam.
Davies, E., A.L.C.M., Bronygàn, Towyn, N. Wales
Davies, E., J.P., Plas Dinam, Llandinam, Mont
Davies, G., Troedyrhiw, Gold Tops, Newport
Davies, H., The Schools, Treharris, R.S.O.
Davies, H. P., London Wharf, Newport

Davies, H. W., Camden Cottage, Brecon
Davies, J., F.S.A., Pandy, Abergavenny
Davies, J., c/o. Davies Bros., Newport
Davies, W., Brynheulog, Neath
Davies, W. B., P.O., Cross Keys, Newport
Davies, Lewis, grocer, The Garn, Nantyglo
Davies, W., Penlen, Talybont, Cardigan
Davies, M., M.D., 10 Goring Street, Houndsditch, London
Davies, T. Witton, Principal, Baptist College, Nottingham
Davies, J. Hathren, Cefncoed, Merthyr Tydfil
Davies, J. A., Ida Place, Ebbw Vale
Davies, T. Ifan, Llanuwchllyn, Bala
Davies, James, Gwynfa, Broomy Hill, Hereford
Davies, R. L., Alexandra Board School, Newport
Derfel, R. J., 6 Stove Street, Manchester
Downing, W., The Chaucer's Head Library, Temple Row, Birmingham
Duncan, John, J.P., *South Wales Daily News*, Cardiff

Edwards, T. C., M.A., The College, Bala
Edwards, A., National Bank of Wales, Llandudno, (2 copies)
Edwards, W., M.A., The Court, Merthyr
Edwards, O., M.A., Lincoln College, Oxford
Edwards, R., Letherland, near Liverpool
Edwards, Llewellyn, M.A., Ardwyn, Aberystwith
Elliot, W. H., 20 De Burgh Street, Cardiff
Ellis, T. E., M.P., (3 copies)
Ellis, Charlotte, Belgrave, Leicester
Ellis, D. F., 22 Great Dark Gate Street, Aberystwith
Evans, Principal, W. J., M.A., Presbyterian College, Carmarthen
Evans, Stephen, J.P., Neuadd, Llansilo, Newquay
Evans, J., F.L.S., Bow Street, R.S.O., Cardigan
Evans, B. G., Y *Genedl* Office, Carnarvon
Evans, J. Silvan, British School, Llanbrynmair, Mont.
Evans, E., Cross Keys
Evans, D., The Gardens, Quaker's Yard, Treharris, R.S.O.
Evans, J. Gwenogfryn, 7 Clarendon Villas, Oxford
Evans, A. B., High Street, Crickhowell
Evans, Benjamin, Rhuddlan. R.S.O., N. Wales
Evans, H. Jones, Greenhill, Cardiff
Evans, A., National Bank of Wales, Llandudno
Evans, Henry T. J.P., Neuadd Llanarth, Aberayon, (2 copies)
Evans, John, grocer, Pontnewynydd

Francis, M., 41 Castle Street, Tredegar

Gaidoz, H., 22 Rue de Servandoni, Paris
Gay, D. R., Llanwrtyd, Wells, R.S.O.
Gee, Thomas, Denbigh

George, J. E., Chemist, Hirwain, Aberdare
Griffith, T. W., Greenfield House, Llandudno
Griffiths, Archdeacon, The Rectory, Neath
Griffith, E., J.P., Springfield, Dolgelly
Growell, George, Albion House, Brynmawr
Gwynne, R., Kilvey, Swansea

Hales, Prof. W., 1 Oppidens Road, Primrose Hill, London, N.W
Hall, J. H. A., Old Bank, Chester
Harris, Rhys., The Congregational Manse, Narberth
Harris, G. R., C.C., Nantyglo
Hayde, Jno., " St." Peters, Cardiff
Herbert, Richard, Garndiffaith, Pontypool
Hill, Jenkin, Chairman Local Board, Briton Ferry
Hood, Archibald, Sherwood, Cardiff
Hopkins, G., The Hayes, Cardiff, (2 copies)
Hopkins, T., 15 North Church Street, Cardiff
Howell, E., Bookseller, Liverpool
Howell, A., Rhiewport, Berriew, (Mont.)
Howell, T. H., Caerau Park, Newport
Howells, John, Olchon, Longtown, Abergavenny
Hughes, W., 117 Marsh Lane, Bootle
Hughes, R. Jones, P.O., Rhostryfan
Hughes, Craigfryn J., Quaker's Yard, Treharris, R.S.O.
Humphreys, W., 101 Mulgrave Street, Liverpool

Ikin, S., Manager L. & S. Wales Bank, Llanidloes

James, E., 195, Newport Road, Cardiff
James, R. T., Ebenezer House, Bassalleg, Newport
Jenkins, Edward, Gwalia, Llandrindod
Jenkins, J. Edmund, Vaynor Rectory, Merthyr Tydfil
Jenkins, J. B., Sebastopol, near Newport
Jeremy, Walter, J.P., 5 Thurlow Road, Hampstead, London
Jenkyn, Iwan, F.R.H.S., Editor *Glamorganshire Free Press*, Pontypridd
John, J., Elliots Town, New Tredegar
John, T., Llwynypia School, Rhondda
Jones, E. P., c/o Lancaster & Co., Newport
Jones, W. S., Menai Villa, Chepstow Road, Newport
Jones, T., Caedraw, Merthyr
Jones, J., 52, Hemans Street, Liverpool
Jones, R., F.R.C.S., 11 Nelson Street, Liverpool
Jones, Roger W., Lewis School, Gellygaer
Jones, Thos., *(Llallawg Llywel)*, Trelewis, near Treharris
Jones, E. Bowen, London and Provincial Bank, Fishguard
Jones, G. E., Nant Peris, Carnarvon
Jones, Lewis, Taff Fechan Vicarage, Merthyr Tydfil
Jones, L. D., 3 Edge Hill, Garth, Bangor, N. Wales

Jones, Thomas D., (*Rhodwy*) Pontystyllod, Mold
Jones, Thomas B.A., Tawelfan, David's Road, Aberystwith
Jones, R. Prys, Ysgolion-y Bwrdd, Denbigh
Jones, H. L., 12 Queen Street, Chepstow
Jones, B. Jenkin, Broniestin, Aberdare
Jones, Thomas, 2 Clytha Square, Newport, Mon., (2 copies)
Jones, Edward, C.A., Snatchwood, near Pontypool
Jones, E., Tymawr, Aberdare
Jones, Joseph Seth, Holywell, Flintshire, North Wales
Jones-Lloyd, J. F., Lancych, near Boncath, R.S.O., Pembrokeshire
Joseph, M., 43 Plymouth Road, Penarth, (2 copies)

Kirby, C., Borough Surveyor, Newport
Kemeys-Tynte, H., Cefn Mably, Cardiff

Levick, J. J., Dr., Philadelphia
Lewis, R. W., Gelligaer Endowed School, near Cardiff
Lewis, J. H., Penucha Caerwys, Holywell, N. Wales
Lewis, J. W., Hamilton House, Carmarthen
Lewis, Augustus, Inspector of Factories, 8 Brunswick Place, Swansea
Lewis, E., Maindee Hall, near Newport
Llewellyn, W., Court Colman, Bridgend
Llewellyn, W., 3 Morgan Street, Tredegar
Llewellyn, G. H., Official Receiver, Newport
Lloyd-Jones, R. S., (*Llwydmôr*), Bron-y Gân, Llantrisant
Lloyd-Phillips, F. L., Penty Park, Clarbeston Road, Pem., (2 copies)
Lloyd, D., 96 Queen's Road, Liverpool
Lloyd, T., 18 Corn Street, Leominster
Lloyd, J. W., Dentist, Rodney Street, Liverpool
Luck, R., Plas Llanfairfechan

Macdonald, G. Free Manse, 10 Albany Road, Aberdeen
Macdonald, J. R., 10 The Avenue, Brondesbury, London
Maddock, J., Roslyn House, Park Square, Newport
McKinnon, Professor, Edinburgh, per James Thin, Bookseller
May, William, Librarian, Free Public Library, Birkenhead
Morgan, D., Maesycwmmer, viâ Cardiff
Morgan, C. E., Brynderfel, Llanderfel, Corwen
Morgan, W. Kinsey, Solicitor, Newport
Morgan, W. M., Dan y Graig, Risca
Morris, J., No. 4 The Elms, Liverpool
Morris, J. J., Board School, Garth, R.S.O., Brecon
Morris, A., Barnard Town Board Schools, Newport
Morris, E. J., Heathfield Street, Swansea

Neild, Theodore, B.A., Dalton Hall, Victoria Park, Manchester
Newman, A. A., Town Clerk, Newport, Mon.

DDD

Newman, H., Leominster

Owen, J. R., 50 St. Edward Street, Newport
Owen, W. H. Plas Penrhyn, Llanfair Pwll Gwyngyll, Anglesey
Owen, Isambard, M.D., 40 Curzon Street, London, W.
Owens, K. E., 21 Berkeley Street, Liverpool

Parry, D. C., Llanelly
Parry, W. E., Bryn Glas., Whiteladies Road, Clifton, Bristol
Parry, T. Jones, Gwent House, Clydach, Abergavenny
Parry, D. C., Llanelly
Pitt, Geo., Berkeley House, Mitcham
Plummer, E., C.A., Glyncorrwg, near Bridgend
Powell, Dyfrig, Grocer, The Garn, Nantyglo
Powell, T. Eugene, Solicitor, Brynmawr
Powell, J., Waunarllwydd House, near Swansea
Powell, George, Albion House, Brynmawr
Powell, J. E., Hendre, Wrexham
Price, " Mrs.," Glan Twrch, Ystalyfera, Swansea
Price, C., Brynderwen, Neath
Price, Peter, J.P., 12 Windsor Place, Cardiff
Pritchard, L. G., Menai Lodge, Wellesley Road, Chiswick, London
Pritchard, W., Clydach Vale, Pontypridd
Pritchard, R. O., 9 Wylva Road, Anfield, Liverpool
Prys, O., M.A., Trevecca College, Talgarth
Prytherch, J., London and Provincial Bank, Rhyl
Puleston, Sir J. H., M.P., 4 Whitehall Yard, London, W.

Rees, Howell, Tyrbach Garnant, R.S.O., S. Wales
Rees, D., Capelmawr, Llangefni, Anglesea
Rees, J., Bont Board Schools, Ystrad Meurig, Aberystwith
Reynolds, Llywarch, B.A., Merthyr
Richards, D., The Willows, Whitchurch, near Cardiff
Richards, W., (Glamorgan Bank,) 9 Alexander Street, Neath
Richards, R., 25 Arthur Street, Newport
Richards, D. M., 9 Gladys Terrace, Aberdare
Roberts, Charles, Pennsylvania
Roberts, C. F., M.A., Pendre House, Llanfyllin, Mont
Roberts, W. T., 343 Cardiff Road, Aberaman
Roberts, T. F., Principal, University College, Aberystwith
Roberts, J. R., Golenfryn, Cwm-y-glo, Carnarvon
Roberts, W., Talywain, near Pontypool
Roberts, G. L., Crug, Carnarvon
Roberts, Hugh, Oakhurst, Alderley Lodge, Cheshire
Roberts, James, Passenger and Freight Officer, Pontypridd
Roberts, D. W., 90 Dock Street, Newport
Roberts, J. D., Penralt, Newport

Rogers, Owen, 8 York Place, Rhymney, Mon.
Rumsey, William, 5 Tower Street, Crickhowell
Rowntree, Joshua, M.P., Scarborough
Rhys, Professor J., M.A., 87 Banbury Road, Oxford

Shindler, R., Portland Villa, Addlestone, Surrey
Southall, H., The Graig, Ross
Southall, Isabel, Wellington Road, Edgebaston, Birmingham
Southey, H. W., *Express* Office, Merthyr
Spurrell, W., Carmarthen
Storey, R. R., Manager National Provincial Bank of England, Cardiff

Thomas, E., Plasterer, 1 Railway Street, Newport, Mon.
Thomas, A., M.P., Penylan, Cardiff
Thomas, A. H., Crymlun Villa, Llansamlet
Thomas, T. H., R.E.A., 45 The Walk, Cardiff
Thomas, J., Grocer, Allen Street, Mountain Ash
Thomas, D., Upper Board School, Rhymney
Thomas, W., Gwendraeth, Board School, Pontyberem, Llanelly
Thomas, D. A., M.P., Llanwerne, Newport
Thomas, Howell, Local Government Offices, Whitehall, London, S.W.
Thomas, L. W., Pontygof Boys' School, Ebbw Vale
Thomas, E., 282 Bute Street, Cardiff
Thomas, G., Ely Farm, near Cardiff
Thomas, T. H., 45 The Walk, Cardiff
Thomas, Ebenezer, Llandilo
Thomas, Thomas, 1 Stow Hill, Newport
Thomas, A. Garrod, M.D., Clytha Park, Newport
Thomas, Moses, Caron House, Resolven
Thompson, J. W. A., C.E., Llanllwch, Carmarthen
Tredegar, (The Lord) Tredegar Park, Newport, Mon.
Tulloh, A. R., 13 Carlton Road, Putney Hill, London, S.W.

Vaux, Geo., 1715, Arch Street, Philadelphia

Walters, C. H., 7 Manley Road, Newport
Warden The, The College, Llandovery
Watkins, E. G., 6 Alma Street, Newport
Watkins, Howell, Machen, Newport, Mon.
Watkins, J. G., 28 Caroline Street, Newport
Williams, W. Ll., *South Wales Star*, Cadoxton, Barry
Williams, R., 82 Rodney Street, Liverpool
Williams, Thos., J.P., Gwaelodygarth House, Merthyr Tydfil
Williams, Joseph, *Tyst a'r Dydd* Office, Merthyr Tydfil
Williams, Lewis, Cae Coed, Cardiff
Williams, J. E., Rhostryfan Board Schools, Carnarvon
Williams, J. L., Chaplain to Duke of Cleveland, Staindrop, Darlington
Williams, Lewis N., Cambrian Lamp Works, Aberdare

Williams, R., Prof. of Welsh and History, David's College, Lampeter
Williams, J., 63 Brook Street, Grosvenor Square, London
Williams, L., Brynglas House, Porth
Williams, J., Coal Owner, Bargoed
Williams, William, M.A., Chief Inspector of Schools, Bronheulog,
    Aberystwith, (2 copies)
Williams, E., 22 Pearl's Crescent, Cardiff
Williams, W. Edgar, Exchange, Cardiff
Williams, E., Trefecca College, Talgarth, R.S.O.
Wilde, T., Zoar Terrace, Craigberthlwyd, Treharris, R.S.O
Wilson, W., 156 Minories, London